# Grave Measures

## A Case File From: The Grave Report

# R.R. Virdi

**Grave Measures**
**A Case File From: The Grave Report**
**R.R. Virdi**

Copyright R.R. Virdi 2016

*Dedication*

Jim Hurd. A great mentor, inspiration, role model, and most of all— great friend.

## Acknowledgements

My editor Michelle Dunbar. Sorry for putting you through all of this again. You're stuck with me for a long time.

My cover artist, Sarah, you're amazing.

Lacey, for making this version possible. You rock.

As always, my supportive friends and family, thank you.

## *Also by RR Virdi*

### The Grave Report

GRAVE BEGINNINGS

GRAVE MEASURES

### Short Stories

"CHANCE FORTUNES"—THE LONGEST NIGHT
WATCH ANTHOLOGY

"A BAG FULL OF STARS"—ALWAYS STARDUST
ANTHOLOGY

**What reviewers are saying about Grave Beginnings:**

"I believe R.R. Virdi belongs with other Urban Fantasy greats like Jim Butcher. The Grave Report is sure to go far and only pick up more fans with each successful novel. I can't wait to see where R.R. Virdi will take us next."—A Drop Of Ink Reviews

"Fast paced, humorous, with action and drama on every page and paragraph, this paranormal thriller is reminiscent of one of my all-time favorite authors. This is like Jim Butcher's The Dresden Files but with a flavor all its own. RR Virdi is fame-bound with this series. If you like Jim Butcher, you'll enjoy this one. Highly Recommend."
—CD Coffelt—Author of The Wilder Mage

"A fast paced story with great characters, I loved the story and fell even more in love with the future possibilities… Virdi maintains both the suspense of the case at hand, and the character's past and current transformation, making us feel both for the victim and the investigator. He excels at action scenes - I have rarely read books with such well-described yet fluid action scenes."—Shadow and Clay Reviews

# Chapter One

There's no good way of waking up in a dead body. For starters, you feel like six pounds of crap in a three-pound bag. You have no idea where you are, you're nauseated, and everything is disoriented. It's like a bad hangover—with a dead man thrown in.

I blinked several times. Haziness and columns of white greeted me, peppered with the odd spot dancing across my eyes. The warmth spreading across the back of my neck prompted me to turn. "Ackh," I sputtered as rays of sunshine shone onto my face, forcing me to squint.

I wriggled my body in an attempt to loosen it up and discovered another reason why it sucks to wake up in a dead body. My arms were bound. And not in the fun and kinky way.

They were stretched across my chest in an awkward self-hug. Now I'm all for healthy self-esteem and loving yourself—straitjackets—not so much. I struggled with the restrictive coat, thrashing like I had been tasered. Nothing came of it. The durable canvas held together. Of course it would. I mean, that's what it's made for right?

My efforts succeeded in, first, exhausting me and, secondly, producing a trickle of moisture on my upper lip. A moment later, the stream of liquid trickled into my mouth. I tasted salt and copper. I let my gaze drift over my coat-covered chest. The muscles in my neck strained as I stretched and brushed my nose against the coarse canvas. Crimson blotched with darker hues of garnet smeared across the fabric.

Dead man's blood.

I didn't expect to be spilling my borrowed blood this early into a case. Sitting up was a challenge as my balance wavered and my body teetered. I rocked from side to side in a cross-legged position. Nausea surged through my body. Bile built in the back of my throat. I fought the urge to retch violently.

*What the hell killed this stiff?* I rocked again, enduring all manner of gastronomical discomfort. A few moments of deep breathing through my mouth and my body settled itself. "'Kay," I panted. "Jacket."

I mulled in silence as to how I was going to get out of the constricting piece of canvas. Straitjackets aren't known for being easy to get out of. But situations like this are easy for me. One of the perks of being a wayward soul with no body of my own. I've got a whole library of information rattling around my noggin. Mostly useful tidbits left over from the people I've inhabited. I can get out of just about any situation so long as I can dig up the right memory.

I blanked...

*Shit.*

And sometimes finding the right one is a crapshoot. One of the many side effects of my countless cases. Don't get me started on my personality issues.

I took several breaths to steel myself. I didn't have any idea of what to do. Well—no good ones. Mel Gibson's voice rang through my head: *Don't try this at home, boys and girls!*

I was going to dislocate one of my borrowed shoulders. Not the brightest idea.

My teeth clamped around a large wad of the canvas. It wouldn't mute my scream, but it would soften it. I breathed heavily through my nose. My heartbeat skipped. Eyes shut, I cursed the stupidity of my plan. I fumbled within the confines of the jacket as I tried to grab my left wrist in my right hand. It took a moment but I managed to take hold of my other hand through the thick material.

*Crap, crap, crap*, droned through my head. I held firm on my left wrist and lifted and pushed against the jacket. It stretched ever so slightly before contracting to its old and limiting shape. I pushed several times, earning myself a small amount of room to maneuver. I secured three inches of room to work in. It wasn't a lot, but I'd make it work.

I resumed my flailing and thrashed with all the vigor I could muster. The fabric gave me a momentary reprieve. It would have to be enough. A small whimper of hesitation left my throat as I tightened my grip on my wrist. I inhaled a final massive breath.

Visualizing my left shoulder, I rolled it forward to loosen it up. The joint pushed as far as it would go without causing me severe pain. It felt like ropes were fraying between my rotator cuff and clavicle. A small prelude of the pain to come. I paused for a moment, keeping my shoulder on the edge of dislocation, letting out a silent curse before continuing.

I squeezed the insides of my shoulder hard. In one sharp motion, I jerked violently on my left wrist, putting more force on my shoulder. It was smooth. A single vicious motion and it was done. Well, it was smooth if you don't count the countless sounds ringing out during the dislocation and after.

A sickening pop drowned my muffled scream, letting me know my shoulder had indeed left the socket. The urge to puke my guts out returned. I fell onto my right side, my good side. Sharp and dull throbs panged from shoulder to collarbone. The small wad of canvas came out of my mouth. I lay there for a moment, listening to my ragged, strained breaths as I tried to collect myself. Growing numbness overtook my left arm, leaving it feeling like a distant thing.

Bleach. It was faint but still there. It came from the walls like a noxious and head-dizzying perfume. My eyes fluttered open. The walls hung around me like freshly laundered sheets: crisp, clean, without so much as a scuff, and looking every bit as soft. They weren't some jarring white, but something lighter and easier on the eyes.

The room was homey; at least, I think it was. It's kind of hard to judge a room when you're lying on your side, incapacitated.

Just trust me on this one.

It was cozy. A singular window sat in the wall I had been leaning against. It was a rather simple thing, split into four sections with a few rays of warming sunlight coming through. The floor was a plush carpet, sandalwood, now stained from the driblets of blood my nose had been producing. The bed was a twin size. The bedding and sheets looked as if someone had gone through a nightmare under them.

I was garbed in a simple half-sleeve tee of light gray.

The pants matched. They were the sort you'd expect a patient to wear. Light and comfortable.

The pain subsided enough that I tried to get to my feet. I achieved wobbly success. Vertigo assailed me the instant I was fully righted. I teetered as the room went through the spin cycle. Once I ended my act as a top, I worked on slipping out of the jacket. My left arm came over my head rather easily. It helps having the arm out of its socket. I brought the various buckles and latches to my mouth and tore at them with my teeth. All that tearing worked wonders on my wrecked shoulder. Each tug sent unpleasant vibrations through the damaged socket. I gritted through it; I didn't have a choice.

After several painstaking minutes, the latches around my arms came undone. They were still bound within the jacket but no longer clasped together. I had more movement now. Bowing my head, I used my right hand to undo the buckles behind. My fingers fumbled at first. It didn't take long to unlock the buckles running down the middle of my back. Flaring my shoulders and chest stretched the semi-opened jacket. I grasped the collar and yanked hard.

There was more room now that the upper portions of the jacket had opened. Thanks to that and my Gumby shoulder, when I pulled on the canvas coat, it slid up. It was just a bit, but still, it was more than before. I exhaled, shrinking my torso as I wrenched again. The jacket slipped up and over my head, coming to hang before me with my arms still inside. I bit into the fabric with my teeth and freed my right arm, using it to release my damaged left.

I breathed a sigh of relief as the heavy coat crumpled around my bare feet. My attention turned back to my shoulder. I grimaced at the thought of putting it back into its socket. It's not the most enjoyable of feelings. In a toss up between what hurts more—dislocation or putting the joint back in—it's a damnable tie.

My feet dragged as I shambled to the nearest wall, preparing to snap my arm back in place. I leaned forward, letting the shoulder rest against the wall with the lightest amount of pressure. I reared back to slam my shoulder against the solid drywall before me—

—The doorknob jostled. A mechanical click sounded

and the door drifted open without force.

I didn't move as lazily as the door. I snapped about. My disjointed arm launched itself across my torso, coming to rest atop my good shoulder. It looked as if I were giving myself a strange half-hug. The door opened halfway when a voice rang out.

"Charles?" The woman's voice had mixed inflections of confusion and concern.

Well, at least I had gotten the victim's name this early into the case. I didn't even have to do much to get it. Only tear my arm from its socket and have a nosebleed. Who knew it could be that easy?

I got a full view of the woman behind the voice the second the door hit the stopper. She was plump and matronly, or at least under normal circumstances she would be. Her hazel eyes widened as she gawked at me. The woman's pear-shaped face twisted into a mask of horror and bewilderment. A few rogue locks of ruddy brown hair hung from her neatly packed bun. Her jowls quivered as she tried to make sense of what was going on.

Most people don't expect to walk into a room and find a guy patting himself with his own dislocated arm. Not to mention the blood that had leaked and dried above my lip, and the fact that Charles' straitjacket was lying on the floor. It was a fairly odd situation, even by my standards, and—trust me—I've seen odd.

There was a heavy *thud* as she fell back against the door. The nurse sank to the floor.

*I hate it when they faint,* I thought with a resigned sigh. It happens way too much in my job.

I lurched forward in a stooped and uncoordinated manner. My limp arm fell from its perch and swung without control as I shuffled towards her. Once I reached the nurse and finished my Quasimodo impression, I gave her quick look over. Her chest moved in sync with light breaths. Satisfied, I stepped out of the room and into the hall. A cool sensation ran under my bare feet from the mottled marble below.

There was no debate in my mind about whether I should stay to examine the room or leave. As much as I wanted to gather more information, I couldn't risk it. One nurse was already out of it. I had no intention of letting more people walk in on that situation. Gripping my damaged shoulder, I hobbled down the hall in search of a chapel. It was the one place where I'd be able to get my bearings in this case. And maybe some answers if I was lucky.

I didn't stop to snap my arm back in its socket. The resulting scream would only draw more attention. I was relying on my injury taking care of itself, like they normally do. Well, not so normally. There's really not much normal about a bodiless soul.

My feet beat across the cold, hard marble as I swayed drunkenly. Steadying myself was a difficult feat, especially when the floor looked like it was moving. This body must've been whammied pretty good if I was feeling the lingering effects. I had no idea what killed him, who he was, or if Charles was even his legal name. It wasn't much to go on, but it was more than I'd had this early on in other cases.

Beggars, choosers and all.

Between my dazed thoughts and battered body, I had miraculously stumbled into the hall leading to the chapel. The fact I had found it without bumping into a single person was a heckuva relief. I braced my good arm against the nearest wall, reveling in my newfound balance.

"Noaow, fo' shum anshaws," I slurred in drunken triumph. I drew nearer to the chapel and was all but five feet away when electric pins-and-needles blossomed within my dislocated arm.

I frowned. That didn't seem right. Not that anything was right about waking up the way I had.

My jaw felt like it'd taken a good punch. Nausea returned and clearly a cannonball had been dropped on my chest. Nothing else could explain the pain. It felt like a balloon was lodged in my chest and expanding fast. My sternum grew fuller and my chest was too tight for my insides. Every bit of strength rushed out of my body.

Naturally, that's when I collapsed.

There was a resounding impact. A great big thwap! It was the floor's way of letting me know: Floor − 1. Vincent Graves − 0.

Stupid floor.

The side of my face was numb, whether from the fall or whatever was happening to me, I didn't know. My breaths grew shorter and shallower as the seconds ticked by. I couldn't even mutter my frustrations about dying this early into a case. Losing the ability to breathe properly does that.

The chapel doors opened and light rolled out. It wasn't something just to be seen, it was something to be felt. It bathed the hall in gold-infused white. It wasn't the sort of glow that illuminated the chapel ahead of me. Nope. This was the kind that caked everything in a blinding and opaque white. It was the kind that forced my eyes to clamp shut in pain. Heat washed over me and staying conscious became more difficult. Every inch of my borrowed body told me to sleep.

I refused. I'm stubborn like that. This was not normal—even for me. A light at the end of a tunnel? Well, a hallway. *I am not going to be killed by a freaking cliché!*

Footsteps—light but audible—forced my eyes to snap open. I couldn't see anything but horrid light for a moment. Khaki coloring came into my beer-goggle view, clarifying into a pair of legs, and legs only. Given the state and angle of my head, I couldn't see above their waist. Hell, I couldn't see their shoes either. My vision was limited to the middle of their thighs and lower. I settled for the halfway point, and developed a sudden and intense hatred for their kneecaps.

Granted, it's not as intimidating shooting a death glare at a pair of knees. I hoped their knees got the message to back off and relayed that to their brain.

Apparently not. Kneecaps aren't all that great at transmitting messages. They kept getting closer. I flailed in protest. It didn't do me much good. A few more steps and they were out of my fishbowl sight. I would've released a sigh of relief if a tugging sensation didn't envelop my good arm. A panicked, dry wheeze left my lungs and I struggled to free my arm from their hold.

No dice. The stranger's grip was frozen steel.

The floor slid beneath me and I realized I was being dragged rather unceremoniously. A thought crossed my mind. *The way to hell involves being dragged, doesn't it?*

*Screw that!* I thought in uppity defiance. If I was going out, I'd go out being the biggest pain in the ass I could! I stopped struggling and allowed myself to do what I had been resisting this whole time—relax. I went limp, becoming one, big, dead weight—literally, if you think about it. All sense of color faded as I heeded the light's message to sleep.

Blackness rolled over me.

# Chapter Two

Salmon and red replaced the sea of onyx before my eyes. Rogue spots of white danced within my lids. Someone must've taken the liberty to slather adhesive between my eyes. They felt gummy and refused to open at first. When they did, I woke to solid and unforgiving wood running beneath me.

Light, much gentler than the halogen-powered assault I had just endured, wafted in. The glow of sunlight put on an interesting show in the air above. Particulate matter hung, bobbing and dancing around. Every now and again, the occasional dust speck sank to the floor. It felt nice, lying there—watching, letting the warming rays spread over me.

My attention returned to the rigid board I was on; it was so uncomfortable I had lost sensation in a certain part of my body. I muttered about all good things coming to an end. I shifted to remedy the situation. It worked, sort of. Prickling orbs of feeling burst into life across the skin below my lower back. Once I was confident my ass was no longer sleeping on the job, I propped myself up for a better look. The hard wood of the pew wasn't too welcoming to my elbows.

A pleasured groan left my mouth—"Ohhhhmagod"— as a series of relieving cracks ran up the length of my spine. With a smack of my lips, I twisted and turned, loosening my torso as I observed the chapel.

It was rather simple, but that wasn't to say it wasn't nice. It was.

The carpet, moss in color and texture, tickled as it brushed along the arches of my feet. It blanketed the entirety of the chapel floor, running below the butt-numbing pews. At the front stood a waist-high altar, possessing the dimensions of a small coffee table. A large stone basin, carved and smoothed to give it the appearance of a river stone, sat atop. Behind it hung a bedsheet-sized cloth of pale gold, the only adornment on any of the tawny walls. Rows of unremarkable lighting fixtures were held above. For the moment, the job of illuminating the chapel was left to the handful of arched windows.

Frantic scratching emanated from behind me. A lopsided grin made its way across my face as I turned to face my rescuer—boss—friend. Well, friend was a stretch. Acquaintance.

His modelesque features made his geeky ensemble look like one gigantic, ironic fashion statement. From his collared, checkered dress shirt to the khakis I had seen earlier. All the way up to the...pocket protector nestled in his shirt.

I'm not joking.

The scratching continued as his hand darted across the page of his journal, the metallic tip of his pen on the verge of tearing the sheet. He scrawled at a furious tempo, paying no attention to me whatsoever.

That bit wasn't a new experience. He ignored me all the time.

I cleared my throat pointedly.

The movement of his hand ceased with mechanical precision. His gaze rose from the diary and he greeted me much as he always did. It was hard to tell if he was handsome or beautiful when his pearlescent teeth gleamed at me. I wouldn't have been surprised if there had been an animated sparkle with an audible *bling*. As usual, renegade curls of thick, blonde hair obscured his eyes. With a slow and measured hand, he brushed the locks away to reveal a pair of eyes I've always found creepy.

Think of azure waters freezing over. A blend of arctic blues, grays and whites. Icy. Clear lenses, wrapped in a dark frame, surrounded those frozen peepers and accentuated his fair skin. His androgynous good looks and dress were the outcome of a social experiment: If Models R Us met Geek Squad.

"Dear diary," I said in a soft, feminine tone. "I've woken up and come face to face with my rescuer, my hero. He's so...dreamy."

He didn't feel obliged to respond right away. He snapped his diary shut and moved to put it away. A simple click and the pen was stowed inside the pocket protector. My teeth grated as he continued ignoring me, going so far as to remove, breathe on, and wipe his glasses before addressing me.

He released an exasperated sigh. "Vincent," he called me by my assumed name. I've been doing this gig so long I can't remember my real name, so I gave myself a new one. "Most days your poor sense of humor possesses some degree of charm. Not today." He sighed again. "I'm tired."

Feigning hyperventilation, I clutched my chest. "Pah—poor sense of humor?" I gasped. "I think I'm going to have a heart attack…again."

Before he could respond, a notion occurred to me. "Speaking of which," I blurted out, before pausing to mull over my next sentence. "Did you…" I trailed off as I pointed to my head, chest and left arm. I hadn't realized until that moment, but my limbs were coursing with a barely noticeable and comforting heat. The kind that radiates from a hot water bottle, the kind that apparently had healed my dislocated shoulder and heart pain.

Tall, blonde and geekily handsome answered with a silent nod.

"Huh," I grunted. "Well, thanks for making a girl feel all warm and tingly on the inside."

"Graves," he groaned, using my last name.

I threw up my hands in a placating gesture. "Alright, alright," I conceded. "I'll stop the smartassery—"

"Thank you." He looked mildly relieved.

"If…you finally tell me your real name." I was curious to see how he'd take my ultimatum.

He didn't miss a beat. He did exactly the same the first time I'd asked him. His lips pursed as he cast a gaze around our churchly surroundings. A twitch of the lips let me know he was holding back a smile. "Church."

*You're not as witty as you think*, I grumbled inside my head.

"Neither are you, Vincent."

I blinked.

When Church did things like that, it caused me to have serious reservations about him. I mean, he never shared his real name, how he knew what I was thinking, or even his damned zodiac sign.

"Pisces," he chimed.

I narrowed my eyes and visualized punching him on the nose, wondering if he'd pick *that* up.

He stared back at me, a beacon of all things still, calm and...without blinking.

Church did that a lot, and, as creepy as it was, I had somewhat gotten used to it. What really disturbed me was what I saw in his face. For the slightest fraction of a second, Church's unnerving and unblinking mask...slipped. When it did, I got a good glimpse beneath the pretty-boy veneer, and it rattled me. In that singular moment, Church's eyes lost their frigid clarity and strength. The deeper tones of blue faded away to softer shades of gray; his eyes were a thin fog. They seemed disconnected, weary...weak.

He was tired.

That wouldn't seem like a big deal to most. It was terrifying to me. Church mentioned he was tired, but he's said that a lot over the years. It means he's annoyed...with me. Now, I could see it for myself. In all the time I've known him, I have never seen him tired. Hell, I didn't know Church *could* be tired.

"Vincent?" he asked in his always soft and polite voice.

I snapped out of my reverie and debated whether to ask him what was on my mind.

Without an exchange of words, Church gave me a knowing look. Translation: *Shoot.*

I resolved to be a bit more serious. If something was giving Church a rough time, it was bad news. "Um..."

Church waited with mannequin-like stillness as I stumbled to find the right words.

"What's wrong?" That's me, master of eloquence.

"Work," he replied in monosyllabic ambiguity, failing to answer my question. Another one of his irritating habits.

"Ain't it a bitch?" So much for serious.

He released a weary sigh.

I took the hint.

"So, um, where are we?" I tried to change the subject and glean some info while I was at it.

The nausea returned when he answered. "New York."

Oh.

Crap.

# Chapter Three

New York: great city, good food—shopping too. Amazing hotels—when they're not on fire.

Last time I was here on a case, the situation went from bad to unbelievably worse. Liken it to a weather report and it rained fire and hailed crap. A certifiable, flaming shit storm.

My last investigation in the Empire State was full of fun surprises. I woke up and nearly suffocated. My soul got thrown into a magical tug of war match and was nearly ripped from the body I was inhabiting. There's the bit where Grumpy Cat wanted to make my bones into wind chimes. I was ambushed butt naked in the bathroom by something that wanted to feast on my eternal and oh-so-witty spirit. Oh...and a five-star hotel almost burned to the ground.

Not my fault. Directly anyways. I claim accidental arson by proximity.

And a good woman died...

All and all, this was not my favorite place to be at the moment. But then, I didn't really have a choice in the matter. I never do.

"So..." I turned my attention back to Church. "What are we dealin' with here?"

"*We?*" He arched a golden eyebrow. A hint of a grin played on his lips.

"Fine," I grumbled. "What am *I* dealing with?"

The micro smile vanished from his face and his expression slipped into complete neutrality. Well, almost neutral. Amusement shone in his eyes.

Right, why give any answers to the guy working for you? Why make it easy?

"If it were easy, Vincent, I wouldn't need you."

I didn't know if that was a compliment or not. But I was starting to hate him a teensy bit.

Church took on the tone of a parent lecturing a child. "The thing about hate, Vincent—"

I waved him off. I didn't have time for a philosophical lesson; I had a monster to hunt.

"What the—" A familiar and unyielding grip took hold of my forearm. I nearly buckled from the hydraulic strength Church exerted—with no visible effort, I might add. The blistering heat that followed wasn't much fun either. A sickly-sweet smell tickled my nostrils. It smelt of hair and skin.

Forty-four. Big, black and bold. The number adorned my arm in the fashion of a tattoo. Never mind the surrounding circle of pink, sensitive skin. It itched something terrible.

Church's grasp loosened and I jerked my arm back. "Gee." My lips peeled back into a sneer. "Thanks, Church, what would I do without you?"

"Fail and die." He said it like it was a matter of fact.

…Douche.

"Don't be too hard on yourself, Vincent."

Church gestured to something behind me before I could think of a response. I followed his finger to the large basin atop the altar.

"Water."

"Huh?" I am the very definition of clever.

"It helps with burns. Metaphorical and literal." I could almost feel him smiling.

I whipped around to confront him.

He was gone.

There wasn't a sound, any hint of motion to tip me off—nothing. Church vanished from sight without the slightest indication he had done so. Now that alone isn't the most remarkable of feats. Great stage illusionists can do so, as well as the many supernatural creatures I deal with. Also, ninjas. But to pull it over on me is something else.

I've inhabited a plethora of people with a vast array of skills and picked up a great deal of knowledge from them. Coupled with years of fighting monsters as well as being hunted by them, I have an amazing sense of awareness.

Apparently Church didn't give a shit about that.

When I had finished fondling my ego, I realized

something. "Hey!" I growled at nowhere in particular. "Damnit, Church. My journals!" I don't know why, but I had the distinct feeling that wherever he was, Church could hear me. Several moments went by without so much as a disembodied response. I gave up.

"Urghall mrrfle grussel!" My incoherent grumbles echoed throughout the chapel as I stomped toward the basin. By the time I got there, I no longer needed its watery contents to soothe the burn. It took care of itself. A courtesy of my ability to heal and regenerate the bodies I inhabit. To an extent of course.

I've survived broken limbs, being burned, falling out of buildings—even gunshot wounds. If it doesn't kill me outright, chances are I'll recover from it. Job perk from whoever Church's boss is. It guarantees that I at least have a shot at taking down whatever monster I'm chasing. I'd be of little use if I couldn't take the punishment the job doled out. The only thing I didn't have was the ability to influence the state of the bodies at the beginning of my case.

That was Church's job; somehow, he made sure they were cleaned up and passable as human. Bodies don't look too great when they've been dead for a while. Granted, I only inhabit the bodies of the recently deceased. Still, some of those poor souls have been killed in truly nasty ways. It's easier if the bodies are put back together so I don't look like a zombie when I'm out on a case. They're also supposed to be free from the remnant effects of whatever killed them too.

I glared at the ceiling. "Like the nosebleed, headache and heart attack." I was going to have to talk to Church about that one. I could've sworn there was some sort of clause about maintaining a ride before someone else picked up the lease. Still, at least it gave me some clues as to what killed "Charles," the man I was occupying.

There's never a clean way to say that.

I may not have known what those clues pointed to, but I would—eventually.

That declaration brought my focus back to the case and I tilted my head to look inside the bowl. It enlightened me on the mystery of *who* I was.

My features were stretched and distorted by the water.

It looked like someone had flattened my face out. Sharp, almost avian features stared back at me. The skin wasn't as fair as Church's, but it was close. Earthy brown eyes gave me a hollow stare. They weren't indicative of having gotten eight hours of beauty sleep. Not-so-neat hair ran across the stark cheeks and jawline as a few days' growth of beard. Oak in color, much like the short, ragged mess of hair up top. My borrowed nose was the most redeeming feature. It was almost perfect, straight-edged.

I released a Neolithic grunt as I finished the appraisal of my features.

"There!" someone shouted. The voice was accompanied by panting and hasty footsteps.

Someone shouting, "There!" is never a good thing.

The muscles along my neck and spine tightened as I turned around.

Three disgruntled looking figures sprinted toward me. At the front of the trio was a slender woman, a nurse judging by her pale lavender scrubs. Her hair, bound into a brunette tail, flailed wildly as she ran toward me. Panic and irritation showed on her freckled face.

Following in tow were two men who could've passed for identical twins if it weren't for the difference in skin tone. The pale one bore the same twisted scowl as the dark one.

It wasn't a comforting notion to see those behemoths jogging toward me looking all scowly. Hell, I'm surprised they *could* run. They had the body mass and proportions of frickin' gorillas! Shaved, thick solid heads sat atop meaty necks you usually see on power lifters. Cantaloupes sprouted on both sides of their massive necks, what I assumed were their shoulders. Nobody should have shoulders that monstrously big. The sleeves of their scrubs barely contained their arms, which were thicker than my legs. Slabs of pectoral muscles pushed against the thin fabric of their clothes, as did their strongmen bellies. Oh, and they were tall—freakishly so. The guys dwarfed most NBA players.

Just because they were built like cartoon characters didn't mean they were inhuman. But people should not— cannot—be built like that. Normally at least. The only reason I ruled them out as monsters in disguise is because of their faces. They were utterly devoid of any intelligence. It seemed like it took all their brain capacity just to scowl and run at the same time.

I relaxed my body, assuming the most non-threatening posture I could. Gorillas may appear gentle and playful like in zoos, but in the wild, the big ones—males especially—can get pretty nasty. And, like all primates, they possessed the strange inclination to hurl fecal matter.

Fair to say I didn't want anything of the sort to happen to me.

The young nurse came to a stop several feet before me, panting from her frenzied jog. The lumbering goliaths barely seemed winded, but I'll be damned if their breathing didn't sound animalistic. Primal sounds, the sort you'd need colossal lungs to produce.

My neck and back stiffened further.

"Charles," huffed the nurse. "We were worried about you!"

I wasn't aware that worried and waspish were interchangeable.

"We've been looking all…" She trailed off. Her head tilted and a puzzled look crossed her face. "How did you get out of your jacket?"

How do you respond to that? I've learned over my past cases that smartassery works well. In fact, it's never failed me.

Stepping backward, I bent at the waist and thrust my arms to my side in an exuberant manner. With a flourish of my hands, I pronounced in my best stage voice, "Call me Harry!"

When I straightened, one of the nurse's brows arched higher than the other. Behind her, the pair of walking monoliths chuckled in unison.

Of all the people to get the joke!

Good humor is wasted on some people.

When she regained her composure, her eyebrows furrowed and she took a step toward me. "That's not funny!" she barked. The anabolic duo chuckled again.

Their mistake.

She whipped about in her pint-sized fury, fists balled as she glared at them. Without a single word she told them to shut up and go back to being intimidating. It worked. They stopped laughing and adopted surly expressions.

The nurse brought her attention back to me. "You nearly gave Kat a heart attack!"

I flinched as a small amount spittle left her mouth. She did me a service though; I had another name. Kat. I worked on the assumption that she was the plump nurse who had walked in on me earlier. It's always nice knowing people's names, especially if you have to speak to them later. No one liked being addressed as, "Hey…you?"

Nurse Ratched pulled a one-eighty when her features softened. Chest swelling as she took a calming breath, speaking in a lighter tone. "I'm sorry for yelling, Charles."

I didn't respond per se, instead inclining my head in an understanding nod.

She gave a genuine smile before turning to whisper something to Yeti and Sasquatch. They grunted in stereo and lumbered to either side of me.

That wasn't worrying at all.

Both of them hooked their Popeye-like arms around mine.

"Hey!" I protested as they walked forward. They were clearly under the assumption that I would follow.

The hell I would!

For the record, those guys were strong. "Let me go, you asswheels!" I kicked the air as they plowed on. I never was much of a follower, so in a repeat performance of earlier, I let my body go limp. Neither the Incredible Hulk nor The Thing seemed the least bit perturbed by my gesture of rebellion. They treated me like I weighed nothing. I resigned myself to releasing a disappointed sigh as my shins and feet dragged across the floor.

"There had better be food where we're going," I muttered.

# Chapter Four

I hobbled to the door muttering a string of obscenities. Another latex *thwap* filled my ears from behind. My ass twitched and the rest of my body stiffened on pure reflex. I turned back to the nurse removing her glove. Upon catching my gaze, she shook her head and smiled.

I scowled, thinking of something witty to say. What do you say to a woman who, in essence, just violated you? A stupid grin crossed my face and I gestured with my fingers. "Call me."

Her wry expression faded, replaced with one of confusion. An angry huff of breath left her mouth as she stumbled for a reply

Point to Graves. Suppository Lady — nil.

The scowl remained on my face as I stomped down the hall, drawing strange looks from patients and staff alike. I continued my curmudgeony walk toward a nearby water fountain. Having one of your orifices desecrated makes a guy thirsty.

I slurped down the water and came to a disappointing realization. My "check up," was the closest thing to intimacy with a woman that I could remember. I sighed. "I need a new life."

"What's wrong with the one you've got?" asked a sincere voice. One that sadly did not emanate from the confines of my head. It would've been better if it had. Believe me. I reacted in the manner you'd expect from a seasoned, intrepid paranormal investigator.

I leapt away from the fountain as if my hands had been scalded, stumbled backward and adopted an awkward Kung-Fu pose. I was sorely tempted to release a shrill howl as I channeled my inner martial arts master.

The man behind the voice regarded me with simple curiosity, which is good. He was a big guy. I didn't want him

getting hostile. He was taller than the human growth
hormone brothers from earlier, but softer looking. Not to
be rude, but he looked like a ginormous baby. His features
were cherubic—smooth fair skin, lengthy lashes, and
enormous hazel eyes. Either he was smuggling Jell-O in his
cheeks, or he had never outgrown his baby fat. Coupled
with his shaved head, he was like a life-sized baby doll, but
dressed in garb matching mine.

I straightened and held out my hand. "Um, hi?" He
didn't shake it—rude.

Hooking a thumb to his pudgy self, he said, "Gusbert."

I struggled not to laugh. I failed. "Your name
is…Gusbert? I sure hope you gave your parents hell for
that!" I laughed even louder.

He joined in and I swear to God, even his laugh was like
a baby's. It was infectious. We laughed for a good while. A
nurse passed by and gave us a strange look. We must've
looked insane. Well, more so.

"You're funny," he said, breaking the silence as he
extended his fleshy hand.

Finally, someone who appreciated my humor. I could
like this guy. "Charles," I said, shaking hands.

"Friends call me Gus," he said with a childlike smile.

"Wow, friends already. Things are moving so fast."

Gus let out an echoing belly laugh.

Yup, definitely liked this guy. Maybe he could help me
too. A patient might've seen or heard something I could use
to narrow down my search. Any bit of information at this
point was gold because I had nothing.

I dropped my voice to a gentler tone. "Hey Gus, can I
trust you with something?" He nodded. Throwing an arm
around his shoulder, I led him down the hall. "With a
secret?" I impressed the importance of the words with a
whisper. He nodded harder. "I'm on a case, and I could use
your help."

He gasped, and his face lit up with glee only a child
could muster. I showed him my tattoo, which remained a
black forty-four. Good. I hadn't chewed up an hour of my
time being "poked and prodded" by the nurse.

After a moment of staring at it, he gave me a befuddled
shake of his head.

"It's magical," I explained. He answered the way I'd expect anyone to: he raised a questioning eyebrow, debating my sanity. But then again, everyone here was some degree of crazy, so what the hell, right? I had nothing to lose but maybe, just maybe, I had something to gain. "It is. See, every hour the number changes, counting down until I solve the case or I...."

Silence. It went on until his curiosity got the better of him and overruled any logical sentiments he might have had about my magical tattoo.

"Or what?" he leaned closer, eyes wide and darting from my arm to my face and back again.

"Die."

That had an effect. Mentioning death normally does.

I could see him working through everything, so I gave him a bit to ponder it over. Once he was done, he spoke. "Case?"

I gave a solemn nod. "I'm investigating."

"What?" His voice dropped to a conspiratorial whisper.

*Here goes nothin'.*

Leaning forward, I matched his hushed voice. "A monster."

His eyebrows rocketed upwards and his eyes ballooned. "I knew it!" he hissed in triumph.

Not gonna lie, his reaction surprised me. People don't jump for joy when you tell them you're hunting a monster. Nor do they say, "I knew it." That's just not right.

"Uhrm...whaa? You knew it?"

Gus nodded faster than a bobble head on crack. "Yup."

Hell, this was easy, which made me instantly suspicious. The job was never easy, and it was definitely never *this* easy. Clues within the first hour? It was never *that* easy. A part of me wanted to believe it could be. It was the part of me that ignored caution and often got me into trouble. And yet, I listened to that rascally part and pursued the matter.

"What do you know, Gus?" I kept my features as neutral as I could. It was hard. My heart was performing a drum solo.

"People are dead." His face hardened into a grim mask.

I figured that much. Hell, I was inhabiting one of them. But, I didn't want to be rude. I rolled my hand in a gesture for him to continue.

"Too many heart attacks." His gaze drifted to the ground. Shaking his head, he added, "Not heart attacks."

Well, that was something. If Gus was to be believed, whatever this thing was, it made the deaths look like heart attacks.

My impatience got the better of me. "How many so far?"

He opened his mouth to answer. A shrill voice interrupted.

"Gusbert!" the woman snapped.

We turned our heads in unison.

It was Kat—the nurse who witnessed my Houdini-esque escape. She reminded me of a lunch lady. With her plump figure, wobbling gait, and pear-shaped head, she would be right at home slapping mystery meat on a tray. Her mouth twisted into something reminiscent of a scowl, probably because of me. I've been known to make people scowl.

She bustled over to Gus. Her face softened upon seeing him. Kat muscled her way between us and took hold of his arm. There was a warm, almost motherly manner in the way she treated him. "Come on, honey." She pulled on his arm, trying to lead him away.

"Uh, Gus," I protested, holding up a finger. He spun around, a giant grin spreading across his face. "The thing?" I shot him a knowing look.

Kat seemed intent on keeping Gus and I apart. She moved quicker than I would have thought possible for a woman her size. Whirling about, she stepped in front of Gus and jabbed a chubby, accusatory finger toward me. "You!" Her jowls trembled. "You should be in your jacket for what you did!" Kat's hazel eyes flashed.

Which had me wondering, *what the hell did Charles do?*

"Stay away from Gus!" He winced as her nails dug into his pudgy arm; she stormed off with him in tow. All Gus was able to do was mouth a silent apology.

I was left alone in the hall with my thoughts. At least I had no shortage of things to think about. Gus had given me a ton of clues to mull over. There was just one issue. Too many creatures and supernatural practices can trigger a heart attack. Narrowing down the pool of possibilities wasn't going to be easy. But it made my next course of action simple: I had to learn more about the body I was inhabiting. It was a good bet Charles' room could give me something to go on. At the very least, he had died there; it was possible the monster responsible left some trace.

It wasn't hard to remember my way back to Charles' room. That didn't mean the trip was without its annoyances. I got my fair share of looks along the way. Some were confused stares; others were downright nasty glares from the staff. Whatever Charles had done had pissed off a helluva lot of people.

The door was open from my earlier escape. Glancing around, I fought the urge to sigh. The room was clean. Well, not counting the minor bloodstains from earlier. Nothing was out of place, no signs of struggle, but then, would Charles have struggled? He died in a straitjacket. Convenient for whatever killed him.

Bleach tickled my nose and snapped me from my reverie. The closer I got, the stronger the smell. It wasn't the odor from before. The walls had been cleaned—again.

*Why?*

I placed my hands on the wall and slid the right one around, feeling for anything that seemed out of place. Pausing, I shook my head to overcome the head-jarring smell from the cleaner. The wall was soft, like a light dusting of powder coated it. No doubt worn that way from years of being drawn upon and cleaned.

I rubbed more of its surface, pretty much molesting the wall as my hands slid over it. It seemed odd, feeling up a blank wall, but something *was* there. Call it a gut feeling, but in all my years as an investigator I've learned to trust those instincts. I haven't been steered wrong once.

My hand ran over something subtle. A slight canal in the wall. It was the shallowest of scratches. *No, not scratches.*

I traced the faint grooves with my index finger. These were more than angry cuts in the wall. This was a carving—a message! I all but buried my face in it, examining the faint lines with laser-like precision. I was close enough to taste the bleach, but my focus paid off.

A black fleck of something caught my eye. I dug at it

with a fingernail, managing to get it out. It was a scrap akin to the remains of a sharpened pencil, save for the color and texture. Dull, black, and waxy. I compressed the material between my thumb and forefinger, smearing it across the tips.

*Crayon?*

A sharp *pang* lanced through my skull. The force was strong enough to rock my head. I took a step back, pressing my palms to my eyes. Everything turned pixilated and my vision blurred. What I saw next wasn't before me; it took place in my mind. But it might as well have been happening in real time.

A hand darted across the walls in a frenzied panic. A pointed black tip protruded from its grip. The crayon darted across the light grooves carved into the wall, giving color to shapes. It was like a rudimentary children's drawing, simple wavy lines that meant...something important.

Knuckles cracked as my fingers formed a fist tight enough to bury my nails into the soft tissue of my palm. I struggled to control the overwhelming desire to soften up that wall a bit more. Something needed punching! This entire case, like many of my cases, was throwing riddles in my face.

I hate riddles.

Still, I had gotten some information. A memory from Charles, a handy gift I possess. Whenever I inhabit a victim's body, I gain access to a slew of their memories. Of course, I have no control over when and how they're triggered. Not to mention how deep they take me, or how frickin' painful they can be. That last one hurt like seven kinds of hell.

With a vigorous shake of my head, I banished the thoughts and pain. I had work to do. Dropping to my knees, I swept the floor with manic desperation. I scampered across the sandalwood carpet. My hands clawed its thick mossy fabric. Frayed bits of material went airborne as I searched for the item from my vision. Something rolled against my fingertips and slid from my grip. I buried my hand into the carpet around the small cylinder with such force the tops of my fingers stung.

As much pain as I've endured over the years, carpet burn still smarts.

I willed the itchy pain away and thrust the dark crayon into the air like I had freed Excalibur from a boulder. "Ha!" Bounding to my feet, I nearly flattened the colored piece of wax in my exuberance. I pressed it against the wall and matched the frenzied motion from my vision.

Dark lines filled the shallow grooves and suddenly, the walls weren't so clean. Those wavy lines from Charles' vision stood out, spreading across the drywall like streams of black ivy. There were dozens of the damned lines.

I sighed. "You couldn't have just left a message…with words?" I resumed my frantic tracing, nearing the end of the carvings. Or so I thought. Upon reaching the end, I realized there weren't dozens of lines etched into the wall.

There were tens of dozens. My teeth ground.

Hundreds of waves stretched across the wall and I had only colored in a few dozen. This was going to take time, a commodity I was never given a lot of. I needed to solve this case and fast. I was tired, violated, and clueless.

Peering at the wall, I tried to make some sense out of the mass of curving black lines. Nothing.

Squinting at something doesn't help you understand it any better. All it does is make you look incredibly stupid— or constipated. Knowing all of that didn't stop me from doing it though. Minutes passed. I still had no answers and had essentially just lost a staring contest with a wall.…

Coolness arced across the back of my knees and my legs snapped rigid. The metal frame of the bed sent chilling waves through my lower body. I tried to get a different and larger perspective of the surreal scene in front of me. Staring at it for a bit longer, I finally came to understand it.

"Squiggles." I sighed to no one in particular. "It's just fucking squiggles."

My body felt heavy, stretched thin, and wobbly. I sat on the bed and let my palms rest on either side of me. The mattress compressed a bit. It wasn't some unforgivable slab, but it wasn't memory foam either. I'd like to think it was a happy medium, but it wasn't. Thank God for that. I leaned more toward the squishy and oh-so-comfortable side. I could almost feel my ass utter its thanks after sinking into the bed. There was still a hint of resistance. It was a box spring set-up, one where the springs had gone soft with years of use.

I released a comfortable groan. My head *thudded* against something like thick cardboard. Frowning, I rose and twisted around to see what I had hit. There were two books, the smaller of the pair stacked on top of the other. The larger one was about the size of a boxed DVD case. Its leather matched the brown hue you'd find in high-end European sports cars. The quality however was nowhere as nice. Rough, ragged bits of leather sprung and curled from its surface. The journal was battered. And it would be. It's been through a helluva lot with me.

It was the journal I'd used through innumerable cases. Inside was every bit of supernatural knowledge and lore I'd ever come across. The pages were a mess, festooned with newspaper clippings, pages torn from old mythology books. Yes, I'm a heathen like that; I've torn pages from books. It was for the greater good. Pictures—taken, drawn and printed out—were paper-clipped throughout it. In it, my greatest weapon—knowledge.

Knowledge. Is. Power.

Knowing what a creature is, what it feeds on and how—you can find a way to stop it. This was a 'how to gank 'em' manual.

The thinner journal was more along the lines of a pocket notebook. It was bound under another leather cover, the sort of burgundy found in darker wines. Church had given it to me during my last case in New York. It was so I could record my cases and keep my memories straight. As you can imagine, bouncing through dead bodies and picking up bits of their memories hasn't been so great for my own. I've lost a great deal of my original ones that way, along with them—my original name. This little book was to ensure I kept my mind from becoming "it gets the hose again" crazy.

I racked my brain on how Church had gotten into the room to leave the journals, or how he had ditched me earlier without making a sound. Failing to figure it out, I cast his ninja moves from my mind.

My face broke into a grin. Picking up the journals, I cast my gaze to the ceiling. "One of these days, Church, I'm going to figure out how you pull this Batman shit." My hand spasmed. The books slipped from my grasp.

Oddly, the one with all my lore and information landed flat. The other one was a different story. It plopped to the floor and splayed open to the first page. With measured precision, I slid my index finger beneath the spine of the book, lifting it up to see.

I frowned. Stuck to the page was a small Post-It note. It read: "No you won't." It was Church's handwriting. My forefinger and thumb rubbed against it as I thought for a moment. Adhesive peeled away from paper as I yanked the smartass note from my journal. Tearing it up may have been a petty indulgence, but it felt damn good. I flung the shredded bits of paper across the room without ceremony.

Content with my paper butchery, I fell back onto the mattress. Flipping through my journals was going to take time, but it's not like I had anything else to do. If I kept staring at the incomprehensible squiggles, I would lose my mind and need a stay in the asylum for real.

With a flick of my finger, I flipped my mythology journal open. Less than a third of the pages tumbled by. There was too much lore and knowledge on monsters for me to start from page one. I had heart attacks as a clue; it'd have to be enough.

As I perused, I came across something old—familiar. A name and a bit more. I frowned, hoping it wouldn't be necessary, but memorized the information written there.

Footsteps, fast, hard and getting louder, prompted me to act. I snapped the larger journal shut and tossed them both under the pillow. Bounding to my feet, I took a position facing the door, brandishing the whittled down crayon like a weapon.

The source of the footsteps entered the room…and he wasn't paying the least bit of attention to me. My feelings were seriously hurt.

I would've pegged him at about average height if he could keep a decent posture. His shoulders sagged. The strength in his upper back seemed nonexistent. He was a wiry guy, Ichabod Crane-looking. Clad in a white coat that screamed, "doctor", the middle-aged man with the beaky nose continued to ignore me. His bespectacled gaze was focused on the clipboard in his slender hands.

Without glancing up, he sniffled and addressed me.

"Charles, I've decided it might be best for you to come back to the group." His voice was something else. This guy made Ben Stein look like a color commentator for a women's wet t-shirt contest.

I wanted to answer, "s'what?" but kept my mouth shut. I figured it wiser. A flat card laminated in plastic identified the man as Doctor Eric Cartwright.

Dry scratching sounds filled my ears. The doc's free hand rested in a claw-like grip atop his head. His fingers ground back and forth through the fishing-wire-thin strands. More pepper than salt made up his hair. He looked work-worn. His hair and lined face didn't help. Weary, almost bored brown eyes finally regarded me.

A violent percussion rang through my head the instant our eyes met. I nearly forgot how to stand, much less remain balanced. Horrible contortions gripped my muscles. My body tensed, ready to spring. An unnatural compulsion urged me to throttle the doctor.

Another vision. Charles grappled with the man before me, taking him to the ground. The doctor's arm sprang out in panicked protest. The soft meat of his inner forearm struck Charles' mouth. Things got savage. Charles opened his mouth, sinking his teeth into the doc's arm. They screamed—the doctor in a wide-eyed animalistic wail, Charles in frenzied glee.

What in the hell?

I get visions all the time; the intense ones cause me some cerebral discomfort. This was something else entirely. I *felt* Charles' anger. I *never* feel anything from the victim.

Okay, that's not entirely true. I get a vague sense of feeling from them. Basic opinions, like they care about this person, or that person's fishy. That's about the extent of it. What I don't feel is how profound their hatred for someone is, and it's never had a physiological effect on me.

Until now.

What the hell did this guy do to prompt Charles to go frickin' Lecter on him? A shiver-inducing train of thought went through my mind. What if the doctor *was* what I was hunting? Why else would Charles attack him? It was a fair bet to assume Charles had been restrained after his attack and confined to his straitjacket. Immobilized, isolated—

perfect prey for later. It all tracked. I was missing only one thing.

Proof.

If I tried to gank the doctor now, I could wind up murdering an innocent person. Not only would that not be all-too-groovy with my bosses up top—whoever they are— but I couldn't bear it. I'm not in the hurting people business.

"Charles?"

His simple question brought me back to the squiggle-infested room and the notion of "group." I made sure my first response would put me back in his good graces. Biting a fella doesn't make you all that endearing to them. "Sorry," I mumbled. I hoped it came across as both sincere and sheepish. I wanted Charles to appear contrite because, let's face it, I sure wasn't sorry the doc had got chomped.

"Sorry?"

"For..." I gave a simple nod to his arm.

His gaze followed mine, and he comprehended. With pursed lips, he mulled over it for a moment. A satisfied look fell over his face. "That's good," he said. "I was hoping you'd apologize. If you behave, we won't have to put you back in the jacket." I was surprised he didn't bring up my escape, or the fact I had defaced the walls. But, hey, if a cop lets you off with a warning, you don't question it, right?

His voice took on a solemn tone. "Just remember you're on probation. I won't tolerate another violent outburst."

I gave a curt nod.

"Good. The group is waiting." He beckoned with two fingers.

I waited for him to turn. There was no way I was going to walk side-by-side with him. He didn't seem perturbed about leaving his backside exposed to me. Considering Charles had attacked him once already, his decision spoke volumes. There were two options. He was a monster and incredibly confident that I was no threat to him, or a vanilla mortal that believed I—Charles—was sincerely remorseful about assaulting him. So I followed Dr. Cartwright, who may or may not have been a monster, to group.

The grounds were beautiful, not the stark surroundings people expect when they hear the word "asylum." Not dark, desolate and full of overgrown, untended shrubbery. Spring light shone over a vast, neatly manicured lawn. All manner of trimmed hedgework festooned the place. Some were shaped in serpentine lines snaking to a conical top. Others were less intricate but no less pleasing to look at. A series of perfect cubes, their bases left bare, ran in parallel lines, forming a wall of sorts.

A playground sat to the right—the sort you'd see in public parks—where several patients seemed content to play. It was adorned with swings, monkey bars and spinning blocks with the letters X and O built into a frame. The entirety of it was set in a rectangular field of woodchips.

We headed to the far end of the grounds where columns of trees stood at the outermost edge in a tight formation. I stopped as we drew closer to the woods. My eyes narrowed and I leaned forward, trying to peer into the trees. That was a prime location for something to hide. Even from where I stood, I could tell how dense the woods were. At night, it'd be impossible to see in them. Perfect hiding spot or hunting grounds if patients or the staff ventured out late.

I glanced down to my forearm on instinct. I had lost an hour.

Forty-three left.

A ring of people sat up ahead. I suppressed a groan upon seeing the metal folding chairs. Near the group was a circular fountain that wasn't working at the moment. Doctor Cartwright waved an amicable hand toward an empty seat.

I followed his gesture and sat down, studying the members of the group as the doc took a seat of his own. A thin man with a wiry shock of dark hair sat closest to me. He gnawed compulsively at the nail of his middle finger. Humming drew my attention and caused me to turn to its source.

The noise came from a stunning woman. Shoulder length blonde curls flitted in the breeze. A few flopped over her eyes of polished turquoise. Fair-skinned with one heck of a smile. A gentle vibration emanated from between her teeth as she hummed, all the while rocking in her cross-legged position atop the seat.

My weight shifted as I leaned over to strike up some

dialogue. For investigational purposes, I swear.

Doctor Cartwright cleared his throat and all attention was instantly upon him…including that of the pretty blonde. I was starting to get an idea of why Charles had bitten him.

My focus shifted to everyone else around me, trying to take in everything I could. I had summed up enough about the doc for the moment; I wanted to take mental notes of how everyone reacted to him.

"We'll begin with you." He gestured to one of the patients I hadn't bothered to look at yet.

My mistake.

"Well," she said and I froze. She paused after that singular word but her voice clocked me with the force of a baseball bat across my skull. My stomach sank into an endless pit and my blood ran a few degrees cooler. "I was…involved in something terrible about six months ago," she went on.

The muscles in my neck rusted and fought my decision to face her. As they ground away in objection, I willed my eyes to look at her.

My heart followed my stomach into that pit.

Even in this place she retained her striking beauty. Her face was slightly longer than it was wide. The sunlight complemented her skin perfectly—beige tinged with shades of gold. A warm glow danced through waves of chestnut tresses, loose and hanging to her shoulders. Her hair looked disheveled, unkempt. Eyebrows, a bit smokier in color than her hair, were furrowed together in deep concentration. Her jawline ended in a rounded chin. Her lips were pursed. She did that when thinking. Occasionally she chewed on them. They weren't perky or pouty, but full. Her lips were lengthy, wide, defined and shaped by her entire mouth. Attractive.

Her molasses eyes no longer carried steely resolve. They were softer now, unfocused—lost. Garbed like the rest of us, her posture carried less strength.

She caught me staring and I couldn't break contact.

"Ortiz."

# Chapter Five

Camilla Ortiz.

The FBI agent who had crossed my path during my last investigation in New York. Six months ago I had gotten her involved in my pursuit of an Ifrit, a form of malevolent Djinni from Middle Eastern culture. It had killed people by granting wishes that went horribly wrong. Example: you're an elderly gentleman wishing for oodles of money and a hot piece of tail to shag. Sounds great...until your heart gives out during a heavy romp.

Ortiz went through a hellish gauntlet because of me. She was almost immolated by an Elemental of fire. A pack of Salamanders tried to reduce her to a pile of goo with their corrosive spittle. Her car blew up. Then there was the bit where I tossed her out a hotel window.

Don't look at me like that; it was a good idea at the time.

And I had gotten her killed. It was only due to a miracle that she was still alive. The worst part? My ineptitude caused her death and I wasn't even the one responsible for bringing her back. I couldn't save her. I didn't save her. Someone else did, and they had paid the price.

Imagine swallowing sand till your throat runs dry. Add a sledgehammer to the temples and, for the cherry on top, screwdrivers to the eyes. That's what it felt like looking at her after what I put her through. She didn't recognize the man staring back, what with my new body and all. Ortiz didn't hear me whisper her name. Thank God.

"I saw—experienced things," Ortiz continued. "And it's strange; I know how to deal with them but…"

One thing I'd learned about Camilla Ortiz is that she was made of iron and all things strong. Looking into her eyes now though.... Well, it would've been wrong to say she looked weak. Ortiz had never been weak but she looked vulnerable.

"I can handle what I endured," she said. "But it's the choices that just...they hurt."

"What choices?" The first bit of emotion showed in Doctor Cartwright's empathetic tone.

White teeth flashed as her lips folded under them, and she began her habit of chewing. Ortiz answered after a moment. "Choices between work and doing what's right. And then there are the answers." Ortiz twiddled her thumbs, and looked away for a second. "I was led to believe I would've finally gotten some when things were over. I didn't."

Ouch. I had promised her those answers at the end of the case. Instead, I had left her, unconscious and alone on a church pew. No answers, no one to help her deal with it. My fault.

"People died." She wore a pained expression, one that I mirrored. "And...I can handle what I saw when I'm awake, but at night...I can't control the nightmares." Her voice was a whisper. Admitting that was hard for a person like Ortiz. She was one helluva tough woman. But as strong as anyone is, it's still not that hard to feel lost.

When you go through a crucible like the one I'd taken her through, you don't come out of it with answers. You're left with questions—questions *I* failed to answer. Unanswered, they had buried themselves in some far corner of her brain and found their way out at night, plaguing her with the worst of notions.

"The man who I thought had the answers..." She paused to reconsider for a moment, and I went rigid. "I thought I could trust him. I was wrong."

The knife in my gut twisted. My lips compressed as I rubbed them in a fervent manner. Listening to her was hard. I debated getting up and leaving, but that would be suspicious. My job was never easy; this was taking it to another level. I'd worked alone for the longest time and Camilla Ortiz had changed that. I could trust her, and she had trusted me. I had broken that trust. There were moments when I could have told her it all. I didn't. Now she was here.

The doc's hand enveloped hers. "Thank you," he said,

before scratching away on his clipboard.

Ortiz gave a gentle bob of her head before taking up silence. That's how the rest of the group session proceeded for me.

Silence.

Oh, people talked—they shared their stories—but I heard none of it. Everything was muted. Ortiz's soft whisper and trying tale had deafened me. Guilt's not so light on the brain. It's a pillow weighed down by lead, suffocating all thoughts. It leaves you empty.

When "story time" progressed to me, I waved a hand and motioned to be skipped. The doc gave a reluctant nod to the next person, the attractive blonde beside me. I had lost interest in her since Ortiz had spoken. Group ended minutes later and we dispersed.

It was still light out, so there was time to enjoy the day. Some patients wandered to the edge of the woods, talking genially with one another. A handful went off to the playground. The rest remained single and shambled off to wherever. Even the doc had gone, leaving me with Ortiz.

Soundless—that's how she approached. No *whisking* of her clothes as she walked, no *crunch* of grass. Silent. I didn't move. I wanted to walk away, to continue the case, but leaving her again... I couldn't do that. It's not that she would've known, but I would.

"Charles." She smiled. It was genuine and made me feel shades of anguish and pleasure.

Returning it in an equally sincere manner wasn't easy. My cheeks felt like rubber, refusing to stretch. Her smile deepened and something churned in my stomach. It felt like a lie when I grinned back.

She hadn't lost any of her strength. I could feel it as her arms wrapped around me in a tight hug. Ortiz may have been struggling with some issues, but she was still an iron wrought gal deep down.

"Hey," I said, finally remembering how to speak.

"Hey."

I didn't know what to say. What do you say to a woman like Ortiz after putting her through hell? *"Hey, sorry about exposing you to the world of deep dark nasties, but thanks for tagging along. Sorry about giving you the swan dive treatment out of a window?*

*Oh, and the nearly turning you into an extra crispy FBI agent? Sorry about that. The car thing? My bad. Didn't mean to get it blown up. You got good insurance? And yeah, the whole getting you killed thing—no hard feelings?"* Is that what you say?

"Charles?"

I snapped back to her. "Yeah?" I croaked. My throat had lost all sense of moisture.

A breeze wafted by, casting some of the chestnut locks off her shoulders. "Nothing," she said. "You just seemed lost."

I didn't answer.

"I was worried, you know. Some of us heard you screaming last night."

Charles had been screaming? *So why didn't anyone go to help him?*

"Nightmare?" asked Ortiz. I picked up something in her voice. It wavered slightly. Of course, she had been having nightmares too. Talking about them probably wasn't her favorite subject at the moment.

"Not sure." I shrugged.

She gave an understanding nod. "I'm sorry about the jacket. It was harsh. At least you're out of it now." She flashed me a reassuring smile. "They didn't take your drawings though. That's a good thing, right?"

*Drawings?*

"Where are they?" Charles might have seen something before dying; maybe he was being stalked and caught a glimpse of the creature.

My sudden response caused Ortiz to blink in surprise. Her gaze faltered and drifted down to my waist, then to my arms. Her head sprang up in an almost Rock'em Sock'em Robots fashion, eyes narrowed.

The soft flesh of my forearm panged as she took it in an industrial clamp grip. "What the fuck is this?" Those attractive lips peeled away from her teeth like a wolf baring fangs.

Shit!

She gestured to the tattoo. It had changed again. Group had cost me an hour.

Forty-two left.

I don't know what compelled me to give her the answer

I did. Stupidity, likely.

"The answer to the ultimate question of life, the universe and everything?" I suggested with a hapless shrug and smile.

Nails burrowed into my arm. A row of acute pressure ran along my skin. Guess Ortiz wasn't a fan of the book.

"I knew a guy with a tattoo just like this," she said, her voice guttural. "He took me through a monstrous shitstorm...then left."

I winced. She must've assumed it was from her talon-like grip, because it loosened. For a second, I feared Ortiz had put it together and realized who I was.

I widened my eyes, feigning surprise. "Yeah?"

"Yeah." Her voice was a low growl as she glared at me. "The guy left me alone and asleep in a church. Kind of hurts a girl's feelings."

I would've appreciated the joke if she wasn't staring daggers at me.

"When I woke up, there was a body." Ortiz's gaze faltered for a moment.

That would've been Norman, the man whose remains I'd inhabited at the time. When I finish a case, I sort of leave it behind. My work has a strict carry-on policy. No bodies allowed after you're done with 'em.

"The man I was working with was dead." Ortiz placed a great deal of weight on the last word. Her eyes fell back to my arm. "He had a tattoo like that."

"Like what?" I shrugged nonchalantly.

"One with numbers that counted down by the hour."

"That's crazy!" My voice didn't quite give credit to the lie. It was a bit too put on.

Her eyes narrowed further, becoming angry slits. Ortiz was smart; I figured that out early on. She wasn't like most people. She didn't try to rationalize or delude herself when it came to monsters. Yes, she was a bit thrown at first, but who wouldn't be? After that, she had come to accept their existence. That took guts and brains.

She reaffirmed my notions a second later. "There's something going on here, isn't there?"

"No."

"Liar." Ortiz didn't miss a beat. She didn't even

consider the possibility I might have been telling the truth. From what I could gather, Camilla Ortiz seemed to possess a rare talent that let her separate fact from fiction with an uncanny ease. It was damn near instinctual. She could not be lied to. I'd forgotten about that.

Ortiz kept her heated stare on me. "Last time I bumped into someone with this tattoo, there was a monster involved." She paused. "Monsters," she corrected. I could see the wheels turning in her head. "That's what's happening here, isn't it?" She looked at me for an answer, an honest one.

"Yes."

A slight tremor coursed from her shoulders to her neck. I barely noticed it. Ortiz was on edge and I felt sick for causing it.

"Oh, Charles." Her voice was a cocktail of concern, fatigue, and sadness. "How'd you get wrapped up in this?"

I shrugged. Lying wasn't an option. "Long story."

"One you'll tell me later." It wasn't a suggestion. A bit of the old Ortiz came creeping back—curious, tough and resolved.

I gave her a weak smile. I didn't know if I'd get the chance to. And if I did, there was no way to guarantee Church wouldn't interfere again. The smile would have to be enough.

"So we're going to get this thing?" It was a question, technically, but the way she phrased it she might as well have said, "What are we waiting for?"

"Damn right!" I growled.

That elicited a reaction from her. The metal returned to her eyes, strong, like they had been six months ago. She released the grip on my arm, and flashed me a wolfish grin. I responded with a smile of my own.

"Alright," she breathed. "What do you have, Charles?"

"Squiggles."

She shook her head, eyes fluttering for a moment. "Squiggles?"

"Yup."

Ortiz shut her eyes. A hand went up to cradle her forehead and temple. Without answering, she walked toward the asylum.

"Wait up, Ortiz!" I jogged after her.

Ortiz stopped. "Camilla," she said.

"What?"

"You've always called me Camilla."

I swallowed. Her eyes glimmered and I could almost see the thoughts looping around her head. Smooth, Graves. "First time for everything, right?" I chortled weakly.

Ortiz watched me intently. I cleared my throat and passed her by as I made my way to the asylum. After a moment, I heard blades of grass whisking against her clothes as she followed.

"Where are you going to start, Charles?"

"Drawings," I said.

# Chapter Six

The rec room had a comforting aura about it. Maybe it was the familiar pieces that made it feel that way. Grey carpeting, the sort everybody's seen at least once in their lifetime, spread across the floor. Clean walls with half a dozen windows let the sunshine in. Some had been opened to allow cool drafts of air inside. Tables topped with favorite childhood board games. Easels, paper and all manner of arts and craft supplies were lying around. In the corner, a makeshift theater with chairs packed tight and full of people staring at a cheap projector screen. And, most of all, it was quiet.

Not a disturbing, hushed silence. It was calming, content; you could feel it, like falling asleep under warming sunrays. Part of me wanted to nestle down in the carpet, curl up and go to sleep. But I had work to do.

Still had forty-two hours. Not too bad.

"Where did you say my drawings were?" I arched an eyebrow at Ortiz.

"I didn't."

I gave her a knowing look and she rolled her eyes. "There," she pointed to a chalk-white shelf. It wasn't lined solely with horizontal boards; it was sectioned off vertically as well, creating a series of cubes.

Ortiz followed me as I walked over to it. "So, the tattoo thing?"

I grunted in acknowledgement of her question.

"Like I said, the other guy had one too."

Grunt.

"That like a club or something?"

"Sort of," I answered absently. My attention was focused on the cubbies stuffed with papers and crafts, little animals made of fuzzy pipe cleaners. Some of the cubbies were hoarding crayons and markers. People really need to learn to share.

"How do you join?"

I couldn't help it. My lips spread into a broad grin. "Go to Church."

"What?'

Now I knew how Church felt giving answers that no-one understood. It was somewhat pleasing. I'm a terrible person. Well, technically I'm a soul, so I guess I get a pass.

I was about to give up searching when a game of pinball erupted in my head. The hard corner of the shelf dug into the tender meat of my palm as I gripped it for support. I was crouched over, struggling to keep my balance. Another vision.

Charles panicked. His hands were a flurry as he tore through one the cubbies. Papers went flying—his drawings. He shoved them below another set of artwork. The name Mindy was visible in fluorescent marker.

I shook my head. That was the second time a vision had walloped me. Was something happening to me, my body, my powers? It was one helluva disturbing train of thought, one I pushed aside for the moment. Mindy's name caught my eye. Carefully removing the stack from her cubby, I set them down and searched.

A gentle weight fell on my shoulder; strong, caring, and one I'd felt before. "You okay, Charles?"

"Yeah." My voice was rough, partly from the vision, partly from that shoulder squeeze. I hated not telling her who I was. Nothing was stopping me of course, except maybe my fear of Church. I wasn't so much afraid of him as I was of what could happen. Church had already told me Ortiz deserved to know the truth, to meet him even. Only, she wasn't ready yet, whatever that meant. So I kept her in the dark. "Yeah," I repeated.

Ortiz adopted a cross-legged position on the floor beside me. She regarded the drawings and arched an eyebrow at me. "You know, Mindy isn't Charles, right?" She smiled and her eyes shone with amusement.

I mumbled under my breath in mock discontent, but it was nice to see her smiling again.

Two thirds of the stack were a mass of bright neon marker. The remaining bit were significantly darker. Charles hadn't scrawled his name anywhere, but I could tell they belonged to him. Sinister lines of black marker, crayon and even paint streaked across the pages. Some of the sheets looked like they were connected, images that ran from one to another. Not squiggles, I realized—tendrils.

I had no idea what they meant, or if they were connected to the monster. It was possible, but then again, Charles *was* crazy. *A crazy man who covered his wall in markings, was murdered, and screamed the night of his death.* It was all I had at the moment. Well, not counting the wall. Everything felt disjointed. The visions were kicking my butt, and I had clues that left me clueless.

A scream tore through the room. Everyone's attention belonged to it now. Paper crumpled as my hands balled around Charles' artwork. I tore off in the direction of the shrieking. Ortiz followed. As I barreled out of the rec room, I realized something. Everyone else was calm. Not a single soul seemed the least bit perturbed by the noise. Two elderly gentlemen had looked up, pursed their lips, and returned to their game of checkers. A nearby nurse shook her head before motioning to nearby orderlies. I heard her say something about sedation.

How the hell were they so calm? There was a monster around. I knew it. Ortiz must've known it. Why didn't they? Gus had told me too many heart attacks were occurring. Didn't that set off bells in anyone's head?

Guess not. My legs hammered across the carpet and onto the marble of the halls as I charged ahead. I could hear Ortiz's breaths behind me. They were calm, the controlled breathing of a frequent runner. Pent up in here, what else did she have to do but run and train in her free time?

Another scream—louder. A prickling sensation erupted over my skin. We had made it outside the room. A normal person would've forced their way in. I wasn't normal and I wasn't stupid. The door was a pale blue steel. I couldn't have forced my way through it no matter how badly I wanted to. So I concentrated elsewhere.

Like the rest of the doors in the asylum, this one had a pane of glass for viewing inside. Only, the keyboard-sized bit of glass needed a good cleaning. A substance like black paint beat and swirled against the glass. It was doing a great job of obscuring what was going on inside. That's not normal. There was definitely a monster in the room.

Another scream. It didn't last as long as the ones before. It had been muted near the end.

"Fuck this!" I snarled.

Charles' drawings fell to the floor as I made a fist. My knuckles cracked right before I sent my hand into the window with ballistic force. Glass shattered. My fist sailed through the shards as somebody screamed. A heavy throb resonated through my fist and into my wrist.

There's a reason punching things isn't always the best option. Human hands aren't the greatest weapons. They're littered with nerve endings, and filled with tiny bones that are easy to break. Oh, and if you *do* smash the window, you let the frickin' ominous black stuff out!

"Holy shit!" I yelped.

Arctic coolness assaulted my fingers. The bones in my hand froze as numbness coursed upwards. My forearm grew distant, like it was no longer part of my nervous system. The black whatsit snaked up my arm, leaving frigid paralysis in its wake. Worse, there seemed to be no end to the stuff. The mass that shot out of the window did nothing to diminish the amount of fog in the room. I couldn't see a damn thing.

"Ackh!" I spat as my free hand beat my ick-covered arm. *Squelch squelch squelch* went the tar-like goop each time my hand slapped it. Every time I pulled away, wisp-like threads of gunk trailed between my arm and hand. Talk about being clingy.

Spreading my fingers into a clawed grip, I attacked my gook-covered arm, digging through the black gunk. My good fingers slowed, growing rigid as the substance congealed around them. A snarl left my throat as I worked through the numbing chill. My hand tensed and I tore at the blackened, jelly-like substance in a savage manner. It fought back, refusing to be parted. Just when I managed to rip the first hunk of the stuff off, something went wrong.

Go figure.

A flash. A vision. A brutal one, but I glimpsed something. Black tendrils writhed and flailed toward me. There were hundreds of them. A pale mass at the center, too bright to be seen properly, contrasted violently against the shadowy backdrop. One of those industrial crushers reserved for junkyards worked on my head. The pain brought water to my eyes.

And then it was gone. That was by far the most painful and quickest vision to course through my head. I had just seen the black tendrily masses of frickin' Cthulhu!

Everything around me had a submerged look to it once I could see again. Stupid tears. A strong grip under my arms hauled me up.

"Erngh," I groaned as Ortiz helped me to my feet. I wasn't aware I had fallen. A spasm erupted in my arm. I felt it again and looked down to see it was clean.

I shot Ortiz a "what gives?" look.

She shrugged. "It sort of…went away."

"What?"

Ortiz's face twisted into a mask of horror. I stumbled as she let go of me and shoved her face toward the window.

"No!" I grabbed her and pull her away.

The room was empty, save for the body inside.

Every bit of the ominous black fog was gone. Whatever it was, it had done its job. The creature had claimed another victim.

She was pretty, the type that attracted men old enough to know better, as well as ones too young and stupid to care. She was at an age hovering between late teens and early college. Ringlets of wheat flowed to a hidden length behind her shoulders. Pale skin—tall. The gal could've modeled if she had chosen to. Only now, her face was frozen in anguish and terror. Her eyes were wide open. Trickles of moisture hung down her cheeks.

I looked at Ortiz. Her face mirrored the young woman's. It's never easy finding a dead body. It's worse when you could've done something to stop it. Ortiz had helped me through a situation like this six months ago. Someone had died and I felt responsible. It was my turn to help her, but first we had to move.

I laid a gentle hand on her shoulder. "Come on."

Ortiz turned and stared.

"We can't do anything for her."

She kept staring, her face pained.

"Look, orderlies might show up any second now. We're

standing in front of a dead body and a broken window."

She remained silent.

I was angry. So was she. I could feel my features harden and my eyes followed. "We will get this thing. I promise."

That galvanized her. The silence was replaced by a steadfast, fiery look I'd seen in her before. "Let's go," she agreed.

Scooping up Charles' scattered works, I bolted. She followed. We hoofed it until we were several halls away. Ortiz rested on one leg, bracing herself against the wall. Her breathing was cool, calm and effortless despite sprinting. That was impressive.

It was quiet. That happens after you see a monster murder somebody. The worst part was that we didn't even *see* the monster. All I saw was endless black obscuring whatever killed the poor girl. That wasn't much to go on, but it was more than I had an hour ago. Tendrils, Charles' drawings, heart attacks, and black fog. Not to mention the unfinished Pollock back in his bedroom.

The hell was this thing?

Ortiz had the same idea—great minds and all. "What the hell was that thing?"

"Honestly?"

"Honestly," she said.

"I have no clue." I gave a fractional shake of my head.

"Yeah, neither did the last guy with one of those tattoos."

Okay…that was a low blow and she didn't even know it.

"Do you have anything we could go on?"

"Apart from what we just saw and these"—I broke off as I held up Charles' drawings—"not much."

Her lips twitched. She wasn't happy, but then again, neither was I. An innocent young woman had been murdered and neither of us had a clue what had done it.

"My bedroom. Come with me," I said as a notion crossed my mind.

Apparently the wrong one crossed Ortiz's. "What?" She crossed her arms, tilting her head and eyeing me askance.

"I have an idea," I tried to clarify.

"I don't think I'm going to like it."

"Just come on." I left to make my way back to Charles' bedroom.

With a push of her heel, she rocked off the wall and followed behind. During the walk, Ortiz kept asking questions. I answered them with traditional ambiguity. It's the way to go on questions you don't want to—or can't—answer. By the time we reached Charles' room, Ortiz was knotted in frustration.

"Are all you tattooed guys assholes?"

I turned, flashed a smirk, and waggled my fingers in a mysterious gesture.

Scowling, she huffed and twisted her hips. Ortiz's heel bounced off the metal door.

Charles' room was still in the mess I had left it. Trails of black crayon covered the wall opposite the bed. The fact Charles had scrawled across the wall meant he was aware of the creature, at least in some regard. He must've known about it for some time. There's no other way he could have left so many signs.

The worst part was that Charles *had* known and still died. If he had asked for help—told somebody—who would listen? He was a patient in a mental institution. Seeing monsters was common enough here. Hell, this creature was ingenious. An asylum was the perfect ground for claiming victims.

While I was busy working things out, Ortiz surveyed the room. "Interesting décor." The corners of her mouth quirked.

"Yeah," I muttered, not really paying attention. "I call it Pollock and The Paranormal, one of my seminal works."

"Cute," she said in an offhand manner.

"I can be," I shot back, cracking the joke on pure instinct.

Ortiz froze. She stared hard at me.

*Shit.* I turned to regard the wall again, trying not to break into a cold sweat. Ortiz's eyes burrowed a hole into the back of my head. Me and my big witty mouth.

Staring at nothing for a long time is a heckuva job. Well, there were squid-like appendages to stare at, but I couldn't at that moment. I was too wrapped up in the fact that Ortiz might have figured me out. So I remained motionless. It was like that scene from Jurassic Park. Don't move and the T-Rex won't spot you. I also resolved to never let Ortiz know that I had compared her to a dinosaur. I'd seen her angry before. It wouldn't end well for me.

After an uncomfortable amount of time spent in silence, she stepped beside me, looking right at me. Something was at work behind her eyes; I could see it. She was starting to put things together. Maybe she wasn't there yet, but if I didn't shut up, she'd get there a whole lot sooner.

Church would be pissed.

Changing the subject seemed like a good idea. I pointed to the marked-up wall.

Ortiz shook her head in confusion. "*What* is it?"

"A clue."

Ortiz's lips folded and I saw her fighting to hold back the smile. Her eyes danced with amusement. "I can see that," she said, adopting the tone a mother would take when dealing with a child who had just stated the obvious. "What is it?"

"Tendrils."

"What?"

"Tendrils." I waved my arms in a fluid wavy kind of manner. "You know, tendrils, squids, octopuses—"

"Octopi."

I scowled. "Whatever. Tentacles of doom!" My voice took on the ominous tone reserved for cartoon villains.

"Tentacles of doom?" Her lips twitched and an eyebrow arched in amusement.

I ignored her. Tentacles of doom sounded appropriate to me.

She gestured to the wall. "Why'd you have to draw so many? Couldn't you have just *written* tentacles?"

I couldn't answer that question without revealing myself, and I couldn't lie to Ortiz. She was a walking polygraph test.

So I ignored her.

Walking over to the bed, I retrieved the crayon from earlier. I turned and thrust it toward Ortiz.

She arched her dark eyebrow higher, regarded the crayon, then me.

I nodded towards the wall. "Well, get coloring, there's

more."

"Why didn't you finish it before?"

"Reasons."

She scoffed and took the crayon. Ortiz's arm moved deftly across the shallow white grooves in the wall. The springs in the mattress pushed against me as I sat on the bed. There was enough room on the mattress for me to spread Charles' drawings over it. After I had done so, I wished I hadn't.

I had no clue what I was looking at, but they terrified me. The same writhing tentacles that had latched around my arm covered a page. Swirls of black marker ran over another page in what I assumed was the peculiar mass of fog I'd seen. One page had a series of simply drawn men, every inch shaded in black. Shadows had been sketched several times across the page. And then a message. "The shadows stare," he'd written. "They watch."

Whatever the hell that meant. It was disturbing nonetheless.

The last page caused my heart to break the world's vertical leap record. It almost got caught in my throat. Thick lines of purple, nearly black, streamed out from the center of the page. Clouds of that dark fog colored the background. Words like "shadows" dotted the page. Bullseye center of it all was an undefined white shape—lengthy and slender. A replay of the vision I had experienced when trying to rescue the poor girl. Charles' drawing might as well have been a Xerox of what had flashed through my head. Somehow, not-so-loony Charles had managed to record everything with startling accuracy.

I was left with one problem: making sense of it all.

So many clues, so few answers. I was tempted to whip out the larger of my journals and go through it. Maybe I could come up with something. However, with Ortiz standing a few feet away, I couldn't risk it. She had already seen those journals; hell, she'd gone through them. If there was ever a way to tip her off to me not being who I claimed to be, that was it.

"Uh, Charles?"

I turned away from the littered pages of spooky art and faced Ortiz. Someone filled my lower jaw with lead. It sank when I saw the wall. I'm pretty sure my eyes had gone full Warner Brothers, increasing several sizes. Charles was one hell of an artist before he'd been killed.

Faces, a few sizes smaller than they would be in actuality, peppered the wall. They were a heckuva improvement over Charles' other work, akin to a forensic sketch artist. There was enough skill involved to identify the faces. The first two were unknown to me, a portly bald man and a pretty young gal. An intense pressure developed behind my eyes as I gazed upon the third and fourth sketches. My heart, the ever-so-rhythmic musician, thumped away in my throat.

Ortiz matched my saucer-eyed gaze as she traded looks between the wall and my face. The third picture was familiar. It should've been. I had been looking at him not too long ago. A few days' growth of scruff lined his jaw. A near perfect nose offset his stark appearance. Ortiz had good reason to be doing a double-take between me and the wall.

Charles' face was on it.

The face beside it didn't help. Long ringlets of hair framed a face of early adulthood. I blinked and thought of the young woman Ortiz and I tried to save earlier.

Gus had told me several people had already died. The young woman I knew for a fact was dead. Then there was Charles. He had predicted his own death. I was left with more questions and not too many answers. Like, when had Charles found the time to practice poetry? He had left one heck of an incoherent message.

> *Water makes them come and makes them go.*
> *With more water I can make them show.*
> *Shadows sitting, watching, always they stare.*
> *Coming at night, to fill me with despair.*
> *It comes at night; it comes at night.*
> *Silent but screams, quiet and out of sight.*
> *Watch the shadows, be careful, beware.*
> *Follow fear down below, down below elsewhere.*

Just once, I wished someone would leave a note behind: "This is what killed me. You're welcome."

"Charles?" Ortiz pulled me away from my inner

grumbling. "You have any idea what this means?"

*No frickin' clue.*

"Yeah," I frowned. "It means I have to make a phone call."

# Chapter Seven

"Phone call?"

"Yeah, you know those things you put to your ears to talk to people with?" I gestured with my pinky and thumb near my ear.

Her eyes went flat. "The other guy had a journal full of information. Don't you?"

I froze. Denying it was not a good idea. She'd see straight through the lie and I'd be in trouble. Well, more trouble. There was still a monster breaking into rooms and killing people.

No biggie…

I made sure to change the subject. "Trust me, this is one of those things I need to make a call for."

A huff of agitated breath left her mouth, but she gave an understanding nod. "Wait here. I'll fetch one."

Wait, what?

"Uh, you'll…fetch one?" I blinked as she left the room. My plan had been to find a way to use one of the receptionist's phones. But hey, if she had access to a phone, it made my job easier.

Once I was convinced Ortiz wasn't anywhere nearby, I reached under the pillows and retrieved one of my journals. With a flick of my wrist I sent the brown leather cover and pages within it, tumbling open. I licked my thumb and flipped through page after page. Nothing. I had the severe inclination to hurl my journal at the wall. Several soothing breaths later, I decided against committing such sacrilege.

My journal was the paranormal equivalent of Wikipedia. Scrolling through it always led me to some conclusion or provided a clue. You'd be surprised how little it takes to start an avalanche of thoughts that can lead you to the right answer. All I needed was a hint. If there was a place to look for signs, this was it. Its handmade and yellowed pages nearly had it all, but none of it was helping.

The hell are you supposed to make out of shadows, water, tentacles, black fog and heart attacks? Most disjointed clues...ever.

My arm itched and I sighed. Forty-one hours left. That was still a good deal of time to close the case. If I had an idea of what was going on.

I shoved my journal in its hiding place as Ortiz entered into the room. I muttered a silent thanks to whoever was listening that she had failed to notice me hiding it.

"Here." She handed me a rather outdated-looking cell phone.

Arching a quizzical eyebrow, I stared at the device, then her. "How'd you get a cell phone in here?"

Her fingers waggled in a spooky gesture. "Trade secrets."

I blinked. Did she just steal my line and moves? I sniffed and took the phone. My thumb slid over the power button. I paused before pressing it.

"Ortiz," I said. She regarded me, waiting for my question. "What are you doing in here?"

"I told you at group." She shrugged, but I waved her off.

"Isn't this going to hurt your career?"

Her voice went flat. "I never told you about my career."

Oops.

"Well..." I looked around the room, at the drawings, at the floor, anywhere but her face. I smacked my lips together and risked meeting her eyes. "Won't it look bad on your record for wherever you work?"

"Oh, that, yeah." She gave an absent wave of her hand.

Whew, saved.

"I called in a couple of favors," she went on in the same nonchalant tone. "I work for the FBI. I have a good history with some of the higher ups. They've made sure my little 'visit' stays off the books."

Which explained how she managed to sneak a phone into a mental asylum. Don't get me wrong. They're not maximum security prisons. You're just not allowed to have cell phones, sharp objects—those sort of things. But if you happen to be an FBI agent who can call in some favors, I'm pretty sure you can have a phone smuggled in.

"My dad was a big player back when he was working. He made a lot of friends—enemies too."

I didn't know her father had been a Fed.

"What happened to him?"

"Died." Her beautiful features sank into a melancholy mask.

Nice, Graves.

"Sorry," I said with as much sympathy as I could.

She gave a simple shake of her head. "Don't worry. You didn't know." Walking over to the side of the bed, she plopped down beside me. I noticed she was looking at the phone with a great deal of intent.

I tilted the phone so the numbers were out of her view and dialed. She shot me a frown before leaning over, her expression curious. I scooted over a bit and waggled an admonishing finger. "Nah ah ah."

Her eyes narrowed dangerously and I had the feeling that if I kept it up, she might have bitten my finger off. So I issued a retreat warning to my uppity digit.

The phone rang. It kept on ringing. Then it stopped.

"Seriously? Voicemail!" I spat in disbelief.

"Who was it?" Ortiz leaned over further, peering at the screen.

I motioned at her to pipe down. She adopted a threatening posture. I quickly shot her an apologetic glance. No point in dying before solving the case. That's plain stupid.

I dialed again. Somebody picked up. There was no answer. Guess that left the hellos to me. I was okay with that though. I am an excellent conversationalist. "Get his ass on the line—now!" See? Excellent.

No answer, but the line was still on.

"I know you can hear me. You tell that little shit he can't just hang—"

Click.

Well...crap.

I redialed and resolved to be more diplomatic.

Somebody answered. "Graves," said a deep, gravelly voice.

"Gnosis?" I whispered, uncertain if I was talking to the

eldest of Gnomes or not.

"Obviously." Somehow he made it sound like I was an idiot. "And why are you whispering?"

I cast a nervous glance toward Ortiz. She looked back at me with an almost predatory gaze. She didn't like it when people held out on her with info, and here I was talking to the George Soros of the paranormal world.

Gnosis was probably the biggest information broker of the supernatural on our plane of existence. He knew a ridiculous amount of things and possessed an equally ridiculous amount of wealth. And he would. Gnomes are the best when it comes to dealing with gems and wealth derived from the earth. He was also the oldest Gnome in existence, mostly because he was the first. That, and no one had killed him—yet.

He was also a colossal asshat, which is saying something for a being of his stature.

"She didn't hear a thing, Graves."

"You...know?" I blinked. How could he have known something like the fact Ortiz was right beside me. Maybe he and Church attended eavesdropping classes together.

"There won't be much for her to hear anyways. This conversation will be short."

See? Rude. Asshat.

Motion cut my conversation with the curmudgeony Gnome short. A blur darted across the wall. It was gone. I knew I had seen it—hunched and insanely fast. I blinked, making sure my vision was clear. It was. The hell did I just see?

"Graves?"

"Yeah." My reply came out a bit gruffer. "Yeah," I repeated after clearing my throat.

"What do you want?"

"Answers."

He didn't respond, not right away at least. I could hear him breathing on the other end of the line. It was deep, slow and calm. He was thinking. Which wasn't a good sign. He was debating whether he would help me or not. Soon, I was wondering the same thing. Seconds later, I got my answer.

"No," Gnosis said in a stone-like voice. It was a weighty, solid answer.

"No?" I could feel reverberations in my throat as I growled. "The hell do you mean, 'no'?"

"As in 'no'. As in to not comply; to refuse." He sounded like he was talking to a dimwitted child.

I ground my teeth.

"My debt is paid, Graves—in full—but there is the small matter of you being indebted to me. You could, of course, offer compensation for such information, *if* you had anything to offer. The last option you are left with is placing yourself further in my debt."

My growl deepened. I could feel him smiling on the other end of the phone. Gnosis had a crooked nose; I suspected someone had broken it for him long ago. I wondered if I could straighten it out with another punch.

"Does that option appeal to you, Graves?" Pure pleasure filled his voice.

I gave him one hell of a reply. "Go fuck yourself!"

A heavy sigh emanated from the phone. "Well, it seems we are at an impasse. Goodbye, Graves." Click.

"Thanks for nothin', you little shit," I muttered as I lobbed the phone up and down in my hand. I had the urge to throw something…again.

Ortiz decided to comment on my little conversation. "So that, um, went well."

I glared at her. The corners of her mouth struggled not to spread into a wide smile. I glared harder. "What happens if I throw your phone really hard at the wall?"

Her lips pursed and she thought for a moment. "Well, first, my phone breaks, then I kick your ass." Her voice was perfectly neutral.

"Oh." I handed the phone back.

She accepted it with a self-satisfied grin. Her attention turned to the miniscule screen, and her brows furrowed. "I've seen that number before."

"Really?" I feigned surprise.

"You're a *really* bad liar." She scowled as she pressed the redial button. The phone rang, and I tried hard not to burst out laughing. Seconds later—the inevitable. Frowning, she turned back to me. "No longer in service—again?"

Raucous laughter erupted as I lost the battle to hold it in. Ortiz had tried that trick last time and Gnosis had given her the same reply. She couldn't even get through to him. I found it hilarious; sue me.

A dull fist-sized throb manifested in my shoulder. I stopped laughing, sort of. "Hey!" I exclaimed through the last bits of laughter.

Ortiz sat there, fist balled, her mouth twisted in an amused expression. "You tattoo guys suck."

I laughed again. She joined me. It felt good. Laughing always does. There's no pain in this world that a little laughter can't help with. Trust me. We finished our laughter and things got quiet.

"So...what now?"

I shrugged. "Dunno, that was my best bet." Although that wasn't entirely true. Gnosis wasn't my best bet—just the safest. Well, that part wasn't true either. It would've been more accurate to say he was the least dangerous. I really needed new friends....

"Don't tell me you're giving up?"

I tilted my head, looking at her like she was crazy. "The hell I am!"

She nodded. "Good. I have an idea."

"All ears."

"They've probably found the body by now," she said. I gestured for her to continue. "I thought I could take a look at it and see if anything's, you know...weird."

"I was told by one of the patients that the deaths looked like heart attacks."

"Sure didn't look like a heart attack to me." Her face tightened, lips pressing together as she thought on it. "Bunch of black smoke and tentacles? How does that equal a heart attack?"

I shrugged.

Ortiz chewed on her lips. "Okay, how about you go and see what you can learn from other people, and I'll go check out the body."

I raised a hand. "Uh, shouldn't I be checking out the dead body? My area of expertise, you know." I hooked a thumb to my chest. "I deal with the paranormal." I pointed to her. "You interrogate people. Part of your job being a Fed and all."

An eyebrow arched and her face took on an amused

look. "I'm sorry, did *you* go to medical school?"

"Well, no." I paused before blinking several times. "Wait...did *you?*"

She smiled.

Woah, impressive.

"Okay then, uh, you go check out the body, I'll go ask questions."

Ortiz snorted. "That's what I thought. Meet back here in an hour?"

I nodded.

"Don't come back empty-handed," she said as she turned on a heel and left.

"You too!" I called after her.

Once Ortiz left, I pushed myself off the bed and headed toward the rec room. It made sense. The largest concentration of people were going to be there. I just had to make sure I was subtle in my questioning.

I can be subtle....

Following leads makes one thirsty. I stopped by a fountain in the hall. "Bleckh," I sputtered as a stream of warm, stale water lobbed into my mouth. It was like it had been sitting in a bucket in direct sunlight—all day. Water fountains do not, and should not, spout warm water. Heresy!

But I was parched, so I took another swig. I let the water slosh around my mouth before swallowing with a grimace. When I had taken my fill, I turned around, freezing as something whipped past me. Startling speed didn't even come close to how fast that freak had moved! Supernatural, sure, but even that did it no justice. The only glimpse I got was a shadow, and it was a poor glimpse. I stared at the wall, resolute not to blink.

A blur.

I blinked.

Another glimpse, another shadow. This thing was freakishly fast...and taunting me. Pressure surged through my gums from the force with which I clenched my teeth and jaw. Eyes narrowed, I stared harder at the wall. If this dick wanted to play games, I'd play along, right up to the moment where I'd kick its ass!

"Who's winning?" asked a voice in equal parts

amusement and genuine interest.

I swore, whirling about to face the source. Big, cherub-like and smiling, Gus stood there watching me. "What?" I said in a half-shout as my head whipped back to the wall, hoping to catch another glimpse.

"The staring contest. You, the wall?" he explained.

I broke away and turned back to face Gus, laughing as I did. Not often I meet someone who can match my razor-sharp wit and crack out a funny like that. I gave a slight bow of my head in admiration for his witticism. He flashed me a childlike grin and extended a meaty hand. I shook it. "Good to see ya, Gus." I grinned.

He *thwapped* me on the shoulder with a pat that nearly sent me sprawling. Okay, the giant man-baby was damn strong.

"Good to see you too."

Grimacing, I rolled my shoulder. It didn't hurt that much. I'm used to all manner of pain, having fought the supernatural for so long. Still, ask someone to slap you on the back pretty hard and tell me it doesn't sting a bit.

"Yeah," I said, my voice coming out a few shades rougher than expected. "So," I said, trying to ease back into the conversation from earlier. "Anything else you can tell me about the…" I trailed off, letting my voice drop to a whisper. "The monster?"

His features sank and he gave me a disheartening shake of his head. "No, sorry."

I sighed. Of course not. I never catch a frickin' break.

Gus must've noticed my reaction. "Sorry," he repeated.

It was an effort to flash an honest smile. "No worries."

"Maybe someone else has seen something?" he supplied in half-suggestion, half-question.

"Possibly," I murmured as I pondered the notion. Charles had noticed the strange occurrences. Ortiz had quickly grasped what was going on, and then there was Gus. It didn't seem like a stretch for others to know of it. In fact, it was starting to seem like I was the only one without a clue, despite actually having a plethora of them.

Irony sucks monkey wang.

Something else occurred to me. "Hey, Gus?"

"Yeah?"

"You know that something strange is going on here, and…you don't seem too worried. Why not?"

He shrugged. "I don't know, but that's why you're here, right? To help us?" I could hear it in his voice. He honestly believed I was here to help. It was a real, authentic belief that I *could*—and *would*—do something to protect the people here.

I set my jaw. "You're damn right it's why I'm here."

He smiled. It lasted a second before it shifted into a frown. "Aw, I have to go. Late for my group." Before it even registered with me, Gus crossed half the length of the hall.

"Oh, okay, uh, erm, bye?" I waved after him. "Guess I'll do the investigation...monster hunting stuff myself," I mumbled.

Another blur. Another shadow.

Icy needles pricked my skin. Either I was finally starting to lose it—my years of monster hunting were catching up to me, or worse, I was being stalked.

Great.

I developed a newfound respect for the sport of speed walking as I hoofed it to the rec room. My pace was not determined by the fact that a monster might've been trailing me. Nope. Paranormal investigator. Fearless. I just needed a brisk—really brisk—walk. Get the blood flowing and all.

The rec room contained a little less than a dozen people. It's hard to do an accurate headcount when you're being pursued.

I maneuvered to the center of the room, targeting a lonesome table topped with a checkerboard. Being in the middle gave me the best view of the entry points into the room—all two of them. It also meant I was surrounded by witnesses if anything happened to me.

*Wait, why am I worried?*

Something wasn't right. I was afraid. I was on edge, manic, and…had been biting the fingernail of my thumb.

What the hell was going on?

Sure, things scare me on occasion. It happens. Now, though, something was plain wrong. I was beginning to feel like I belonged in this place. Doing my job didn't seem important anymore. Being safe was more important.

Cold sludge rolled through the insides of my skull. I could feel it pressing against my mind. Those weren't my thoughts.

*I. Am. Not. Chicken shit!*

The pressure increased. I fought harder. Beehives—plural—erupted within my noggin. Convulsions wracked my body. My vision blurred the harder I fought.

*Fuck this!* I was not going to have my ass kicked by a supernatural headache. If anything was going to kick my ass, it was going to be me. So, I did.

Checker pieces went flying. A resounding *thud* emanated from the table, and my vision went red. My skull ricocheted off the board. Spots danced in front of my vision and the strange thoughts...ceased. Groaning, I cradled my throbbing head, holding it until the room stopped seesawing. I got a few strange looks. Screw 'em. They weren't the ones being brain-addled. I made it all the way up to a hundred deep breaths before my noggin settled.

A blur.

I debated head-butting the table again. Church would be irked if I died from a self-inflicted aneurysm, so I didn't.

A blur.

Whatever it was, the message was clear. It could move faster than I could see and it could get at me whenever the hell it wanted. I couldn't help it. I spoke in my best Luke Skywalker impersonation. "Your overconfidence is your weakness." I smiled to myself.

A blur.

I exhaled through my nose in frustration. "Whatever." I shook my hand in a dismissive wave. "You feel like coming after me, I'll be right here," I said in a challenging manner. Kneeling down, I took the time to recover the checker pieces I had sent flying and set up the board.

Another blur.

The ridges atop the coin-like piece tickled the underside of my finger as I rubbed the edge.

My gaze drifted to the opposite wall. Another blur. My teeth grated. Narrowing my eyes at the far wall, I nudged a piece forward with my index finger. I was ready for one helluva staring contest.

"Game on, bitch!"

# Chapter Eight

"King me!" I roared in raucous triumph. I maneuvered my piece to the other end of the board. I was winning oh-so-effortlessly. I had already won six games. I had also lost six.

"Enjoying yourself?" chuckled a sweet, amused voice.

The hem of a white coat over casual clothes came into view. Lengthy toned legs with a recent tan were next. I'm a detective; I notice things like a nice pair legs.

"I am now." I smiled.

She matched my smile, making it reach her eyes of periwinkle infused with gray. "Do you mind?" She gestured to the empty seat across from me.

My opponent was pretty much letting me win, so I figured it best to let the pretty lady sit. "Not at all."

Loose waves of noir tresses bobbed as she eased into the chair. She placed a clipboard across her lap. "Who's winning?" The edge of her mouth quirked in a bemused expression.

I hooked a thumb to my chest. "This guy."

Her reaction wasn't quite an entertained snort, but it was close. "I figured."

Okay, pretty women don't normally come over and chat me up. It's not unheard of, but it's more common for gorgeous gals to form a line to kill me. My clothing felt a tad restrictive. I shifted uncomfortably. "Eh, what's up, doc?"

"I'm here for our session."

"Session?"

"I'm assigned to you for individual sessions, remember?"

"I thought Doctor Cartwright did all that stuff?" I made an offhand wave.

"He's busy running group sessions."

I made a mental note of that.

"So what can I do ya for, doc?"

"How are you?" Her voice changed ever so slightly, adopting a clinical tone.

"Uh, fine?"

"You're not sure?"

My lips twitched and I bit back my sharp response. "Fine." The word came out solid.

She nodded more to herself than me and scrawled on her clipboard.

Motion on the far wall drew my attention. Something flickered by.

"How are the nightmares?"

"Better," I lied, leaning over to look past her.

She noticed, turning her head to watch with me.

"Charles?"

"You…see something?" I eyed her for a second before turning back to the wall.

"No, did you?"

There was a loaded question.

"S'nothin'." I shrugged.

She refused to give me a moment's reprieve to think. First, she asked me to remember my name. Confirming the basics, over and over. The only thing that stopped it being an interrogation was her gentle tone. A rhythmic tapping colored our conversation. Then, it stopped. The piece I had been banging on the table dug into the meat of my palm as I squeezed it.

"My name is Vincent Graves," I growled. "I lost my body a long time ago due to—well, I don't know what the fuck. Trust me, I'd love to know. Because of that and a clerical error at the pearly gates, I'm stuck here. I'm a soul without a body. I'm assigned cases and inhabit the bodies of those killed by the supernatural. Those bodies are cleaned up before my soul gets shoved inside so that they're not all zombie-looking. When I'm in a body, I have the ability to heal from normal wounds. Right now…I'm on a case, and lady, you're really getting in my way!" My chest heaved as I labored for breath. That was cathartic though. It felt good to let it out. Therapy works.

The doctor didn't know how to take my outburst. She sat there, wide eyed and swallowing saliva. Without a word, she rose from her seat, didn't bother to push it in—rude—and left.

I felt the urge to shout after her, "You can't handle the truth!" I didn't. I remained the definition of calm and composed—if you don't count the outburst.

Something irked me. I hadn't seen a single blur while she quizzed me. I know I hadn't imagined any of it. I *saw* what I saw. A solitary man sat near the wall opposite me. Elderly guy, a few ragged wisps of hair, lined face. His view was fixed on the television across from him. He was seated in front of a window, sunlight bathing his form.

His shadow was on the wrong side...

The show ended and the old man rose to his feet, hobbling off down the hall. His shadow didn't. It stood there, unmoving—watching me.

Don't ask how I knew the shadow was watching me. Everyone knows what it feels like to be watched. There's a gentle pressure that envelops your body, and you can't quite pinpoint what it is. You just know.

The shadow stood with military erect posture. What I took to be the head faced me. I can't honestly tell you how long passed. We just stared at each other. I didn't blink the entire time.

The shadow walked off.

That roused me from my trance. I shot out of the chair, upending the table and sending checker pieces hurtling through the air—again. The shadow walked at a leisurely pace down the hall opposite the one the old man had taken. It sped up—so did I.

A blur, and I saw it. The shadow covered the length of the hall and all I caught was the end of it. It stood there, stone-like—waiting.

"Who am I, Peter Pan?" I huffed and sped after the shadow. It turned the corner and I followed, barreling into something.

"Ow!"

My abdomen smarted a bit. Lying at my feet was a young girl. She sprawled out on the floor, partially lying over a stuffed rabbit nearly the same size as her. I knelt and extended my hand. It felt like the right thing to do after having toppled her over.

She was adorable, with thick, shag-carpet-like hair. Curls of black fell to her ears. She had the look of a child on the verge of her preteens but not quite there. Her eyes seemed a bit too big for her face. Their appearance had nothing to do with the big mean man who had rammed into her. They were almond in color, a sweet, warm brown. Her complexion was splotches of tawny and fairer skin. It needed some evening out. Given some years, it would. She was holding onto some baby fat, and not just in her cheeks. But she wasn't chubby.

"Come on," I said in the most reassuring and gentle tone I could.

She looked at me, wary, then at my hand. She didn't take it.

I cracked my best smile. "Come on."

Pushing herself up a bit, she took my offer. I enveloped her delicate hand within my own and eased her to her feet. For good measure, I exerted a bit more force at the end. The little gal shot up from the ground in surprised glee, giggling as she landed.

I knelt again, my hands working to straighten her rumpled garments. Picking up her rabbit, I handed it back to her, jiggling the toy as I did. She embraced it with a tight hug.

"You okay?" I asked.

She nodded. "Yeah," she replied in a distant and somewhat ethereal voice. Maybe she was a relative of Church. Simple answers—soft voice. Now if only she insulted me, we'd have a winner.

"Sorry," I kept my tone gentle.

"S'kay," she mumbled in a sleepy manner.

I flashed her another grin. "I'm Charles."

"No you're not." She said it with such definitiveness I might as well have told her I was MacGyver. Well, that one would've gone over her head. What do kids watch these days anyway? "Charles is dead," she stated in a matter of fact tone of voice.

That caused me to rock backward. Maybe Ortiz had a kid she didn't know about. "How do you…" I trailed off.

"Charles told me," she beamed.

"Uh, what?"

She ignored me. Her eyes turned to our surroundings. The little mystery girl was amazingly observant. I'm a detective but was astounded by how carefully she looked at everything around us. "You're looking for the shadows, right?"

"I, uh, yeah, wait, huh? Shadows?"

"Mmmhm," she hummed, "I was following one of them too!" There was a disconcerting level of cheer in her voice considering that she had been following a monster.

Ice water coursed through my body. *Them*—plural. There were more of these freaks.

"Did…Charles tell you about those too?" I was uncertain of what her answer would be.

"M'no, I saw them."

Oh, well that works too.

"Uh, why were you following a shadow?"

"My sister told me they were dangerous." An innocent and amused smile was plastered across her face.

She was told they were dangerous and still went after them.

"Yeah well, maybe you should listen to your sister and… Wait, how does *she* know about them? Does everyone in this place know what's going on but me? Did I miss a memo or something?"

My complaints sailed over her head. She stood there smiling, humming, content in her own little world.

"Uh, kid?"

"Elizabeth, but friends call me Lizzie. You're a friend, right?"

I sighed. This was going to take a lot more patience than I had at the moment. "Yeah, kid…Lizzie, yes I am."

She nodded. "Charles said you were."

Charles seemed to know a lot more than I did, and he was dead. I hate my bosses, whoever they are. I swear they enjoy watching me flounce around without a clue.

"Uh, Lizzie—"

"Mhmm," she interjected.

I breathed a couple times. She was a kid. I was mad, but there was no way in hell I was taking my anger out on her. You just don't do that—ever. "Lizzie, mind telling me how Charles told you all this?"

"His ghost," she said as if it were obvious. For the record, it wasn't.

"His ghost told *you*?" Most people would've gotten lost right there. The fact that she brought up ghosts would have told normal people all they needed to know about her. It was clear why she was here.

"She's crazy," they'd say.

They'd be wrong.

People have been known to see ghosts. It's not some fake phenomenon like some "experts" claim. What do they know? I'm the paranormal expert. There are several reasons why someone would be able to see ghosts. More often than not, unfortunately, it's personal—immensely so.

The most common reason: loss of a loved one. People are more likely to see the ghost of a family member who left something unresolved. Ghosts aren't complete. They're imprints of who that person was. They can act like they did before perishing, but they're not whole. Some ghosts are stuck in perpetual loops related to their deaths, acting out scenes over and over again, unable to move on—unaware. It's sad really.

But Lizzie claimed to have spoken to the ghost of Charles, which was something. Speaking to a ghost not related to you takes a rare talent. That's power. Ghosts are an untapped reservoir of knowledge. The ones that are more aware can interact and are more complete. They see and hear a lot. And if Charles was indeed roaming around here somewhere, Lizzie could help me gain a bunch of helpful info.

"So Lizzie, is Charles here now?"

"Mhmm, no."

Damn. There's never a helpful ghost around when you need one. My life is complicated like that.

"What about your sister? She here?"

Lizzie shook her head. "Her ghost's not here right now."

A concussive blast hit my chest. Something just about broke in me. "Oh kid." I exhaled. "Sorry."

"S'okay." Her voice still sounded like it was far away. "Mom and Dad left when I was little. She took care of me before she died."

"Why are you here?" I croaked.

"Because I see dead people."

I blinked. Right. To the rest of the world, that wasn't normal.

"But my grandma's going to take me soon." She beamed. "And I still see my sister sometimes."

Kids are amazing, wonderful, pure things. After all she had been through, she was still happy she could see her sister. I had to clear my throat and blink pretty hard to make sure no tears came out. I'm a manly monster killer, not a wimp.

"So, Lizzie, do you know something that can help?"

She shook her head. "Follow the shadows?"

I almost laughed. It wasn't a bad suggestion. Hell, it's what I was doing before. "Okay, Lizzie, I'm going to chase shadows. You go somewhere safe—your room maybe—okay?"

"No."

"No?" Why was this the day everyone was telling me no? "Why not?"

"You didn't tell me your real name."

"Oh right, it's um, Vincent. Vincent Graves."

"Okay," she mumbled, content. Lizzie turned and wandered back down the hall, dragging her large, stuffed bunny behind.

Shadows, ghosts, muck and heart attacks. This was a serious supernatural mess. I needed help. Gnosis was out on account of being a diminutive dickwheel. But I had other options.

"I hope you're in a talkative mood, Church," I said to no one in particular.

I walked past the rec room. Something caught my eye when I entered the receptionist's office. A young nurse had her eyes trained on the screen before her, paying no mind to me. Mid-thirties, plain-faced with a hint of freckles and a brunette ponytail.

I cleared my throat pointedly. "Who's that?" I pointed to a small frame on the desk.

The nurse looked at me, then to where I was pointing.

"Kat."

The photo showed a much younger, leaner Kat. Her

face didn't have the generous mass it did today. It was shallower, gaunt and weary. What was more surprising was what she was wearing. She wasn't garbed in nurse's attire. She was dressed like a patient.

The nurse must've noticed my puzzled expression. "Katherine was a patient here for the longest time. Her son died as an infant. She took it hard, withdrew and slowly got worse." Her features sank as she paused for a moment. "Kat was sent here for treatment. She was rough for a lot of years, but slowly, she got better. She eventually became one of the nurses. She's Doctor Cartwright's greatest success story. Patient to nurse! Can you believe that?" She smiled as she looked at Kat's photo.

"So why does she keep that photo here?"

The nurse shrugged. "Maybe it reminds of what this place can do? Or maybe what she lost?"

My gaze drifted back to the photo. Two sets of initials were written across it in marker.

"What's K.R stand for?"

"Katherine Robinson."

"And G.R. is…?"

"Her son's name, I guess. She doesn't talk about it."

I nodded but let the conversation drop. Kat had been a patient here once. I wondered if she knew anything.

Filing away everything I learned about Kat, I headed toward the chapel. The walk wasn't long, but shadow chasing and checker playing had carved out another slice of my time.

Forty hours left.

Still, the chapel was directly ahead, and with any luck, Church would be there. As far as I could tell, that was his job. Apart from annoying and belittling me that is. But if I showed up at a church, Church was supposed to be there.

I reached the doors and pushed my way through. Stepping onto the mossy carpet, I scanned for Church. Dim evening light shone through stained glass. Church, however, was nowhere to be seen.

Sighing, I walked forward and plopped onto a pew, which would undoubtedly make me lose touch with my butt after a while. Squirming in discomfort, I craned my head. Still no sign of him.

"Uh, Church? You here?" No response. My lips twitched in annoyance. Church was supposed to be the "go to guy" on my cases. He wasn't really living up to that part since I couldn't contact the jerk.

"Hey, Goldilocks!"

Nothing.

I let the weariness I had been holding back wash over me. My posture collapsed and I slumped further into the pew.

"Please don't refer to me as Goldilocks."

It felt like I had fallen into a pool of liquid nitrogen. I rocketed out of the pew and whirled around. "Holy shit!"

Church stood there, calm and collected. He had the makings of a small frown on his face. "Vincent," he began, "I'm quite certain one is not supposed to swear in church."

He pulled a ninja move on me, freaked me the hell out, and was admonishing me for cursing? "Yeah, well…fuck," I replied.

Church sighed and walked around the pew. He sat beside me and avoided my stare. Instead, he chose to rest his chin atop clasped hands. His gaze was held by something nonexistent at the head of the chapel. "What can I do for you, Vincent?"

"Well I'd like to ask you for some answers, but I'm pretty sure you can't give them to me, right?"

Church smirked but otherwise remained silent.

Shrugging off the day's weight with a roll of my shoulders helped release some of the tension. "I guess since you can't answer my questions flat out, I'd like a talk."

"That I can do, Vincent."

I was hoping that would be enough. A chat with Church, while annoying, always seemed to point me in the right direction. I didn't know if it was luck, brilliant manipulation on Church's part, or something else entirely. Whenever I finished a conversation with him, I always seemed to know what to do next.

"Gnosis was a bust." I let the words hang in the air.

Church didn't reply. His gaze was still fixed on that imaginary spot, but there was something in his face which let me know what he was thinking.

"Ohhhhh, you knew, didn't you?"

"Gnosis is a businessman," he said. "It was expected. He was indebted to you the last time. It seems it's the other way around now. He had no reason to help you. As far as he's concerned, you're an investment."

I don't know how far I'd whittled my borrowed teeth down, but it must've been a good deal as I ground away. I didn't know who was a bigger ass—Gnosis for turning me down, or Church for knowing it would happen.

"I didn't know he was going to make me owe him one!"

Church arched a golden eyebrow and stared.

"Okay, yes, he's a slippery douche weasel. I knew that."

He blinked. "Vincent, I don't think I've ever met a person with such an affinity for creative profanity."

"I know. I'm damn near artistic with it. My foul wordage needs an exhibit at the Louvre."

He sighed. I took the hint.

"'Kay, back to Gnosis. He was willing to deal, but I would've had to owe him another favor."

Church listened in silence.

"I mean, it's worth it in a way. The knowledge he could've offered might help me save some lives but…"

"What if Gnosis compels you to do something that could potentially put people in harm's way in the future?" Church reasoned.

I nodded.

"It's a possibility."

"Did you know Gnosis would try and make me owe him one?" I watched his reaction carefully.

He didn't respond but his lips twitched. He had known.

"I thought you were supposed to have my back? How could you let me walk into that? Hell, you suggested it in a way."

"Vincent"—his tone was still gentle—"I didn't *let* you do anything. You chose to. There is a reason free will exists. You know that, don't you? You were and are responsible for your choices and the outcomes—not I. However, did you ever stop to wonder if becoming indebted to him might be a good thing?"

I snorted. "How's that?"

"Because, Vincent, that was his reason for turning you down."

I rolled a hand, motioning for him to continue.

"Now you are forced to find another way to procure the information you seek. Perhaps Gnosis wouldn't have been the best option. You should learn to have a little more faith in the way things play out."

I snorted again. Faith and I aren't the best of buddies. "So now I'm stuck with less than stellar options. I mean there are tons of information dealers I can contact, but I would've preferred Gnosis. He's a businessman—practical and trustworthy…ish."

"How did dealing with him the last time end up for you again, Vincent?" His eyes gleamed behind the lenses of his glasses.

My fist was shaking. I reached over with my other hand and grabbed it tight. Church took note of my rather melodramatic struggle. I wanted to punch him oh-so-badly.

Church ignored my threatening hand motions. "Gnosis wasn't the only one who owed you for a deed. If you are afraid of incurring more debt…" Church trailed off. I knew whom he was speaking of.

"Oh…" There wasn't a trace of enthusiasm in my voice, "Her." Most people would've been excited there was another source of information they could access. Not me.

"You don't seem pleased."

"Yeah well, things didn't end all too well between us. I don't know if she'll help me or kill me." I told him.

"It was *your* fault, Vincent—"

"The hell it was!"

"She does owe you for aiding her in the first place."

"That just means she'll have to work harder to repay her debt *and* kill me. She's an opportunistic bitch."

Church fought hard not to smile. I was right and he knew it.

Grunting, I pushed off from the pew. "Thanks for the talk, Church. Guess I'll go play with fire now."

"Vincent," he called.

"Hmm?"

"Didn't you promise to meet up with Miss Ortiz…more than an hour ago?"

Oh…man.

Ortiz was going to be pissed.

# Chapter Nine

Keeping a woman waiting is never a good idea. It just isn't. I was not at all eager to enter Charles' room.

"Look who showed up, the man without a clue…or a watch." Her face slipped into a tight mask.

My hands leapt into a gesture of placation. "Sorry," I mumbled.

Ortiz glared at me. I could hear the seconds ticking in my head. She relented after a few moments and breathed, releasing her frustrations. "So, you find anything?"

"A bit. You?"

Her lips twitched in annoyance. "Not what I was looking for."

I arched a single eyebrow, silently asking the question.

White teeth flashed as she chewed on her lips. "The young woman from earlier"—she paused—"I checked her out. It's not right."

"What isn't?"

"We saw how she died."

I nodded in agreement.

"There was no sign of that—no black gunk, no marks, nothing."

"Nothing?" I found that hard to believe. I was there. We both were. We saw a helluva lot more than nothing. But Gus had told me the deaths were made to look like heart attacks. I had no idea how something could pull that off, and more importantly, what that something was.

"If you remove what we saw, it looks like a heart attack." Ortiz frowned.

The more information we gleaned, the more obscure things seemed to get. It was becoming apparent that I was going to have to get in touch with the paranormal contact Church had hinted at.

Those meetings always went well.…

"We both know it wasn't a heart attack," she said, snapping me out of my thoughts.

"Yeah." My voice came out rough enough to sand stone.

Ortiz gestured at me with a little nod. "Your turn— share."

So I did. I told her about the odd movements I'd seen. Chasing shadows and coming up empty. I conveniently forgot to mention my run-in with young Lizzie. Ortiz had enough on her plate with this case. I didn't need to overload her with the existence of ghosts or the young girl who could see them. Not to mention I didn't want to drag a kid into this. Last time someone got involved in my world, she died. Only due to a small miracle did she come back from the experience. And that journey led her to a mental hospital.

I was not going to send a child into what I had put Ortiz through. No way in hell.

"A shadow?" said Ortiz.

"Shadows. Plural." I stressed the second word.

Her body shook a bit as she suppressed a shiver. I couldn't blame her. I had effectively told her that an unknown quantity of supernatural creatures were moving throughout the facility posing as shadows.

That's bound to send a tingle down anybody's spine. My hand fell on her shoulder and I gave her a reassuring squeeze.

A mix of emotions passed over her face but she reined them in. Her face hardened, then settled. "So these shadows...think they're what's killing the patients?"

Tough question. It was possible, but I hadn't seen a single shadow do anything aggressive. The only interaction I'd had was it making me feel like a cat chasing a laser pointer. That and dicking around with my field of vision when they darted around.

I answered Ortiz the best I could. "I don't know, but I'm going to find out."

A tingle. I shot a glance down to my forearm. I had lost another hour.

Thirty-nine left.

Ortiz caught my glance, followed it and gave me a look.

"Fast," I added. "I'm going to find out fast."

"You got an idea?"

I waggled a hand in a so-so gesture. I did have an idea. I didn't think it was a great one—or safe. A notion I shared with Ortiz. "Yeah, I do, but it's dangerous."

"So what is it?"

"Going to have a meeting of sorts." I paused before adding, "With a contact."

"Let's go." She took a few steps toward the door.

"Alone." The single word carried a lot of weight. It wasn't the right thing to say.

"What?" she snapped like a whip crack. I flinched.

Something about speaking the truth even if your voice shakes entered my mind. "I said...I'm going alone." Ortiz's temper could be a scary thing, and that's coming from someone who ganks monsters.

Balling her fists, she placed them on her hips. It was a pose women took up when giving men a chance to change their mind. Most men would've taken the opportunity. I'm not most men, nor too bright, but I had my reasons.

I made my voice as flat and hard as possible. "You're not coming."

"Like hell I'm not!"

"Do you trust me?"

"The last time I trusted one of you tattoo guys things turned out bad."

Ouch. She was right. I'd taken her through hell, which was exactly what I was trying to spare her from this time. I gave voice to that concern. "This is going to be just as bad. It'll be dangerous."

"I'm not a china doll," she growled.

No, she wasn't. I had fought right beside her. She was made of steel and fire. That still didn't mean I wanted her to go along with me. Ortiz's trust may have been shaken, but her moral senses weren't. I appealed to those.

I looked her in the eyes. "Ortiz, you might not trust me—fine. I can live with that. Look me in the eyes and tell me if I'm lying when I say that I'm trying to help people here."

Her eyes didn't waver. She looked me straight on and I could see her struggle. Ortiz knew I was telling the truth.

"Believe me when I tell you that I should do this alone.

That it's for the best." A moment passed before I added the magical word, "Please."

That did it. Ortiz's posture softened and I could see her work through several emotions, mostly frustration. Finally, she resigned. "Fine, but I don't like being left out on this."

"I know. I'm not leaving you out altogether—just on this." I gave her a weak smile. "Maybe you can find out something I missed during my search."

"You want me to take a crack at questioning some of the patients?"

"Sure." I shrugged. "We need leads. Just be careful if you see those shadow things, 'kay?"

Her head turned to the window. The honeyed, orange glow of evening poured over her, doing beautiful things to her skin. "It's getting dark," she said in a hushed tone.

"And with the dark comes dark things. Muwhahaha!" The ominous laugh echoed in the small room.

Ortiz shuddered, and I instantly regretted the joke, especially when her eyes flashed. The look she shot me could've been weaponized. "Not funny!"

"You're right," I agreed, throwing up my hands in a gesture of defeat. "But seriously, I don't know how these things will act during the night. Be careful."

"You too." It wasn't a suggestion. There was an undercurrent of threat in that tone. If I didn't come back in one piece, she'd kick my ass. Knowing Ortiz, she'd make good on the threat.

My jaw tightened and I gave her a nod.

She slipped past me, and, as she made it to the door, turned her head back. "Don't keep me waiting this time." She gave me a wolfish grin. "Or else."

I swallowed as she left the room.

I was starting to wonder who was more frightening—Ortiz or the unknown monsters. I figured it would've been rude to deny either first place, so I called it a tie as I fell to the mattress. Without looking, I sent an arm snaking under the pillows to fetch one of my journals.

My forefinger blurred as page after page flicked by. All manner of supernatural information filled my vision. I ceased my frenzied finger flippin' when I found a certain image. Intricate, old, dangerous knowledge. And that was just the picture.

I didn't know how long Ortiz planned to take, but I had to go slow. Common sense dictated that I bring my journal along. It'd certainly make things easier. My job's never been about easy though. Bringing my journal could be a recipe for disaster. I could lose it, which would be bad. Worse, it could fall into the wrong hands. My heart lurched at the thought of that. The amount of information contained in my journal could lead to a whole lot of trouble for someone unaware of the paranormal. More terrifying, if they were perfectly aware. Then I'd be handing them a contact list and a hunting guide. All the more reason my journal had to remain behind.

I memorized the complexity of the image before me— every wayward line, symbol, and spacing. I had no idea what would happen if I got this wrong. That was a damn good reason to get it right.

Time passed. My eyes felt like they were being compressed and my temples throbbed.

The journal *thwapped* closed. I shut my eyes and took a ten count of steadying breaths. It was a struggle to lift my lids. Someone had sewn a shot of lead into them. Church may have given me a heck load of time on this case, but I was falling apart nonetheless.

The great thing about being me is the restorative ability I possess. So long as I don't die outright, I'll heal from nearly everything. Too bad every part of my brain was falling to pieces at the moment. If I didn't deal with this, more people were going to die. Maybe Ortiz; maybe Lizzie—a child.

That settled it.

My hand pulled at the thin skin beneath my eyes as I rubbed my face. It may have been spring, but the evening light was straight out of autumn's handbook. I slid my journal back to its spot beneath the pillows and rose. It was getting darker and there was something that needed doing.

Time to summon a monster.

\* \* \*

I managed to get outdoors without arousing too much

suspicion; only being stopped once by a nurse who reminded me curfew wasn't too far away. The grounds were no longer littered with people. Empty. A different scene from my earlier group session. I didn't have time to appreciate the sky and what it did to the woods at the end of the grounds. My attention was fixed on a small playground set in a sizable ground of woodchips.

I sprinted to the edge of the closest tree, snapping off a branch thicker than my thumb. I hoped it was sturdy enough not to break with what I had planned. After making it to the field of woodchips, I knelt and brushed away at the surface.

"What I wouldn't give for a can of spray paint," I growled as I cleared a space large enough for several people to lie in. Jamming the stick into the dry, gritty dirt, I inscribed from memory.

Evocation, the art of summoning a supernatural creature, does not take an ounce of magical ability. It takes knowledge. Lots of it. Starting first with how to make a Summoner's Star. It's not some simple circle with a pentagram scribbled inside it like on television shows. There's so much more to it than that.

Like the number three. It plays a massive role in the supernatural world, and for good reason. Think of triangles, three-sided, strong, just like the number—indivisible. That's what the number three is in the supernatural world. Strong, resolute, ironclad. You have to take that into account when making a proper Summoner's Star.

I formed three circles, each successively smaller than the next. At the center I formed a triangle. Frowning, I tore at the section of stick held together by strands of weak bark. I knew the damned thing would break. I carved another triangle, inverted, forming a star of sorts. The ends of the star were triangles themselves. The center was an upside down pentagram. Within that I carved one last triangle. Three in total. At the center of it all, I made an archaic letter.

Sometimes I wish I had a mat with these printed out on them. Unroll it and toss it to the ground—done.

I willed away my fantasies and peppered the ground with minute circles, each with a symbol inside. Running along the outside of the thing was a script that could've belonged on the One Ring.

It was complete. Almost. Many scripts of magic needed something to give them power, like a battery. This one was no exception. I didn't have the slightest bit of magical power. But I had something else.

Blood.

There's more power in a drop of blood than in a dozen nuclear reactors. The magical kind anyways. Blood is a life force, and there's nothing more powerful than life.

The soft skin of my forefinger slid between my teeth as I clamped down. I winced for a second. A drop no bigger than a pinhead welled up. Turning my finger over, I held it atop the circle. The drop clung stubbornly to my finger. I squeezed the digit with my other hand and a proper-sized drop of blood fell.

The ground hissed spitefully, like a freshly struck match. Every line I scrawled flared into existence with a fluorescent red shimmer. A flash and then it subsided. The Summoner's Star looked as if it had been scorched into the ground. Everything was set. I just needed one more thing.

A name.

Proper evocation takes a name. What good is it summoning something if you don't have its name? Names hold power. Don't believe me? Try calling out someone's name the next time they're around. They'll instantly whirl about looking for the source. It's not conditioning. It's something more. It's an identity. There's a form of magic in that. A link between a person and who they identify as. Something I've lost over the years. When someone identifies with a name, it's part of their being; it's a magical connection to something deeper. So when evoking a spirit or creature, you call their name.

Calling it once or twice is like a gentle invite; but like I said, three's the magic number. Saying a name three times in conjunction with a Summoner's Star—that's not a polite invitation. That's a forced summoning.

Most beings aren't a fan of that. You're essentially whisking them from wherever they are and dumping their butts into your circle. But I had an inkling that the creature I was about to summon wouldn't answer if I called politely. So the rude call it was.

"Lyshae, I seek your wisdom. Lyshae, I seek your guidance. Lyshae, I invoke you."

Nothing of note happened. There was no magical flare, no thrum of subtle power. Nothing.

Except where once there was an empty circle, there now stood a woman possessing otherworldly beauty.

"Vincent Graves," she said, her voice too rich, too melodic, and utterly inhuman.

Her looks were the same. She couldn't have passed for an ordinary woman if she tried. There was a wildness in her—fierce, something akin to a predatory cat. That same wildness appeared in her eyes. Exotic, canted with vertically slit pupils. Chatoyant gems, flecked with noticeable traces of yellow-gold. A hint of mischief hung within them. She had thick, lengthy lashes of soot that sharply contrasted her porcelain complexion. Her features were sharp, angular, fox-like. A perfect nose sat between wide, full, model-esque cheekbones.

An evening breeze stirred her loose-fitting and lengthy shift. It fell to her feet with a train of fabric running several yards behind her. It would've been a mistake to say her clothes were anything simple. The shift seemed to have been made from strands of pearls, reflecting the evening light with their glossy sheen. Lyshae appeared tall and slender with a ballerina's figure. The cut of her dress revealed a bit more. It may have been loose but it clung to her in all the right places, revealing feminine swell and curves.

"Lyshae." I smiled halfheartedly.

"You...utter and complete sociopath!" She stomped the ground once. Locks of spun gold bounced before her eyes.

"I consider myself more of a puckish rogue." I smiled, genuinely this time. White tails atop her head caught my attention. She wore her hair in an odd style. A fistful of golden hair was clipped up and hung back in a plume of individual ponytails. Nine of them to be exact. The ends of each tail was the color of powdered snow. Nine tails. Nine *white* tails.

"A rose by any other name." Her voice was dry.

"Wait…are you trying to insult me…or flirt with me?"

Her nose twitched in annoyance, as did a pair of things protruding from her head. Two rounded triangles, trimmed in fur matching her white tails of snow. A fleshy color showed within the fur. They were ears—fox ears.

Lyshae was a Kitsune. A Japanese fox spirit of intellect, knowledge and mischief. A particularly important one, indicated by the nine tails she wore in her hair. It was a sign that Lyshae was a Kitsune past the age of one thousand years. That meant if Gnosis was out, she was likely my best bet at gleaning some info. If she was in the sharing mood.

"Charming." She gave me a bemused smile.

"There you go with those mixed messages again." I beamed.

"What do you want?"

I grinned. "To call in that favor you owe me."

She huffed in irritation. "After what *you* did?"

"Hey! I did what you asked. I helped you, and now you owe me!"

"You started a war between the two parties I was a liaison for, you...barbarian!"

That was a gross exaggeration. It was more like a skirmish.... "Oh please." I waved a dismissive hand through the air. "They were looking for any excuse to break peace and start a riot. I may have exacerbated the process a bit," I concluded with a shrug.

"A bit?" Her eyes went wide. Lyshae's ears twitched and disbelief filled her voice.

I held my thumb and forefinger an inch apart.

"You, Vincent Graves, are a self-destructive, violent, narcissistic maniac."

Guess that made me quite the overachiever. My grin widened. "I'm not narcissistic."

Her eyes flashed dangerously before returning to normal. "What. Do. You. Want?"

"I told you, a favor."

One of her eyebrows rose expectantly.

"I'm on a case. Something's going around all cloak and dagger and offing people. I've seen shadows moving of their own accord. Not shadows like magical constructs and illusions. Just shadows."

"Intriguing," she murmured to herself.

"Whatever the hell it is, it can conjure up some black fog-like gunk and I think it's psychoactive. When the junk touched me I lost feeling in my arm, and I started to trip."

"Trip?"

"Ah, hallucinate, see things."

She nodded in understanding.

"For whatever reason, after the thing's done with people, it looks like they've died of a heart attack. So I need to know if you know what this freak is, or if you can help me find out?"

"I cannot tell based on what you have given me, but I'm sure we can figure it out." She smiled. It was the sort a lioness gives a gazelle.

"Good. I've got time but I'd rather not let it dwindle so—"

"But first," she interjected and my stomach knotted. "Let me out."

Bad feeling verified.

"Uh, why would I do that?"

"You wish me to help you figure this out whilst trapped in here?" She gestured to the circle around her.

"Yup. I was thinking of making it a girl's night. It'll be like a sleepover. We'll chat, gossip, slip into our pajamas. Maybe we'll talk about boys, break out the Haagen-Dazs— share dirty secrets."

"What sort of dirty secrets?" She quirked an eyebrow in amusement.

The question caught me off guard.

"Maybe *your* dirty secrets, Vincent?"

"What?"

Her smile deepened. It would've been a lie to say I didn't find it disconcerting.

"What do you know, Lyshae? How do you know?"

"I worked for Gnosis for a while, if you recall."

I had forgotten about that. Lyshae wasn't even close to being one of the oldest brokers of information out there. Gnosis and a handful of creatures easily outclassed her in that regard. Because of that, for the longest of times, Lyshae was employed by more prominent beings in the information business. Kitsunes are fast, masters of illusion, nimble and have unparalleled senses. That makes them premier sleuths.

If Lyshae had worked for Gnosis, it meant she might know more than just things about me. It was entirely possible that Lyshae knew Gnosis' secrets too. Those would be great assets to get my hands on. *If* I could convince Lyshae to part with them. I had an inkling she wouldn't however. I didn't seem to be on her Christmas card mailing list at the moment.

"Let me guess, Lyshae. This is the part where I sign over my soul and you tell me everything I've been dying to hear. Sound about right?"

"So melodramatic," she purred. "Nothing of the sort. Simply release me from my debt and you'll owe me several in return."

Several…. The last time I did her a favor I barely made it out alive. But she made it sound so simple, enticing—easy. All I had to do was agree and she'd tell about my past, hopefully. I'd owe her a few favors is all. A few undefined— potentially dangerous—favors. I twitched and my heart drummed. My breathing sped up. I was tempted, sorely so, and she knew it.

The conniving bitch!

Gnosis knew. She knew. Church knew. That last thought settled the matter for me, as hard as it was. Church knew the truth and had promised to tell me—one day. I gritted my teeth and a string of obscenities rang through my thoughts. "No."

She didn't seem the least bit surprised or even upset. "No?" she said, her tone bemused. "Well, you've always been a stubborn one. What are a few more debts? You've already incurred one to Gnosis."

"The hell do you know about that?"

Her eyes danced with glee but she remained silent.

"There a supernatural information broker weekly seminar I don't know about? If so, how do I snag an invite?"

She chortled. It was rich, musical, and did funny things to my ears. "Do you honestly think you'd be welcome? You have a habit of starting fights, demolishing things and causing everything in the vicinity to develop an immense level of distaste toward you."

I sniffed. Everybody doesn't hate me.

"You still didn't tell me how you knew about that?" I said, changing the subject.

She spoke with an air of nonchalance. "During my time with Gnosis I may have made some acquaintances, and garnered favors of my own." Her smile widened further.

Lyshae had moles within Gnosis' information network. That was seriously a big flippin' deal. And she had told me about it. I couldn't do much with that information at the moment, but I filed it away for later. It could come in handy. It could be used for blackmail or bonus points depending on the circumstances. Not that I was eager to get involved. This was some spy-on-spy crap. Getting caught in that would be terrible for my health.

"That might come back to bite you in your pretty little ass," I mentioned.

She shrugged so casually it was disturbing. Gnosis was not a being you screwed over.

"We're getting nowhere," she said.

She was right. If I wanted to make any progress with this case, I was going to have to let her out. "Give me your word that you'll help me solve this case. That you'll act in accordance to my will so long as you are in my debt. Give me that, and I'll let you out."

Lyshae didn't falter. "Of course." It was too sweet a reply. "I give you my word, Vincent Graves, that I will act in accordance to your will. So long as I am bound in your debt, I will aid you in solving this case."

I grimaced. She might have said the words, but it didn't mean I was comfortable around her. Sliding my foot forward, I broke the first layer of the three-tiered circle. Lyshae regarded me with amusement. My foot traveled further, breaking all three circles, and smearing the triplicate of triangles within.

Hydraulic pressure enveloped my skull and neck as Lyshae took me in her grip and jerked me forward. I felt like I had whiplash. She may have looked slender, but she had supernatural strength. She pressed her lips to mine. It was like kissing honeyed rosewater. A sweet, cooling kiss. Our lips parted as I was shoved back.

"Still wondering if I was flirting with or insulting you?" she purred.

"Uh, yeah, wow, that was—"

My head rocked to the side. This time I definitely had

whiplash. My jaw had nearly been unhinged and the left side of my face was aflame. Her full-armed slap made spots dance before my vision.

"That," she growled, rubbing both hands over her body to smooth her dress, "was for my last job with you."

I tasted iron. My teeth must've cut the soft tissue inside my cheek. "Geez, Lyshae, you play rough."

"You have no idea," she purred again.

Something stirred inside me. I told it to shut up, sit down and go away.

"So, Vincent, shall we begin?"

"Start talking."

She let out a hearty laugh, like I had just cracked one heckuva amazing joke. "Not here."

"What?"

She moved her arm in a simple bisecting motion behind her and a ribbon of silvery white appeared. It hung there, suspended in midair. It was half my length and no thicker than a finger.

My heart trip hammered. "You want me to follow you in *there*?"

What Lyshae had opened was a doorway. A path to the Ways. The Ways were exactly what they sounded like: pathways—roads to be traveled along to a particular place in a world I didn't want to think about. Sometimes it was the other way and something followed them out. Not a nice thought. The Ways were as singularly unique as each part of the world they led to. There were a countless number of them, and each held a different surprise.

"Of course. Where else did you expect to find the best answers?"

"How about Wiki-fucking-pedia!?"

She blinked in confusion. "You didn't specify how or where I should procure the information." Her teeth shone with a predatory gleam. "This is the most efficient way."

*Efficient for you.*

"Do I look stupid?"

"No, Vincent. You look desperate."

I scowled. This was bad. My slip-up had cost me. I should've been clearer on how I wanted her help. I could, of course, terminate the deal, thus freeing Lyshae from her debt. I had screwed myself in my desperation, but I'm nothing if not stubborn. I wasn't going to let her off the hook that easy.

"How do I know I can trust you, Lyshae?"

"I gave you my word, Vincent."

I eyed her askance. Just because she gave me her word didn't mean she couldn't find another way to screw me over. Lyshae was adept at that—wordplay, wiggling out of deals and all manner of backstabbery. Kitsunes are trickster spirits, mischief-makers, and great at being all-too-clever. I continued my oblique stare.

"Very well," she breathed in mock exasperation. "I'll put your concerns to rest, Vincent Graves. Trust me to be myself."

That wasn't comforting in the slightest.

"Trust me to be wholly untrustworthy." Her eyes danced with mischievous delight.

"And that's reassuring why?"

"Because, Vincent," she gave me cunning smile, "you can always trust an untrustworthy person to be untrustworthy, but you never know when a trustworthy person will choose to be untrustworthy. It's the honest ones you should be wary of. I, however, will be honestly dishonest till the last of my days." The impish twinkle in her eyes intensified.

My head hurt after hearing the epic mind fuck. I shook the cobwebs clear. "None of that makes me feel better about following you. I could be walking into a trap."

Those iridescent pools of gold shone with something like madness. Her eyes were terrifying. "Oh, Vincent, it's the possibility that a trap lies ahead that makes this so exciting!" And with that she bounded backward in a single leap, disappearing into the silver-white ribbon in the air.

My jaw worked furiously as I stood there for a ten count. I needed answers and the best option I had was to follow a maniac trickster spirit to the other side.

*Desperate measures, Graves.*

"Damnit." I leapt after Lyshae.

# Chapter Ten

I don't know if such a thing as perfect darkness exists, but if it does, it would definitely apply to where I was. Forget seeing ahead of me—I couldn't see my frickin' self. No amount of time would allow my eyes to adjust to the abysmal darkness. That's saying something, considering what hung around me.

Fist-sized balls of light floated through the dark expanse, pulsating. There were more of them than I'd ever be able to count. They hung in every color imaginable and beyond, with a vibrancy that'd leave master painters stunned. I'd never seen something so simple and yet so beautifully entrancing. The terrifying part...all that light and none of it did a damned thing to illuminate the darkness.

I was in a part of the Neravene, the world beside our own. A world where almost everything out of mythology existed. A place I tried to avoid at all costs. Dark things, eldritch creatures, Gods, Faeries, Elves and more—anything not born of our world—resided here. Everything wonderful and equally horrifying called this place home.

The Neravene was part of our world in a way. It overlapped and stood beside it, but was an infinitely different place. There's no possible way to describe its size. It's not bound by things like time, size or distance. The Neravene is exponentially larger than our world on a scale that no person could possibly imagine. It's a place of magic, and now I was in it, left in the dark—alone.

Fantastic.

The colored orbs continued their throbbing dance. They bobbed through empty space, giving the illusion of light but doing nothing to aid my vision. I kept the nearest of the lights in sight and stepped toward it. Rock crumbled beneath my feet in protest. I stumbled, losing my balance. The familiar sensation of falling overwhelmed me.

*Well, I didn't last that long.*

"Argh!" My left shoulder erupted into fire. It had wrenched. Something enveloped my wrist, its vice-like grip worlds different from the softness of its touch.

"Careful, Vincent," Lyshae teased as she hauled me back to my feet. She was right in front of me and I couldn't see an inch of her. She smelled of something sweet—cherries. "Word of advice, Vincent: don't follow the lights." And she was gone.

"Thanks, Smeagol," I grumbled. "Way to ditch Master."

Sliding a foot forward, I found solid ground, inching just a finger's breadth to the right. Something crumbled. Holy shit, was the ground narrow! It must've been no wider than a yard. If I didn't walk perfectly inline, I'd take another tumble. I had the feeling that Lyshae wouldn't save me a second time. It would be a great technicality if the person to whom she was indebted killed themselves. If I was too incompetent to navigate the Ways and died of my own accord, it wasn't her fault.

"Tricky, sneaky, uppity, conniving, mrffle, urffles," I grumbled as I crept forward. Each step felt like walking barefoot on a live wire. Shocks and jolts shot up my legs as I proceeded. Stone groaned, *crack*, and my heart moved to dubstep.

*Crack, crack, crack, crumble.* I inhaled so sharply it sounded like a panicked wheeze. *Please don't break, please don't break, holy crap, please do not break,* I pleaded silently.

It didn't. I wasn't worried. Intrepid investigator of all things spooky and magical I am.

A chorus of laughs reverberated across the place. I couldn't pinpoint their source. It was eerie in surround sound. Awesome. They rang out again and something occurred to me.

"Lyshae?" I called.

Another chorus of laughs.

"Yes, Vincent?" Her voice came from all directions at different times. Echoes. Great. Now I'd really have a fun time finding her...and the way out.

Grayish-white streaks caught my eye. I turned and backpedaled. Not smart. Stone crumbled, but I didn't fall. It looked like a person—if it were made out of streams of fog.

Slender, emaciated almost. Its features were gaunt and hollowed. A trail of smoke wafted behind, like it was bleeding mist. And I suddenly knew which one of the Ways I was in.

"Holy…shit!"

Lyshae's laugh filled my ears once again.

"This is your idea of answers? Taking me through the Dead-Straits?" My roar went out in all directions, filling the endless chasm of darkness.

More smoke-like beings walked over the air beside me. They drifted by in a grim procession. Their heads hung low, moving aimlessly—sad. They were something between a soul and a ghost. A bastardization of a once-living essence. Souls lost in this place—human souls.

Humans can pass into the Neravene. It doesn't take magical ability to cross over. It's just that those with magical ability find it easier: wizards, witches, druids and so many other magical humans. Though this is not the place to cross over to.

If you fall off the Dead-Straits, you die. It's not a normal death. Your soul's trapped here, but its essence—its identity—slowly strips away. These things were souls once. Now they were worn into dejected memories of their former selves.

If I fell, that would be my fate.

Chilled water ran through my veins. "Fuck that." I shuddered and resolved to walk with more caution. I slinked forward. I didn't want to stay in this place any longer than I had to. I counted as I walked, something to keep my mind off the terrible things around me.

"Two thousand and forty-six," I panted, and everything changed. A hot lance seared my eyes. Having struggled to adapt to the dark, the dim light of evening was blinding. My hands rushed to cover the thin layer of skin around my eyes.

"Such a child," murmured Lyshae's amused voice.

"Such a bitch," I murmured back.

She laughed. "We've still a ways to go."

I ignored her, giving my eyes the time they needed to adjust. They fluttered open. A hint of moisture welled in the corners from the earlier pain. Soft, rich browns of earth snaked before me into a long, wide path. Thick, old-world trees towered on either side. Dense forest lined the path. It was beautiful, something reserved for stories. Tolkien-esque.

I shot Lyshae a glare. "All that to come here?"

"Here, yes. There, no. Remember: we haven't reached the end yet; there's more to go, Vincent Graves."

I stuck my tongue out at her.

Her lips spread, revealing teeth, and she took off. No, that was the wrong word for it. She fucking flew off! She didn't have wings but what she was doing didn't qualify as running, at least not by any definition I've ever heard. Her petite feet were visible beneath her shift as she moved, blurring away. The instant a foot touched the ground, it was back in the air as she bounded forward. She covered distances no mortal could hope to match. It was awing. Lyshae moved with an inherent grace that the world's best dancers, gymnasts, and ballerinas could never hope to achieve.

And suddenly I was alone, again. This time in an unknown forest.

Worst. Guide. Ever.

I snarled and took off after Lyshae. My legs fired like pistons, hammering into the ground as I tried to keep her in sight. I didn't do a great job of that, but the path was straight, or so I hoped. I'd either run into her eventually...or trouble.

As I ran, I remembered something from my earlier trips into the Neravene.I frowned as I examined my forearm. There was always a minor tingle surrounding the tissue of my tattoo. It may have been insignificant, but it was always there. A reminder of its magical power. I didn't feel that at the moment.

Time moved differently in the Neravene and, even then, it never moved at a fixed rate. It depended on what part of the Neravene you were in as well as what kinds of magic were involved. My tattoo wasn't from this side of the world. It was part of mine, the normal, vanilla world. It was bound to the rules of my world, meaning I'd have no indication of how much time passed or would pass. As long as I was here, my tattoo would remain in stasis. But time in the normal world would keep moving. The second I returned, my tattoo would decrease in time accordingly...

If I spent too long here, unaware and lost, I could possibly burn through all the time I had. Church wouldn't like that. Hell, I wouldn't like that. I've never failed a case before. I didn't plan on making this my first time.

I pushed harder and willed my legs to propel me as fast as they could. I was hoping I'd catch Lyshae. I'd been running for fifteen minutes normal time—in my head at least—before I found her. She stood before a tight wall of trees. Everything seemed denser here. The air felt heavier. Massive streams of silken material decorated the trees, forming intricate nets. Not comforting at all. Worse—the sun had set.

"What now?" I exhaled and worked to catch my breath.

"Now, we go through the woods." And she did exactly that.

"Right," I breathed to no one in particular. "Let's go for a nice walk in the spooky cobwebbed woods…at night."

At least I was able to keep my eyes on her this time, which wasn't easy. The amount of webbing intensified the further we went. The moonlight did odd things to the silvery threads. They hung in eerie silence with a ghostly glow. I kept from freaking out. It wasn't as hard I thought it'd be. All I had to do was stare at Lyshae.

She was the definition of icy calm, and that caused a series of questions to shoot through my head. Those questions were the only thing keeping me from turning around and bolting out the damned forest. How could she be so calm?

*Curiosity killed the cat, Graves,* I warned myself. *Ah, but sating said curiosity was worth it. Was it?* The mental badminton helped. *Cats have nine lives.*

"I don't," I growled. All those years, all that body inhabiting and memory borrowing, has left me with some serious multiple personality issues. "I'm not a cat," I spat.

"No, you most certainly are not." Lyshae waved to our surroundings. "We've arrived."

Yippee. I'd be lying if I said there wasn't a part of me that wished the running through the forest part lasted a bit longer. My skin prickled.

I followed Lyshae as she broke through the woods into a clearing, a dirt circle the size of a stadium. A campfire burned in the center, and cobwebbed trees formed a wall around us. The prickling sensation strengthened. It was like I was caught in a heat wave. My skin itched like I'd gone ten rounds with a hornets' nest. Something watched me from within those trees. I'd been spied on enough to know when something was staring at me.

"Uh, Lyshae?" I fell in step behind her as she progressed toward the campfire.

"Hmmm?"

"Uh, what are we doing here? As in like here-here? You know, with the webs, and the spooky ominous trees of doom, foreboding and evil…ness?" I waggled my fingers to accentuate what I meant.

She smiled.

My blood pressure didn't like that.

As I walked, I became aware of presences. Not presence—*presences*. There were more of…whatever was watching me. "I love an audience."

"Good, they'd love to watch you perform." Lyshae grinned.

"Uh, I'm the shy sort. Heck, I can't even take a leak with someone watching, you know?"

She didn't respond. Lyshae walked at a leisurely pace toward the fire, where I hoped we would sit, make s'mores and tell stories. "Sit." She gestured to a spot in front of the fire.

I complied. "Now what? We roast hot dogs or something? Don't get me wrong. I'm all for fun campfire times, but…I sort of need answers."

"You'll get them, Vincent. I gave you my word."

Yeah…because I could trust that ever-so-much.

"Perhaps we should play a game while we wait?" There was a look in her eyes when she said that, a look I didn't care for.

"Uh, well, you know, it's all fun and games till someone drops their wiener in the fire." I let out a weak chuckle.

She stared. Guess she hadn't heard the joke before.

It grew darker and the fire flickered in disapproval. It struggled to stay alight. My worry grew as it waned. "Lyshae?" I turned back to look at her. I don't know how she did it. She was sitting right beside me, at the edge of my peripheral vision. Now, she was gone.

Iridescent baseballs hung inside the depths of the darkened forest. There were half a dozen clumped together. That was one set. At rough count there were more than twenty. Twenty sets of gleaming orbs in the forest. All of them motionless, fixed on a single point, and it wasn't the fire. Nope. They were ever-so-keen on the dimwit backpedaling away from it.

"Lyshae!" I hollered. "Where am I?"

Her voice came back as a distant echo. "Why, in the domain of my mistress, of course."

Crap. Of course. Lyshae had stopped working for Gnosis, but that didn't mean she couldn't have picked up a new employer.

A disturbing choir of noises erupted from the surrounding trees. A non-human chorus of chittering. Whatever was hiding in those trees had got to talking. Three guesses who they were talking about. I tried to ignore it.

Not that easy—take my word for it.

"Who do you serve, Lyshae?"

Echoing laughter filled the air.

"Lyshae! Who do you work for?"

The chittering increased in tempo, now sounding like a swarm of flying insects. I wasn't fazed. Nope, not at all. Stone cold calm and collected I was.

"Lyshae, who the hell do you work for?" I screamed.

The chittering ceased and was replaced by something else. A heavy, rapid clacking. Clogs on wood, eagerly snapping away as it grew darker still. Moonlight cast its shine upon those glowing orbs. They brightened further. There was a ravenous gleam in those things. Don't ask me how I knew. It's like how a rabbit knows there's a fox watching it, thinking of dinner. I just knew.

"Why, the Mistress of Webs," Lyshae answered.

A lead weight fell into my stomach.

"I serve the Mother of Lies and Whispers," she continued.

The pit of my stomach froze solid. Arctic tendrils worked their way into the rest of my body.

"I serve the Mother of Spiders, Vincent Graves."

Where was Admiral Ackbar when you needed him? The

campfire flickered and waned, dwindling further. It was the only light source. The moonlight was weak, unable to brighten the darkening field. The clacking evolved into an intense drone, like a weighty hail.

"You are in her realm now, Vincent." I could almost picture Lyshae smiling.

The campfire went out.

Oh shit.

# Chapter Eleven

The Mother of Spiders.

This was bad. She was a major player in the paranormal world's information network. She also happened to be one of the freestanding lords of the Neravene. A creature of immense knowledge and power. Someone with enough muscle and assets to carve out and claim a chunk of the Neravene. Likened to being a queen, she had her own domain. It was vast, expansive, and, in it she ruled absolute. And I was trespassing. Fantastic.

The Mother of Spiders was the most deceitful, wicked, cunning creature I'd ever heard of. Lyshae was a sweet, innocent wallflower next to her. And that tells you all you need to know about the Mother of Spiders. She was cold, cruel and calculating. Merciless. Lyshae may have been a good source for knowledge, but the Mother of Spiders was one of *the* sources for information. Her webs ran far and wide, and, thus, she was able to build an information network that potentially rivaled Gnosis'.

That sounded like great news. She definitely had the resources to help me. Given her reputation though, she was more likely to kill me—slowly. For the record, I'm not a fan of patience, and certainly not of dying slowly. Or at all if I can help it.

"Come closer," rasped a voice, jarring me from my thoughts. It was disturbing, something like a wet cough, phlegm-filled and disgusting.

I stayed rooted to the spot.

"Come closer," it cooed.

"Said the spider to the fly," I muttered.

A series of...what I could only describe as laughs, emanated from the trees. It was odd, distorted, like whatever was doing it didn't have the vocal ability to laugh. Didn't stop it from trying.

"Fly indeed." It sounded almost amused.

I kept backpedaling.

"Won't you stay for dinner?"

"Uh, no, thanks." I waved my hands. I had no idea if it could see the motion or not. It didn't hurt to be extra clear though. "I'm full. Cafeteria oatmeal. Good stuff. Hearty, healthy, wholesome—you should try it."

"Full? But we are not," it replied.

Gulp.

"Ah well, eat breakfast like a king, lunch like a prince, and dinner like a pauper," I quoted. "Best to eat next to nothing at all, if possible."

More laughs. "Amusing."

"That's me," I chirped. Cold sweat formed over my body. "I think I'm going to go now."

"I think not," said the voice.

The moon was directly overhead now, finally able to cast its pale light and allow me to see clearly. I wish it hadn't. A fucking tarantula larger than a minivan bustled out of the trees. Right. Toward. Me.

I inhaled. That was about all I could do. Trust me, I wanted to run. I just had to remember how. "No more GMO's for you," I breathed. "You've gotten big." Good ol' mouth, when my body freezes, you just keep on going. Way to go—toward getting me killed.

"Leaving? So soon? How rude." The arachnid was grizzled. Scars littered its legs and body. One particular wound stood out. The uppermost left eye was a milky white, unfocused and obviously blind. *Wonder who gave 'em that?*

"Well, I'd hate to be rude but I, erm, have a job to do." I tried laughing in a causal tone. I failed.

"Do stay," it pleaded. "We're hungry."

We...right. A whole mess of these freaks were around me. I didn't think there'd be enough of me to go around.

"I'm not that great for eating. Seriously, I'll give you indigestion. It's not worth it. Have you considered the oatmeal I told you about?"

It...chortled, I think. "Lyshae did well bringing you to us. An amusing meal indeed."

Heat enveloped my frozen body. "Yeah? Well, she screwed me. She gave me her word!" I howled past the overgrown spider, hoping the foxy bitch heard me.

"Did she?" The freak blinked all it eyes. "You valued *her* word?" It laughed.

Okay, that one *was* on me. But still, I'd dealt with Gnosis and it turned out well, sort of. She'd just thrown me into the lion's den—spider's den—spider's hole? Whatever. She played me.

"So, since she broke her word, guess I'm free to go, right?"

It covered the remaining distance between us in a fraction of a second. "No." Viscous trails of fluid fell from its mandibles. I shuddered.

Where was Samwise Gamgee when I needed him?

Clacking mandibles drew me back to the hungry monster. Streams of saliva hung from its mouth. A fist-sized globule broke free and fell to the dirt. Disgusting.

"Eat, eat, eat, eat!" rasped the multitude of voices around me. Guess the jury had decided.

Mandibles snapped together in anticipation of a long awaited meal. All seven of the creature's working eyes trained on me. I didn't know if spiders could smile, but there was enough of a glint in its eyes to let me know it was happy. I wasn't.

Cold adrenaline rushed through me and I moved. My body hit the ground as I tumbled beneath the oncoming freak, hoping it wouldn't trample me with its many legs. I bent my knees, tucking them up to my chest. The spider's legs hammered the ground around me.

The second it passed over me, I bolted. Terror drove me toward the extinguished campfire. I kept my gaze fixed ahead and not on the giant arachnid behind me. Masses bristled within the trees. About a hundred eyes peered through the dark, illuminated by the pale glow of the moon.

"No!" ordered the chief creepy-crawly. "Mine!" it hissed, followed by another series of clacks.

Talk about being greedy.

I covered the remaining distance to the smoldering fire with a dive, arm outstretched to the point where it strained. My ribs took the brunt of the landing but I managed to grab what I wanted. Rolling over, I hurled chunk after chunk of firewood toward the oncoming predator. The creature's movement ceased as a forearm-sized piece of firewood struck the smallest of its fangs. A shrill sound, like a whistle, pierced the night. I didn't know spiders could scream in pain. It must've been like getting punched in the teeth. A pair of furry arms near the front of its mouth pawed at the injured fang in frustration.

In its pained moment of self-coddling, I groped for another piece of wood. It was rough, not having burnt completely. The thing was hefty at one end too. Good. It was club like. I was more interested in the bottom half. Nothing close to a dagger, but it was jagged and fire hardened. It would have to do.

My hand sank, then rose up, sending the piece of wood into the air. It smacked into my palm with a comforting weight.

The spider recovered. Rapid clacks filled my ears while its eyes screamed murder. It charged. I snarled in defiance. "Bring it, Shelob!"

Pincers snapped with the intent of decapitating me. I bobbed my head out of the way. I wouldn't be much use to people without a head.

Darting to the side, I raised the makeshift club overhead, intending to send it crashing down on a massive leg. The air rushed out of me as one of its limbs barreled into me, batting me aside like I was a joke. Dirt washed over me as I rolled on the ground. My hand still maintained a death grip on the firewood. The spider hopped—*hopped*—toward me!

You've got to hate jumping spiders. As if they weren't creepy enough.

I scrambled to all fours, clawing up fistfuls of dirt as I crawled away. The spider landed mere feet behind me, and I silently gave thanks that it wasn't using the metric system to move. Bark tickled the soft skin of my palm as I spun the firewood in my hand. I gripped the makeshift stake tight. Spider-douche raced forward, fangs moving with ravenous purpose. Globs of spittle fell from them.

My legs pounded against dirt as I moved to meet it. I exerted as much force as I could into my jump. We collided. My chest informed me that I was an idiot as a dull pain filled it. I slammed into the spider's beach ball sized skull—

fortunately—above the pincers.

The bristle-like hairs caused my hands to itch like I'd run them through poison ivy. Gritting through the discomfort, I clawed at the creature's body, fighting to keep my grip on it. Spasms shot through my torso as I swayed. The spider flailed its head, trying to shake me. I slid ever closer to its unfriendly chompers. Its eyes trained on me as I moved closer to becoming dinner. I released one of my hands and swung the improvised stake. It connected, driving through bulbous tissue with a sickening *squelch*.

The spider bucked and I was thrown clear. My grip on the stake was so tight that the muscles in my hand spasmed from fatigue. Air escaped me, leaving me to wheeze, as I lay immobile. Fangzilla stomped around in pained fury. Minute forearms, or whatever they're called on a spider, rubbed its face to assuage the damage and pain. Not like it would help. There's only so much you can do when you've been stabbed in the eye. One blinded, one now missing—not too shabby.

I found some relief in its anguished wailing. I'm not the kind of guy that gets a kick out of pulling wings off bugs. Unless they're trying to eat me, then I lose my cheery demeanor. I rolled to my side, pushing myself to a wobbly stand while the spider flailed.

"Lyshae!" I screamed, struggling with what little breath I had. "If I get out of this, I'm gonna kill you!"

"Is that any way to treat someone who's helping you?" Her voice echoed back from wherever the hell she was.

I blinked… I wasn't aware she could hear me. I was venting in frustration. I rubbernecked as I tried to pinpoint the location of her voice. I turned just in time to see arachnosaurus bustling toward me. The remaining six eyes blazed with an insane light. I think it was pissed at losing an eye. Some things just take stuff too personally. I mean, it was trying to eat me! And *it* was mad?

The stake whirled in my grip, now hefted like a poor club. My knees groaned as I sank to a fast crouch. Jaws clacked above me, striking empty air. Rocketing to my feet, I twisted my body, sending the club upwards in a double-handed swing. I ached to the marrow. A jarring force went through my arms as the blow landed. The club struck one of the large mandibles with a crack like lightning hitting an old tree. Another cry from the spider as its pincer fractured, not completely separated from its mouth, but rendered useless.

Deuces, bitch! One eye, one fang.

The beast stumbled backward in another fit of agony.

"Lyshae! Is this what you call helping? I am not spider bait!"

"I. Am. Negotiating. You Neanderthal!" Her voice had an amphitheater-like effect.

Neanderthal—me? I frowned, looking at the club, and grunted. I was not!

Spider-boy skittered toward me and I sighed. It was really keen on eating me. The club blurred into motion as I waved it in a wild pattern, hoping to keep the spider at bay. It didn't work. The spider pressed on, advancing, albeit warily. Guess it didn't want another chipped tooth. That's what happens when you play with your food.

"Lyshae?" I howled in panic. "How's that negotiating going?"

My response came in the form of a burst of light and warmth. The campfire crackled to life. The piece of wood in my hand erupted into flames as well.

I fumbled with the weapon as the broad club-like end became wreathed in flames. The fire's warmth was a small comfort. Its light was helpful, but I was gladdened by something else. Like animals, many of the paranormal creepies don't like fire. If you're an oversized spider, chances are you'll hate it all the more.

The flaming club whirred into a dizzying array of lights as I cast it into wide arcs. The spider gave up ground with every wave. Leaping forward, I jabbed the weapon toward its face. It shrieked and bounded over me. I followed suit. I jumped behind it and swung, managing to strike its butt…abdomen? Whatever. I hit its spidery ass with fire! The arachnid ignited.

My ears were assaulted by an agonized keen. The spider writhed and stomped. Just as quickly as it had been turned into a giant fireball, it was snuffed out. Its body twitched. Mandibles clicked.

"You've got to be kidding me…" I sighed, my shoulders sinking. I raised the club overhead and charged. Thrashing, bustling and all manner of noises sounded off as the entire army of spiders left the trees. I stopped so fast that I almost face planted. I was fully encircled by the freaks. One fiery club was not going to help me out of this.

They rushed past me—toward their fallen comrade. They crawled over him, strands of silk like material trailing behind them. Soon, it was fully cocooned and a pair of spiders took the initiative to haul him off. Its body still squirmed a bit. It was still alive. I shuddered.

"Sucks to be him," I murmured. My mistake. The remaining spiders turned to face me. I wondered if my escalating heartbeat was audible over the otherwise crypt-like silence.

"Stop!" the voice snapped with utter and unquestioning authority. The spiders froze in place. Lyshae stood there, posture straight, calm and undisturbed by the vast number of spiders around us.

One of them reared its ugly head. "Do not presume to—"

I never figured out what it was going to say next. Lyshae's hand cut through the air. An orb of fire appeared from nowhere. The spiders head was engulfed in flames. Its legs beat in panic before Lyshae motioned again. The fire extinguished and the creature fell to the ground, jerking. Its cries stopped. A repeat performance ensued. The spiders eyed Lyshae warily and scuttled over to their buddy. Seconds later, it too was wrapped in webbing and hauled off. A few arachnids hung back, eyes fixed on Lyshae and myself. A ball of fire appeared in her hands. They left.

I breathed in relief.

"Now, Vincent, that wasn't too bad, was it?"

I crossed the distance and took Lyshae in my grip. My thumb and fingers dug into the tissue around her windpipe. Her eyes widened for a fraction of a second before narrowing into dangerous slits. "What are you…" She trailed off as I squeezed harder.

"You screwed me." My chest heaved, matching my rapid breathing.

She sputtered something. I didn't care. I'm not so nice a guy that I wouldn't kill a pretty fox spirit. Lyshae may have had a bit of supernatural strength, but I had her by the throat. And her throat would crush just like anyone else's.

"Please," she managed to say.

I let her go. Lyshae crumpled into a heap. I didn't kneel to pick her up. I don't like it when someone plays me and leaves me to become spider chow. Sue me.

She rose a minute later, smoothing the rumpled pearlescent fabric of her shift. "Well, that was terribly rude of you. I should slap you again." She smiled.

I growled.

"Would you like me to share what I discovered?"

I didn't think she actually did her job. My look must've shown it.

"Please, do you honestly think I would've betrayed you? After I'd given my word? That would be bad for business."

"Yeah, you know what else is bad for business? Leaving me to be eaten by spiders!"

Lyshae's eyes did a lazy somersault, like what I had gone through was no big deal. "Hardly a trial. Besides, I helped you, didn't I?"

I remembered the spontaneous combustion of the campfire and club. Not to mention the fireball she had conjured. I eyed her askance. "That was you?"

"Who else?"

"Except you can't sling fire around," I said, my voice tense.

"Of course not, but illusions serve just as well," Lyshae punctuated the statement with a small laugh.

"Illusions?" I sputtered. "Lyshae, I felt the heat from those things. Hell, I saw what they did…." I trailed off as the realization hit me. Lyshae was well over a thousand years old. Her illusions were practically an art form. They were powerful enough to be felt. Well, powerful enough that you imagined you felt them. "So those spiders weren't burned. They imagined it?"

"Pain is in the mind, is it not, Vincent?"

I blinked. The spiders were fine; well, not counting the one who had lost an eye. They were alive when their "buddies" dragged them off. Alive and going to be eaten. I shivered. "Um, thanks, I think."

She gave a slight inclination of her head, about the closest thing to a bow I'd get from her.

"Before you spill everything you learned, mind telling

me why I had to go through that? If you weren't planning on screwing me, I'd like an answer, Lyshae."

"It was her price." I assumed *her* meant Lyshae's boss, the Mother of Spiders.

"What in the hell?"

"A bit of entertainment, while the grown-ups discussed things." A fox-like grin spread over her face. "While you were busy doing what you're so good at—wielding a cudgel and causing havoc—I was speaking to my lady." She said it so nonchalantly. That is not frickin' normal!

"Entertainment? What if I'd been eaten?"

"Entertainment and a meal." She grinned. "Either would have sufficed." It's never okay to be so calm and collected when talking about someone almost being eaten by spiders.

"Lyshae," I breathed, "I think I hate you."

She chuckled.

"Before I have a stroke, can you please tell me what you learned?"

"The shadows aren't shadows, not truly. Neither are they illusions. They are real, wholly so."

"So, what, they just pass as shadows—look like them? They can definitely move like shadows," I said. "What exactly are they doing here?"

"Doing what scavengers do." Her beautiful features twisted in disgust. "Vultures," she spat.

Vultures don't kill. They feed off whatever scraps are left after something bigger is done with a kill. That meant something bigger was here…something more dangerous than them. I swallowed.

"The shadows aren't killing the patients, are they?"

She shook her head.

"What are they doing here? What are they feeding on?"

"Why, the remains of the patients obviously."

Their remains…but Ortiz inspected the young woman's body. It was in the morgue. I raised an inquisitive eyebrow.

"Not their physical remains, Vincent. What happens when someone dies the way they have? In pain and confusion—issues unresolved?"

Oh, crap. This was getting worse by the second. Ghosts. She was talking about flippin' ghosts! It wasn't bad enough that something was murdering people. Now there was a group of supernatural scavengers picking off their ghosts!

Charles—Lizzie! Charles was a ghost now. He would be an easy target for these things, and Lizzie had seen him—spoken to him. What if she got roped into this? Things were getting out of hand, and fast. There were too many variables. It's not my job to save ghosts, but I wasn't going to leave them at the mercy of those freaks.

"Lyshae, what about the creature, the one responsible for the killings?" I blurted.

She shrugged. "I do not know, not at the moment at least."

"What? I went through all that, and you don't know!" I felt like my hand was going to reach back up and encircle her windpipe.

"There's only so much I glean from my lady, and let's not forget that you did not specify how or when you wanted the information. The rest will take time." She wore a smug expression.

A deep, audible burble formed in my throat.

"Also, I am not overly fond of being choked, Vincent Graves." Her smug smile vanished. A hand flicked through the night and a silvery gleam caught my eye. I turned to look at it, she had opened a door out of the Neravene. I shifted and saw a flash of movement. A wide smile played across Lyshae's face. My gut cried as a petite foot lashed out and the air was knocked from my lungs. "Goodbye for now, Vincent," she said as I tumbled through the doorway.

* * *

I landed hard, staring up at a different sort of dark from that of the Neravene. No disorienting balls of colored light, just the faint and distant glow of stars peppering the sky. Cool air drifted over me as I pushed myself to all fours. My hands dug into the asylum's grass. "Lyshae, you bitch!" I tore tufts of ground and sent them into the air. My forearm tingled.

I hadn't been in the Neravene for more than an hour or two. The Neravene didn't care for my deadline however. I

had lost nine whole hours.
    Thirty left.

# Chapter Twelve

It was past midnight, my body ached, and my mind begged for a few hours' rest. Except rest wasn't part of the job. I hobbled back to my room, taking care to go unnoticed. The second my body touched the mattress, overwhelming temptation came over me. My body sunk into the soft bed. Its contours shifted, welcoming me with an inviting hug. All I had to do was curl up and throw the blanket over myself. I'd only lose six to eight hours. Maybe a person would die in that time, maybe not. Maybe I'd have pleasant dreams.

I groaned, wondering if Church was ever going to give me a case where I could sleep. Crablike, I sent my hand scuttling beneath the pillows, sliding around aimlessly in an attempt to locate my journal. I batted the cover with an upturned hand and let it open to a random page. Sighing, I dug through it, hoping that I'd find something, and soon.

Another hour passed. Twenty-nine left. But a bit of luck broke my way. I wouldn't say it was lucky exactly, but I knew what the shadowy creatures were. I wasn't overly fond of the idea of dealing with them though. My eyes adopted a new level of focus as I scoured the pages.

These things were smart, possessing startling speeds and, worst of all, a pack mentality. An unknown quantity of monsters were darting around the place, and somewhere along with them, was their big dog. If I wanted to stop these things, I had to gun for their leader.

Not a big issue until you factored in that these things weren't the only monsters roaming around the place. Chief Freakzilla was going around giving people heart attacks and conjuring the fog of doom.

A hollow knocking sound destroyed what silent thinking time I had. My heart adopted a jackhammer-like beat. The audible clicking of a doorknob filled my ears and I rushed to stow my journal.

Ortiz's face broke into view. She was blinking more frequently than normal as she fought to stay awake. Slipping into the room, taking care not to make any noise, she sat beside me. My arm throbbed from her punch. I rubbed the area as I shot her an accusatory glare.

"I could've punched you in the nose." She smiled, but it looked strained—tired. "You're making a habit of keeping ladies waiting, not a good one to get into."

Don't I know it?

"Find anything, Charles?"

"Lots of something on one hand," I answered, "and lots of nothing on the other."

She let out an unladylike snort. Ortiz arched an eyebrow, waiting for me to elaborate.

Bowing slightly, I flourished my hands. "Ladies first."

"Fine. Apparently you were right. We're not the only ones to see or feel weird stuff. People claim to have seen shadows running all over the place. Of course the staff dismiss it as hallucinations."

"Wait," I chimed in, "can't the staff see them?"

Ortiz shook her head. "Only patients."

"Fits," I added and Ortiz gave me a curious look. "I'll explain when you're done."

She gave me a satisfied nod. "Some of them said they're feeling worse—more depressed, and negative. And then there are the cold spots and chills—"

"What?" I snapped, drawing a glare from her. Ortiz wasn't fond of being interrupted.

"Cold spots," she repeated, "sudden drops in temperature. I was speaking to someone when all of a sudden it felt like I was thrown into a pool of ice water." She visibly shuddered.

Lyshae was right. These things were picking off ghosts. Hell, for all I knew they might've been pushing people toward becoming ghosts. If I was right, they were responsible for people feeling depressed. It was possible they were psychically pushing people to commit suicide. More dead patients, more ghosts, more food.

"Charles, what's going on?" Ortiz's fatigue seemed to be melting away. She had an inquisitive look in her eyes. She was a hawk when it came to info. "You've got this look on your face."

"Yeah." My throat felt raw. "I've got a lot to tell you, and you're definitely not going to like it. I'm not sure as to how much you're going to believe actually."

"Charles, within the last six months I was almost burned alive, nearly buried, and thrown out of a hotel window. I was murdered, brought back to life, witnessed black fog kill a young woman… I think at this point I'm willing to believe a lot."

Ortiz was right. I had put her through a lot—it wasn't fair. And yet here she was, by my side, again, and willing to help. She may not have been aware that I was the same person from six months ago, but I knew it. Her last adventure had landed her in a mental hospital. Part of me was afraid of what might happen this time. Ortiz didn't deserve to be caught up in all of this. She had the chance for a normal life.

But I was losing time and, as much as it pained me to admit it, I needed help. A silent prayer ran through my head. I begged forgiveness for dragging her into this. I'm not a spiritual person, but for Ortiz's sake, I didn't think it'd hurt to pray a little.

I let out a resigned sigh and spilled what I had learned. "These shadows aren't really shadows. They just look like 'em. I don't think they're killing the patients either. Well, not entirely."

"What does that mean?"

"Hang on." I raised a hand in a gesture for her to slow down. "There are stories of these things all over the world. Heck, radio stations have talked about them. The stories about shadows like this go back ages. Some have said they've been attacked by them. I don't buy that—that's rare. These things don't go after people's physical forms."

"Physical forms? What the hell are you talking about?"

It's a tough thing to explain what ghosts are, mostly because they're so interconnected to souls. I still don't know why I ended up retaining my soul and not winding up a ghost. But don't look a gift horse in the mouth, right? The largest difference between a soul and a ghost is that souls are complete and whole identities of a person. Ghosts are the broken fragments. They linger in our world, lost and confused. Souls don't stay here; they move on. I should've moved on too. Church still needed to tell me why I hadn't.

I worked out what to say and how to phrase it. "These things go after their ghosts," I said, letting the words settle in.

Ortiz's mouth moved but no sound came out. Her face went through an array of motions. I remained silent, letting her work through them. There's no easy way to come to grips with the idea that shadow beings are hunting down the ghosts of murdered patients.

Tingle. Another hour had passed. Twenty-eight.

"Ghosts," she said moments later.

"Yeah. The cold spots you've been talking about—dead giveaway. When people die the way they have here—terrified, lost, confused—their spirits cling on. Ghosts are broken-up pieces of the people they were, fragments of emotions and ideas. Sometimes sorrow, other times—rage. It's not pretty. The angry ones can lash out and hurt people. Most of the time they're harmless. But these things, they're preying on the victims' ghosts, giving them no chance to move on. What's worse, they're trying to make more." Barely audible pops rang out as my fist tightened.

She arched a curious eyebrow. "How?"

"These things are making people feel despair, pushing them along to the ultimate form of desperation."

"Suicide," she breathed.

I nodded. "These freaks poke and prod at your mind. They're drawn to negative thoughts and feelings, and this place is banquet hall for them. But it's not going to be enough. They're picking up the scraps for the moment. That won't keep them content for long."

Ortiz read between the lines. "Picking up the scraps... Something else is here, killing the patients."

"Something worse," I added.

Her eyes clamped shut for a moment. When they opened, they glowed with something hot. She set her jaw. "So, we're going to stop these shadow things and whatever's killing the patients."

"Damn straight we are," I growled.

"How?"

Movement caught my eye and I rubbernecked. The way the light was shining in the room cast our shadows behind us—bedside. Across from us, however, there was a silhouette of black. It didn't appear flat or part of the wall. It protruded. Ripples flowed through its mass as it rose, giving it a Jell-O like consistency.

Ortiz caught sight of it. "What the hell is that?" She scrambled to her feet, adopting a fighting crouch.

The figure stretched to its full height. It didn't look like the other shadow beings I'd seen earlier. It took on a noticeably different shape. The sound of drying glue pulling from paper filled the room. The creature stepped forward, peeling its body from the wall. It shuddered as shadows bent around it. They spread over its neck and sides, giving the appearance of a tattered cloak of midnight. Black strands raced from its shoulders like ivy, weaving around its head into a hood. All it needed was a scythe to be the Grim Reaper sans a bony ass.

My eyes ballooned and I reeled away from it. "It's a frickin' Nazgul!" I couldn't very well call it a shadow-being or person. That's what they were referred to throughout history. It lacked creativity.

Ortiz didn't appreciate my creative naming solution. "You can't be serious?" She remained on guard with her fists balled tight and muscles coiled.

It was good enough for Tolkien, but I decided to come up with a different name lest I be sued.

"Shadow men," I muttered. "Damned shadow men."

"What?" Ortiz blurted. "Now is not the time to be naming things!"

The shadowy creature surged forward. No, surged was the wrong word. It was fast and disjointed, like watching gelatin stretch and snap toward you.

I dove to the side, avoiding its grasp. The creature turned to face me. Directly in the center of its sternum was a hole, almost see-through. I say "almost" because something occupied the basketball-sized cavity. No larger than my fist, it was grim, black and pulsating. It hung connected by wispy tendrils to the surrounding mass. The strands fluctuated in size as a black, ichor-like gel coursed through them.

A heart. A black, morbid, and ever-so-disgusting heart.

Ugly, yes. But it was still a vital organ. One that could be attacked. Myths about shadow beings said their hearts were only exposed at night.

The shadow being's wrist twisted and deformed, rolling around in a manner that confirmed it had no bones. Its mass rearranged itself, and soon, its hand changed shape altogether. It increased in size to become something like a dustpan, wide and unnaturally large. The new appendage sported serrated talons. They looked like tactical knives.

It was the sort of thing to make your eyes go wide. Mine certainly did. Drywall cried in protest. Flecks of it went everywhere as the creature's hand swept toward me. "Fuck off!" I yelped, ducking to avoid a follow-up swipe. "The One Ring's not here!" The shadowy fiend ignored my genius quip. Something about genius never being celebrated went through my mind.

"Holy—" I blurted as another swipe came my way. The creature's hand lodged itself in the floor. I capitalized, sending a haymaker into the thing's face. My fist met what I assumed was the creature's jaw, and sank in. The shadow being didn't fall to the ground. My fist impacted and stuck there. It was like punching a memory foam mattress. Pulling my fist from the spot, I shot my arm straight up, bringing my elbow down hard. I connected with its neck—again to little effect.

"Ooomph," was the only sound that came out of me as the air rushed from my lungs. A weighty blow from the shadow man's free arm drove me back. I shook it off and rocketed toward the monster, arms spread wide. My arms tightened around it as I charged. My momentum carried us to the wall, which crunched. The creature peeled itself from the dent and stepped forward, its attention focused solely on me. That was a mistake.

"Ortiz! The heart!"

She blurred into motion the instant I found myself in an unrelenting grip. The pressure around my throat was unbelievable, but I could still breathe—just. The muscles in my neck begged for mercy. This thing wasn't trying to choke me. It was trying to crush my friggin' throat.

Ortiz disagreed with that idea. Even from where I hung suspended, I could see her move. Lashing out with a fist, she struck the creature's heart. The pressure ceased. I crumpled to the floor and developed sympathy for Lyshae. Being choked is not fun.

The shadow figure's body spasmed and contorted in silent agony. It shifted shapes as it writhed. Ortiz's leg arced with a flexibility I didn't think was possible and impacted the organ again.

Holy Chuck Norris, could she fight.

The creature howled in mute distress, moving with disjointed and startling speed as it hit the wall. It sank into the material and darted out of sight. Panting, I rose to my feet. "Well, that sucked. Nice moves by the way."

"Aiki Bujutsu," she commented.

"Uh...gesundheit?"

"It's a martial art."

"Didn't know you studied kick butt fu."

Ortiz rolled a shoulder in a nonchalant shrug. "Dad made me."

Thank you, Papa Ortiz.

"So..." she said, breaking the momentary silence that had fallen between us. "That just happened."

"Yeah, we were jumped by a—"

"Don't name it."

I sniffed. "Fine, we were jumped by a shadow being. That's what they're called in mythology. So uninspired," I muttered.

"And there are more of them," she added. "Lots more."

I gave a grim nod.

"Ghosts, shadows and something worse...all here," she said more to herself than me. An invisible weight overcame her and she sank to the bed. Part of me wanted to give chase to the shadow creature. I shut that part down and sat next to Ortiz. She slid further back on the bed, adopting a cross-legged position, hands limp on her thighs. Reaching over, I took one of them in a reassuring grip.

"You okay?"

"Yes. No. I don't know." She released a deep sigh. "It's just like six months ago. I thought I was free and clear of this stuff. I knew it was still out there. We dealt with it earlier...."

"But?"

"But, that thing." She shuddered. I squeezed her hand harder and she gave me a weak smile. "It made things sink in more, you know?"

I nodded.

"The thing is, I feel—not lost—uncertain, maybe. Somewhere between no idea and part of one, if that makes sense?"

"It does." I kept my voice whisper soft. "I feel like that a lot."

"With the life you tattoo guys lead, I bet. I don't know how all this can be out there and for me not to be a part of it. That's why I joined the FBI. To solve crimes and help people. But who helps the people dealing with this stuff?"

"I do." My voice cracked a bit.

She shot me another smile, a bit warmer than before. "I know. I haven't met many of you people. How many are there? What about me? I know things go bump in the night now. I don't know if I can just sit on the sidelines and watch."

After everything Camilla Ortiz had been through, she still wanted to get out there and fight monsters. She didn't have to; she *wanted* to. I didn't know how to take that. It was hard. She had suffered so much already. It wasn't my call. It was hers. Still, I didn't want to put her through anymore of this stuff.

It was like she could read my mind. "You're not making me do anything. That's what you're thinking, right? Men are idiots like that. Taking responsibility for stuff out of their hands. It's me, I guess. I can't sit back and watch. It's not who I am. I may not be used to it, but…I am involved." Her words brimmed with steely resolve.

My voice shook. I was in awe of her strength. "Fair enough."

She returned the pressure I exerted on her hand with a squeeze of her own. "So, are we going to sit here holding hands, or are we going to get this thing?"

Snorting, I slipped my hand out of hers. "Hell, yeah. Let's gank us some shadows!"

"What do we know? Or what do *you* know?"

"About shadow beings? Well, apart from the fact they have the most uncreative name in history, I mean that's what they look like for…" I trailed off as I noticed the irritated and somewhat deadly glare Ortiz was giving me. Clearing my throat, I resumed from a more appropriate point. "Erm, well, they feed off ghosts, almost in a vampire-like manner. These things drain their essence into nothingness."

Ortiz's eyes flickered when I said that. No doubt a series of disturbing thoughts and images were going through her mind.

"The stories say they're supposed to be hurt by light—"

She let out a light snort. "The bedroom lights didn't do much to it."

"Because," I said, drawing the word out, "bedroom lights aren't real light." Her face lost focus at that revelation. I waved a hand, motioning for her to slow down as I explained. "It's manmade, not part of the natural world. I'm talking about direct sunlight."

"We can't wait for morning, Charles."

"I know. The other option—which I'm not too fond of—is fire."

Her eyebrows shot up.

"Fire isn't just a purifying source in the magical world. It's one of the purest forms of light besides the sun. Don't get me wrong. Fire is great, but I'm not keen on running around this place with torches."

"What about that black heart in the center?"

"To be honest, I wasn't sure about that bit until I saw it myself. The stories talk about them having black hearts. They're only visible and vulnerable at night."

Ortiz gave me a knowing look, gesturing to the window and the dark skies outside.

"Yeah, I know. They're vulnerable right now. That doesn't mean they'll be easy to take down. Although we could have you going all Crouching Tigress, Hidden Dragon on their shadowy butts. Feel like ripping out some hearts?"

"Maybe." She smiled. "I'd rather find a better way to deal with them than tooth and claw. Any other ways we can hurt them?"

"Well, we know they're not really after us—"

"Uh, all evidence to the contrary there, buddy. It might have slipped your mind while you were getting your butt kicked—"

"I was not getting my butt kicked," I countered with a growl.

She waved me off like I hadn't said a word. "I saved your ass." Ortiz smiled and her eyes danced with amusement.

I scowled. I can fight too. I've inhabited all manner of great fighters in the past. I can't come across as badass all the time.

"Fine," I relented. "Yes, technically they...one of them came after us. I think that's because we're getting involved in their business."

"How do they know that?"

A chilling notion crossed my mind. "Well, they can pose as shadows. They've been darting around the place, listening, picking up conversations—"

"Including ours," Ortiz finished.

"Yeah," I agreed.

"They're that smart?"

I nodded. "They can rationalize. They can understand human speech from what the lore says. They're nearly human level intelligent—well, the leaders are."

"Leaders?" She blinked.

"These things are pack animals. Somewhere in this hospital, there's a chief creepy running the show. The older these things get, the smarter they get. The eldest are normally in charge."

"So...if we take him—it—out?" Ortiz left the question hanging.

"Chances are the rest will bail...or kill us in retaliation."

"Thanks for that little add on, Captain Sunshine."

"This plan is still dependent on taking out the big dog. We don't know which shadow that is," I said.

"Or how to find it. Plus, we're not exactly spoiled for ways to take it out," Ortiz added.

I blinked as a notion occurred to me. These things were feeding on ghosts. They were stalking deceased patients. If we could find their ghosts, we'd find them. It wasn't only that; it was how they fed on the ghosts. It was a transference of energy in a way. They absorbed the ghost's life force, their essence, by essentially opening themselves up and ingesting them—in the metaphorical sense. It's like how a starfish extends its stomach and envelops its prey. It wasn't in the lore. It was more speculation than fact, but while they fed, their soft bellies were exposed, so to speak.

I shared my theory with Ortiz.

"How sure are you this will work?"

I waggled my hand in an ambiguous gesture. "Fifty-fifty."

"Great odds." Her voice was pure acid. "So we still have to find a way to kill it. It may be open, but I don't think bare hands will do it."

"Worth a try though, ain't it?"

She nodded in agreement. "But doesn't this rely on us finding the ghosts in the first place?"

I laughed. I couldn't help it. Ortiz looked at me like I was a madman. That's when the realization hit me that I was trapped in a mental asylum. So maybe I was a madman. I laughed harder. "Ortiz," I said, my tone on the edge of something near maniacal, "there's someone I need to introduce you to."

# Chapter Thirteen

"Where are we going?" Ortiz hissed.

"Shut up." I held my index finger to my lips.

Ortiz glared at me, but I directed my gaze straight ahead.

"We're not supposed to be wandering around this late, Charles."

I ignored her, focusing on the door before us. I peered through the pane of glass and surveyed what I could. Everything seemed okay. Good. If these things were after ghosts, she could've been dragged into the mess. I wasn't about to let that happen. A subtle chill filled my palm as I took hold of the metal doorknob. I gave it a twist. Frowning, I turned the knob again only to have it click in resistance.

"This needs a woman's touch. Move." Ortiz slipped between the door and me. Digging into her hair, she removed several slivers of something that glinted in the night.

"You hid pins in your hair?"

Ortiz flashed a quick smile. "Never know when they might come in handy."

I enveloped one of her hands in a gentle grip, pulling it away from the door. She shot me a quizzical look.

"I don't think we should be breaking into her room. It's late. She's asleep and, like you said, some people are on edge. If we wake her up, well, it could get bad. I mean, imagine it. You're there, conked out in Sleepyville, and two stalkers are standing over your bed watching you. Creepy, right?"

Ortiz bobbed her head in agreement.

"Last thing we want is to startle them and make 'em scream. Might raise attention, might not. I'd rather not chance it."

Ortiz withdrew from the door. She slipped the pins back into her hair.

I flashed her a smile. "But who knows, we might need the pins later. I hear voodoo's handy."

My ribs panged as her elbow glanced off them. Grunting from the blow, I made a fist, rapping it against the door. Gently, I might add. It was night. I didn't want to wake everybody up, just the person inside.

We waited about a minute before a sleepy, soft voice answered. "Who's there?"

Grinning, I plastered my face against the glass pane. I didn't know if she could see me. I hoped it would put her at ease. "It's me," I whispered back. That might have been one of the most ambiguous answers, but she was an astute person.

"Oh, s'okay." The knob clicked. It cracked open an instant later. Lizzie stood there, her eyes pasted shut. Big brown peepers fluttered open seconds later. They were a tad unfocused, but she smiled when she saw me. I stooped to a single knee, putting myself at eye level with her. "Not Charles," she beamed, shaking off her sleepy state.

My eyes went saucer-sized and I developed an arrhythmia. I whipped a shushing finger to my lips. "Shhh on the 'not Charles' thing. Please."

I don't know how much of that Ortiz had heard, but I could feel her eyes beaming through my skull. She was always curious and aware, it seemed. I didn't want my identity revealed by the young girl.

Lizzie threw herself against my chest and embraced me in the sort of hug only a child can give. "S'okay," she whispered in my ear. "Sshh."

I smiled weakly at Ortiz. "Kids say the darndest things, huh?" Her eyes narrowed. I could see an innumerable amount of thoughts processing behind them. I swallowed, hoping she didn't hear what Lizzie had said.

"Oh, hello," Lizzie said when she noticed Ortiz.

Ortiz's narrowed-eyed gaze broke upon seeing Lizzie. The intensity fled her face and was replaced by a smile. "Hello," Ortiz replied in warm and kind tone. She glanced at me out of the corners of her eyes, asking a silent question.

Easing myself out of Lizzie's hug, I made the

introductions. "Right. Ortiz, Elizabeth—Elizabeth, Ortiz." I gestured between the two. "Elizabeth sees ghosts," I chirped. Lizzie smiled and nodded several times.

I don't think Ortiz expected to hear that. Her face lost all expression. Lizzie and I let her work through the not-so-little revelation.

"She sees...ghosts?" Ortiz blinked several times.

"Yeah, she does."

Lizzie nodded again in silence.

"And you know this...how?"

"She told me," I answered.

"And you believed her?"

"Ortiz," I began, "within the last day, you've seen black fog and icky tendrils attack me. You've told me about cold spots all over the place and, just now, we were attacked by a shadowy creature out of mythology. I deal with the paranormal all the time. Lizzie says she can see ghosts. I believe her. She has no reason to lie. She's not getting anything out of it. Heck, she's stuck in this place because of her gift."

Her teeth showed as her lips folded. She chewed on them. "So...Lizzie—Elizabeth—"

"You can call me Lizzie." She beamed. "You're here to help him stop the monsters, right?" Ortiz smiled and bowed her head in agreement.

"Yeah," I chimed in, "she's here to help. But right now, Lizzie, we need *your* help. We're trying to stop the shadows. I don't know if you know, but they're hurting the ghosts. They're—"

Lizzie's weight crashed into me as she threw herself against my chest. Her hug was tighter this time. Moisture tickled my neck and jaw. Her body shook and I noticed tears. "My sister," she sobbed.

Those words hit me hard. "Is she..." I didn't want to finish my sentence. Lizzie had lost everyone, but her sister had stayed in touch as a ghost. I didn't like the idea of her losing her sister as well. No kid should have to go through that.

"No," she sniffled, "but they took her."

I squeezed her for a brief moment. "It's gonna be okay, huh?" I tried to reassure her. I was never good at that stuff.

"Hey." I took her by the shoulders, gripping them tight. "Look at me." I tried to balance my tone between soft and strong. "We're going to get her back, okay? Lizzie, look at me; I promise you." I cast a glance toward Ortiz. Her jaw was set. "We promise you," I amended. Ortiz nodded.

Lizzie sniffed harder, looking up at me with those large, tear-filled eyes. She didn't say anything. Lips quivering, she just stared at me, asking a silent question. I answered her by flashing a smile. There was no way in hell I was going to leave Lizzie's sister at the mercy of those things. I may not have had a plan exactly, but Lizzie and Ortiz didn't need to know that.

My smile widened. "I've got a plan." Lizzie sniffed, more lightly this time. Her trembling lips seemed to still a bit. I may have lied about the plan part, but not about my promise. I was going to get her sister back.

But first things first. I scrunched the bottom of my shirt into a tight wad. Rising from my crouched position, I brought the wad to Lizzie's face, dabbing her cheeks and eyes with it. "Better?" I eyed her.

She sniffed again, but broke into a weak smile. It was still a smile though. I took it, glad to her see her tears gone.

"So, Lizzie." I gave her cheeks one last rub with my shirt. "You don't know where they took your sister, but you can still...sense her?" I was unsure of what that entailed. I was hoping that whatever she felt could be used to help us track her sister down.

It was a gamble and a bad one at that. This was starting to go beyond my expertise. I know about ghosts, but that's far from being an expert on them. Heck, I knew people like Lizzie existed, but I had no idea they could be *that* in tune with a particular ghost.

Seeing the ghosts of family members isn't common, but it happens to those few who have the talent like Lizzie. Being able to sense them even when they're not in sight...that was something new for me. I didn't know the extent of Lizzie's abilities either. If she was that tied to the ghostly world, these shadow freaks could come after her. She was essentially a ghost radar. It didn't seem like they needed help finding prey, but what did I know? The possibility existed, and that caused a frozen lump to form in my stomach. I wasn't fond of dragging a kid into this.

I breathed in sync with a ten-count, planning my next move. "Okay, Lizzie, you're going to have come with us, hmm?" She nodded. Ortiz grimaced, and I stretched a false smile across my face. "But you're going to have to listen to everything I say, huh? If I say run, you run. If I say hide, you hide. I don't know what's going to happen, but it's going to be dangerous. I want to help you get your sister back. Ortiz and I *are* going to get your sister back. Those shadow freaks aren't going to stand by and let us do that. So I'm going to need you to stay by her side, okay?" I nodded toward Ortiz. Lizzie bobbed her head in silent understanding.

"Good."

If anything happened, chances were it was going to happen to me. If not, I was going to make damn sure it would happen to me. I resolved not to let this girl get wrapped up any further in this mess.

I would've made the same resolution for Ortiz, but I knew I couldn't make that—or any other calls—for her. As much as it hurt to admit it, Ortiz was willingly involving herself and I couldn't protect her if she didn't want it. My best option was to entrust her with Lizzie's care. It was dirty and underhanded. I knew Ortiz wouldn't take any risks if she had to worry about Lizzie. Plus, no one could protect Lizzie better. If there were stupid risks that needed taking, I was the idiot for the job.

I was about to speak when the frozen lump in my stomach moved through my entire body. My extremities lost functionality. I couldn't touch my thumb to my pinky. My marrow and blood turned to jelly. My muscles quivered and Ortiz gripped herself tight. I could see Ortiz's breath as she exhaled. It might've been spring in the world around us, but in the room, it was winter. I erupted into a spasmodic dance as something came over my body. It was like having syrup poured over you—thick, gelatinous, liquid nitrogen syrup. It wracked my bones and froze me to my core.

*The hell was that?*

The only person unperturbed by the declining temperature was young Lizzie. The last time I'd felt anything like this was six months ago in Manhattan. I was attacked by a Wraith. I wasn't keen on reliving the experience, but something was off. If it was a Wraith, everyone would be feeling the side effects, even Lizzie. Not to mention I couldn't think of a single reason why a Wraith would be here, or after me. Given where we were and what was involved, I realized what was going on.

"Ghosts." My breath condensed into white fog, dissipating as fast as it formed. The sole window in the room was adorned with crystalline shapes. Intricate flakes ran across it. It was eerily beautiful. I've seen water freeze in the presence of paranormal beings before—heck—even ghosts, but never like that. My previous encounters with ghosts were always with troubled ones—lost, aching, and lashing out. When they entered a room, everything froze over and did so violently. Horrendous cracks formed in glass that then shattered. It's not pretty.

"You shouldn't stand in the way of others," Lizzie murmured, breaking me away from my thoughts. I gave her a quizzical, lost look. "She had to walk right through you," Lizzie explained without really explaining.

I put it together after a second's thought. A ghost had just walked through me. I shuddered, and it had nothing to do with the temperature.

"Uh, Lizzie? What's going on?" My lips trembled. Ortiz's expression mirrored my confusion.

"They want to help," Lizzie said as if everything was obvious. It wasn't.

"Who? What?"

"The ghosts. My friends. They're going to help. They're going to look after us." She seemed comforted by the notion. Comforting wasn't the right feeling or word when you're surrounded by ghosts.

"Oh." There's not much you can say when you've been told ghosts, plural, want to help. At that point I was content to shut up and nod.

"Charles…" Ortiz said, more like a question than anything. "What's going on?" Her hands rubbed against her bare arms.

"Um, I think the asylum's ghosts are going to help us— well, Lizzie," I said, uncertain of whether that was wholly true.

Lizzie nodded agreement and smiled. "Us."

That settled it. We now had a group of ghosts on our side. There's no right way to feel about that. On the one hand, I had a group of ghosts at my back. On the other, I had a group of ghosts at my back. Double-edged sword if I've ever seen one. I've never gotten along with ghosts. If they were there for Lizzie—fine. I couldn't guarantee what would happen when we were done. That bit worried me.

I think the same train of thought crossed Ortiz's mind. She muttered, "Ghosts," like a curse.

It may well have been a curse, but it was one I planned to use to our advantage. Regardless of their temperaments, situations, and stability, or lack thereof, these ghosts knew the asylum. That knowledge was invaluable. My mind may have been focused on rescuing Lizzie's sister and dealing with the shadowy beings, but there was still another nasty hiding in the asylum. Maybe—and it was a big maybe—the ghosts would have some information about it.

"I don't suppose"—Ortiz's teeth chattered—"that the ghosts could help us without the icebox treatment?"

"I feel fine," Lizzie stated, not quite understanding our discomfort. But then she wouldn't.

I couldn't figure out the reason, but whatever it was, Lizzie seemed immune to the chilling effects the ghosts were having on us. A notion occurred to me. She was either immune to their effects, or they were sheltering her from the adverse parts of their presence.

That was interesting. I'd never seen behavior like that from ghosts. Lizzie was becoming all the more intriguing. The manner in which she interacted with the ghosts and they her—I couldn't believe it.

Ortiz sneezed, jarring me from my thoughts.

"Sorry," mumbled Lizzie, her tone apologetic and ethereal all at once. "Sharon says they can't do anything about the cold."

"Sharon?" It clicked a second later. Right. Ghosts. Ortiz came to the same conclusion.

"How does, uh, Sharon know we'd like her to turn it up a little?" Ortiz aimed the question at Lizzie and me.

I piped up. "Even though we can't see them or hear them, Ortiz, they can hear us." Lizzie motioned in agreement. "They're occupying the same space as us in a way. That's why we're feeling the side effects of them being here."

Ortiz frowned. "Speaking of occupying the same space... How many are there, Charles, Lizzie?"

I shrugged and left it to Lizzie. "Six."

The temperature hadn't dropped but it felt colder. Six ghosts. I've had bad times dealing with one really pissed-off ghost. I was praying they liked Lizzie enough to hold back any angst that might have built up since their deaths.

"How come only you can see them, Lizzie?" Ortiz eyed her as she rubbed her arms.

Lizzie shrugged, leaving it to me. "There are many ways a person can see a ghost or ghosts. More often than not, it's because you're related to them or close. In her case, it seems she was born with the gift. She could probably see each and every ghost in the asylum. Before you ask, the reason we can't see them is that they don't want us to. That's it. If you don't have Lizzie's talent, the only way you can see a ghost is if they want you to. Trust me when I say that it's no good thing if they want you to. That happens when they're epically ticked off at you."

Ortiz breathed out. A plume of fog left her mouth. "So, it's a good thing they're not showing themselves right now? They're not mad?"

"As good as a group of invisible ghosts surrounding you can be, I guess. Sure." I gave her a halfhearted shrug.

"They're mad," Lizzie chimed. Not a reassuring thing to hear. "But not at you two. They're mad at the shadow monsters for taking the other ghosts." A hint of a growl edged its way into her voice.

That rocked me. The entire time I had known her, short as it may have been, Lizzie didn't seem to get angry. She spoke much like Church—slow, soft. Seeing the little girl growl was all I needed to know that this was serious for everyone involved, corporeal or otherwise.

A sound like dry twigs breaking filled the room as I cracked my neck from side to side. My joints protested the cold. "'Kay, Lizzie, I know you said you can feel your sister, but do the asylum ghosts know anything that might help?"

She paused for a minute. Her features stilled and she listened with intent to a voice only she could hear. Lizzie's lips folded. A second later, her eyes. "Yup, they know where they took her! They know where all of *them* are."

That was good news and bad. I wasn't keen on tackling every single one of *them*—them being shadow beings—in one place all at once. My priority, well, preference, was to rescue Lizzie's sister. After that, I could deal with the shadowed monstrosities running around the place. Then came the freak show that had killed Charles. I sighed on the inside at how much I had to deal with.

"Lizzie, erm..." I paused for a moment realizing the stupidity of what I had been doing. The ghosts could hear me fine, yet I'd been addressing all my questions to her. I thought it polite to change that a bit. I circled in place as I spoke to the unseen beings around me. I waved. "Um, hi."

It wasn't the best of starts.

Ortiz scratched at the side of her temple, giving me a look. I scowled in return.

"Ortiz and I"—I gestured between the pair of us—"are here to help. I was wondering if you could tell us, well, Lizzie, how to find her sister?" I cast a look over my shoulder towards Lizzie.

"Hmm?" she mused.

"What?" Ortiz and I asked in unison.

"They said that...they're here?" Lizzie's tone was uncertain.

"Here?" Ortiz and I said in stereo. Ortiz moved from her position near the wall, springing toward me. I followed suit, moving toward her. Both of us tensed for a fight. Or to run. It's always a viable option when the supernatural are concerned. It's definitely saved my ass a few times.

"No..." Lizzie trailed off as her face contorted in confusion. "Here, but not here?" Blinking, her puzzled expression grew as she tried muddling through whatever it was they were telling her. "Somewhere like here?" Her face scrunched further. "Here but not here. More like—next to here?" Lizzie still struggled to understand. Ortiz mirrored Lizzie's confusion.

I didn't.

A Formula One event broke out inside my skull. Thoughts too fast to count raced by with deafening roars. I couldn't make anything out. Lizzie's explanation left me with a cold feeling of dread.

The Neravene.

Going through the portion I did with Lyshae was no fun. It was dangerous enough on my own. Bringing Ortiz and Lizzie along—damn, I didn't know what to think. She was just a kid. And Ortiz had already been through so much. I couldn't take her into a place like that now. Worse, I didn't have a clue what waited on the other side.

You can't think of the Neravene as one big place. I went through one part of it with Lyshae. But if we went through from here, it would be something else entirely. It's not connected like roads across a country. It's disjointed, separate realms and domains for whatever inhabits them. There was no way to know with any certainty what we would cross into.

An asylum haunted by ghosts. Ones traumatized by the monster that killed them. Then there were shadows hunting then. It wasn't something I wanted to think about. The side of the Neravene that overlapped with the asylum would be something from a Stephen King novel.

And I'd be dragging Ortiz and Lizzie into it. Enamel ground away as my teeth clenched and slid. Ortiz noticed.

"Something wrong?"

"Yes." I clenched a fist. "No. I don't know."

"I'm freezing, surrounded by ghosts, shadow monsters and more," Ortiz growled. "If you've got something on your mind, I would prefer you spill it before I make you."

"I know where they've taken Lizzie's sister." My voice was flat.

Lizzie's face shifted. Something akin to hope flickered through her eyes.

A smile passed over Ortiz's mouth. "Great."

I shook my head. "No, not great."

The hopeful mask on Lizzie's face slipped and part of me ached for robbing her of the moment. Ortiz's eyebrows arched expectantly.

"Ortiz, the place they've taken her—it's dangerous."

She snorted. "And this place isn't?"

"Ortiz," I breathed in exasperation. All the pent up weariness flooded through me. "Just listen for one second and stop getting uppity with me."

She glared daggers. I was too tired and concerned to care. If they came along and a single slip up happened, someone would die. I'd rather the both of them be alive and pissed at me for an eternity. It beat the alternative.

"Where they are makes this place look like an amusement park." My brief explanation garnered shudders out of Lizzie and Ortiz. I couldn't imagine what was going through their heads. As bad as this place was, they had to start taking seriously the possibility that somewhere worse existed. Their imaginations must've been running wild.

"You want to go alone." Ortiz's face hardened as she realized what I was doing.

I nodded. A look of hurt came across Lizzie. It banded my chest with iron. She looked like I had broken my promise to her. Ortiz's look wasn't any better. Her eyes narrowed to slits. I felt like heat vision beams would burn through me at any moment.

"She's my sister!" Lizzie protested.

"You don't get to make that call for us—for me!" Ortiz bristled.

"You're right." I fought to keep my voice from rising to a shout. "I don't get to make that call for either of you, but I sure as hell wish I did. Believe me, this place is...." I trailed off, not knowing how to impress upon them all that the Neravene was.

"This place is what?" Ortiz's leaned closer. For Camilla Ortiz, not knowing something was an irritation and even more so when it came to the paranormal world. "Lizzie has more right than anyone to know. *We're* going to rescue her sister." Ortiz made it clear that they were in fact coming along. Her mind was already set. "There's no way you're leaving me behind unless you want to have your—" she paused for a moment glancing back to Lizzie, "—butt, kicked in front of a little girl." She forced the word out instead of the easier one that would've come to mind.

I shook my head and smiled. The woman was nothing if not tenacious. "Fine," I relented. "The place is called the Neravene."

It didn't register with Ortiz or Lizzie. Why would it? It was up to me to explain the unexplainable. I took a deep breath. "The Neravene is The World Beside Ours. It's a

place that sits beside our world, but it's not something that
adheres to time, size, space or anything else. Like billions of
worlds inside an even bigger world. A world that's as large
as it needs to be to encompass the ever-growing smaller
worlds. Most of our rules hold very little sway there. It's a
place where every fairytale, folklore and mythology you've
heard of—and some you haven't—reside. They have a
home there. Ghosts carve out their own little niche. A single
ghost gets an entire world of their own there, twisted and
broken, shaped to their mangled mind."

Ortiz's steely gaze wavered for a moment. Her jaw
tightened as she worked through the information. Lizzie, on
the other hand, was a statue—silent, unmoving and
listening. I could see the focus in her eyes. She was taking
every ounce of info in. Anything to save her sister.

People never cease to amaze me. Moments ago Lizzie
was a quiet girl with a calm demeanor, talking to ghosts.
Now I could see the ice water running through her veins
and deep-set resolution in her eyes. That little girl was going
to save her sister's ghost, Neravene and danger be damned.

It bowled me over. If the kid was ready to handle
anything for the sake of her sister, then maybe she did
deserve to come along. But, even with that fire in both of
them, they needed to know how bad it could get.

"It's a heckuva lot worse than that though."

"How could it be worse?" Ortiz's color had paled from
the long exposure to the cold.

"Because, I have no idea what we'll face on the other
side. We're going in blind." I let the truth hang in the air. It
had a sobering effect on us all.

In any world, supernatural or not, knowledge is power.
Fact. I knew it. Ortiz knew it too. And I didn't know what
we were in for. That was something to chill the blood.
Walking blind into anything was a recipe for disaster.
Walking into the Neravene blind was a death sentence.

"Ortiz." I paused, turning to address Lizzie as well.
"Lizzie." I cleared my throat. "I need you to promise me
something." Before they could agree, question or disagree, I
laid out my terms. "If you wanna tag along, you play by my
rules. I make it a habit not to cross into this place unless I
absolutely have to. That says something right there. You

want me to get your sister away from those freaks, then we do it my way. I want us *all* coming out of there in one piece. End." My voice made stone seem soft.

Ortiz and Lizzie stood in silence, letting my words register. They nodded in agreement a second later.

Good. So long as we were on the same page we had a decent shot.

"So… where is this place? How are we getting there?"

I smiled at Ortiz and gestured around the room. "They're taking us there."

"Oh." Lizzie bobbed her head in understanding.

Nothing happened for a short time. Then the asylum's ghosts opened a Way.

# Chapter Fourteen

No two creatures or people, however much alike, will ever open Ways similar to one another. An opening to the Ways is as singular and unique as the one, or ones, creating it. Nothing made that more evident than the Way before me. It was a dead ringer for the one Lyshae had made earlier, except for in every possible way. There was no perfect ribbon of glimmering silver.

Lyshae was grace given form. Her Way reflected that and the ghosts' Way reflected them. It wasn't an opening. It was a tear. My mind conjured images of sharks chomping into surfboards. An eight-foot jagged bite suspended in mid-air. It was a broken and violent-looking thing, which spoke volumes about the ghosts that made it. Part of me twinged to think what they must've been going through. The other part of me was glad my bladder was empty.

Ortiz was transfixed by the sight, eyes locked but quivering in their sockets. She gazed upon the mirrored finish of the Way with a mixture of awe and horror. Gazing back at her, at all of us in fact, was something out of a fun house. Distorted images of the three of us stared back in reflection.

"Charles...wha...what the hell is that?" Ortiz took a cautious step back.

"That...is a Way to the Neravene. Their Way to be exact." I rolled a hand at the invisible ghosts surrounding us.

"And...we have to go through that?"

"You could always stay here." I worked to keep my tone neutral.

She whipped to face me with a heated glare.

I fought the urge to smile. She wasn't staying back because of a moment of confusion and terror. People always freak at the unknown. It's part of what makes us...us. That being said, another part of being a person is seeing, acknowledging and dealing with the unknown. No one I knew could do that better than Camilla Ortiz. She could look danger in the eye, tremble, and then shove her foot up its ass.

Movement caught my eye and I surged forward, grabbing Lizzie by the shoulders. "Whoa there. We go together." It was a brave thing to do, marching off into the Way, but brave often goes hand in hand with stupid. Not that I was going to tell Lizzie that. If anyone was to step through first, it was going to be me. That wasn't chivalry talking; it was common sense. I had the most experience.

Grip slipping from her shoulders, my hand made its way down to hers, enfolding it. I gave Lizzie's hand a reassuring squeeze and craned my neck toward Ortiz. I flashed her a grin. "You comin'? We could use your fists of fury."

She gave me a wolfish smile. Ortiz took my hand and the three of us stepped through.

* * *

This part of the Neravene was a perfect mirror of Lizzie's room—if that mirror was broken. What was once pristine, inviting and white, was now the opposite. Everything—from the walls, floors, sheeting and even the frickin' air—was warped. All of it seemed to be covered in a dense lacquer of melancholy blues and blacks. The floorboards had aged to the point of rot, broken and crumbling like sodden cardboard.

The only things to retain any color that wasn't a chilling blue were the three of us. We looked out of place. Perfect prey for whatever nasties lingered nearby.

Pressure enveloped my hands. I looked at Lizzie and Ortiz. Their faces were masks of carved ice. I let them squeeze their anxiety away. It's not the worse pain I've dealt with. There's nothing wrong with letting someone crush your hand if it brings them a little comfort. Sometimes people just want to have something, or someone, to hold onto while their mind goes on a leave of absence.

"This…this is the Neravene?" Ortiz's breathing picked up.

"A reflection of the asylum." I gestured to the familiar walls.

Ortiz gave me a look that said it sure as hell didn't look anything like the asylum.

"A twisted version," I amended. "A small part of it. Remember what I said about ghosts getting their own niche here? This little nook belongs to the asylum's ghosts."

Ortiz and Lizzie swallowed.

"Every one of them calls this place home. It's going to be as dark, broken, disoriented and violent as they are. This part of the Neravene is going to resemble their minds as a collective. Think about that."

Their grips tightened on mine.

I peeped at my forearm. The number twenty-eight was gone. Twenty-seven hours left. I frowned. My timeline didn't update in the Neravene. It must have changed back on the other side. I noticed it too late. With no accurate way of telling time here, I couldn't gauge my deadline. Every second in the Neravene could translate to minutes or hours back in the real world.

Ortiz caught my stare and followed it. "We've still got some time."

I shook my head and told her about the policy the Neravene kept regarding timepieces. Even my oh-so-fashionable tattoo wasn't exempt. She scowled.

"We have to move, and fast. Lizzie, can you wrangle up the Casper posse and see if they can get a bead on your sister?"

Ortiz leaned in and kept her voice to a whisper. "Why can't we see the ghosts still?"

It was a good question. We were on their turf now. They didn't have to hide unless they wanted to. "Same reason as before. They don't want us to see them."

She didn't respond to that. Who could blame her?

"Lizzie, got anything on the ghost radar?"

"She's somewhere in the building." Her voice was tinged with hope.

I kept my grim thoughts to myself. I wasn't going to rain on Lizzie's parade. The asylum was a big place. There was bound to be trouble lurking somewhere. Not to mention there were still the shadows to contend with.

Lizzie smiled. "But I think I know where to go."

"Good enough for me. Point the way." I slipped out of Lizzie's and Ortiz's grasps as I moved to take the lead. Motioning for Lizzie to fall into step behind me, I gave a nod to Ortiz. She understood. Ortiz moved back and put Lizzie between the two of us. It would be the safest place for her.

Peering through the doorway on both sides, I led them from the room once I was satisfied nothing creepy was about. Well, nothing creepy asides from the group of hidden ghosts that were trailing us. At least the ghosts' icebox treatment had subsided.

Something else took the place of that worry. There was no sound apart from our voices. Every footstep happened in silence. My fist lashed out toward a section of the wall. It fell apart like it was comprised of LEGO bricks. Ortiz and I traded glances. I shrugged. It was a blessing of sorts. If we could move in silence, all the better. It did mean that whatever else was in here would also be muted. I didn't share that thought with the other two. There was no need to put them further on edge.

Flicker. Something darted past. It was hard to tell given the dark blue tinge that hung around us. But I know what I saw.

"Charles," Ortiz hissed.

"I know. I saw it." The shadows had come out to play.

We kept walking. I refused to slow our pace. If the shadowed assholes wanted to jump us, they'd have to follow behind. We weren't going to chase after them. Lizzie's sister was first priority. Stopping the monsters was secondary.

A dark blur blasted past us. Ortiz and I tried to follow its path. A muffled cry filled the otherwise crypt-like halls. Lizzie screamed in anguish and moved toward something. My gut somersaulted when I saw what.

I outpaced her, sinking to the ground and wrapping my arms around her. "No!"

One of the shadows had swum below, crossing the floor and coming to stop behind us. I connected the bodiless cry and Lizzie's scream of protest. One of our unseen guides had been taken out. Lizzie's reaction made sense. She didn't have anyone physical to hold onto. These ghosts were her caretakers. Heck, for a young girl like her, they were probably her friends.

And one of them had died.

I didn't know what happened to ghosts when they "died." All I knew was that they could. They were fragmented memories clinging to life, trying to grasp a second chance. They never could though. They weren't the real deal. They weren't souls. But for many, they were close enough. Lizzie certainly thought of them as more.

She thrashed and screamed in my grip. I held her tight. Ortiz shouted something but I tuned her out.

"Get it!" Lizzie kicked and flailed.

What I saw next caused my entire body to fail me. The shadow launched itself from the floor, taking on its full form and height.

And bolted.

It didn't get very far. It came to an abrupt halt several yards from us. The shadow man impacted an invisible wall. Then it was thrown to the marbled floor with a jarring impact. Tiles shattered in mute protest at the creature's sudden weight.

Lizzie's frantic motions didn't cease. It was a struggle holding her back without crushing the girl. "Get it!" Her feet pedaled in the air as she howled.

Shadowed limbs stretched like strands of glue when pulled too far. They thinned as they elongated. The shadow being's mouth widened to an unnatural size, a cavernous maw as the ghosts tore it apart. The center of its mass sported incisions that looked like a rake had been dragged over its torso. More strands were peeled from its body. The black threads flew into the air and faded to blackened dust.

"Get it." Lizzie's voice weakened in concert with her flailing.

The remains of the shadow man were dispatched within moments.

All was silent once again. Nobody moved.

"Jesus Christ." Ortiz's eyes were wide. Her breathing intensified.

Lizzie's body stilled, becoming a limp weight in my arms.

"You good?" I kept my voice confined to a gentle

whisper.

"Isaac." She looked to a spot only she could see and sniffled.

Her reaction let me know that she and Isaac had been close.

"He was my friend." Her voice was barely audible. She stretched a hand out as if to touch the spot where Isaac had fallen.

My chin came to rest atop her head and I pulled her tighter. "I'm sorry, kid. I'm sorry, Lizzie." It was the best I could do to comfort her. I didn't know what else to say or do. Loss is never an easy thing. Adults have a hard enough time dealing with it. She was a child.

Pain is a miasma. It spreads and corrupts your thoughts and, eventually, your heart. I knew what Isaac's death was doing to Lizzie...besides wracking her with heartache. She was wondering about her sister. If that shadow had destroyed Isaac's ghost, what's to say one of them hadn't done that to her sister? I made it a point of stamping those thoughts out of her mind.

"She's fine, Lizzie." I gave her a quick squeeze. "Your sister's fine and we're going to get her back." I turned her around in my hold, looking her dead in the eyes.

She nodded but didn't seem convinced.

All my fingers save for one, curled into a fist. I extended my pinky toward her. "Pinky promise. I'll get her back." I smiled. She hooked her pinky around mine and gave me a weak smile back. Good enough for me. I rose from my crouch, hauling Lizzie with me.

"Charles, what just happened?"

From Ortiz's perspective, what happened couldn't have made much sense.

"One of those sha—"

"Monsters," Lizzie interjected. Her tone left no room for argument as to what to call the shadow beings.

"Monsters," I corrected. "One of those monsters attacked a ghost in our company. Isaac. He was Lizzie's friend. After that...." I shrugged and trailed off. "His fellow ghosts didn't take it too well. They nixed the freak that did it."

Ortiz moved beside me. "They *listened* to her." She eyed

Lizzie uncertainly.

My gaze drifted down to young Lizzie. She hadn't heard what Ortiz said. She was back to being her withdrawn self. A hint of wariness hung in her eyes though.

"I suppose they did." I gave Ortiz a level look.

I played the events back through my mind. They *had* listened to her. The ghosts had made no move against the shadow creature during the attack on Isaac. It was only when Lizzie screamed at them that they acted. The ghosts *listened* to Lizzie. I felt like I had taken another ice bath. I'd never heard of anyone being able to influence ghosts. I looked down at Lizzie again. Now I was the one with the wary look.

*The hell is this little girl?*

Whatever the answer was, it had to wait. More darkened shapes darted into view.

"Move!" I barked.

I grabbed Lizzie's hand and broke into a sprint. Ortiz lagged a few paces behind. We crossed the hall when another wail rang out. Another ghost had fallen, though I was certain it wasn't a one-sided fight. I saw what the ghosts could do in retaliation. I'm sure they were evening the odds.

I shot a look over my shoulder. "Give 'em hell," I murmured. I looked at Ortiz and Lizzie. "Keep going!"

We moved through another hall. There wasn't a single dark mass in sight. I slowed my pace, motioning for Lizzie and Ortiz to stay where they were as I moved ahead. I lost all coherent thought when I peered into the next room. It was a strange version of the recreation room. My hands went numb as I stared at the scene. I managed to coax my right hand into beckoning Ortiz and Lizzie.

They stood at either side of me, gazing into the room with the same puzzled mask I wore. The rec room was empty, sort of. Katherine the nurse, Doctor Cartwright, and several patients I had seen earlier in the day were there. As we watched, the light-skinned member of the muscle-head brothers passed through the room. The problem was that they sure as hell weren't in the Neravene. So what the hell were we seeing?

Grayscale.

That was the only way to describe them. Someone, or

something, had removed all traces of color from their bodies and clothing. Every inch of them was comprised of morning fog in the shape of people. They were distorted, yet behaved exactly like they did on the other side—the normal side. Doctor Cartwright scrawled furiously on a clipboard. A pair of nurses walked by, chatting to one another, their voices unheard by us. An elderly man sat and rocked in a chair before the television. Katherine Robinson looked like she was speaking to thin air. She reached out to pat a spot only she could see.

"Uh," Ortiz blinked several times. "What's going on?"

"It's how they see it," Lizzie said. "It's how the ghosts see us back home."

Everything shifted when she said that. People morphed into something else entirely. Doctor Cartwright went from fog to a man of stone. He ceased all movement. His skin grayed, becoming gravel. He looked like a cold and uninviting person. Uncaring, distanced, stony and hard. That's how the ghosts saw him.

Another nurse walked by. Her features twisted into golden light, radiating warmth. She looked like bottled sunlight.

The old man at the television changed too. His skin took on a plastic-like sheen. Water roiled inside the confines of the surface. He was a bag holding too much water. His outsides strained to keep themselves together as pressure built and he weakened. He was frail and falling apart.

Katherine turned to polished glass, gleaming in perfection. Until I looked closer. Millions of deep but minute cracks webbed through her body. One forceful tap and she'd shatter. She mouthed a single word in silence. A name. Gus. I filed it away for reference.

"Let's keep moving." I nudged Ortiz and Lizzie. They agreed silently.

We passed through the rec room. Our eyes were wide and alert. The second we made it out, the three of us breathed a sigh of relief. Even Lizzie had been overwhelmed. That was some creepy crap. And I know creepy.

I led the way in silence. It had nothing to do with the fear of attracting more shadows. My mind was growing numb from what I was seeing here. I had warned Ortiz and Lizzie about the dangers of the Neravene, but I was struggling myself. I slowed my breathing and clenched my fist several times. It helped to steady my heart. Everything I thought I knew was being rewritten.

Ghosts acting in new ways, listening to a little girl and tearing apart shadowy monsters. They had insight into the inner workings of staff member's minds. I had a lot to learn if I wanted to make it out of this case alive. And I didn't have long to learn it.

"What's with this place?" Ortiz muttered under her breath.

"Like Lizzie said, it's what *they* see." I pointed to a space of air where I imagined a ghost could be occupying. "This bit of the Neravene is their take on the asylum. It's the last home they knew and they're clinging to it. The older and more warped they become, the more the asylum follows suit. Like I said earlier, most ghosts get their own piece to call home. With so many dying here it's like they've co-opted the place and formed one big chunk. Every person who's ever died here shares their experience with the others. It all gets twisted along with them. Countless ghosts—their views shaping this place."

"They have that much effect on something like…" she trailed off as she eyed the walls around us.

"Yeah"—I followed her gaze—"they do. And they can affect more than that. They can affect our side."

"Like the cold." She nodded in understanding.

"A side effect of when they come through to our side. That's how they feel—cold. It's hard for them to see things as they are and not how they remember them. People move on with life. They can't. The ghosts feel cold, alone, and it spreads to their surroundings." Just talking about it made me want to shiver. "It's the one bit they can affect. It's a part of them in a way. They're spreading their feelings—" I cut myself off as something horrible occurred to me.

"What's wrong?" Ortiz's remarkable intuition went to work.

"This place isn't just a mirror for what the ghosts see. It reflects their feelings. This part of the Neravene reacts to the feelings of those who inhabit it. That's what we saw—back

there with Doctor Cartwright and the others. It isn't just
about how the ghosts see them; it's about how they feel
about them too. Any presences in the place can affect it,
somehow, for good or ill. Though, looking around, I'm
gonna go with more ill than good."

"Charles, aren't we occupying this space too?"

Cold electricity went down my spine. I huffed in
agitation. "Oh, fuck." Ortiz gave me a reproachful look, her
head tilting toward Lizzie. "Sorry kid. Best you plug your
ears. There's bound to be more cussing from me."

"Hmm?" Her attention seemed focused on her own
thoughts.

"Uh, exactly." I shook my head. If she didn't hear me
swear I guess it was okay. I turned to Ortiz. "Yeah, we've
got to be on guard with what we're feeling. I don't know
how our feelings could affect this place. They could change
things on a tangible level."

Ortiz eyed me and raised an eyebrow. She mouthed the
word, *tangible.* "Big word."

I scowled. "Keep your feelings in check." I turned to
Lizzie and softened my voice. "Hey, kid, watch what you're
thinking and feeling, okay? This place can do horrible things
with them. I think. Anyways, rein it in. Don't think fearful
thoughts."

"Pink elephant much?" Ortiz's tone could've dried
paint.

Right, I effectively put the notion in their heads. Now it
would be harder to avoid it. "Fine," I growled. "Ortiz, think
about pink fluffy teddy bears. You seem like the kind of gal
to like those." My quip earned me a heated stare. I turned
away. "Lizzie, just…be you."

She seemed like she was still in cloud city. "Okay." She
turned to watch the empty halls.

Got to love kids. So simple. Tell 'em to do something,
and they'll do it…some of the time at least.

I motioned for Ortiz and Lizzie to follow me as we set
off. The hardest part wasn't moving through the place
without attracting attention. It was keeping myself in check.
I was out of my depth, surrounded by hostile paranormal
creatures and probably running low on my deadline. Not a
great series of circumstances for one's mental state. The last

thing I needed was some of my fears manifesting. Doing this job for as long as I have leaves a person with a handful of nightmares.

Another vision of black darted in and out of sight. An anguished howl echoed and everything fell silent again. That wasn't frightening at all. My muscles changed their consistency to water.

"Breathe, man," I muttered. I reminded myself of my obligation to bring Ortiz and Lizzie out of the Neravene whole and sane. I couldn't do that if I was the first one to freak out. I tried to move my mind away from the shadows to something less spooky—like the posse of ghosts around us. "Lizzie, we still got a non-corporeal escort service?"

"Huh?"

"Uh, is there still a gang of really mean and tough ghosts ready to kick butt following us?"

"Oh, yes." She bobbed her head and grinned before retreating to wherever she went in her head, humming all the while.

Good, good. So long as we had our invisible group of potentially dangerous ghosts around us, all was well....

Somebody panted. I turned to Ortiz and lost the words I was going to say. Beads of sweat matted her face.

"Ortiz, you okay?"

She tugged at her collar as if it was too tight. Ortiz swallowed several times and one of her hands drifted to her stomach.

"Fine." Her voice rasped like dry, crumbled leather.

Droplets cascaded down her face. She looked like she'd run a marathon through the Sahara—without a coating of sunscreen. She was suffering from what looked like heat exhaustion. Not the thing I'd expect here. Hypothermia maybe, if the ghosts kept up the chill treatment. Heat exhaustion—no.

I grabbed Ortiz's biceps as her balance wavered. They felt like stones left in the desert heat. "Ortiz, hey!" I shouted point blank, but she didn't seem to hear me.

"So hot," she murmured. A sleepy look filled her eyes. More of her weight fell on me; she was losing the ability to support herself.

"Hey, don't faint." I brought her down gently to rest on

the floor. I fanned her with my hands. A part of me knew it wouldn't do much good. That wasn't the point though. If you can ever do something to help, no matter how trivial, you do it. The top of my hand brushed against her soft, sweat-stained face. I might as well have held it over an oven. The heat radiating from her wasn't natural. It felt like she was going to combust from the inside out.

"Lizzie!" I screamed, snapping her out of her reverie.

She was beside us in an instant. Her features shifted, adopting the same worry on my face. "She's hot."

"I know." My voice was weak. Slipping out of my shirt, I stretched it between my hands. I resisted the urge to wipe away the sweat drenching her body. I needed the sweat to help her. Moisture conducts heat away faster than air itself. It's why we sweat in the first place. The shirt whipped as I fanned her body.

"Lizzie, isn't there anything your ghost pals can do? Please!" I begged as my arms pumped. Molten rock coursed through my muscles from the effort. I willed away the fatigue and kept going. "Lizzie, tell them to make it cold. I don't care. Ortiz can scream at me later for it. Do it."

My theory was that the ghosts would be able to influence the Neravene much more than they could our world. It made sense. They were more connected to it than they were the other side. Just like any other paranormal creature, this was their domain and they held power here. If they could make it frigid in the real world, they could make it damn near arctic here.

I was right. Cold fog rolled in from nowhere, obscuring my sight. I didn't care if there were any shadows waiting to sneak up on me. If they tried it, they could freeze their asses off with me. A blanket of gray-white hung around us. The floor iced over and Ortiz began to cool.

I sighed in relief.

I rocked Ortiz with the same care I'd handle a baby. "You okay?"

Her eyes fluttered as they refocused themselves. She groaned. "Where are we?"

Ooooh boy, how do you answer that one? "*Hey, we're in a part of the Neravene, which belongs to pissed off ghosts. We walked, we talked, and you burned up and fainted. It's all good now.*" Is that what you say?

I settled for the important part. "You fainted." I bit my tongue to keep from adding, "Again." It was hard concealing my identity from her. Mentioning that she had fainted in my presence before would be a slip up I couldn't afford. So I kept the focus on her. "What happened?"

She shook her head, cradling it with one hand. "Fire."

# Chapter Fifteen

"Fire?" There wasn't any fire from where I was kneeling. Quite the opposite. I glanced at the thick, icy fog that filled the hall. Something wasn't right. Ortiz's body had cooled, but not enough. She was somewhat coherent, but part of her was still lost somewhere. "Hey, what's going on?"

Ignoring me, she craned her head to one of the open doors nearby. She was transfixed on something within the room. I followed her gaze but saw nothing. "Ortiz, what are you looking at?"

She muttered something in a voice too low for me to catch it all. I was able to make out a single word. "No." The word rang with tones of denial.

With a burst of unexpected strength, she tore herself from my grasp. Her feet kicked against the floor as she moved away. Her body broke out into sweat again, despite the chilling fog. "We killed it."

"Killed what? Ortiz, you're not making a lick of sense!" I slid my hand over hers, squeezing it as hard as I could without causing pain. Whatever she was going through, she wouldn't be alone. "Tell me what you see!"

I got my answer. I wished I hadn't. Heat pricked at me, something akin to a sauna. It escalated from there—fast. One second I was hot; the next, the room before us burst into flames. I had no idea where it came from. A place like this should not spontaneously combust.

They also shouldn't be harboring eldritch creatures of fire. There may have been an inferno before us, but icicles pierced my gut. A figure I wasn't aware of before made its presence horrifyingly clear. A petite woman with fiery locks of orange, red and yellow hues. Her eyes were pools of flames ridged with obsidian. Something cracked and I noticed a whip-like tail swaying. It was made of frickin' fire.

So was the rest of the creature.

An elemental. They were fire given form, with a demeanor to match. Ortiz and I had faced one six months ago. It wasn't pretty. Our encounter resulted in the partial incineration of a five-star hotel. I say partial because technically some of a building was left standing. It took a lot of bullets and a Ford Bronco—long story—to finally take the creature down. Now one of them was standing yards away from us, whipping up a firestorm.

My luck blows more than a porn star making balloon animals.

Something tingled in my head, but I pushed it aside. I didn't have time for it. If I didn't figure out what the hell was going on, Ortiz and I were going to be charbroiled. I kept my hand over hers while we both freaked out. I chanced a look at Lizzie who somehow remained utterly composed. Her attention was down the hall, not on us or the fire. The tingle came back, refusing to be ignored.

*Holy shit!* I realized what was happening. The Neravene was playing on her fears—our fears. Elementals are creatures of fire; they wouldn't be found in a place like this unless they were compelled to. Not to mention the fact that this was not their domain. You don't barge into other creatures' home in the Neravene. There's so much subtle magic and more going on. It's like fighting the home team on their turf, their advantage. Plus, there was the bit where an elemental *couldn't* have wormed its way into where we were.

Not unnoticed at least. But there it was. I found myself wearing a grim smirk. The Neravene manifested Ortiz's fear of the elemental. Truth be told, I didn't think she could feel fear. Surprise—sure. Anger, definitely anger, of that I was aware. Fear though? On my last case with her, I couldn't recall a moment where she was truly paralyzed by fear. She soldiered through all of it—grit, gore and more.

But nightmares never strike in the moment. They linger and get you down the line. A pang ran through me as I remembered it all. It was my fault before, and it was again. She had told me I couldn't keep her away from this. That wasn't true. I could've if I really wanted to. I could've ditched her, lied—anything. A part of me—and I was ashamed to admit it—had wanted to bring her along. I trusted her and, hell, could rely on her. Because of that, she was going to die. We both were.

"Fuck. That!" I snarled. I'm not good with the whole lay down and die shtick. This wasn't real. It was a byproduct of Ortiz's fear and a bit of my own. So long as we gave it power, it had power. That's how fear works. You feed it—it grows. The way to beat it: starve it. All I had to do was convince Ortiz that the monster wasn't real, and it would cease to be.

Easier said than done.

My hand exerted the sort of pressure reserved for macho male dominance handshakes. It wasn't enough to crush her hand, and she was no pushover. She could take it. I was trying to make it hurt. Pain is a great way for your mind to change its focus. One second you're worried about the fiery woman who could burn you to cinders. Next you're wondering why some asshole is trying to crush your hand?

It worked.

Ortiz's horrified look faded as her eyes shot down to her hand, then to me. With a growl, she withdrew it and shoved me. "What the hell are you doing?"

"Holding hands." I gave her a goofy grin. "That's what couples do."

"Keep smiling. It'll make it easier for me to knock your teeth out."

I shrugged. "It got you to stop thinking about *that* for a second." I pointed to the elemental.

Her eyes ballooned and she scampered back a step. "Shit! I thought it was a bad dream." She put a hand to her head, wiping away some sweat.

"It is." I waggled a hand in a so-so gesture. "I told you about this place. It draws on your thoughts, feelings…fears."

Her face went through a myriad of expressions, finally settling on one indicating deep thought. "I was thinking about the elemental." She put it all together. "I have bad memories of it, so…."

"Yeah, which is also why it's not moving." I pointed to the creature. It stood there in the definition of stillness, minus the swaying tail. Flames licked their way up the walls of the room but no further. Not a single wisp of fire left the confines of the bedroom. It was waiting on Ortiz. If she gave into her fear any further, it'd take action. Or, she could dissolve it right there.

"It's in your head Ortiz." I gave her shoulder a reassuring squeeze.

"Easy for you to say," she growled. "That thing nearly killed me."

It almost did. I was there. I couldn't tell her that though. "Yeah, but it didn't, did it? You're still here, and the only reason it is is because you're letting it. It's got rent-free accommodations in your noggin. You beat this thing. You killed it." My voice picked up enough heat to match the inferno before us.

"I don't—"

"Hey!" I shouted. My hand slid to grab her forearm. "It's. In. Your. Head! Nowhere else. Stop being such a little girl!" Those last words elicited a reaction from her. A fist lashed out and my arm throbbed.

"Who are you calling a little girl? You're freaking out just as bad as me." Her face hardened but her eyes shone with a hint of humor.

Good. Better that than fear. I could work with that.

"Pssh, look at your clothes." I waved two fingers at them. "You pretty much wet yourself."

Another jab, another dull throb stacked atop the previous one.

"Seriously, if I break all the teeth in your mouth, will you still be such a monumental smartass?"

I put on my best Shakespearean accent. "To be…or not to be!" I even lifted my hand to the sky all-theatrical-like. Seriously, I could've won an award. It was that good.

She shook her head and muttered something that sounded like, "Bat-shit." But she smiled. "This is all in my head," she whispered to herself.

"It is," I said. "Keep it there, not here." I squeezed her arm. "I'm here."

She chewed her lips and shut her eyes.

"No pressure," I whispered. "It's not like if you fail, we get cremated."

Her eyes never opened, but I could feel her glare. That

was frightening—a supernatural ability in its own right.

My breath caught halfway down my throat, unable to find its way to my lungs. The flames dwindled. She was doing it. I resolved to keep quiet and allow Ortiz the concentration she needed to work through her demons. It wasn't easy.

Fire waned. The elemental flickered in and out of view. Seconds later, the entire scene vanished like a white car driving into early morning, mountain fog. It faded from sight and we were left there, sweating.

"You good?" I gave her a gentle shake.

Her eyes fluttered open. "Yeah, I just need a minute."

I didn't say anything. I rose from my place beside her and walked over to check on Lizzie. My body shivered as I drew near. The sudden chill prompted me to wring my shirt and slip it back on. A veil of icy moisture hung around her. She was surrounded by ghosts. I reached and tapped her on the shoulder. "Lizzie, you okay?"

No response.

Her eyes were shut, head craned to the ceiling in an odd, esoteric pose. She seemed oblivious to everything that had happened.

"Lizzie?"

"Hmm?" She sounded like she'd woken up from nap time. "Sorry, I…." She trailed off, her face riddled with confusion. "The ghosts were helping me."

"With what?"

"To not see. That's what they said."

They sheltered her? If I understood her correctly, the ghosts had spared her from being drawn into Ortiz's nightmare. I didn't know they could do that. This might have been their chunk of the Neravene, but to interact with it that much? I was at a loss for words. Then there was Lizzie herself. The second I thought I understood her connection to ghosts, all my notions were shattered. I was starting to wonder if she was even human. I decided to keep a better eye on her after this case ended, if I could.

I carefully drew back from Lizzie. Something impressed upon me to give her a bit of space. I gave both women some time to themselves, choosing to investigate the room the elemental had inhabited.

I gagged as I stepped into it. It smelled like brimstone. The previous shades of solemn blue were blackened. The entire room would've been overkill for even the most hardcore of Goths. Acute pressure enveloped my upper arm. Fingers dug into it, making sure I wouldn't move. "Ortiz, what gives?"

Her voice dropped to a dangerous low whisper. "How did you know I killed an elemental?" There was a dangerous light in her eyes.

Shit!

I hadn't been thinking when I said that. I had been so worried and spoke to reassure her. No good deed and all that. I could tell her I was with her when we pancaked the elemental. Or I could lie.

So I did. "You told me."

The light in her eyes deepened. "No, I didn't."

It nearly slipped my mind that Camilla Ortiz was a human lie detector. "It was implied," I said.

"No, it wasn't."

Come on, Ortiz; give a guy a break, jeez.

"Word travels?" I gave her a hapless shrug.

"No, it doesn't." Her grip tightened. She was done playing around. "You're lying to me." Her voice made it clear that she knew it as fact. Well, it was fact.

Ah, what the hell.

"Yes, I am."

"Why?" Her voice held notes of a plea.

"Can't tell you." I didn't mean for it to sound so rough. I was surprised my voice didn't crack. Every ounce of me wanted to tell her the truth.

"Can't? Or won't?"

"Yes." I gave her a look saying that was as much as I'd explain.

Her eyes narrowed, and her grip tightened to more than just discomforting. "Why? I'm right here beside you. *Here!*" she stressed, gesturing to the warped asylum. "I'm fighting shadow people and whatever other monsters are in this place—with you."

She was. My stomach churned. I didn't voice that guilt however. "You chose to come." I let the harsh words hang in the air.

Smoky chestnut eyebrows rose. Her eyes widened, and the vice-like grip—faltered. "Yes, I did," she whispered. "Because *I* wanted to help. *I* couldn't sit back and watch people get hurt. *I* didn't want someone like you to go in alone and possibly get hurt, or worse."

Every word she spoke was a hammer to my gut.

"Don't you trust me?" She looked away for a second and her lips folded. She looked pained.

That question hit harder than any of them. "It's not about trust. You've seen the world that I deal with. Knowledge here is power, but it's also dangerous. It's not about trust, damnit. Ortiz, I *do* trust you, a helluva lot."

"Then what?"

"Honestly? Part of it's personal. No, scratch that. A lot of it's personal. Part of it is that I don't want to get you involved, despite the fact that you are. This life is dangerous. The answers you want.... They might not be dangerous in their own right but, trust me, they can get you involved in some pretty nasty stuff." I was right though. If she knew the truth about me, the knowledge itself wouldn't hurt her, but it could draw her into the crossfire. I've made my fair share of paranormal allies and contacts over the years. I've made a good deal of enemies, too. That was the problem.

Even if Ortiz hadn't ruffled any supernatural feathers herself, I sure as hell have. That could blow back on her if she was affiliated with me. All she needed was to know my identity and she would become a target. The supernatural aren't known for playing fair. Anyone close to me could become a target.

I have the advantage of being hard to find. I'm always bouncing between bodies and location. Ortiz probably had a place of permanence. That made her easy to find, easy to get to. If there's anything the nasties of the paranormal world love, it's easy prey.

"And that's your call?" Her voice was dangerously quiet.

"Some of it is. Some of it isn't." I shrugged. "The part I can control is not telling you things you don't need to know, or shouldn't."

"And if I want to know?"

"Tough luck. Until I decide to tell you, that is."

Nails dug deeper into the flesh of my arm. "That's

bullshit! I have a right to know! I'm getting involved in this crap with you!"

"Yeah!" I shot back, my voice rising. "You did. *You* did!" I made it clear that it was her choice. "I'm glad you're here. I really am. But if it means you getting hurt, I'd rather you were on the other side of the planet right now! I mean, damnit, Ortiz, what—"

A simple yet resolved voice cut through our argument with ease. "Stop fighting," she said in an odd balance between soft and hard. Like a feather sharpened to a sword's edge.

Ortiz and I turned to Lizzie. She stood there, her face as firm as her voice. Big brown orbs sparked with heat.

"She's right. We've got a job to do." My voice was gruff. "We can talk later."

Ortiz's grip tightened for a second, making a point as she nodded. "Later." Her tone left no room for argument. We were going to talk later, no matter what.

Yippee….

Lizzie turned and moved in complete silence, leading the way as Ortiz and I hung back. We moved down the halls, wary of anything that might try to sneak up on us. None of us were in the mood for any other surprises. Too bad life doesn't hold what we want in the highest of regard.

Our progress came to a halt when we came across a surge of black. It was a cloak of shadows arcing from the ceiling to the floor. Wall-to-wall blackness obscured what lay beyond. The grim veil gave me a good idea of what was lingering on the other side.

"We're here." Lizzie's body quivered in anxiety.

"Yeah." I licked my lips. Cold emanated from the barrier of black, but not the sort we experienced with the ghosts. It wasn't something chilling to make you shudder or pale. It was something else—something worse. It was the sort of cold you feel when you go numb emotionally. It was akin to apathy—not caring. Trust me when I say that's what made it feel more unsettling.

Ortiz's hand reached out toward the veil. I lashed out and grabbed her by the wrist. "What is it with you and wanting to touch the icky black stuff? No!" I pulled her hand away from the dark, paranormal curtain.

A look of confusion flickered across her face. I could see that she was thinking something. Whatever it was, she kept it to herself. Good. So long as she didn't go touching the spooky wall of shadows.

That was for me to do.

I extended my arm, holding my hand a hair's breadth from the surface of the shadow wall.

"What are you doing?" Ortiz looked at me like I was nuts.

Guilty.

*Something stupid.* "What you seek lies beyond, heroes!" I said in my most animated of voices.

Ortiz muttered something I couldn't hear and shook her head. Lizzie stifled a laugh. Glad to know my humor is appreciated by someone.

Something thrummed from the wall, a vague sense of energy. I wasn't attuned to magic. I can't recognize the faintest trace of the stuff. I wasn't able to make much out other than I needed to be cautious around it. Spreading my fingers, I placed them against the surface and pushed. The wall gave. It wasn't much. Then it pushed itself against my fingers. It resumed its shape. The stuff was like Flubber. Black, ominous, creepy Flubber.

I was betting it wouldn't have the friendly and exuberant nature of Flubber though. Nor would it try to help me win a basketball game.

I pushed harder. The wall gave in further, giving the impression my hand would make it all the way through. It may have been exuding hostile vibes, but so far it hadn't done anything terrible. I guessed the shadow dicks were somewhere on the other side of the barrier. So was Lizzie's sister.

I hoped.

My fingers curled and tightened. I launched my fist into the black curtain. I met some resistance, but I can throw a damn good punch. My hand made it through to the other side. It hung there for a moment before I pulled it back. Examining my hand and arm, I saw nothing wrong. Guess it was safe to pass through. Although I was certain that whatever was waiting on the other side wasn't so safe. It never was.

"Didn't you just say not to touch the disturbing black stuff?" I could picture Ortiz frowning behind me.

"No, I told *you* not to touch it." I hooked a thumb to my face. "I'm an intrepid paranormal investigator. I can touch whatever I want." I waggled my fingers in a mysterious manner. Ortiz rolled her eyes as I turned back to face the wall.

Somewhere over my shoulder, I heard Lizzie mutter, "Boys."

Ortiz snickered as if she understood what that meant. I sure as hell didn't.

"Just follow me," I growled, "and stay close." I tensed my muscles and pushed against the wall. The wall resisted, but only for a moment. I was through.

# Chapter Sixteen

The blues and grays of the asylum were gone. A black veneer replaced them and dimmed all light. My eyes struggled to adapt. I could barely see a thing.

Something flickered past my vision, or I thought it did. I wasn't sure. The human mind is adept at playing tricks, running wild with your fears. Although, considering where I was, it was possible that *my* fears were being brought to life. I tightened my body in response to the shiver that wanted to break loose. If there was something, or a bunch of somethings, watching, I wasn't going to let them see me scared.

Show fear in the sight of a supernatural predator, and you're asking to be dinner.

A puckering sound drew my attention to the wall behind me. Ortiz popped through the darkened veil, bringing Lizzie along by her hand. I couldn't completely make them out, only the faint outline of their figures. They were likely squinting, as I was, trying to adjust to the dark.

"Where are we, Charles?"

"We're in the part of the asylum the shadow beings have holed up in. They're corralling the ghosts here."

"They don't belong here," Lizzie snarled.

I eyed her askance. It was odd to see the normally happy girl snarling. "No, they don't," I agreed. This place was the domain of the ghosts in the Neravene. The shadow beings were trespassing, but that's what they did. They were parasites, breaking into the domain of others. Mostly weaker-willed paranormal creatures they could feed off. Ghosts are broken things. What better prey than something broken? First rule of hunting: go for the weak, the slow, the elderly, the helpless. The ghosts may not have been completely helpless, as demonstrated earlier, but they didn't have it easy either.

It's difficult to fight something that feeds on your essence.

And here, it definitely seemed like the ghosts were at a disadvantage. The entire place was cloaked in shadows. The shadows could be hiding anywhere. These things could move through walls. Hell, for all I knew, they could have been the walls themselves. That thought caused all manner of nausea. I gave the room a suspicious look.

"Lizzie, I don't suppose there's anything your ghostly buddies can do about the dark?"

She scrunched her face and furrowed her brows. "Sort of, but you're not going to like it."

I arched an eyebrow. "What's up?"

"Some of them will have to stay back," she said.

I wasn't keen on leaving any of the ghosts behind. They were the only edge we had in this place. The asylum's ghosts knew the place well. They could fight the shadows and God knows what else. Losing one would be a pain, losing some...not great for our odds. But neither was fighting an unknown amount of shadows in an abysmally dark room.

I sighed. "Not a fan of the idea. How many ghosts would we have to leave behind?"

All I saw was a faint motion I assumed to be Lizzie's hand. It rose up and I could see vague outlines.

"Uh, Lizzie, I can't make out what you're doing."

"Oh." She seemed startled by my admission. "Two." She flashed her fingers.

Two wasn't a terrible sacrifice, especially if it meant being able to see clearly, or clearer at least. It did mean that we would have two fewer ghosts to help us take down the shadowy fiends if it came to it.

I grimaced. "How many ghosts do we have following us?"

"Eleven."

It wasn't an army, but a pack of wolves can take down much larger prey. I just had to hope the group of shadows wasn't larger than our group of ghosts. Knowing my luck, we would be facing a legion of these things.

"'Kay Lizzie, can you ask some of them to hang back and help with this darkness crap?"

"They heard you." She waved around us.

Of course they did.

The effect wasn't instantaneous, but it was close enough. Darkness seeped away. A flood of depressing blues, grays and whites wafted past us. Within seconds, the area returned to its previous grim coloring. Whatever the ghosts were doing sailed forward, illuminating the hall ahead of us. I wished it had stayed dark.

There were dozens of the freaks! They were dispersed through the hall. Some leaned against the walls; others busied themselves with other things. If the shadows had been bothered by the change of scenery, they didn't show it. Their attention was fixed on a series of unseen things. I had a good idea what those things were. The shadows' movements were languorous. It was an almost-pleasured and lazy state. I'd seen similar behavior in heroin addicts.

These things were feeding on ghosts, slowly. The way they moved suggested as much. It was a group of uncoordinated shadow people, stumbling about. Some of them were on all fours, pinning something to the ground. The shadow beings didn't have to feed fast and hard like the attack on Isaac. These monsters wanted to string the pleasure out, draining the ghosts. They not only fed off a ghost's essence but their negative emotions as well. They were like Wraiths in a way. Part of me wondered if they were related. The captive ghosts probably didn't have much strength to fight back. There was a single blessing in all of that. None of them were focused on our little trio.

"No!" Lizzie shrieked.

So much for the element of surprise.

She tore off. The kid zipped past us, screaming as she charged dozens of monsters. There's nothing quite like seeing a young girl stampeding off to face monsters.

"Ah, what the hell." I let loose an animalistic bellow of my own. Roaring, I surged forward. My long strides carried me up to and past Lizzie. Out of the corner of my vision, I saw Ortiz sprinting in tow. A wild grin appeared on my face, soon replaced by another maniacal howl that shook the shadow beings from their reverie.

Stirring from their leisured feeding, the shadow beings shambled without coordination. Something impacted me around the midriff. Breathing was difficult and I found myself staring at the ceiling. Apparently the shadow monster pinning me down had some adversity to being strung out, because he wasn't slow at all. I glared up at the perfect reflection of a shadow man and lashed out with a fist. I struck its jaw and the creature reeled. I sat up, snaking my arms around its torso. With a jerk and twist, I took the creature to the ground. From my newfound position on top, I rained hammer blows on the creature's skull.

Frantic movement caught my eye. I didn't stop my assault. Every sort of hell imaginable had broken loose. My fists slowed as I took in the scene of carnage. In one corner, a shadow was suspended, spread-eagle in mid-air. Thin strands of tissue elongated where its limbs met its trunk. Moments later, its limbs fell to the ground. Nearby, a trio of shadow beings grappled with what seemed to be thin air. They sank to the ground, wrestling with something, before their hands shifted into small rakes. Clawing like dogs retrieving a buried bone, the shadowed monsters dug into the ghost. A pained wail filled the air. It was silenced a second later.

I gasped as five tendrils of steel took hold of my throat. The creature squeezed as I batted its arm without result. I had forgotten something in coming to the Neravene. We had left at night. Though time moved differently in the Neravene, this particular spot mirrored the asylum. If it was night there, it was probably night in the warped asylum as well. My gaze slipped from the creature's arm and wandered down to its chest. A hole the size of a basketball greeted me. It wasn't empty. A fist-sized pulsing mass of black hung there, ichor dripping from it.

I reached out, trying to encircle the beating mass. I would've had better luck trying to grab grease coated with baby oil. That sucker was slippery. So I did what I'm oh-so-adept at. I punched it. The pressure around my neck vanished. The shadow being backpedaled, clutching its chest. I intertwined my fingers and sent both my fists crashing into its chin. The creature's head snapped back and it lost its balance. It collapsed. I brought my heel up and sent it plummeting down. There was a wet *squelch* as the blackened heart was crushed.

"Ortiz!" I shouted.

No reply.

"Lizzie?" My head swiveled with enough speed and force to wrench the muscles. "Lizzie?" It was a fustercluck and I couldn't see her anywhere. Shadowed figures filled my sight.

Somebody screamed and it wasn't me.

Lizzie was held up by one arm, flailing and kicking as she dangled from the creature's grip. Snarling, I ran toward them. No way I was letting that freak hurt a little girl. Ortiz beat me to it. She bounded into view as she sank and kicked out with a leg. She swept the monster off its feet and was back on hers as Lizzie fell. Ortiz caught Lizzie under the shoulders and let her down gently. Ortiz's attention shifted to the fallen monster. I almost felt sorry for it—almost.

The monster swatted at Ortiz with dagger-like claws. She batted the blow aside with a series of strikes of her own. Her foot snapped out and caught the shadow being under the chin, driving it back. I covered the distance and jumped atop the rising creature, bringing it back down. As I struggled to keep it down, I saw Lizzie take off, again.

"Sarah!" she screamed in equal part horror and relief. Lizzie darted further down the hall. There was one problem. Well, more like a dozen problems. There was still a sizable group of shadow beings left. None of that mattered to Lizzie. She scampered as fast as her legs could carry her.

*Into the maw*, I thought. But she wouldn't be alone. "Ortiz!" I barked, nodding my head toward Lizzie. She broke her attention off the creature I was pinning down, and took off behind her.

"Fuck!" I yelped as my forearm was lanced with needle-like gashes. The shadow being's fingers had lengthened, becoming slender scalpels. "You nearly wrecked my tattoo," I growled as I brought the weight of my knee atop its arm. Having trapped it, I pummeled its face. It may not have been the most effective thing, but it was satisfying. Heaving, I palmed at the fiend's head, taking it up in both hands. I bashed it against the floor. It didn't take long for it to cave.

Moans and cries of agony reverberated through the hall. Ortiz and Lizzie were surrounded by a group of shadow monsters. Lizzie's screams were audible over the sounds of ghosts being devoured. I rose from my position and hoofed it over to Ortiz and Lizzie. I wasn't needed.

I heard deafening crashes like waves breaking over boulders. The walls caved in. Shadow beings were sent hurtling into the asylum walls. Some were slammed into the ground. The remaining ghosts didn't take too kindly to Lizzie and Ortiz being surrounded. Tiles cracked, drywall crunched and, soon, we were alone.

The remains of the shadow beings faded and the three of us stood in eerie silence. My arm itched. I glanced down at it and frowned. Worry took hold of me. The time hadn't changed. Of course it hadn't in this place. That wasn't a reassuring fact. I could've had fifteen minutes left for all I knew. Not great.

A sniffle pulled me away from my anxiety-riddled thoughts. Lizzie's face was without tears, but I could see the mix of emotions in her. She moved slowly. A mixture of disbelief and caution weighed her steps down. Lizzie stopped about two feet from a broken wall where one of the shadow beings had lingered earlier. Then she threw herself forward…

…and connected with something I couldn't see.

Lizzie's face widened as she smiled, emphasizing her cheeks. Ortiz gasped and I inhaled sharply. It—she—stood there smiling down at Lizzie, who had an arm wrapped around the ghost's waist like she was completely solid. Ghosts have the ability to become tangible, but only under certain and quite specific circumstances. Anger is usually the easiest. Lashing out becomes addictive to them. It's why ghosts have the stigma for throwing and or knocking things over. It's the easiest way to garner attention. The ghost standing before us was not angry in the slightest.

She was in perfect control, and she was beautiful. Around twenty years old, the resemblance to Lizzie was all there. She was an indicator of what little Lizzie would grow up to be: an attractive young woman. Dark, thick hair hung loose to the middle of her back. Eyes much like Ortiz's, a rich syrup-like color. She was barefoot, wearing a dress of pale blue. Lizzie's sister appeared clear and vibrant, not some distorted thing.

People have this odd notion that ghosts are translucent beings of grayish white, like a pale fog. That's not true at all.

Ghosts are just like people. Different personalities manifest in different ways. The way a ghost will and can appear all depends on them. A fractured and broken ghost will show up as such. One like Lizzie's sister—the definition of calm and clarity—will appear the same. And that's massively impressive. To end up a ghost and hold the composure and mindset Lizzie's sister did, it spoke volumes about her. Sure, not all ghosts ended up violent and broken, but most do, at the very least, end up a little lost. There was none of that showing in her sister's face. Maybe a hint of worry about her situation, but that was it.

That took immense strength. I was starting to wonder if it wasn't just Lizzie who was special. Lizzie's sister looked up at us, flashing a warm smile. She didn't say it, but I picked up on the silent, "thank you." Ortiz shot a smile back and I grinned stupidly.

Lizzie gave voice to her sister's sentiments. "Thank you," she said. Her voice was a mixture of the emotions one could expect after they rescued their ghostly sister from being fed upon. It's not a common problem.

Kneeling down, I cupped one of Lizzie's hands between mine. "No problem." My grin widened. "We promised, didn't we?"

Before Lizzie could respond, her sister's form flickered, losing its clarity for a moment. One second she was in perfect color, almost solid, the next instant she was translucent. The ghost shifted her body from facing us to looking down the hall. Her mouth moved in the form of a silent hiss and her features flickered out of clarity again. The ghost's skin blanched, mimicking chalk, while her hair, nails, and sclera became pure black. Her body was visibly tense. A cat on edge.

Following her gaze, I realized why. The far end of the hall was darkening in the wake of an oncoming mob comprised entirely of shadow beings. Mob was an understatement. It was more like a metric fuck-ton, which is always more than enough to kill you. I couldn't even see a gap in the progressing horde.

At the head of the group was the hooded, robed shadow who had attacked Ortiz and me earlier. Their stampede halted. The chief shadow-douche extended his arm. Its shape liquefied as it morphed. The limb narrowed, lengthened, and curved wickedly. The oversized sickle plunged into the nearest wall. Its scythe-like arm inflated, then compressed like a pump. Tendrils of dark matter flowed into and through the wall. There was a flash of black and the asylum was plunged into absolute darkness.

"Crap," I spat.

Where the hell was Aragorn with a torch when you needed him?

*Torch...fire...son of bitch*! Spurred by the chain of helpful thoughts, I recalled as much as I could about shadow people mythology. Their history is fragmented, but seeing shadow-like people is an old phenomenon. People have recorded sightings for hundreds of years.

The most prominent and helpful of the mythologies are from the Native Americans, notably Choctaw. It was from their mythology I had learned about the shadow people's hearts being visible and vulnerable at night. According to the myths, pure forms of light hurt the monsters. It could be sunlight, firelight, or flames. Too bad we didn't have access to any of those.

The myths did touch on something else though. It's been said that someone encountering a shadow person can rely on another form of light to protect themselves. An inner light. The idea was that a person could picture themselves bathed in pure light and it would repel the shadow being. You couldn't just envision the light; you had to believe in it. It was a matter of faith.

Faith itself has been, and can be, a great form of protection against the supernatural. The problem with theories is that they need testing. I didn't think the current situation was the best of times to do so. But in the asylum's corner of the Neravene, thoughts of fire and light didn't have to remain as thoughts.

In the abject darkness of the asylum, there was no way to tell how close the shadow beings were. Given their ability to move at darting speeds, we didn't have much time.

"Ortiz, I've got an idea how to gank all these suckers in one go."

"I'm listening, but I've got a feeling I'm not going to like it." The doubt was clear in her voice.

"No, you're not going to like it at all." I told her my idea, confirming her apprehension.

"That's a terrible idea!"

"You got a better one?" I spat. "We're facing an oncoming horde of monsters that has seen Lord of the Rings way too many times. We can't see, so what have you got?"

"Keep talking. That's how guys get false teeth," she snapped back.

"Look," I began, working to keep my tone light. "I know you don't want to do this—"

"Of course I don't. It's stupid and will probably kill us!"

"That's not it and you and I both know it." My plan wasn't stupid. Okay, it wasn't completely stupid. But the real reason Ortiz was avoiding it had to do with her. I understood that. Enduring it the first time had been bad enough. The second time, when the asylum manifested her fears and memories, had been tough. Asking her to deal with it a third time was too much to ask, and I knew it. That didn't stop me from asking anyways.

"Ortiz." My hand fumbled in the dark for hers. They were warm, slender, but still strong. I slipped my fingers through hers and gave her hand a squeeze. "I know I'm asking a helluva lot." A lump formed in my gut. Guilt always weighs a ton. "But if we—*you*—don't do this…" I trailed off as I swallowed. "Well I'm not a fan of the alternative."

Her voice had dropped to a hush. "I'm scared."

Break every bone in my body. Tear off my skin. Hell, burn me alive, but don't ever ask me to endure that again. Hearing a woman like Camilla Ortiz say those words? It gnawed at me from navel to spine. I would rather have faced the horde alone than ask her to go through with it. Although that wasn't exactly plan A. Everyone gets scared. They just do. I don't care how big and badass you think you are. It's normal. But to see someone struggling with that fear, to see someone slipping—that's hard.

"I know," I whispered back. "So am I. Hell, I'm always scared in dealing with this side of things and the freaks involved. It's not a crime to be scared, Ortiz. The only shame is if you don't do something about it and you can." I squeezed tighter. "I'm here with you. So is Lizzie. You wanna know what I'm most scared of right now? I'm scared that if we don't do something, we're going to die. I don't know about you, but I'm allergic to death, dying and things that aim to kill me."

She snorted. That was a good sign. "Pansy."

"A pansy who's gonna live," I retorted. "What about you?"

"For the record, I hate you." There was no heat in her voice.

"Duly noted. Now get with the fire startin'!"

Her grip tightened on mine for a second. "Don't let go."

"I won't." I'd hold on forever if I had to.

Cold moisture trickled down my body in anticipation of the oncoming wave of shadowy freaks. For all I knew, they could've been an inch from my face.

It started in my palm. An uncomfortable sensation like biting insects spread over it. Ortiz's hand was slipping within my grasp. Heat prickled my fingers, but I held on. Ortiz fingers were strips of molten iron, gripping tightly, and seriously hot.

The burned hand teaches best. Every instinct of self-preservation was telling me to let go. Good thing I'm a slow learner. My arm was pulled down as Ortiz sank. Her hand desperately tried to slip from my grip, but I held on. The heat worked its way up my arm now. It was a taste of what Ortiz was going through. None of it served to dispel the chunk of ice that formed in my stomach for asking Ortiz to relive the nightmare.

A tendril of orange flickered to life in the dark. It wafted up like one of those sped-up reels of growing plants from nature documentaries. The single tendril burst into a crackling fire, spreading over the floor and creating a shallow pool of flames. Going from sudden darkness to the bright light of the fire wreaked havoc on my eyes. Once my eyes stopped watering and adjusted, I threw my head back and laughed. It worked.

On the other side of the flames were the group of shadow people. Their dark outlines hovered a safe distance from the light. One of them was brave—or stupid depending on how you viewed things. I settled on stupid.

The creature edged towards the fire. There was a *hiss-crackle* as a spark made contact with the shadow creature. No screams. Only silence as its body became engulfed in flames. It writhed until there was nothing but smoke and ash.

I laughed harder, maniacally so. My voice sunk to a deep bellow and I roared. "You shall not pass!"

The hooded shadow being stepped toward the fire. Its sickle-like arm nearly touched the flames. With a quick motion it blew away a section of the fire, allowing the group to pass through as long as they formed a narrow rank.

Figures. The Balrog did get one up on Gandalf, sort of. So I pulled something else out of the Tolkien handbook.

Scooping up Ortiz, I tensed the muscles in my legs, praying they'd be able to handle the run. "Fly you fools!" I shouted. "Lizzie, run!" I added in case the reference went over the girl's head. Ortiz's body was riddled with sweat, most of it conveniently drying itself on my clothing. She was burning up and if I didn't haul my spirity keister faster, we both would be.

It's not smart to turn your head back when you're running forward. I did it anyway. The shadow people stepped through the slender gap in the flames, huddled rather close to each other. They may not have had distinct facial features, but the way they were gingerly moving made me wonder if they were afraid.

A pair of shadows experienced a bout of bad luck. They were moving back to chest when a rogue flame licked at the leg of one of the creatures. It ignited instantly, setting a nearby shadow ablaze as well. The lead shadow person didn't care. It passed through the fire while the remaining shadows hesitated. Guess they didn't want to end up briquette like their buddies. Good call.

A rapid and rhythmic sound forced me to turn back to Ortiz. Her breath was shallow and fast. I spat a curse, hoping she would pull through. I chanced a look at the little person running beside me. Lizzie was keeping pace, hardly straining at all.

Energy is wasted on the young.

Fire moves fast. It can keep up with a person and even pull out ahead. Not a wonderful thing if you're the person trying to outrun it. A stream of fire snaked its way ahead, cutting us off. Behind us, the procession of Ring Wraith costumers drew closer. At least they couldn't move with their usual freakish speed. A raging inferno sort of makes it hard to dart around. An all-too-familiar wail made my head snap toward the fire. Fear tickled the back of my throat. It tasted like bitter, stale coffee.

Strands of flames coalesced into a pillar that shot up to the ceiling before collapsing on itself. It stood about the average height of a woman, filling out to the form of one as well. The elemental was one fired up bitch. She didn't know when to stop chasing a guy. Except she wasn't chasing me. The creature stood there, unmoving.

Fear clouded my judgment. It took me a moment to remember the elemental wasn't real. Well, technically it wasn't. It may have been several yards in front of me, fully tangible and possessing the ability to roast my ass. It still wasn't a *real* elemental. More importantly, it wasn't the one Ortiz and I had faced six months ago.

Who says illusions are cheap? If this played out right, we'd have a serious win. If Ortiz gave in and allowed herself to be consumed by fear, we'd be boned. The elemental would probably come after us. Not ideal considering we already had problems to deal with.

"Hey, Ortiz, dunno if you can hear me, but hang in there." I gave her a gentle shake.

The saliva in my mouth turned to ash. I hated doing this to her. I felt hollow and stretched thin. Hot weights fell into my stomach. We needed this though. It was our only shot. And none of that made me feel a damn bit better about it.

The elemental was rooted in place, blocking our path. But it didn't show any signs of hostility. That was a blessing of sorts. The place was still on fire, but I try to take my silver linings when and where I can. Whatever happened next would depend entirely on Camilla Ortiz and her ability to work through whatever haunted her mind. Whatever monsters she was facing inside her head, I resolved to make sure she didn't go though it alone.

It's been said that positive messages get through to comatose patients. Words of strength and encouragement help. That's all I had to offer. I crossed my fingers that it'd be enough.

"Ortiz," I began, "whatever's going on inside you, remember that's all it is—inside you. I know it's not easy to deal with, but you've dealt with it in the real world. In there, inside yourself, you're the boss. Those things can't hurt you when you've already survived them on the outside," I lied. Sometimes it's what's inside you that hurts the most. It clings and lingers like a meat hook, refusing to let go. You try to pull at it, tear it away, but you end up tearing bits of yourself along with it.

No one ever said getting over fears was easy.

Between the heat, fear, and Ortiz's body pressed against mine, my body was riddled with sweat. I may have been a soul inside someone else's body, but there were still rules I had to play by. Some of them had to do with dehydration and heat stroke. Just because I could heal from wounds didn't mean I could ignore the fact I was sweating precious fluids. I'm as susceptible to harm and danger as anybody else…unfortunately.

Instinct told me to risk rushing the elemental and getting the group out of there. It was my faith in Ortiz that kept me planted to the spot. She *was* going to work through it, and I was going to be right here with her as she did.

"Ortiz, you're bigger than this, better than it. I know you. I've seen you fight things that were well out of any vanilla mortal's league. Trust me. I still have nightmares about this sort of thing. They suck. But that's all they are—nightmares. Sometimes we'll beat 'em. Sometimes we won't. Even then, it doesn't matter. In the end, even if they knock you down, even if they win, you can still keep moving. So long as it doesn't kill you—you're still in the fight. Last time I checked, you're still here."

A small hand, containing a hint of pudginess, reached up and placed itself on Ortiz's body. Lizzie joined in on the Tony Robbins seminar. "You can do it," she said in her oh-so-soft voice. It may not have been the most rousing of speeches, but sometimes the simple things are the best.

The elemental moved. My eyes abandoned Ortiz's curled body and focused on the being of fire. It took a single measured step forward. Behind us, the group of shadows inched closer. Another step. Every muscle in my body coiled with industrial spring tension. If things got dicey, I was planning on hauling it past the elemental and taking my chances.

The elemental moved forward. I gritted my teeth as its hellishly hot body approached mine. I could feel my skin redden. There was no look on its face to say it had seen or even acknowledged our presence. It stepped up to and past us.

Exhaling, I urged Lizzie to start moving. I cast a wary glance at the living hibachi. The cynic in me said to check if the elemental was going to pop us from behind. It never broke its stride. Nor did it turn to face us. Its arms spread wide as it approached the oncoming gaggle of shadow beings. Upon seeing the woman of fire, they stopped. Even their leader ceased moving.

Things were getting interesting. If the shadows didn't move, the fire would consume them. If they did, they could possibly push the elemental into a hostile reaction and end up deep fried anyhow. I couldn't help but grin.

"It'll be okay." Lizzie patted someone I couldn't see.

My grin slipped. Fire was a purifying force in the supernatural world. It could hurt a plethora and kill just as many. The shadow beings weren't the only creatures lurking in that spot of the Neravene. There were the asylum's ghosts, too. In everything I had encountered about the lore of ghosts, nothing suggested they could be harmed by fire. But this wasn't an ordinary fire. It was a unique mixture of the Neravene bringing Ortiz's fears to fruition. That was a recipe for all manner of unknown things to happen. Here, in a place where everything was out of whack and broken, I had no idea what could happen.

"Lizzie, are the ghosts okay?" I gestured with a thrust of my chin to the fire.

She didn't respond immediately. "Yes." She paused for a moment. "And no."

"The fire?" I already knew the answer.

"Yes."

*Damn.* There are many ways to harm ghosts. Salt, iron and a handful of other things can do the job. There's a particularly special way to hurt a ghost too.

Make it personal.

Find out what killed them, what they're afraid of.

Ghosts often fear the thing that killed them. That fear can be used as a weapon. The fire here could kill a ghost.

It was a bit of a stretch to assume that many of the asylum's ghosts had pyrophobia, but it was likely that there was at least one. From Lizzie's answer, I assumed one of them had met their end in this blaze.

It's odd feeling sorry about the loss of a ghost. It's a distant lack of sensation. You didn't know them. Hell, they weren't even human. That's when the realization washes over you that they *were* human at one point. They didn't ask to die, to become the lost things they ended up as. In many ways, ghosts are larger victims of the paranormal than myself. I may have been murdered and left without a clue about my original identity, but I was still myself. I was still complete.

They weren't. Not entirely so.

The elemental's keen was on the edge of human hearing. It was just audible enough to cause my eardrums to consider bleeding. The shadow figures bristled in place, wary of taking any rash actions. The elemental's body flickered in every imaginable hue of fire. Blues gave ways to whites then oranges, yellows and reds. Leaning forward, she exhaled. A cone of fire shot from her mouth.

Ortiz's body bucked, and I almost dropped her. I shuffled awkwardly to keep her in my arms. The length of fire that had blocked our path was gone. I looked over my shoulder. My view of the standoff between the elemental and shadow beings was clouded by steam and smoke.

A cool swell of air made its way across the nape of my neck. My body spasmed in response. You don't feel cool breezes in the midst of a fire. It made more sense when I realized that there wasn't a fire.

"Hmm," Lizzie pondered.

"Uh, yeah." I blinked as I tried to make sense of the scene before me. The hall behind us was no longer covered in steam, smoke or flames. There was no woman wreathed in fire. No mass of shadow beings ready to kill us. They only thing that kept me from doubting it had happened at all were the remains. Ash and a series of dark stains pooled across a small section of the floor where the shadow monsters had been.

Ortiz coughed. I looked down to see her body shake. Her eyes didn't flutter open like I expected. They opened slowly, as if something were pulling back on her eyelashes. Another cough wracked her body before she muttered in a sleepy soft tone, "Hey."

I smiled. "Hey."

"We win?"

"Something like that." My lips quirked at the edge, becoming lopsided.

"Mind letting me down now? I'm a big girl. I can stand on my own."

My inner caveman released a grunt. "Me like holding woman; no want to put her down."

Ortiz snorted and eased herself out of my arms. I helped her fall to her feet, supporting her as she wobbled a tad. She blinked several times as she surveyed the asylum. "What happened?"

"Your fear of the elemental happened. Good job by the way, setting the place on fire. It spread, nixed some of the shadow beings. Elemental appeared, ignored Lizzie and I, and nuked the shadow beings. Then poof—all gone. Dunno why. Here we are," I prattled.

"I...did that?" Her eyes grew in size as she worked through the unbelievable chain of events.

"Look at you." I let out a light laugh. "You little fire starter, you!"

Ortiz then asked the question I'd been asking myself. "Why didn't the elemental come after you two?"

My lips and nose twitched as I thought it over. I had nothing.

Young Lizzie supplied the answer, sort of. "You weren't afraid of it anymore?" It sounded more like a question than a statement.

I raised an eyebrow and stared at Ortiz, wondering if that was true.

"I wouldn't say that." She shifted uncomfortably in place. "I'm still afraid of that thing. It just wasn't important anymore."

"Huh?"

"I'm not so sure myself." She made a mild shrug. "It's like putting something aside. It's still there, just not in view.

Not repressing it," she added upon seeing my expression. "I don't think this is the sort of thing you can just get over all at once. It was my first experience with the supernatural and it was a bad one. I don't know if I'll ever get over it. I know I'll never forget it. But...I can put it in its place, which isn't at the front of my mind. There are more important things, you know?"

That was the Camilla Ortiz I knew and expected. "I know." I bowed my head in acknowledgement. What she'd done was impressive. It's never easy to conquer your fears. Instead, she buried them. They could come back to haunt her later. And she knew it. Doing that takes another kind of strength.

"But none of that explains why you and Lizzie weren't roasted by the elemental."

"Yes, it does." Once Ortiz removed the elemental from the forefront of her mind, it no longer carried any weight in her thoughts. The Neravene couldn't do much with a fear that a person willed away. So, the elemental ignored Ortiz and company, just as she learned to ignore it. That left only one thing for the eldritch creature of fire to do: take its anger out on the shadow beings' asses. I shared this with Ortiz and Lizzie, leaving out the part about asses for the younger member of our group.

"Oh," Ortiz breathed.

"Yeah."

"What now?"

"Dunno." I rolled my shoulders, working through the tightness. "Now that the Shadowvores are done, we can focus on whatever nasty is killing the patients."

"Shadowvores?" Ortiz arched a questioning eyebrow.

"What?" I held up my hands in defense. "Throughout every trace of lore they've been referred to as shadow people, shadow beings, shadow things. You think someone would've given them a proper name by now."

"Shadowvores?" she repeated.

I sniffed. "I like it."

Ortiz didn't reply.

I turned to Lizzie, and ignored Ortiz's ignoring of me. "Can you convince the resident ghosts to open us a Way back?"

"She can do it." Lizzie bobbed in place.

A hauntingly beautiful twenty-year-old came into view. With a motion of her hand, the air before us parted. A powder blue line shone. It was as finely crafted as Lyshae's opening, not mirroring the earlier ghost's Way in the slightest. Lizzie's sister may have been a ghost, but her Way made it abundantly clear—she was not broken in the slightest.

We stepped through.

# Chapter Seventeen

Needles jabbed mercilessly at my forearm. My skin felt raw. I glanced at the affected area. The news wasn't good. My timeline updated. I had lost seven whole hours.

Twenty left.

Our foray into the Neravene couldn't have been more than an hour's trip at most, but that didn't matter. I had played by its rules there and was paying for them here.

"Why are we back here?" Ortiz surveyed the room. "We didn't leave from the same point we entered."

"Doesn't matter. Ways can take you anywhere if the opener has enough skill. Apparently"—I nodded towards Lizzie's sister—"she does."

Lizzie's sister didn't say anything, but a smile appeared on her lips.

"Now we deal with other things." Ortiz's jaw clenched in determination.

I pointed to Lizzie. "Now *you* can get some rest." I glanced at Ortiz. "And you can watch over her for a bit."

"And you?" Ortiz eyed me.

Time was dwindling away. My body was torn between being stiff and Jell-O-like. I slipped my fingers over my eyes and rubbed them. A yawn escaped my throat. "I need a drink. Then I'll scrounge around, see what I can dig up."

"I'll join you in a while," said Ortiz.

"Maybe you should rest too." I stopped myself short of adding, "You could use some." I didn't think she'd appreciate that. As tough as Ortiz was, she was still human. There's only so much a person can go through. I may well have been pushing her to the brink. God knows I didn't want to.

"I'll join you in a while," she repeated, her tone settling the argument.

"Sure. I'd love the company." I tried to keep the sour

notes out of my voice. I failed.

She smiled.

I left Ortiz with Lizzie and her sister and stepped out of the room. Faint rays of golden light filtered through the halls. Groggy and starving, I stumbled past the morning nurses. My timeline was pressing, but I couldn't solve the case on an empty stomach. The last time I ignored my gastronomical urges I ended up being attacked by a tiger.

Shambling into the cafeteria, I maneuvered toward a counter with metal bins. A dazzling array of colors greeted me as I stared at the sugary grains. Grabbing a bowl, I eyed the first container of cereal. Yellow, crouton-shaped pieces amidst red and blue artificial berries. I had no desire to shred the interior of my mouth to a bloody mess.

The rest of the breakfast foods were equally unappetizing until I came to the last one. Simple grains mixed with colorful marshmallows. Deciding my luck could use a boost, I heaped the Lucky Charms into my bowl. I narrowed my eyes and cast a glance around me. I palmed a second bowl, filling it as well.

I was hungry. Sue me.

I navigated my way to a table in the far back. I didn't need or want company. What I needed was my stomach filled and time to think. My eyes were closed as the first spoonful made its way into my mouth. The cereal hadn't absorbed enough milk to become soggy. There was a satisfying crunch mixed with soft marshmallows.

"Breakfast of champions," I muttered as I chewed.

It may have tasted good, but it did little to abate my hunger. I tore into the second bowl without thought, eating mechanically. I swallowed the remaining cereal and milk. My stomach grumbled in protest at the lack of filling food.

Petite cups were lined across a container. They were filled with something gelatinous. I placed a hand over my discontented stomach. "Pudding."

My stomach's protests ceased as if hearing the word was enough to placate it.

I put my bowls away and grabbed my share of pudding. I returned with not two, but four cups. One simply cannot eat a single pudding cup and be sated. It's a law of life. I savored the first dollop of chocolaty goodness; the rest of the cup was inhaled. The cup of vanilla followed in the same way. I blended the remaining two into a half and half concoction in the empty cups. They were divine.

Brushing the plastic containers to the side, I leaned over, resting on my arms as I thought. The connections were there; I just couldn't see 'em is all. Something linked the Shadowvores to whatever was killing people in the asylum. Shadow beings are drawn to places of fear, negativity, depression and the like. While they could feed on people, it was rare and difficult. Ghosts were the easier target and allowed them to remain out of sight. After all, who'd miss a ghost?

The way the young woman had died didn't offer much. A shroud of black fog hid the creature doing its work. Then there was the way it seemed alive, snaking its way up my arm and causing me to hallucinate. I sighed and got to my feet, leaving a mess of pudding cups behind.

My mind and body ached for sleep. A fifteen-minute nap would've been blissful. I reminded myself I couldn't afford to waste even that with so little clues to go on. My mental objections became verbal grunts and grumbles as I walked down the halls. I stopped when I noticed a fountain.

I bent at the waist and brought my mouth toward the spout. I guzzled for a good while, allowing myself to become lost in the simple action.

"Thinking?"

I pushed myself from the fountain. "Yeah. How are you, Gus?"

He scratched idly at his chin. "Not good."

"What gives?"

"Someone else died," he replied in a somber tone.

"What? When? Where? How?" I blurted.

His face contorted in confusion as I overwhelmed him. "Heart attack. This morning. I heard her screaming." His voice grew hollow near the end.

My hand fell on his shoulder, giving it a squeeze. "Sorry."

His head sank and his gaze fell to our feet. "I thought you said you could help."

Such a simple sentence, but he might as well have hit me with a freight truck. It was the same damn thing from where I was standing. "I know." My voice was that of a stranger's, far off and unrecognizable. "I'm trying."

"Try harder." His face shook a bit. He wasn't visibly angry, but that didn't make it hurt any less. "Good people are dying."

"Well, then, why don't you help me out, pal?" Spittle left my mouth. My knuckles ached and my fingers dug into my palms. "It's easy to stand there and tell me to try harder. Don't you think I'm doing everything I can? If you've got a lead, then share it with me. Otherwise, fuck off!" I waved a hand down the hall.

Gus may have been trying to help, but his last words had an effect on me. I was tired and without a clue. He wasn't the only one feeling the loss. Their deaths hurt me too. How did he think I felt? I was the one who was supposed to make sure no one else died.

It was my job.

And I was failing.

Gus' mouth moved to voice his response. I didn't give him the time. I spun on my heel and took off down the hall. He was right about one thing. I could try harder and I was damn well going to.

Charles' bedroom contained his unfinished drawings. Hopefully they'd shed more light on the case. And if it came to it, there was still Lyshae. Not that I was keen on another meeting with the trickster fox spirit.

It didn't take long for me to make it back to Charles' room. I made a point of stopping by the rec room to grab a box of crayons. Upon stepping into his room, I realized grabbing an entire box was a good decision. Bleach hit my nose. The walls had been wiped clean—again. Everything else was untouched. The good news was that my journals were still hidden beneath the pillows. The bad news was that I'd have to highlight his work once again.

The paranoid cynic inside me screamed the words "cover up." The small and nearly nonexistent, logical side argued it was simple practice. Most hospitals aren't big fans of graffiti, especially the sort that could rile up sensitive patients. It was plain that a member of the cleaning staff saw the disturbing images and scrubbed 'em clean. It was applaudable—keeping the place clean. It also interfered with my case.

My forearm tingled. Another hour had passed. I couldn't believe it; I hadn't been back that long. The only explanation was that I was already a good bit into it upon my arrival. Nineteen hours left and a whole lot of doodling before me.

Wonderful.

Hot aches filled my elbows as my hands and arms blurred across the wall. Black lines quickly undid the bleach's work. There was no measured action in my movements, just desperation. The first crayon wore to a nub after a minute of my furious tempo. The second crayon served to recreate the scene from before. The third, a pastel blue, fleshed things out a bit.

Charles message was clear once again, only now it made more sense. I understood the mention of shadows, but the fear part still left me without an answer. Then there was the elsewhere reference. He could have been referring to the Neravene. It was a similar concept. "Follow fear down below." That meant…something important.

"Follow it down," I mumbled to myself. *Down where?*

Parts of it made sense. The Shadowvores operated in that manner. They may have been popping into the asylum, but they were holed up in the Neravene. The creature responsible for the deaths could have been doing the same thing. Hiding in the Neravene only to pop out to nab victims. If that was the case, things were going to be harder.

I had already made two trips into the Neravene. Somehow, a third trip didn't feel like it'd be a charm. I hoped I wouldn't need it. Ortiz and Lizzie had been in enough danger. If the creature responsible was in the Neravene, the only options I had were to consult the asylum ghosts. Or I could visit Lyshae and possibly be thrown into a bottomless pit.

I was spoiled for choices.

I shook my head clear of the slew of ideas. My musings could wait. Charles' drawings needed to be finished. Pale blue lines brought the faint carvings to life. The particular area I was working on became interesting as a shape began to develop. Narrow limbs came into being. It was the appearance of a slender being. A thin man of sorts.

Something about it tickled the back of my brain.

White spots danced before my eyes as a violent kick rocked my head. A fog of black blinded me, and something held me down in an iron grip. My feet kicked in the air, occasionally tapping a frantic beat on the floor. A coolness enveloped my leg as something writhed over it. It felt like a large snake had wrapped itself around the limb. I caught a glimpse of pallid flesh amidst the fog. The flesh was a chalky hue that blurred with my vision. My body felt the urge to sleep.

I gasped as the memory faded and my vision cleared. "Holy shit." I stood there and heaved.

My heart drummed like a bass tester. Something crawled against the back of my throat. Setting the box of crayons on the bed, I left Charles' room. There was a fountain nearby. The water helped as it rolled its way down my gullet.

I blinked as I examined my hand. I didn't remember getting a cut. A gash the length of my pinky finger ran from the base of my thumb. It was all the more bothersome when I realized the gash lengthened of its own accord. The beating in my throat picked up. Who knew my heart could jump so high? The skin of my hands—both of them—began to shed. I reeled from the fountain, rubbing my trembling hands together.

*The hell's going on?*

More skin fell from my fingers as the color of my hand resembled that of an old corpse. My arms followed suit, going so far as to lose sensation. Every step I took sent an electric jolt through my body. My legs wobbled and I stumbled, losing my balance. Everything was falling to pieces. *I* was falling to pieces. Moisture trickled from my eyes and rolled down my cheeks.

Over all the years I've worked as an investigator, this was one of my fears. I was forced to inhabit the bodies of the dead by some higher power. Whatever that power was, it restored the bodies to their pre-death state so I could occupy them. That process held firm throughout every case. All of those things meant nothing if the body failed to hold itself together.

*Like now.*

Something gnawed at the inside of my head. Gasoline

burned within my skull. Tears streamed from the pain, and
there was a fear I couldn't get a hold of. I lurched down the
hall as my borrowed body failed me. Patients gave me
puzzled looks—some were horrified. They should've been.
Seeing a body fall to bits isn't pretty.

"Charles?" The voice was concerned and mystified.

I looked up. Doctor Eric Cartwright's features twisted
into something out of a zombie flick. His skin stretched into
pale leather pulled tight over too large a surface. Strips of
flesh were missing and what bits remained were gangrenous.
His hair thinned, matted and frayed, hanging to his
shoulders. Bile built in my throat but I held it back.

My head panged as I envisioned a memory from
Charles. It was the same one from earlier: Charles taking the
doctor down. My ears pumped with blood. My skull
throbbed and my knuckles *popped*. Charles had attacked the
doctor before and no good had come of it. I had no proof
the doc was a monster. All I had was Charles' anger.

"Charles?" The doc sounded like he was underwater.
He extended a wary hand.

I slapped it away, stumbling back as I did. My hands
flew to my ears. I turned and hobbled away as fast as my
deteriorating body could take me. My vision clouded every
few seconds before snapping back to clarity. The floor
seemed uneven. Every step, no matter how measured,
caused me to fight for balance.

*Come on, Graves. This isn't real.* The pressure increased. A
familiar feeling filled my head. It wasn't real. I just had to
convince myself of that. My abilities and borrowed bodies
have never failed me. There was no chance they'd start now.

There was one notion that carried me through—
Church. He wasn't the sort to let crap like this happen to
me. The last time something had tried, he'd intervened. That
may not have seemed like much to most people, but for
Church to actively get involved in a case was major. He was
more of the quiet, on-the-sidelines type of guy. If Church
wasn't rescuing me, there wasn't nothing I needed to be
rescued from.

Something hard jarred my knees. Floor tiles. I sank to
my side. My teeth ground as I gritted through the pain. I
pinched my nose shut in an effort to still my frantic

breathing. Seconds later, I released my finger and thumb, allowing myself to take in several slow breaths.

"Hey," someone said. I couldn't identify the voice.

Hands took hold of my shoulders and stopped my shaking. Their grip was surprisingly strong and yet gentle as they helped me to my feet. I blinked away the hazy clouds and let my eyes settle. "Gus?"

The baby-faced man nodded. "Sorry."

I arched an eyebrow the best I could. "For what?"

"Earlier." He rolled his shoulders.

"Oh, that." I blinked owlishly. "Yeah," I said, my voice gruff. "Me too."

An awkward silence hung in the air. Men aren't programmed to deal with the process of making up. There's too many emotions and thinking involved for our brains. Hugging it out isn't an option.

We shrugged in unison and Gus spoke. "You okay?"

"Yeah, just tripping. I think the Lucky Charms are loaded with acid."

"Stay away from the mushroom marshmallows," he said in solemn tones, but the corners of his mouth twitched in something near a smile.

I let out a sharp bark of laughter and realized something. The pain had faded. My body wasn't falling to bits. I laughed harder. People underestimate the power of a good laugh. It's a salve for the worst of things. Laughter is pure. It can help you through a great deal.

"What are you doing?" The gruff voice seemed strained from stringing so many words together.

"Oh...you." My eyes narrowed on light-skinned gorilla orderly. "I'm having a conversation and a laugh. You know what those are, don't you?" I scowled.

His eyes narrowed to match mine. I couldn't tell if he was angry or straining his brain to understand my reply.

"Aww, what's the matter? Mongo not like big words?" I teased. "Too many syllables?"

"Calm down," Gus whispered.

I looked over my shoulder to him. "Fine."

The orderly followed my gaze to Gus, then glanced back at me. He shook his head in disgust. "Nut job." With his half-baked insult uttered, he waddled his meathead self away.

Nut job? Me? Like hell! Just because I was in a mental hospital didn't mean I was crazy. "Asswaffle," I sneered as he left.

Gus gave me a curious look. "Interesting word."

"What can I say? I'm a creative genius when it comes to the art of cussery."

"That's not a word."

"The hell it isn't," I growled.

Gus opened his mouth to speak, but a scream carried through the halls—or tried to. Something cut it off. I was already in motion. My rapid breathing strained my haggard throat. I didn't know where the scream had come from, only the general direction. I kept my eyes peeled for anything out of the ordinary as I ran.

Another scream and a series of thuds rang out. The source seemed to be a room a few doors ahead of me. I sprinted toward the door, thrusting my face up to the small viewing pane. The room was shrouded in black.

"Bingo, you son of a bitch!" I snarled as my hand slipped over the door handle. I was rewarded with a full turn instead of a click of resistance. As soon as the lock disengaged I wrenched the handle. It flung open, bouncing off the door guard. I dove into the murky fog in search of whatever it concealed.

"Bwah." I flailed as chilling tendrils of the black gunk clung to me. I was not ready for another paranormal drug trip. "No, no, no." I growled as I swept my hands in wide arcs, trying to feel my way through. My fingers brushed against something smooth, cold and moving.

"Whoa—oof!" Something struck my midsection— something strong. The air was knocked out of me. A hint of paper-white flesh stood out within the dark mist. It moved with startling speed.

Groggily, I righted myself and plunged further into the darkness. I grabbed only air. There was a clang above me. I couldn't see what exactly made the noise. The muck was taking hold. I lost track of time and visions flooded my mind. Colored spots danced in front of me as ten kinds of pain wracked my head. Sharp stabbing sensations, dull aches. Something pummeled my noggin with blunt force.

Faces swam before me, people I knew. Not me—people Charles knew. A young woman with fairer shades of hair than Charles. She was creamy-skinned and freckled. His daughter. A portrait of a woman resembling his daughter, older, smiling. A lone lily sat before the picture. Charles' wife. My heart throbbed in remembrance. It panged shortly afterwards.

He had a family. I had never thought about that. The poor guy had lost his wife, then his own life. His daughter was alone out there somewhere. Something boiled inside me. This monster had taken a father away from his daughter, and not long after she had lost her mother.

*Screw this.* I set my teeth and thrashed. I became dimly aware of something restraining my frenzied motions.

"Calm, Charles. Calm," someone urged.

I stopped my fit and my breathing slowed. The visions faded and I found myself staring at the ceiling. There was a face in the corner of my view. It had lost its zombie look but that didn't make it anymore welcoming of a mug.

I coughed. "What's up, doc?"

His mouth formed a thin line. "Charles, what are you doing here? This is not good." His head sank. He looked tired. "Tragic," he muttered.

My head lolled like a newborn as I looked around. I wanted to ask what he was talking about, but a metal square caught my attention. In the far corner of the ceiling was a barred grate, large enough to accommodate a child.

The ventilation system. That's how the bastard was moving through the asylum. It had to be small in stature to pull that off. Most ventilation systems, contrary to Hollywood, aren't large enough to fit a full-grown man.

"Charles?"

"Yeah." I swallowed a fit of coughs.

"You didn't answer me. What are you doing here?"

I groaned as he helped ease me into a cross-legged position. I told him the truth, most of it anyways. "I heard screaming and came to help."

"That was nice of you." He gave me a thin, patient smile. "But you shouldn't have done that. Andre suffered a heart attack. His problems got the worst of him, I'm afraid."

Yeah, a heart attack caused by a frickin' monster.

"Andre was a paranoid schizophrenic. Do you know what that is?"

"Yes." I tried to keep my tone from becoming scathing. It wasn't easy.

"He thought he heard voices, had delusions of monsters, ghosts, and God-knows-what other horrible things."

"What if he was right?" I eyed the doctor askance. I wish I hadn't.

Doctor Cartwright blinked. It took a few seconds for him to collect himself. "Charles, there are no monsters."

"Right." I didn't see the point in arguing.

"Good," he said more to himself than me. "Let's get you up. You should go get yourself checked over by the nurse. You were out of sorts when I found you."

"Sure." My ass twitched at the mention of the nurse. I wasn't interested in going back.

"Good." He nodded to himself.

I blinked.

His skin was losing its color. His sockets recessed and his eyes sank deeper. The irises darkened into pools of black. His skin had bleached to the purest of whites. Every trace of hair was gone. He looked every bit a monster. I knew it had to be a lingering effect from my exposure to the fog.

Something didn't add up. I had encountered the doctor earlier and left him behind. Doctor Cartwright must've been several halls behind me when I heard the scream. It was muffled for me. There was no way he could have heard it. He also arrived far too quickly. Just after the creature left through the grate in fact. It was a stretch to believe he could fit through the vents, but then I wasn't so sure about that either. I didn't see the creature go through it.

It was genius really, operating under the guise of an asylum doctor. The creature could move around without suspicion. It could visit any patient at anytime. That God-awful pressure returned. A hive of insects swarmed my mind.

I lunged. The pale creature struggled beneath me. I snarled, sending my fist arcing toward its ugly head. I connected with its jaw. It struggled beneath my weight, not putting up much of a fight. My fingers dug into the doctor's clothing as I tried to keep it from wriggling away from me. "No, you don't!" My lips peeled back.

The force of a linebacker threw me off the creature and sent me rolling across the floor. The fair-skinned, pill-popping orderly advanced toward me.

"The hell are you doing?" I shouted. "Are you blind or just that stupid?" I pointed to the creature. The giant freak of a man grabbed me in an unbreakable grip. Well, not so unbreakable. I was sure I was going to break if he kept it up. My legs kicked against his, trying to find his shin, or even his groin.

There are no cheap shots in a fight.

"Don't let him loose!" ordered the monstrous doctor.

"Fuck that!" I thrashed. "Let me go!"

The creature approached me. There was a narrow glint of silver in its hand. Something slipped into my arm, but I shook and fought it. My vision clouded. The creature took several cautious steps back, regarding me carefully. My body felt too heavy. My vision dimmed further.

Blackness followed.

# Chapter Eighteen

Something tugged me awake. Well, awake was the wrong word. Sluggish consciousness maybe. My head felt like it had been filled with wet sand—muddy. Something itched at the back of my mind. Dim lights swam before me.

Another tug, sharper this time.

I let my head flop to the side. Whatever they had injected me with was powerful. Drugs don't have the greatest of effects on me. They're not tailored for souls. That doesn't mean they can't knock me out.

"You okay?" The face attached to the voice was a blurry mess.

"I get knocked down," I sang off-key and drunkenly. "I get back up again," I slurred. "You're never gonna keep me down."

"He's fine," proclaimed another voice.

My vision cleared from the slew of pharmaceutical whatsits in my system. I was able to make out a tawny young face. Large almond colored eyes peered at me with childlike curiosity.

A roughness rubbed its way across the skin of my wrist. Lizzie tugged on a heavy-duty saddle-brown strap of leather.

"Why," I breathed, trying to speak slow and clear, "Am I strapped. To. A. Bed?"

"Because you attacked Doctor Cartwright, genius." The other voice was now discernible.

"Ortiz?" I groaned.

"Who else would come rescue you?"

I mumbled something incoherent about not needing a rescue.

Lizzie fiddled with the straps holding me in place. I developed an immense dislike of whoever put me in these situations. The easy answer was to blame Church. I awoke in a straitjacket the first time and was now tied to a bed.

Whoever orchestrated this must've had a BDSM fetish they needed to work out.

"Here, let me." Ortiz nudged the struggling Lizzie aside.

Everything snapped into clarity as my body worked its way through the suppressing effects of the drugs. I almost wished it hadn't.

I had lost two hours. Seventeen left. No pressure.

Ortiz pulled harder than Lizzie had. A sliver of metal slipped out of a hole with a *clink*, striking the belt buckle and freeing my arm. Ortiz unfastened the ones around my waist and my other arm before tackling the pair at my ankles.

It was a struggle to right myself. Luckily, I didn't have to do it alone. Lizzie and Ortiz were there, helping me up. I didn't know how to react. I'm rarely at a loss for words, but that simple action did the trick. I still wasn't used to working with people. Six months prior, Ortiz had been the first person I had worked with in a long time.

It changed a lot. Working with her through that case reminded why I did what I did, aside from the bit about having no choice in the matter. I did it to help people. To save them from the nasties out of stories. I learned I could count on people—trust them, lean on them if I needed to.

Now here was another person, Lizzie, a girl around the age of eleven, helping me. I tried to swallow, but a series of dry coughs racked my throat. I waved Lizzie away as she stepped forward to help me. I let the coughs finish their bout. Clearing my throat with as much force as I could muster, I felt the saliva work its way down.

"Thanks," I said, finally able to speak with ease.

I thought about having now dragged another person into my work. Guilt filled me. Lizzie had her whole life ahead of her. I couldn't guarantee what would happen to her. And, yet, a portion of me was relieved to have someone else watching my back.

"So, what happened?"

"What happened what, Ortiz? You already know I attacked the doc."

"Yes, but why?"

"Would you believe me if I said he was a monster? At least, I think he is." I shook my head. There was just a hint of medicinal cobwebs left.

"Are you...sure about that?" I understood her hesitance. Doctor Cartwright was the head doc in the asylum. He was responsible for helping many of the hospital's patients recover. It was likely he worked with Ortiz as well. She already had trust issues because of our last case together. Casting doubt upon the doctor helping her was probably a hard thing to accept.

"I'm sure of what I saw." I kept my tone neutral.

White teeth flashed as Ortiz's lower lip folded back. She chewed on it.

The ever-curious Lizzie leaned on the bed. "What did you see?"

"It was after I left you two back in your room." I nodded to Lizzie. "Bumped into Gus first. Had a talk—an argument really and—"

"Who's Gus?" Ortiz's eyebrows knitted together in confusion.

I described him.

Ortiz gave Lizzie a questioning look. "You know him?"

Lizzie shook her head.

"Huh?" I eyed the pair of them. It was a big place. I shouldn't have been surprised they didn't know every last patient.

"Keep going." Ortiz rolled her hand for me to continue.

"Uh, yeah, after that I went back to my room, tried to think about what could be doing the killings. I left to get a drink, and that's when I heard a scream."

"Yeah," Ortiz whispered. "We heard there was another death."

"Another heart attack." I scowled. "I saw the thing feeding on him—"

"Wait, you saw it?" Ortiz's eyes went wide and she stared.

I waggled my hand. "I saw bits of it. Whatever it is, it's chalk white. Fast, slender and has weird appendages."

"Define weird."

"I don't know, Ortiz—weird! It's a monster. Something wrapped around my leg. Sure as hell wasn't an arm!"

"A tentacle?" Lizzie leaned closer.

"Uh, yeah, maybe. Wait, how do you know?"

"What you said." Lizzie sounded as if everything were

obvious.

I raised an eyebrow.

"It sounds like a Narrowman." Her voice dropped to a conspiratorial whisper.

Ortiz and I responded simultaneously. "A what?"

"A Narrowman." Lizzie stared at us as if we should've known. "They're tall, thin, have tentacles on their arms. They can turn invisible, but kids can see them. They wear suits—"

"That freak wasn't wearing a suit. Trust me, Lizzie. I—"

"Their skin is really white," she continued as if I hadn't spoken. "They make the air smell funny and they can make you see things."

"Hold on, Lizzie. How much do you know about this thing?"

"A lot."

I shook my head. The sludge slid from side to side within my skull, trying to settle. "'Kay," I huffed, hopping off the bed. "Let's head back to my room. I have something to show you."

"Just...be discreet, okay?" Ortiz eyed me. "You attacked the head psychiatrist—again."

I had almost forgotten about that. Charles *had* attacked the doctor before. I pored over what info I could as we walked. He must've believed the doctor was some sort of monster, if not *the* monster.

But that didn't fit. If Cartwright was a monster, why didn't he kill Charles for finding out? Although, it was possible that he *did* kill Charles. I still didn't know the exact circumstances of his death.

Something was off though. The doc didn't seem surprised by "Charles'" return. Nor did the doctor attempt to kill me the many times he'd seen me. He had me alone in Charles' room at one point. *That* was a perfect opportunity.

The more I thought about it, the more it didn't seem to fit. He wouldn't have needed an orderly to subdue me if he were a monster. Hell, he could've killed me then and there, scoring a two-for-one meal ticket. None of that ruled out the doc as a monster one hundred percent. All it meant was that he might—might—not have been a monster. That...or he was exceptionally clever at concealing his identity.

But I had learned over the case that there were some things you couldn't hide from in the asylum.

"Hey, Lizzie." She turned her head to regard me. "Is there any chance you could get your ghost buddies to do me a favor?"

Almond pools quaked.

"Not your sister," I added quickly.

That didn't do much to placate her.

"Look, I know the ghosts have been through a lot. They've helped us a bunch. I'm grateful. I really am. But..." I paused, feeling sick at the hand I was about to play. "But, Ortiz and I helped them out too. Is there any chance, please, they can do something for me?"

She stared at me for what was probably seconds but definitely could've passed for hours. When she spoke, her voice sounded heavy. "I can ask." She sounded like it was the last thing she wanted to do.

My stomach twisted, nauseous from having manipulated a child like that. But it needed to be done. Lives were at stake. Maybe if I kept telling myself that I wouldn't feel so bad about it. "Thanks."

Lizzie turned her head without reply.

I led the way in silence. It took us minutes to get back to Charles' room. Fortunately, I didn't draw any attention to myself. The last thing I needed was to be restrained again and lose more time.

"Close the door." I gestured to Ortiz.

She shut it and turned to the markings I had brought to life through the power of Crayola. She smiled. "Ever think of taking art up as a profession?"

Because I'm a mature paranormal investigator who would never stoop to petty remarks—I stuck my tongue out at her.

"That's a Narrowman." Lizzie pointed to the wall.

We followed her finger to the coloring of a rather slender figure. Looking at the markings Charles had made, I recalled all that Lizzie had said. Gears slotted and clicked into place. "What do you make of that, Ortiz?" I pointed to Charles' cryptic message from earlier.

She shrugged.

I grimaced. "We're not dealing with a Narrowman."

"What?" Ortiz stared at me in uncertainty.

"How do you know?" Lizzie eyed me in the same manner as Ortiz.

"Trust me. I think I know what's behind this and, man, do I hope I'm wrong."

"Yeah?" She arched a quizzical eyebrow.

"Yeah. Just how good are you with dead bodies?"

Her eyebrow rose higher.

* * *

I eased my way into the morgue. Ortiz followed and—despite our objections—Lizzie as well.

The kid was nothing if not obstinate.

At first I thought there might have been ghosts lurking about. My breath was visible as I exhaled. My teeth weren't clacking together yet, but the air nipped at my bare arms. It wasn't the temperature that made it feel cold. Not entirely. I think it had more to do with the notion of being in a room *for* the dead.

A morgue isn't solely a place where dead bodies are carved up, analyzed and shipped off from. It's not just a room where the temperatures are chilling. It's a home, no matter how temporary, for the dead. At least until they are given a more permanent form of rest—burial, cremation, whatever. There was a little bell going off in my head reminding me that we were trespassing in a place reserved for the dead. Knowing all of that is what made the cold feel so prominent.

And yes, because the thermostat was also set to Gravescicle.

Ortiz pointed to a nearby examination table. "Who's that?"

My eyes tightened as I tried to recall his name. "Andre?" His skin had already lost its color. His features suggested that he might have been several shades darker, like a rich stained wood. Someone had done him the politeness of shutting his eyes. Hair fell down to his ears, losing none of its black polish-like luster.

Ortiz edged closer and pulled the sheet off his body. An

unremarkable, average build greeted us. It was without marks of any kind. Ortiz made a puzzled face. "Whatever killed him did it without a trace," she mumbled more to herself than the rest of us. I didn't know what prompted her to lean closer. "Well..." She chewed on her bottom lip. "Autopsy? I'm assuming that's why we're here?"

I nodded.

"If we're caught..." Ortiz eyed me askance.

"I know." I dragged my thumb across my neckline.

Ortiz gave me a look, then cast a quick glance to Lizzie before settling upon me again. I took the hint.

"Hey, Lizzie, you sure you don't want to—"

"No," she interjected. Her answer might as well have been written in stone.

Obstinate.

I didn't want to expose a kid to someone being sliced open, but then again, she had seen worse. I don't know if that made it any better, or if it made me a terrible person. The world I work in isn't kind to people, especially children. As much as I wanted to shelter her from whatever I could, at the end of the day, I wasn't her father. I had no right to tell Lizzie what she could and couldn't do.

So I slipped my hands under her arms, picked her up without asking, and carried her to the door. Her legs kicked out. One of them glanced my ribs. Kids can kick. I dropped her outside the room and shut the door behind me, locking it as I did.

Ortiz stared. I answered it with an exaggerated flourish of hands. "Proceed, Bones."

"Damnit, Jim, I'm an agent, not a doctor!" she growled. A light smile touched her lips.

I snorted.

She moved around the morgue, picking up implements and laying them atop a metal cart. "I don't know if I should do this."

"Why not?"

"Well for starters, won't it be odd if a physician walks in and finds an autopsy already done? Especially when there's no record of it being completed."

I shrugged. "So forge the record."

She rolled her eyes.

"It's not our problem. We're trying to save lives."

"And that means you can break the rules?" There was a dangerous undertone in her voice. Ortiz was a Fed. The law—rules and order—meant a lot to her. She didn't see things my way, and I didn't expect her to.

"If it means helping people, then yes." I set my jaw to let her know where I stood.

She turned her head without responding. I knew she was weighing things. I left her to it. A moment later, she picked up a scalpel and pressed it to Andre's chest. A V-like incision appeared seconds later. She made a simple linear motion, creating the full Y and stopping at his navel.

Poor Andre opened like an oyster. Having been around too many dead bodies to count, I've developed a detachment when it comes to looking at them. I've also gotten used to the smell. Something pungent, meat-like, tickled my nose. Despite it, I watched quietly, trying to take note of whatever I could. There was no trauma from what I could see, but then I wasn't the one with a medical background.

There was a chorus of noise like breaking bone and sinews tearing. I buried the sounds and focused on what was important.

"Anything?" I arched a brow and waited for her answer.

Ortiz, engrossed in her examination, ignored me.

"Anything?" I peered closer trying to figure things out for myself.

"Nothing." Her eyes never moved away from Andre's body. "What I saw looked fine." Her face furrowed. "In fact, everything looks fine, but I never finished med school so I could be missing something. I also don't have a handbook on how monsters kill." She gave me a look.

Holy shit. I wondered if Ortiz had found my journals. Was it possible she knew? When she didn't say anything further, I exhaled through my nose as silently as possible.

She put the scalpel aside and stood there like she was wrought from stone.

"The young woman before—she died of a heart attack, right?"

"According to what I found and what you said, Charles, yes." Ortiz shook her head in agreement.

"How could you tell?"

"Well, you suggested what it might be, not to mention what we saw—"

"We saw a monster." I gave her a level stare.

"Yes, but there were no other signs of trauma. When that happens, most people rule it as a sudden heart attack."

"Any other signs?" I hoped something would turn up.

Her eyes turned to the floor. She brought her thumb and forefinger to her chin as she thought. "There were some hemorrhagic areas. The heart wasn't only stressed, but looked bruised."

"Anything else?" I needed more.

"Yeah." Her eyes widened for a second and she swore.

"What?"

"There was discoloration around the heart. I passed it off as nothing, but it wasn't right."

"Wasn't right?" I blinked, lost with what she was getting at.

My eyes felt as if they had been jabbed. Something flashed through my mind. My nose felt like I had gone ten rounds with a professional boxer with my hands tied behind my back. I shut my eyes and shook off the rather powerful vision from Charles. It was what I needed though.

Ortiz pressed the scalpel to Andre's heart. The surgical blade pierced the muscle with ease. Blood didn't spurt out. That's always the first thought when it comes to hearts. This heart wasn't pumping any longer. The blood pooled out in a dribble, like an overripe fruit being punctured.

Only, dead man's blood didn't seep out, not alone at least. A purple fluid, the color and consistency of children's cough syrup, oozed out. The smell that came with it was the sort reserved for vinegar factories. It was an overwhelming sourness to the point of being sickening.

I fought the urge to retch. Ortiz's body shook for a moment. "Check his nose." I gagged, resisting the smell as best I could.

"What?" She eyed me like I was crazy. "You want me to puke?"

"I thought you were a med student." I eyed her back. "Step up."

She shot me a glare and made no move to do as I asked.

"I'm serious. Check his nose."

She breathed in exasperation but relented. Ortiz picked up an obscenely long swab and stared at me. "I hate you."

I smiled the best I could, trying not to retch as my mouth opened.

The cotton-tipped stick slid into Andre's nose. Ortiz paused before jostling it a bit. She moved it toward the outer side of his nostril, and Andre's nose deformed.

"Um, that doesn't seem normal," I said.

"It's not," she frowned.

"Aren't there supposed to be bones preventing that sort of thing?"

"They're...broken?" She blinked several times.

"Pull it out, check his ears." I wanted to be wrong, I *had* to be wrong.

"Why? Do you know what did this?"

"Just do it!"

Her eyes widened, first in surprise, then with a dangerous light flickering through them.

"Please." I held up a calming hand and gave her a weak smile.

The cotton swab slipped out of his nose. A trail of syrup followed it out.

"His ears," I croaked. I was going to be wrong. As soon as she checked his ears...I was going to be proven wrong.

She inserted another swab into his ear canal, removing it seconds later. I wasn't wrong.

God, I wasn't wrong.

Purple ichor coated the cotton tipped tool.

My face must have betrayed my thoughts because, when Ortiz saw it, her features mimicked how I felt. "Charles?" Uncertainty rang in her voice. "What did this?"

My spine was thin ice, ready to be shatter with a simple tap. "A phage," I whispered. "A Babylonian phage."

# Chapter Nineteen

"That's not a good thing, is it?"

"No," I breathed. "No, it's not."

"How bad is it?" She inhaled sharply as she waited for my answer.

I swore.

"That bad?"

I swore again.

"What are they?"

I swore again, completing the charm.

Ortiz's forehead creased. Her jaw tightened and her arms folded beneath her chest. She gave me an impatient look.

"They're... Ah hell, I don't even know where to start. They're bad, so frickin' bad. They're a type of phage."

"And phages are...?"

"You know how vampires feed on blood?"

"They're vampires? Wait, vampires are real?" Her posture loosened and her eyes grew several sizes.

I shook my hand. "In a way. Remember vampires are creatures that *feed*." I placed emphasis on feed. "They are too many types of vampires to count if you look at it that way. That's what phages are, a type of creature that feeds and lives off a certain essence. For the traditional and well-known vamps, that's blood. These things though—they feed on fear." I let the revelation sit with her.

"Which explains what it's doing here."

I nodded in agreement. "This place is a captive pen. It's an all-you-can-eat buffet."

Ortiz nodded. "Plus, who's going to believe a patient when they scream, 'Monster'?"

"Yeah."

"Tell me more." Her lips folded and pressed tight. She didn't look like she wanted to hear more.

"These things are old—biblical old. I mean, they hail from Babylon. *The* Babylon. You know the stories about the Tower of Babel? Babylon's collapse and the speaking in tongues bit?"

"Yeah?"

"It wasn't the wrath of God that did that. It was these freaks. Lore goes that they drove the populace mad. It's one of the things they can do. They foul the air around them. They don't just make it smell like a vinaigrette fest; they taint it. Breathing in the same air space as them can cause hallucinations, drive people insane and cause paranoia. In this place—amplify that. The patients here are already on edge. This thing can and will push them over. Back in Babylon, mythology suggests these monsters corrupted the water supply…" I trailed off as Charles' cryptic warning began to make sense.

"What?" Ortiz stared at me as if she knew I was onto something.

"The water, damnit," I growled. "They've tainted the water supply!"

"You're not making any sense, Charles."

"Every time I've freaked out and had a hallucination, it's been right after having a drink of water."

"That's insane. If that were the case, how come everyone else isn't having hallucinations?"

"I think they are, to some extent at least. It might not be the same for every person. It's not always about causing mass hysteria. Think about it. If this place collapsed into sudden pandemonium, what happens to your food source? Most of the patients would be hurt, killed, or the asylum would shut down. End result; no smorgasbord. The water may be corrupted, but the creature is only reaching out to a select few at a time. Easier to control, manipulate, and make it look like accidental deaths."

"They're that intelligent?" She repressed a small shiver.

"They brought about the collapse of one of the most prominent empires in history," I said.

"Dangerously intelligent," whispered Ortiz.

"Yeah," I mumbled as my thoughts drifted. Why were they affecting me so greatly? It clicked. Charles had died under their influence. That also explained why I had felt so bad waking up in his body. The vertigo, nausea and the frickin' heart attack. Residual effects of being fed upon by a nasty phage. They pumped their victims full of whatever cocktail they created during feedings.

Charles died struggling, most likely alone, frightened, trapped in a room with a nightmare. It could've been nightmares in fact. Babylonian phages were notorious for plaguing a victim's mind with every horror imaginable, right up to the moment the person died.

None of that explained how Charles had known about the water, why he attacked the doctor, or scrawled over the walls. There was no way of knowing what Charles' hallucinations had been. I recalled a bit of lore that could let me turn the tables in a way.

And it wasn't a great way.

"You've got a plan," Ortiz said. It wasn't a question. She knew me well, which was saying something considering that she didn't know the truth.

"Yes," I admitted.

"What is it?"

Seeing how I couldn't lie to Ortiz—well, not without her knowing it was a lie—I told her. "Story goes that a person hallucinating under the influence of a Babylonian phage can give themselves wholly to the taint and—"

"That's a stupid idea. I'm not surprised you came up with it!" she snapped.

I sniffed in defense. "It's not stupid, and let me finish. If I drink enough tainted water, I might be able to see the creature if I pass by it. Not only that, but I might be able to find it."

"How?"

"The taint works two ways. It makes it easier for the phage to find its prey. It's like a marker, a scent trail. It also means the victim can see the monster, among whatever other monsters their mind makes them see."

"Like I said, stupid idea." If Ortiz's tone were any more scathing, it would've stripped my skin.

I scowled. "You have better ones?"

She shook her head. "That doesn't mean you get a pass to be a dumb ass. Tell me more about this thing."

"'Kay, well." I tried to remember whatever else I could.

"These things don't just feed off fear. Phages like these feed off the person's bodily fluids, fluids flushed with hormones secreted when they're afraid. They pump a slew of toxic garbage into the victim's bloodstream as they feed. To them, nothing's better than feeding off a person who's losing their mind. They want their victim to suffer, to undergo all manner of horrors while they suck 'em dry. They've got a sweet tooth for brain juice."

"Cerebral spinal fluid," Ortiz said.

"Yeah, that stuff." I waved my hand nonchalantly. "The myths also say"—I hesitated to tell her the next bit—"that children have been known to be able to see them. These things can't look like humans, but they can make us see them that way. It's not real though. With them, it's a hallucination. They can make us see them as anyone." I didn't mention the doc because Ortiz didn't seem to want the doctor to be guilty. I couldn't blame her.

But Charles' attack of Doctor Cartwright never left my mind. It could've been the doctor *was* the monster. It could've just as easily have been that it was part of Charles' hallucinations. From the monster's point of view, it was a masterstroke. Cast doubt on the person trying to help the patients.

"You said a child can see it?" Ortiz's tone was carefully neutral.

"No!" I knew where she was going with this.

"She could help, Charles."

"She's just a kid."

"A kid who can see and talk to ghosts. Hell, she can order them around! She's a kid who just walked through a world of shadow monsters, ghosts and fire. She's not the sort of kid you're thinking of." Ortiz kept pushing. Even as she said it, I could see her lack of conviction.

"She's just a kid," I repeated, my tone weak—tired.

"I know," Ortiz relented. I knew she wouldn't push it. She wasn't that sort of person. "I just... I don't know, Charles. I can't see this place lose another person."

"It won't." I made my voice as hard as stone. "We won't let it."

Her lower lip folded back and she bit it before nodding. "No, we won't." Iron resolution filled her voice. "So, let me see if I've got this right. This creature can cause people to hallucinate, drive them mad—madder in this case. Can stalk them. Is able to commit genocide if given the chance. Can taint the air and water. It's ridiculously old and intelligent. And it seems to be gunning for you, if your hallucinations are as bad as you say they are. It must be marking you, right?"

"Seems like," I agreed.

"How does it kill?"

"They're roughly humanoid, agile, strong, and have tentacle-like appendages."

Ortiz's neck and shoulders went visibly tense. There's something about tentacles that bothers people down to the core. They're odd, move in a freaky manner, and have always been associated with frightening things of the deep.

"They use these"—I wriggled my fingers as if they were squid-like limbs—"to feed. It's how I knew about the nose and ears. They force them into any orifice that leads to the brain. Jam 'em up, scramble and feast."

"Okay, apart from that disturbing piece atop the laundry list of things they can do, anything else I should know?"

"Yeah, I have no idea how to kill it...."

Silence. As if a morgue wasn't quiet enough.

"So," Ortiz said after a minute, "we've got work to do."

I nodded.

The door shuddered. A bang echoed through the room. Lizzie's voice filtered through. "Someone's coming!"

Waving my hands, I shouted, "Cover him up or something!"

Ortiz shoved the cart to the side. It crashed into the wall with a *clang* and I flinched. Grabbing the sheet, she threw it over Andre's body, muttering under her breath as she did.

In the quiet of the morgue, the doorknob turning might as well have been a resounding *click*. The sort to make your blood freeze and your joints turn to cement. The door opened. Ortiz and I tensed.

A woman in her late twenties with the figure of a gymnast stood there. Someone must've filled her body with the same concrete that held us in place. We gawked for a moment in silence before she spoke. "What are you two doing here?"

I threw my hands up in the air and shouted, "Captain Crunch!"

I panicked. Can you blame me?

Ortiz followed my lead, albeit with less enthusiasm. "Oh captain, my captain," she said in a voice that could've been used as a sleeping aid.

The nurse's head swiveled from me to Ortiz before she shook it, letting her posture sink as she did. She sighed. "I'm too tired for this shit. Come on." She beckoned us with a wave of her hand. "Let's go."

I shot Ortiz a triumphant look. "Maybe I should've dropped my pants and shouted pudding?"

Ortiz snorted. "Yeah, that would have worked great."

I scowled. True genius is never appreciated.

We followed the nurse out of the morgue. I scanned the hall but couldn't see Lizzie anywhere. She must've bailed. Smart kid.

"So, how about I take you two to get some cereal, and you two promise to stay away from places like that?" The nurse smiled. "Deal?" She eyed me as she added, "Captain Crunch?"

"Lucky Charms," I demanded.

The nurse's eyes widened and her mouth moved soundlessly for a moment. "Uh, okay, fine, Lucky Charms."

I nodded gravely.

Three bowls of leprechaun endorsed cereal. I was either going to have one helluva lucky day or terrible indigestion.

"Charles," hissed Ortiz. "Monster?" She arched an eyebrow.

I chanced a look at my forearm. Sixteen hours left.

"We'll handle it," I hissed back.

Ortiz pursed her lips, looking like she was going to counter, but she remained silent.

I was soon greeted by the familiar sight of breakfast cereals as the nurse delivered on her promise. She was even kind enough to bring me the bowl of Lucky Charms. Who says hospitals don't have wonderful service?

Ortiz was handed a bowl of the crunchity cereal that dooms mouths. She looked at it like it was sludge.

The nurse left, giving me a weary smile and an

admonishing finger wave.

"What am I supposed to do with this?" Ortiz grumbled, placing the cereal on the table as she sat across from me.

"Eat it?" I supplied through a mouthful of marshmallow goodness.

Ortiz eyed it like it was dangerous. "I think I'll pass." She slid the bowl to the side. A small wave of milk formed and sloshed out of the bowl. "So, what now?"

I devoured my cereal as I thought. It wasn't an easy answer. We knew what the creature was and what it could do, but that was about it. We still had no idea where it was. Not to mention that I had no idea who it was, if it was under an illusion at all. Worse, I had no way to kill it. So even if we did come across it, the most likely deaths would be Ortiz's and mine.

"I don't know," I told her. "We have some bits of the larger picture, not all of it. Not a whole lot we can do with that."

Ortiz frowned. "No, there isn't. Any way you—we—can find out more?"

I paused, the spoon hovered half an inch from my face. I let it sink back into the bowl. "Possibly." I knew where I could get more information. Lyshae could've given me more answers. For a price, of course. I wasn't so sure if I wanted to pay that price, much less find out what it was.

"What about Lizzie?" Ortiz suggested. "The ghosts might be able to find out something."

"Maybe," I said uncertainly.

"But you're not sure?" she pressed.

"I'm not. It's possible, but I don't think they'll come across much, now that I think about it."

"Why not?"

"Because these things aren't interested in feeding off ghosts, nor can they. They're interested in the gooey bits up top." I rapped a fist on my skull. "I don't think there's any interaction between them and the ghosts."

"So why did the shadow monsters come here then?"

"This is a place of fear, despair, depression and more. Not all of it, of course. Some of the folk here are doing fine. But we're talking about both sides of the veil here—mortals and ghosts. When there's a fresh kill around, every predator notices, and there will always be scavengers waiting. The ghosts of the asylum were easy picking for the shadow beings. 'Nuff said."

"Not so easy." Ortiz gave me a wolfish grin.

I mirrored her grin. "No, not so easy. But the idea's the same: creatures that prey on fear will often end up in the same spots. This place is a beacon. We're not playing for just one side here. It wasn't and isn't about the ghosts or the patients. It's about both. If we don't stop the phage, this place will be housing more ghosts. If we didn't take care of the Shadowvores, those ghosts would be fed upon."

"Again with the Shadowvores?"

"They need a name," I said in defense. "I don't see you coming up with one."

She waved me off as if it wasn't important. For the record, it was. Monsters always need names, especially those with crappy ones.

"Fine, ignoring my brilliant name—"

Ortiz snorted.

"Ignoring that," I continued, "there's too much going on here to be certain of anything. Half of me would like to take some time, play it quiet and smart. I'd like to find out more."

A soft grip enveloped my hand, lifting it out and away from underneath the table. Ortiz traced a circle around my tattoo with a finger. "I don't know if we can afford to play it quiet and smart. Sixteen hours isn't a lot considering we don't know where to find this thing or how to kill it."

"Kill what?" a voice asked.

I nearly upended my bowl of Lucky Charms, almost incurring a bazillion years of bad luck. "Lizzie, what the hell?"

"Kill what?" she repeated.

"The phage."

Her face twisted in confusion.

"The thing you're calling a Narrowman."

"Oh." She nodded in understanding. "How are you going to kill it?"

I sighed. "I have no idea."

"But you might have a way to find out." Ortiz stared. There was an undercurrent in her voice of something more.

She either thought I could find out more, or knew I could.

"Yes. I'm not overly fond of that option though."

"Why not?" Ortiz could've burrowed holes through my noggin with the way she watched me.

"Because they'll screw me, or kill me, or screw me then kill me." I wasn't wrong. Lyshae was an overachiever in bitch-craft.

"Not if we come with you." Ortiz's face made it clear that it wasn't a suggestion.

"Bad idea. It could be dangerous."

She shot me a look which settled the debate.

"'Kay," I groaned. Reaching into the bowl with a finger, I scooped up a lone green marshmallow. I flicked it into the air toward Lizzie. She caught the clover and gave me a puzzled look. "For luck."

"Oh." She stuffed the soggy marshmallow in her pocket.

"Erhm, yeah, you hold onto that, Lizzie." I turned to Ortiz and beckoned with a nod of my head. "Come on."

"Where?"

"Outside. But it's morning so we'll have to go into the woods to avoid drawing attention."

"What are we going to do?" She looked at me with a hint of wariness

"Have a chat with a fox."

# Chapter Twenty

The asylum grounds were as close to empty as they could have been. I was nursing a hope they would've been devoid of all people. It would've made things easier. With everything that was happening, I didn't want to chance an evocation in the woods. Hell, even a meeting with Lyshae, secluded in the tree-covered grounds, was a dangerous proposition.

Lizzie trailed behind Ortiz as I led them to the thicket. We passed a man with dark, shoulder-length hair. He rocked on a swing and spoke to himself. His eyes twinkled with merriment. An elderly woman sat nearby. Her eyes were closed, expression serene. Seeing those two made me smile.

It's something about people, I've noticed. No matter the hardships, no matter how long they've been endured—people persevere. It's not always loud triumphs and accomplishments. Sometimes it's about the quiet things, the simple things. It's about the little smiles while sitting in a field of green grass under the morning sun. It's about being five years old again, swaying back and forth on a swing. I hadn't realized that my feet had stopped moving. I stared at them for—well, I don't know how long. Everything was still, the calm sort. The sort I've never really known.

A hand fell on my shoulder. "You okay?"

"Yeah," I replied, my voice a bit rougher than expected.

"Sure?" She gave a gentle squeeze. "I know that look. I've seen it before."

"Yeah?"

"Yeah," she said. "Six months ago. Last paranormal case I was wrapped up in. The guy looked at a young couple walking down the street like that. You could see the longing in his eyes, to be normal, to want to live like that."

"Yeah." She was right. I did have that look on my face.

"You guys don't have it easy, do you?"

"No."

"Sorry." She punctuated the word with another squeeze.

"So am I, Ortiz." I stood rooted there for another few moments, letting my thoughts run away with what it'd be like to be normal. Lizzie sniffed behind me and I snapped back to reality. I turned and walked off in silence. I kept my eyes fixed on the copse, not wanting to chance a look back.

The woods drew nearer. I didn't have much of a plan but I went through all the possibilities of what could happen. It never hurts to have a plan. Knowing how Lyshae would react, and what she would do a second time, was like trying to guess the future with a magic eight ball. There was no real way you could do it. You couldn't trust the outcome either. She might be more cooperative if I summoned her in a circle. Or she could be exceptionally hostile and even more unpredictable. Believe it or not, supernatural creatures are not overly fond of being summoned on the whims of a mortal. Nor are they fans of being trapped.

Go figure.

The best chance I had of Lyshae helping us was if I called her—politely. No Summoner's Star. I risked losing leverage, but she might be more amicable.

I hoped.

We reached the end of the asylum's well-manicured grass, stepping into the thicket. My vision corrected itself as we strolled through. The morning sun struggled to make itself known between the tight-knit trees. Canted pillars of light shone through here and there. Leading Ortiz and Lizzie further inside, I wondered how they'd react to Lyshae. Horrible monsters are easier for people to imagine and accept than nice ones. Well, nice was a stretch for Lyshae. Morally ambiguous, but not keen to rip one's face off. Oh, and a backstabbing bitch.

"How much further?"

"Not far, Ortiz." Technically we didn't have to be far in at all to call Lyshae. However, the further in we were, the less likely someone would stumble on our talk. It'd be one thing for Ortiz and Lizzie to meet Lyshae, but for one of the asylum's patients... That would be awkward.

I stopped after another minute of walking.

"What now, Charles?"

"Now, I call up an acquaintance." I dropped my voice to a whisper. "And hope she's in a helpful, not murderous, mood." I kept my voice low as I called, "Lyshae." I turned back to see if Ortiz had heard me. She didn't. We may have needed Lyshae, but I didn't want Ortiz knowing her name. If Ortiz knew Lyshae's name and watched carefully enough, she'd figure out how to call the Kitsune by herself.

Without a Summoner's Star to keep Lyshae at bay, Ortiz would be screwed. I didn't doubt Ortiz's toughness. She'd proven that on a several occasions. Regardless of what she believed, she was still ignorant about the paranormal world. Lyshae would prey on that ignorance and naivety. Ortiz was naturally curious; Lyshae would fuel that curiosity until she could easily manipulate her. That wasn't going to happen.

"Lyshae." It didn't matter how quiet my summons was, Lyshae would hear it; that's what mattered. So long as Ortiz didn't pick up on them, everything was fine. "Lyshae," I called for the third time. "Come on, you conniving bitch."

A gentle gust blew. Branches swayed like a genial wave from a close friend. I closed my eyes and relished how comforting the breath of wind was. It was easy to imagine that it was that little draft that swept up my calls and carried them to Lyshae. Of course, the wind had nothing to do with it. It was simply the act of uttering her name. Once got her attention. Twice was an annoyance. Thrice was a firm, yet polite, invitation. Well, invitation's the wrong word. Having said her name three times, she didn't have a choice but to show up. The question was: when?

The breeze picked up and my hairs stood on end. I let myself shiver for a moment. A flash of white bounded into view with speed and grace beyond human or animal.

It was roughly the size of a Labrador Retriever, which is saying something, considering most foxes weren't. Thick pelt, immaculate and pure white. A fan of slender fur trailed behind the creature's body. Nine lengthy tails, their tips gold. The fox covered the final six feet in a single leap. Its features shifted in midair. The transition was seamless. A fox had sailed into the air, but a woman landed in front of us.

Lizzie gasped. Ortiz bristled, moving halfway into an aggressive pose before reining herself back in.

"Lyshae." I made a small bow.

Her lips quirked, and her eyes filled with amusement. Returning my slight bow, she added a polite inclination of the head. "Vincent," she said in that melodious voice of hers.

"Who's Vincent?" Ortiz eyed the pair of us.

Lyshae's head tilted to the side as she observed the situation. Her eyes widened as a look of understanding came over her. "Oh," she breathed, eyes alight with childlike pleasure. She smiled. "That's interesting."

I gave her a look. Her mouth shut, but the pleased look remained. It was the look of a fox that had stumbled into a chicken coop with no one around.

Ortiz didn't relent. "Who's Vincent?"

Lyshae made an offhand wave of her hand. "Another name, another man. Similar—very similar. I'm afraid my memory is not quite what it used to be." The master lie-smith gave a smile that edged on too sincere.

"Well," Ortiz said dryly. "That was almost the truth."

I was glad I didn't rubberneck like I wanted to at that moment. Ortiz picking up on my lies, or anyone else's, was impressive. Picking up on Lyshae's on the first time was impossible. It was easier for me to admit it was dumb luck than anything else. Lyshae wasn't just a masterful liar. She was beyond that in a supernatural way. She was a Kitsune, a trickster spirit. Lying was as natural to her as breathing. Not to mention she had her own magical ability interwoven with her skills at telling non-truths.

That delighted look returned to Lyshae's face. "Oh, you have a hint of talent about you." Lyshae moved with slow, precise motions as she brushed passed me. She circled Ortiz with the measured caution of a predator. "And what, if I might inquire, is your name?" She gave Ortiz a fox-like grin.

"No," I grated.

A golden eyebrow arched as Lyshae glanced at me, then toward Ortiz. "I believe I asked her." Her smile grew.

"And I believe I gave you an answer. How did it go again? No!"

Lyshae let out a huff of breath and ran her hands over the shift, smoothing the already straight material. "Fine, to business then. I'm assuming that because there's no Star binding me, I'm entirely free to go if I so choose?"

I grinned. "You know what happens when you assume, Lyshae? You make an ass out of you."

She blinked before adopting her usual smirking facial expression. "Should I take that as my cue to leave?"

"You could, but..." I let the word hang in the air, drawing her curiosity. "You'd lose out on a chance to make me owe you one."

Her pleased mask slipped, but she kept circling.

Fish sees bait.

Lyshae muttered something that I couldn't make out. She slowed her pace and faced me. "What do you require of me?"

Fish. On. Hook.

"We're hunting a phage."

Lyshae rolled her hand with an air of indifference. Most phages weren't something to be noticed by her.

Before I spoke next, Lizzie approached Lyshae, her little hand outstretched. We all stopped to watch as a beaming Lizzie let her hand fall on Lyshae's iridescent shift.

Lyshae's discomfort was priceless. "What is the little mortal doing?" She furrowed her brows in confusion.

"I think," I said, fighting the laughter, "she's petting you."

Lyshae frowned. "Please stop."

"No." Lizzie made her point as she rubbed Lyshae's leg.

I couldn't help it; I broke into rolling laughter. Ortiz joined in.

Lyshae took Lizzie's hand within her own. She patted Lizzie on the head with her free hand. Lizzie smiled. Lyshae returned it. It was what Lyshae did next that caused me lose it. Lyshae bent and motioned to slide her arms underneath Lizzie's to pick her up.

I covered the distance in a microsecond, putting myself between the two. I brushed Lizzie back a pace from the Kitsune. My voice dropped to a dangerous growl. "No way in fucking heaven, hell, or in all the damned Neravene will I ever let you pick that child up." If my words weren't enough warning, my glare certainly was.

She took a step back and raised her hands in a peaceful gesture. "Honestly, I'm not a Kappa." She rolled her eyes. "I don't whisk children away." Lyshae flashed another smile.

Kidnapping children may not have been part of Lyshae's resume, but lying came too easy for her. She was a spirit of information and Lizzie could, at the very least, commune with ghosts. There was no end to the potential information Lyshae could glean from Lizzie. A child like that would be an untapped and wonderful resource for the Kitsune to exploit.

We weren't meeting under a truce. There was nothing binding Lyshae. If she wanted, she could try to take Lizzie. Chips of ice slid down my back as I wondered what would happen to the young girl if Lyshae took her—if Lyshae raised her. I gave a silent thanks that she wasn't aware of Lizzie's gifts.

"No, you're not a Kappa." I gestured to the kid with my head, then to Ortiz. "Hey, why don't you scuttle over to her." Lizzie did as I asked, and I breathed a sigh of relief. The further I could keep the two of them away from Lyshae, the better. I gave Lyshae a level stare. "You'll forgive me if I don't take your interest in my friends as just that. There's always more going on with you."

With a slight bow of her head, she agreed. "I have never once tried to conceal that from you. You, on the other hand, have your fair share of secrets, don't you?"

My finger slipped inside my collar and I gave it a light tug. It may not have been tight, but it felt it. I cleared my throat pointedly. "Beside the point. I called you here for help. Remember, I'll owe you one."

She remained motionless save for her foxy ears twitching. On Lyshae, that simple ear twitch might as well have been a poker player screaming victory.

When she didn't say anything, I continued. "We're after a phage. A Babylonian phage."

"Hm," Lyshae mused but otherwise offered nothing helpful.

"It's been killing the patients here. Driving them crazy and reaching out to them. We need a way to find it, fight it, and gank it. Anything you might know or can find out would be of help."

"And for that information, you would render me your services?" A hungry smile appeared on her face followed by a discomforting light in her eyes.

"Once."

Lyshae's smile grew in tandem with the lump in my stomach. "Mmm, no." She shook her head. "For that, you'll have to give me more."

"The hell he will," snarled Ortiz. "Charles, don't make a deal with this freak. She's a liar."

"No arguments here, Ortiz, but we need her."

Lyshae spoke as if my exchange with Ortiz hadn't occurred. "I can tell you a few things about the phage. They're older than I, significantly so—"

"Makes you seem young in comparison. Must feel nice," I muttered. Lyshae's ears jostled, but she didn't seem perturbed by my aside.

"They exude a hallucinogenic in the form of black fog. It's a type of Myrk in actuality."

That made sense. Myrk is a supernatural weapon of sorts. A great number of creatures implemented it. Its effects varied depending on the creature. Some used Myrk to obscure light sources, veiling them in an ink-like fog. Myrk doesn't have a singular use because it's more than a mass of black mist. It's alive.

Myrk is a living thing much in the way trees are. Trees may not be able to speak or physically interact with a person, but they live and grow. Myrk is the same. It feeds off light sources. It can grow. It can evolve. It's shaped to the creature that uses it, which is what makes is so terrifying. The Babylonian phage used it to hide, but, more than that, simple contact with it could cause nightmares. It had reacted to me. The gunk had latched onto my arm and refused to let go, inducing one hell of a panic attack.

The phage was a creature of fear. If its Myrk adapted to it, there was no telling how far it could twist a person's mind.

Lyshae spoke as I thought, going over details I was already aware of. I let myself ease back into listening, hoping she had something new for me.

"—incredibly agile. They can manipulate their bodies like master contortionists. They have hearing better than that vast majority of beings I've encountered. It's one of the ways they hunt."

My eyed widened. "By sound?" That was an impressive

way to hunt.

"They have little in the way of facial features, *Charles*." Lyshae drew out the pronunciation of the name like it was a new sound for her.

I narrowed my eyes.

"They have no eyes, no noses, and barely a mouth. Though they don't need one. They don't have ears that fit any definition I'm aware of, and yet their hearing is close to my own. Killing one is problematic."

"How so?"

"Because"—she grinned—"there is only one way to kill a Babylonian Phage." The grin became predatory and she chose that particular moment to fall silent.

I waited, teeth grinding as I did. I peeked at my forearm. Another hour had passed. Fifteen hours left. The pressure in my jaw grew.

"A stake made from the wood of a cypress tree, coated in olive oil, then run through a flame until the oil has burned."

"Where are we supposed to get that?" Ortiz piped up.

I shrugged, but Lyshae had the answer of course.

"I can procure what you need...at a cost." Lyshae's smirk remained.

"I bet." I scowled.

"Finding the creature," she said, "will be more difficult however. A Babylonian phage cannot linger on this side for long. They have to retreat to the Neravene to rest."

"They pull themselves over through force." I was catching on.

Lyshae bowed her head.

Some creatures like the Babylonian phage aren't just tied to a place, but a time as well. It hailed from Babylon. Not the physical location, but what it represented way back when. It was born there and was a part of *that* particular Babylon. That empire may have fallen, but the creature lingered on. When the home of a creature like that fades, the only option they have is to seek refuge in the Neravene. They can leave to feed, but that's about it. It was probably holed up in its own little bubble of the Neravene, hopping over for an easy meal. Coming over and operating on the mortal plane took considerable energy—energy that had to be replaced by feeding. It was that or starve.

Monsters never choose the starvation route.

I had suspected the phage was operating that way, but I hadn't known why. Now I did. It explained how and why the creature took its time with the killings. Why there were a handful of deaths versus dozens. It tainted a select few, let its toxic Myrk work its magic, and then fed. It was slow, measured, and effective. With the phage's ability to contort itself and its already slender build, it could move through the vents with ease. All of that meant it limited its exposure a great deal, as well as minimizing risks to itself.

The phage could've chosen to stay longer on our side, but that meant expending more energy, which meant more meals. All of that would definitely arouse suspicion. It was as smart as I'd figured. It reasoned well. The notion occurred to me that I would also run the chance of engaging the thing in the Neravene. That was going to be a problem. This thing was dangerous and could toy with my mind. In its own pocket of the Neravene, I wouldn't have a hope.

And I wouldn't have a choice, either, if it came to it. People were dying, and my timeline continued to whither away.

"What's she talking about, Charles?"

I told Ortiz everything I knew about the creature and its home in the Neravene.

Ortiz's hands slid up to rub her biceps and shoulders. "I don't want to have to go into a place like that again, not unless we absolutely have to."

The feeling was mutual, but I kept my objections silent. Ortiz was as solid as they came but even she was susceptible to fear. So was I, as well as Lizzie, and this thing preyed on fear. I didn't need to showcase any of the doubts I harbored.

Lyshae spoke. "Finding the creature while it's in the asylum will be problematic. There are two ways it can be done. Neither are without their dangers." She went silent again, waiting.

I motioned for her to continue.

"How is the water here?" Her eyes shone. She knew the answer to that.

I confirmed her suspicions anyways. "Tainted. The freak's contaminated the water supply."

"As I thought. The first option you have is for one of you to ingest large quantities of the fouled water. Whoever is under its influence will be able to see the creature, should it be near, and they will be drawn to it. Drinking enough of the water forms a link between the phage and mortal who consumes it."

"And turns the person into a flare," I said. "The phage would find them easily. Not to mention the fact they'd be out of their minds and couldn't put up a fight."

"No risk, no reward," Lyshae replied.

"Second option?" I asked, blowing over her reply. Part of me didn't want to ask the question. I already had an inkling what the answer would be.

"The use of a child," said Lyshae. The lump in my stomach grew.

"I knew I could help," Lizzie chimed.

"No!" Ortiz and I shouted in unison. Lizzie pouted, crossing her arms and adopting a haughty posture. Nice to know she wasn't always airy-fairy.

"Keep the kid out of it." My lips almost peeled back from my teeth.

Lyshae's brows rose as her eyes grew. "Why?" She sounded genuinely surprised. "Children can see the creature regardless of their condition. Babylonian phages favor children. They find nothing sweeter than a child's blood rich in fear."

That was wrong on so many levels.

"Bait," I whispered. "You want us to use the kid as…bait?" Air popped within my knuckles as my fingers dug into my palms. I inhaled several times, reminding myself with each breath that I needed Lyshae. I told myself that pummeling her for even suggesting that would do no good. Well, it would make *me* feel good.

Lyshae shrugged. "Then you have only one option."

"Seems like," I agreed, my voice gravel-like.

"About the stake…" Lyshae's voice rang with undertones of something more. "We should speak—in private." She slipped off to move further into the woods.

"Charles, don't," Ortiz warned.

"Relax." I flashed her a grin. "I'll be fine."

Ortiz bit down on her lip but didn't argue further.

Lizzie, on the other hand, moved to follow. I stopped her with a shake of my head. Her posture sank, but she was a smart kid; she understood.

Flashing her the same smile I'd given Ortiz, I walked over to Lyshae and her outstretched hand. I hooked my arm around Lyshae's. "Shall we?"

"My," she breathed, letting a hand fall to her chest. "So polite."

"I can be."

Lyshae released a huff of breath that edged on laughter. "Not nearly enough, remember?"

I adopted dignified silence. That fiasco wasn't my fault.

We passed through an array of younger and slender trees, some no thicker than paper towel tubes. I struggled to keep up with Lyshae even though we were arm in arm. She navigated the woods with a grace I couldn't imagine having. Stepping past an upturned root here, avoiding a sunken patch of earth there. All the while I stumbled along. My foot snagged on that same root. That piece of sunken earth worked ever so hard to twist my ankle. The uneven ground made me fight for balance. Lyshae's innate skill brought to us a clearing no larger than a hot tub.

It was a rather intimate place. No more than ten paces would've taken me out of it. To be in such a tight place with a creature as beautiful as Lyshae gave my anatomy ideas. I told it to shut up. Lyshae was the sort to take those ideas, spin 'em into a wonderful fantasy, then push my ass off the imagined cliff.

For once, I let my actions speak in place of my words. I arched a brow and let my head fall to the side as I regarded her. She picked up on the question I posed.

Lyshae waved her hand more elegantly than I thought possible, and yet the making of the gesture seemed so casual for her. For a second, the air resembled a desert mirage, bending visibly. I felt the touch of something sap-like engulfing my body in an invisible cushion. My ears received a liberal heaping of the feeling. It felt like they were clogged with Vaseline.

"Out of sight," Lyshae murmured in perfect clarity, "out of mind."

"Lyshae…did you just veil us?"

She inclined her head no more than a millimeter. Had I not been so focused on her, I might've missed the action entirely. "From eyes and ears," she commented.

Veiling was a magical art that did exactly what the name suggested: obscure one from sight, even sound. We weren't truly gone. Someone could've bumped into us. We were simply masked. Simple was the wrong word. There was nothing simple about what Lyshae had done. Illusion-based magic takes skill, patience and a deft hand. Lyshae had all of those in excess. But the ease with which she performed the act wasn't something to be taken lightly.

That took a level of skill that put many practitioners to shame. Many creatures I've met can perform veils to hide voice *or* sound, not both. Nor could they do it so effectively. That performance gave me a new respect for Lyshae's abilities. She'd picked up some neat tricks in her thousand years of existence.

"Wow," I breathed. "Didn't know you could pull ones off like that."

"Honestly, Vincent." She gave a little shake of her head.

"Right, sorry, should've known," I muttered while rolling my eyes.

"Now that we have some privacy, let us talk about a new bargain. One," she said, pausing for a moment, "that will put you in my debt."

My teeth slid across each other. This wasn't going to be good.

"I will help you, Vincent Graves, but you will be in my debt, and you will fulfill said debt." It wasn't a question.

I ceased eroding my enamel, instead swallowing my anger and feigning a smile. "'Course."

She held up three fingers.

"Three?" I sputtered. "What makes you think I'd agree to three debts?"

"First, because I am not obligated to help you. I am choosing to. That warrants a debt. Second, helping you stop the creature is not the same as procuring and delivering the means with which to kill the creature."

"It sort of is," I countered.

"It is not. I have already informed you how to do so, and have done so in good faith, I might add. If you desire, you can retrieve a stake made of cypress yourself. You are also free to prepare it yourself, to my description. That is, of course, if your limited schedule allows you the necessary time to do those things."

I scowled.

"Lastly, I could have—and still can—reveal the truth of your identity to the woman called Ortiz. The sole reason I did not is because you might be of use to me. Better use if you're not compromised in any way. That young woman is adept. If she finds out who and what you are, it could be troublesome."

My scowl deepened, my posture tightened, and I imagined what Lyshae would look like with a broken nose. I believed in chivalry, but I also believed that it didn't apply to supernatural women who'd tried to kill you. "You're blackmailing me."

"Of course," she said through a peal of musical laughter. "I am myself. It's to be expected, is it not, Vincent Graves?"

"Bitch."

She laughed harder.

"Lyshae, have a heart. People are dying here."

"People die all the time. After a thousand years, I've learned that. What makes this so different? A monster, a non-human one, is doing the 'murdering'? Spare me." She waved her hand. "Your kind has bred monsters in its own right. Many times a finger wasn't lifted to stop the killing."

She was right about the last bit. That didn't make her right about all of it.

"I'm not going to argue semantics with you, Lyshae."

"Then, what? If you aren't opting to strike a bargain, what else is there?"

"Lyshae." My voice dropped to a hushed whisper. "People are dying, damnit! Don't pull this crap."

Lyshae remained resolute. The frickin' icy bitch. "I am not your friend, Vincent Graves. I am not someone you can call upon for favors without expecting to owe me in return. You dealt with Gnosis. He provided information and you reciprocated by placing yourself in his debt."

Technically that wasn't true. The little asswaffle slipped that into a conversation. He had hung up before I had time to counter. True, I didn't argue the point anytime after that; it was still a dirty move. But then again, so was blackmail.

"You and Gnosis should get a room—two peas in a pod of assholery."

"This isn't getting you anywhere. As you said"—Lyshae broke off to tap her forearm—"people are dying, and you are running out of time."

Damnit, she was right. I didn't like the idea of being blackmailed. I liked the idea of owing her even less. Not to mention it'd be three frickin' debts. Three atop of the one I owed Gnosis. But that was the problem of being a soul who never knows where he will wake up.

It's near impossible to plan ahead. I can't exactly have a tool kit ready to slay monsters with me everywhere I go.

I exhaled and loosened my posture. I unclenched my fist and noticed the row of marks left by my fingernails. "Right," I grated. "Let's deal."

Lyshae's smile wasn't one of overwhelming glee or surprise. It was of quiet confidence, of surety. It was a smile of triumph. "Your word, Vincent Graves."

"Is good."

"Give it, please." She smiled and batted her eyelashes coyly.

She enjoyed watching me squirm.

"Your word," she repeated.

"Contingent on you giving yours. No offense, Lyshae. It's not that I don't trust you. It's just that I don't trust you."

She let out a rueful laugh, covering her mouth with a hand. "Very well then." Her hand blurred into motion faster than I could follow. All I could see was the trailing ripples of her shimmering shift. A glint of silver made its way towards me. My wrist was wrapped in an iron grip. She upturned my hand and made a fast horizontal swipe. I reeled. A paper-thin stream of heat enveloped my palm, running across the length of it. Crimson seeped from my flesh.

Before I had finished shouting, "Lyshae what—" she turned her own hand over, doing the same. I couldn't tell what stood out more in contrast—the porcelain flesh against the blood, or the blood against the flesh.

*The hell'd she get the knife?*

As soon as I thought it, Lyshae fanned her hand like a

magician doing card tricks. The knife vanished. Either she was adept at slight of hand, or she veiled the knife as well. Both were disturbing.

I waved my bleeding palm. "The hell?"

She took my hand within hers—gently, I might add. I didn't expect that after she nicked me with a knife.

Women are complicated creatures. Supernatural ones all the more.

She solidified her grip. We were essentially shaking hands. But it was more than that.

The idea of blood pacts stretches far back into human history. Normally interwoven with tales of dealing with the devil. In this case it might've been true. This wasn't some macabre handshake. It was an ironclad agreement. We were forming a link. If Lyshae broke her word, she'd suffer consequences. If I broke mine, it wouldn't be pretty.

For a being like Lyshae, the side effects could range from diminishing her power a bit, to losing it altogether. It depended on the severity of her transgressions in breaking her word. It also depended on the wording of the contract between us. I tried to slip my hand out from hers. The grip wasn't painful, but she was strong.

"I, Lyshae, swear upon my power to render my services to you, Vincent Graves. I swear upon my power to aid you solely in stopping the Babylonian phage within the asylum walls. I swear upon my power that I shall give you the weapons necessary to kill the creature preying on the people here. I swear to supply you with any knowledge that will aid in stopping the phage. I swear upon my power and name so long as you, Vincent Graves, place yourself in my debt—thrice." She held up three fingers with her free hand. "As reciprocation for my services."

I honed in on the word "*solely*" as she spoke. That was a limiting word, a bit of a loophole she'd worked in. It was smart. Wordplay was Lyshae's strong suit. I tried to recall all that she had said exactly as she'd said it. If she had left herself any wiggle room to screw me over, I needed to know about it.

"I am waiting." She smiled.

I exhaled through my nose. "I, Vincent Graves, abide by those terms. I swear it by my name to place myself in your debt thrice, so long as you live up to your offer of services. So long as you do not reveal my identity to"—I trailed off, catching myself before disclosing Ortiz's full name—"the woman I call Ortiz. And so long as you stay the living fuck away from the young girl who was in my company." I figured I'd throw in my own conditions.

Lyshae's features shifted into a frown and back to neutral with startling speed.

Good. If she wanted this deal so bad, I was going to make her suffer for it.

"I, Vincent Graves, swear by my name and life, to place myself in your debt."

A multitude of expressions flickered over Lyshae's face. They went by faster than I could register. It was never easy to understand what she was up to, but that little display sent a low voltage current down my body. It made me conscious of my wording in the pact. I tumbled through all I had said. If I had slipped up somewhere and didn't amend it, Lyshae would capitalize on it, twisting it to her advantage.

The injured tissue of my palm contracted and pulsated violently. A horrible mixture of arctic ice and skin blistering heat filled the wound, spreading up my hand. As it worked its way into my forearm, the muscles broke into a spasmodic dance, twitching in painful bursts. My veins were visibly clear, engorged and darkened as if filled with a sickly wine. They ached like braided cords of steel ran through them.

Lyshae's face might as well have been carved in stone. It betrayed no emotion. But her posture did. Lyshae's arm may have been hidden beneath the loose and lengthy fabric of her shift, but she had to be feeling what I was. Supernatural strength or not, it was damned painful and her sinking posture said that. It was a small pleasure to know that I wasn't enduring the agony alone.

Sharing is caring.

Despite the pain, our grips never faltered. Lyshae and I held onto one another in grim determination. It was a contest of wills. Using her hand as a cushion, I squeezed, digging my fingers into her. The skin around her eyes tightened. The next moment, her hand exuded a dangerous amount of pressure as she reciprocated. The delicate bones in my hand cried out for relief. They were rewarded.

Seconds to my pain threshold being exhausted, the excruciating sensations ceased. The bulging veins subsided and we broke contact.

We each took a cautious step back, putting the slightest bit of distance between us. Physically, it may not have been much. Lyshae could've crossed the distance before I could react, if she chose to. It was more of a gesture to put the other at ease after our machismo showdown.

Nonplussed, Lyshae ran her hands down the lower half of her shift to smooth it. "The bargain is struck," she said in a soft and carefree voice. Her mouth split into a smile and she bowed deeply.

It was the first time Lyshae had done so with serious intent. It was a measure of respect.

"I cannot recall, in all my years, more than a handful of beings who've endured the binding as you did, Vincent Graves." There was a note of surprise tinged with respect in her voice.

I answered with a deep bow of my own. It seemed proper.

Lyshae's smile grew. "Well," she murmured, "you can learn manners."

"You know, next time you want to have a big dick contest, you can just ask me to drop my pants and we can skip the special handshake." I winked.

She arched a delicate eyebrow and shot me an oblique look. "I'm afraid that I'm more interested in another piece of wood at the moment. Or have you forgotten? Also, I've noted in my time that males of any species seem to have an overinflated opinion on the size of their"—she paused for a moment—"offerings. It's rather a shame that that same inflation never seems to make its way farther south." She gave me a rueful smile as her gaze fell on the area just below my waistline.

Did Lyshae just make a joke? Did she just call my borrowed junk small?

"Low blow," I muttered.

Lyshae let loose a torrent of uncharacteristic giggles. She actually giggled! "I think our meeting is concluded. Before I depart to fetch your weapon and whatever information I can glean, some advice."

"Oh?" I perked up.

"Remember, Vincent, in this place, no matter what is felt, what is seen, nothing here is as it may seem. Phages prey on the minds of people. Many here who seem whole are broken. Many who seem broken are whole. Remember that fears can bind you, or they can set you free. And most of all, Vincent Graves, do not let the phage pull you into its domain within the Neravene. Do not die before I get back. It is rather a long trip. I'd hate for it to be a waste, especially as we have such a wonderful bargain now." There was a smile on her lips that revealed a flash of white teeth.

With a careless flick of her hand, Lyshae opened a Way. A strand of silver streaked through the air, parting it. She bounded backward with a singular step.

Before she disappeared into the Neravene, I shouted, "How do I find this thing?"

"Drink deeply," she called back. Then Lyshae was gone, vanishing into the ribbon of silver.

The instant she left, an odd rippling feeling went through my skin. It felt like the layer of oil-based lubricant that had coated me was dripping off. The pop associated with air-based travel went off in my ears. I had forgotten about Lyshae's masterful veil. With her gone, it was lifting. Maybe there hadn't been anything physical covering me, but I squirmed as the veil dissipated.

"Whoa," someone breathed.

Ortiz stood within the row of trees that formed the clear circle Lyshae and I had been standing in. Lizzie was a step behind her with half her body obscured behind Ortiz's.

I waved. "Hey." My voice was a bit drier than expected. Dealing with Lyshae can leave a guy with a sore throat and a bitter taste.

"How'd you do that?" Ortiz motioned her arms in a wide and encompassing arc.

I raised an inquisitive eyebrow.

"We followed you," she explained. That didn't come as a surprise. Even though I told her to give Lyshae and me some privacy. I guess she couldn't keep her inner Fed at bay. "We lost sight of you, and then we came here and...nothing. Now you just appeared out of nowhere. Explain."

So I told her. I described Lyshae's veil and how it hid us

from sight and masked our voices. Ortiz's face tightened and she grimaced.

Her gaze narrowed. "What did you talk about?"

I pinched the bridge of my nose, eyes tightening as I thought. I could tell her the truth, which would piss her off. I could lie, which would piss her off. Or I could say nothing, which would piss her off. "She agreed to help," I answered.

Ortiz tilted her head, eyes still narrowed as she surveyed me. "Why would she agree to that? She didn't seem very willing before." Ortiz continued her hawk-like appraisal of me as she waited for my response.

I didn't give one.

"You made some sort of arrangement with her...a deal, didn't you?" Comprehension dawned on her face. "You said something about owing her. I saw her face when you said that. She took it seriously, like you owing her a debt is a big deal."

It was, and I didn't owe Lyshae one. I owed her three. But Ortiz didn't ask, so I didn't mention it.

"Why did you do it? You know you can't trust her, Charles."

"I know," I said, my voice tight.

"Then why'd you do it?"

"People are dying." I struggled to work some moisture into my mouth. The lining of my throat went dry. I felt stretched, hammered and compacted all at once. All the running, clawing, and lack of sleep was taking its toll.

"Yes, yes they are," Ortiz breathed. "But no more will." She spoke in steely tones. "We're going to find and stake it." Her eyes glowed with determined heat.

"Yeah we are," I agreed.

"How?" Lizzie chimed.

Ortiz gave me a questioning look. "Did your *friend* tell you how to find this thing?"

I shot her a knowing look. "We already knew how to find it."

Both her eyebrows shot up. "Oh...."

"What?" Lizzie inquired.

"This is a terrible idea," Ortiz said below her breath.

"I'm going to need a drink. A big one."

# Chapter Twenty-One

The black number on my forearm read fourteen. Another hour had passed.

"Did I say what a monumentally stupid idea this is?"

"Yes, Ortiz, you did," I sputtered between mouthfuls of water.

I clung tight to the sides of the fountain to ensure I didn't quit. My stomach cried out against the rush of liquid filling it. I ignored it, drinking to the point where I realized if I didn't solve this case in time, I'd lose a kidney. Rubbing the back of my wrist across my mouth, I wiped my face clean.

"Wanted it to be noted."

"Noted," I said dryly.

"I can help. It should be me," protested Lizzie.

"No." I groaned and placed a hand over my stomach to settle it. It felt like I'd replaced the organ with a water balloon, one filled far beyond its capacity. The lining stretched as excess water sloshed inside. *Maybe this wasn't such a great idea.*

Lizzie refused to relent on the matter. "You said children can see the monster."

"I did," I managed to say between something that worked to be a belch but didn't quite make it up.

As right as Lizzie was, I didn't want her being the one to look for it. She'd been roped too far into the paranormal world for my liking. She may not have had a choice as far as seeing ghosts were concerned. That was out of my hands. What I could control was ensuring this kid had a shot at a normal life. Well, as normal as it could get for a girl with her talents. She didn't need the nightmares, the cynicism and the danger that came with my line of work.

I gave her a stern look. "You're staying here."

She looked like she was about to pout for a moment.

Instead, she turned to Ortiz and flashed her a look for help. Ortiz didn't come to her aid. She wouldn't have anyways. She felt the same as I did. Neither of us were going to put this girl through anything she didn't have to endure.

Ortiz left Lizzie to stew in disappointment and turned to face me. "Someone should go with you."

"You're right," I admitted. "They should."

Ortiz stared at me, waiting for me to add that it should be her.

I didn't say that however.

"You should stay with Lizzie."

"If this thing gets the drop on you—"

"I'll be screwed, the same as if you were to come with me. We have no way of fighting the phage yet." I raised my voice to speak over her. "If you come along, we'll both get hurt. That's pointless. I'm just going to find out where this thing's holed up and anything else I can while I'm about it. As for killing it, that's what…my associate is for." I worked to keep myself from sharing Lyshae's name. "Stay with Lizzie, huh?"

Ortiz's lips pressed together tightly. "Sure."

Lizzie bristled. "I can take care of myself."

"I know you can," I agreed in a soft voice. "But still, I'm going to worry. It's a grownup thing. She's not staying so much for you as she is to give me peace of mind. Get it?"

The kid was smarter than I gave her credit for. She didn't buy what I said in the slightest. She rolled her eyes, but didn't argue any further.

"Be careful," Ortiz said as I turned to go. Lizzie remained silent but gave me a look carrying the same message.

I grinned and headed down the hall, waiting for the hallucinations to start. I walked for ten minutes. Nothing. No horrifying visions, no flashes of random imagery— nothing. I wondered if the information from my journal was wrong. As much as I hated the notion, it was a possibility.

But Lyshae had told me the same thing. She wasn't the sort to get things wrong. Information brokers who spread misinformation don't have lengthy careers—or life spans for that matter. The possibility that she had intentionally given me bad information crossed my mind. I quickly banished the thought. Lyshae and I had bargained. There'd be no reason for her to screw me over now. I was in her debt; there were no benefits to me failing this case or, worse, dying. If she pulled one over on me, she would incur a penalty upon herself at the cost of her powers. Not to mention the fact that she wanted me in her debt. That only worked if I made it out of this case intact.

I paused as I came across a familiar room. The door was left open. I walked through the doorway and came to rest on Charles' bed. My gaze transfixed on the mass of lines covering the far wall. The simplistic image of the Babylonian phage burned itself into my mind the longer I stared. I had to blink several times to verify that I was seeing what I thought I was. Charles' wall had been drawn all over; the majority of the images were tendrils that spread over the white surface. Only now they weren't behaving like scribbles of crayon.

For one thing, crayon markings are inanimate, or they're supposed to be. The ones before me swayed ever so gently. The writhing black lines seemed ominous. My right eye twitched and shut tight of its own accord. I knew why a second later.

An area no larger than a dime, directly behind my right eye, erupted in agony. It was like an ice pick had been jammed into the tissue deep inside my forehead. The sharp throbbing caused my hands to fly up and press against the area in hopes of dulling the pain. The heel of my palm came away wet. My eye shuddered as I reeled from the horrible ache.

My good eye watched the lengthy slender appendages waving over the wall. Trickles of what looked like molten wax dribbled downwards as the tentacles grew tired of being two-dimensional. They peeled themselves from the walls and worked their way across the room.

"Shit!" I kicked myself back across the bed. Sheets fell and my head banged into the drywall behind. Both eyes shut as I worked through the jarring impact to my skull. My left eye opened in time to see the tendrils making it halfway across the room, hanging above empty space. I shook my head to the point where my neck ached. "I'm hallucinating. This isn't real."

I ground the heels of both palms into my eyes as hard as possible, anything to numb the excruciating sensation. The muscles in my jaw strained as I clamped my teeth. I fought through the pain the best I could and reminded myself of what I had done. I recalled drinking ridiculous amounts of tainted water. I knew it would lead to something like this. My breathing slowed, becoming steadier as I repeated the mantra that this was an illusion. The stabbing needlelike pain abated.

Once I was certain my eye hadn't been impaled, I rubbed the back of my thumb underneath the lid, wiping away the tears. At first, I blinked to aid my eyes in readjusting to my surroundings. Then I blinked because of the stranger hovering an inch outside Charles' bedroom.

My palms found their way back to my eyes, exerting enough pressure to clear them up. When the man didn't fade, I knew I was still under the effects of the toxic water. Real people don't walk around an asylum clutching a rust-tinged cleaver. I shifted uncomfortably as I realized that it wasn't rust on the blade. It was dried blood. The only thing that held me back from charging was his demeanor.

The cleaver hung in a loose, relaxed grip. There was nothing threatening about his posture. Well, maybe his size. His girth took up the majority of the doorway, with shoulders broad enough that he'd have to pull them together if he planned on entering. He had the short beefy arms of competitive power lifters, and the belly to match. The man possessed the face of a flabby toad that had somehow learned to grimace. His skin was unnaturally pallid and greasy-looking. Meaty fingers scratched at several days' worth of stubble. Other than that, he loomed there, staring harmlessly.

A person I couldn't make out passed by in the hall without pausing to regard the cleaver-wielding man.

*Yup, illusion.*

The apparition thrust his index finger at me, beckoning me closer.

"Uh, no offense there, big guy, but most people aren't keen on getting near somebody with a bloody cleaver in their hands. I mean, I'm sure you're a nice fictional guy, but I'm going to stay right here." I jabbed a finger to the bed.

He raised his cleaver and I sprang from the bed. I paused when he brought it toward his chest. His lips came together as he frowned thoughtfully, eyes glancing down at his midsection. With his free hand, he pulled at the thick and grimy apron he wore. The next second he pinched the culinary garment over the sharp edge of the cleaver, running the blade through it several times until it came back clean. The weapon fell back to his side and once again he motioned for me to come closer.

"Smartass," I mumbled.

He didn't respond. Instead, he turned and shuffled away.

"Hey! If you think I'm going to follow you back to your van..." I trailed off as I lost sight of him. "Damnit," I muttered, sprinting toward the doorway. I caught sight of him lumbering away down the hall. "Hey, wait, jerk off!" I tore after him, sidestepping awkwardly to avoid somebody as I did.

The "Butcher," as I dubbed him, did not give any indication he heard my calls. He plodded toward his unknown destination. I lagged far behind. Someone stepped in front of me. We collided and I threw a quick apology their way.

"Charles?"

It was Gus. "Can't talk now. Chasing an illusion. My only clue."

His face sank deeper into confusion. I set off after the man with the cleaver before Gus could utter a word. The apparition turned a corner and I picked up my pace, hoping to keep him in sight. I was dimly aware of the odd glances I was getting as I barreled through the hall. I was getting close to shoving people out of my way. As I rounded the corner, I saw the butcher nearing the end of the hall. His body flickered from opaque to a vaporous translucent blue. That gave me pause. I wondered if he was an asylum ghost here to help. Or, was he truly an illusion? I hoped he didn't have a more nefarious purpose, like leading me to the phage.

Technically, that was what I wanted, but not this way. I would've preferred the element of surprise and a chance to plan. I spat a curse as I realized that regardless of his intentions, I didn't have a choice. Without him, I'd be back to nothing.

The notion spurred me to spring after him. I huffed random obscenities as I ran. Strangely enough, he paused at the end of the hall this time and turned to face me. He stood eerily motionless as he waited for me to catch up.

I stopped a few feet from him and panted. "You're in pretty good shape for a husky guy."

He stared.

I sighed in exasperation. "You take lessons on communication from Church?"

He disregarded me and swiveled his head to a hall on the right. He even went so far as raising a meaty hand to point to the way ahead. I followed his finger down the hall and had to squint. The end seemed miles off, obscured in the haziness that accompanies a mirage. What I could make out was a pool of tar like material spread across the floor. Noxious-looking vapor rose from it.

I gave him a quizzical look. "What gives?"

With a single finger, he pointed down, bobbing his arm to make sure I got the gist.

"Hate to break it to ya, pal, but there's marble tiling under that gook." I stomped the floor to make my point. "I can't go down." As soon as I said it, the entire floor began exuding a black vapor. I shielded my mouth on instinct. The stuff ensconced me and I had to remember that I was hallucinating. I let my arm fall from its mask like position and inhaled. The black vapor refused to deviate from its course. It sailed up and past my nostrils, failing to enter. The dark steamy substance didn't look to be a threat. "So what is this stuff?"

The silent butcher breathed in, exaggerating the effort by wafting his free hand beneath his nose. His belly expanded to monstrous proportions as he continued to take in air. Just when I thought his illusory ass was about to go St. Helens, he exhaled. His frame started shrinking back to normal. After the display, he pointed a finger to his temple, sending it into a circular motion.

"Ah. This stuff's what's driving people crazy…er. Wait, I thought it was the water?"

He gave me a patient stare.

Two fingers bounced off my skull as I tapped my

forehead in realization. "Right. This is—what? A representation of the taint in the water." I looked around at the rising charcoal mist. "It's in the water and coming from below this place. What's down there?"

The butcher blinked, running his fingernails across his stubble in a soundless scratch.

"Fine." I sighed and pulled the muscles in my shoulders together as I stood up straighter. "Let's go into the spooky dark below," I said to the apparition. Since he wasn't really there, I was actually talking to myself. I waved at the smoke-like vision, trying to clear the air as I walked down the hall. A slicing heat swept across the back of my hand. I pulled back. "What the hell?"

The butcher stood at my side; his cleaver sported a thin stream of crimson.

"The hell?" When he didn't answer, I sent a fist hurtling toward his amphibious face. I winced as I became aware of the fact I was punching an apparition. My eyes shut tight in anticipation of colliding with the wall behind. Something connected with my knuckles. A brick coated in layers of putty. When I opened my eyes, my fist was lodged in the soft tissue of the butcher's cheeks.

"Holy shit! I hit you!" That shouldn't have happened. I recoiled from the large man wielding one helluva of a culinary implement. "Uh." I held up a pair of hands in an effort to calm him. "No hard feelings, right? I mean, you're a big guy. You look like you can take a punch."

He didn't twitch. The giant stood there, watching. It was reminiscent of Church in a way.

Well, if Church started the Crisco diet anyways.

His movement brought me back to attention. The large man pointed down the hall, waggling a finger in admonishment.

"Wait, I can't go down that way or something?"

He rested one of his giant fingers along the base of his neck, slowly dragging it across. A warning about the phage.

I snorted dismissively. "Not if I kill it first."

His eyebrows shifted and he turned his head. He gave me a dubious look.

Really? Now I had hallucinations doubting my ability?

"I'm going," I resolved with a low guttural growl.

He gave me the "Nice knowing you" look.

Everybody's a critic, even the imaginary.

I flashed him an extra wide smile and flipped him a finger of my own. Call me petulant, but I'm not one to take crap from illusions, especially my own.

I left him behind and made my way toward the far end of the hall. My hand moved of its own accord at times, trying to brush away the nonexistent fumes. The pool of tar drew closer. I had no idea what to expect. Sure, it was an illusion, but it had to represent something. At least, I believed it had to. After all, they weren't solely hallucinations, but a tool to lead me to the phage. Or to lead it to me. I didn't know what I'd be able to do if the phage got the drop on me. I had no weapon. Then there was my condition. Tripping on supernatural psychedelics isn't the best state to be in when confronting a monster.

I was an arm's length from the pool now. Its surface roiled like a flame was beneath it. My fingers waggled in anticipation and I reached toward it. Every bubble forming on its surface erupted. Geysers of thin motor oil sprung toward the ceiling, attaching themselves like strands of a grim cobweb. They collapsed on themselves, shrinking in thickness and flattening out. A sickly black curtain spread before me. A noticeable seam of white ran down the middle. Seemed simple enough.

Except I'd learned over the years that when the paranormal are involved, nothing is what it seems. And nothing is ever simple.

I formed a pair of stiff shovels with my hands and thrust them into the sludgy seam. I pulled. I met some resistance as the gooey material clung together. It refused to part no matter how much I huffed and puffed. Leveraging more of my weight, I leaned into the wall and used the muscles in my back as well as my arms. The curtain spread, peeling away from itself and leaving clinging trails of gook. I reminded myself that this, too, was imaginary and stepped through the tendrils of foul gunk.

My arms spun in circles as my legs almost cut out below me. Teetering, I flailed, trying to regain my diminished sense of balance. My vision adjusted and I stared down a spiraled stairway of stone. My feet hung well over the first step.

"This is one hell of an illusion."

I stepped down to the next stair. I wondered if I was, in reality, descending a flight of stairs. If I was, where in the asylum had such a place? A layer of chilled cotton clouded my thoughts as I tried to recall the path I had taken to get here. My chest strained as I worked my way down. Breathing became a laborious task and my arm tingled.

"No," I panted through clenched teeth, denying the heart attack. But the heart attack never came. I cracked a smile, telling myself that this time, what I felt were the symptoms of my warped mind. Calmed by my understanding of it I took another step.

Apparently the heart attack was indeed a Jedi mind trick—one meant to distract me from my legs. The second my foot contacted the floor, it continued bending. My leg collapsed on itself like a bit of rope. Walls and steps passed by as I tumbled. I didn't even have the chance to blurt out a string of ever-creative obscenities before hitting the bottom.

The first impact sent me into a world of varying reds and whites. My vision went haywire. Everything from electric bursts of pain to sharp jabs and heavy thuds filled my body. I don't know how long I fell. You lose track of time when you're being subjected to skull-jarring impacts. One agonizingly-long moment I was bouncing down the stairs like a Graves slinky; the next, I was staring at a ceiling that was spinning with no sign of stopping.

Time has a funny way of escaping when you're in the Neravene, or when you're under the influence of magical LSD. My forearm rested atop my eyes as I lay prone on the cold stone. I pulled it away and noticed my tattoo had lost the four. Thirteen hours remained.

Normally that would have spurred me into action, but every instinct objected to that. It felt nice to rest and let my thoughts wander. As used to pain as I am, I'm not fond of it. Nor am I keen on constantly absorbing it without reprieve. My breath came in deep, calming inhalations that did nothing to ease my aching body.

*How the hell did I lose another hour, and so fast?* Even thinking about it sent a twinge lancing through my head. There was only one conclusion that fit. My ingestion of the phage's toxins hampered my perception of time. My senses were dulled. A flare of pain rolled through my ribs as I entertained the thought of moving in slow-motion down the halls. God knows how long it actually took me to get as far as I did. All the way to the bottom of a stairway.

Talk about progress.

All manner of body parts cracked, groaned, and cried out against my sudden motion to rise. The joints from my shoulders to my wrists quaked as I tried to push myself up. Molten globules burned within them. Folding my tongue between my teeth, I bit down—lightly. I redirected some of the pain to my tongue and strained the muscles in my arms. A forceful huff of wind left my nostrils. Something warm tagged along. The stone floor bore a minute splattering of ruby jelly. Using the knuckle of my forefinger, I rubbed it against the soft cartilage. It came away red. Thankfully it wasn't broken, just battered.

My left arm responded a bit late after my fingers dug into it. A few motions with it reassured me that, while injured, it was functional. Good thing too. Another set of repugnant-looking curtains blocked my path. Vibrations rang through my throat as I summoned up a glob of saliva. My face twisted in contempt as I spat at the wall. Of course it didn't react. I wasn't expecting it to.

For the second time in an hour, my balance wavered as my heel crashed into the curtains. They absorbed the impact and exerted a force of their own up my leg. I lost the battle and fell. The ground greeted my ass with an impact that made its way to my jaw, rattling my teeth.

I shot up, willed away the pain, and launched myself into the wall of demonic Play-Doh. I didn't peel it apart like before. I barreled into it, trying to separate it with sheer force. My knees struck the wall and it faltered. I didn't let up. I swung at the wall, releasing the frustration I'd accrued over the case. With a final surge and crash, I plowed through the seam, falling into a scene from Tolkien.

# Chapter Twenty-Two

Hanging gardens don't belong in mental asylums. Despite my certainty of that fact, a masterwork of stone and flora surrounded me. At least...I'm sure it was a masterwork at some point in time.

Someone had forgotten to pay for garden maintenance. My fingers trailed over grass that brushed against my knees. Columns of stone losing the battle against time reached for the sky around me. Beams of aged wood ran between them. It was a miracle the wood still held together. The place made my stomach feel like it was nursing a bundle of agitated snakes.

Antiquated vases of brass hung from chains that looked close to breaking. Exotic plants sprouted from them in varieties that only a botanist could identify. In the distance was a mass of deteriorating stonework that could easily have been a city at some point.

"Fuck me," I breathed as it struck me. "Babylon." The hallucinations were giving me a vision of Babylon. *Or its fall*, I reasoned. The crumbling architecture, neglected grass and deserted city made it clear.

A coolness no larger than a penny hit my head. My fingers dug into my hair. One of them came away with a moist sheen. I looked up and found channels of pitted stone hanging in canted angles. Another sphere struck my face. My fingertips slid over my cheek with abrasive intent after I saw what emanated from the aqueducts. Tendrils of blackened vapor rose from the old stone.

I bounded forward. It was a battle for level surface as I navigated the cobbled stones masked by stalks of grass. I may not have suffered any consequences from inhaling the mist-like gunk with the butcher, but I had felt the water dripping on my face. I wasn't going to take a chance. It was likely it was tainted, but the question of how I'd even felt it occupied my mind.

Illusions were and are just that—illusions. The list of creatures that can conjure something you can interact with is short. My mind pulled up images of the Ifrit from my last case in New York, and the shadow it had summoned. It was a type of apparition that was as close to real as it could get. But that took a level of power a Babylonian phage didn't possess.

There were two options: the grass and water were real, or I believed I was feeling them. That fit more within the realm of what I knew about this breed of phage. They couldn't whip up actual horrors, but they could make the mind believe them, and that's enough. The mind is a terribly potent and wonderful thing. It can subject you to a myriad of emotions—all with physical effects.

Anger may not have a physical form, but you can sure as hell feel it on the inside. Your heart picks up in tempo. Your temples drum as a slew of chemicals race through your blood. It's the same principle behind phantom limbs. A person loses an arm or a leg in some tragedy, yet they have moments where they can feel their missing limbs. A Babylonian phage exploits the most powerful organ in the human anatomy—the brain. It perverts one of the most fantastically exciting and petrifying things humans possess.

The ability to feel.

The tainted water was manipulating my brain on a level where I thought I was *feeling* things. The only thing real was the ground beneath me. Unable to shake off the effects of the drugs, I legged it, reminding myself that I was still within the asylum. No matter how powerful the hallucinations were, I refused to let them jeopardize my case. I was using them to find the phage, not the other way around.

*Maybe if I keep telling myself that, I'll believe it.* The grim thought echoed through my skull.

A low whistle left my lips as I made my way to an upright block of stone that would dwarf a shipping container. The thing would've taken dozens of cranes to move and yet somehow, it was raised to stand vertically. Walking past it, I entered the ruins of what I assumed was the fabled city. My intestines knotted as I moved through the maze-like remains. The air felt almost like syrup, thick and heavy. No sounds filled my ears as I progressed. Soft earth muffled my footsteps. The scene, the silence—all of it was dissonantly beautiful. And that, most of all, is what sent a tongue of grease slithering down my neck.

I walked through the remains of one of the greatest cities in the world. A city brought low by paranormal creatures that didn't just inspire horror, but generated it. And it was as tranquil as a fucking Disney movie.

*It's quiet. Too quiet,* giggled a voice of insanity.

"Fucking clichés," I spat.

Something chalky white raced along the edge of my vision. Strands of muscle worked like rebar to keep my neck from tearing as I swiveled my head. I turned in time to catch sight of...nothing. No monster. No dirt or dust kicked into the air—nothing. The rocks were undisturbed. A couple of spindly-looking flowers swayed in the wind.

Which would've been fine if there was any wind. I may have been sort of tipsy, but something *did* move through there. This freak might've preyed on fear, but fear works both ways. It doesn't render you completely helpless. With fear comes an edge of hyperawareness. Every possible ounce of human potential is squeezed out. I risked shutting my eyes for the briefest of moments, taking in several breaths. I wasn't working to decrease my fear. I was taking control of it.

The hairs on my arms stood at attention. Miniscule bumps formed over my skin. Breathing sent a menthol-like chill through my nose, but there was no actual drop in temperature.

"Okay," I breathed. "It knows you're here, and you know it's here." I spread a wary gaze over my surroundings. No movement. No sounds. I found myself sympathizing with Arnold. I now knew what if felt like being hunted by the Predator. Except, in his case, it was a giant guy in a costume. I doubted I'd be so lucky.

So far the phage had avoided direct confrontation. That was a plus. Given how fast the thing could move and what it could do to my mind, I wasn't itching for a fight. At least, not a fair one. I needed one hell of an advantage if I was going to take on that freak. I clenched my fists several times to loosen the tension in my body.

A blur of white zipped by.

I refused to react. The thing was baiting me, trying to unnerve me. Another cooling rush of air sailed up my nose. I let it settle there for a bit before exhaling. This thing could've attacked me already if it wanted to. So I ignored the motions and moved on.

I passed through a narrow alley and stopped. There were markings on the stone. Rudimentary in design, they still got the message across. A roughly humanoid shape—slender, chalky white with lengthy appendages—covered the wall. The ends of each limb trailed off at odd angles. The drawings were the products of haste...or something else.

Peculiar writing accompanied the markings. Akkadian if I had to guess. I couldn't understand the language. The way it was written told me it probably wasn't legible in the first place. It had the look of something scrawled in a panicked flurry. I peered closer. The stone bled.

Color seeped from the walls, shaping themselves into all manner of images and words I couldn't discern. All of them made one thing clear: Charles didn't lose his mind. It was broken. And the guy still managed to ID the phage while losing his marbles. That was an impressive feat. One I was going to reward by ganking this monster.

I tore myself from the wall and moved out of the alley. A long stretch of dirt greeted me. It was puzzling deciding where to go next.

Screams filled the air. I turned and saw a pair of children rushing towards me.

Their ruddy faces were caked in grime and tears. They ran from some unseen terror.

I waved. "Hey!" They showed no signs of hearing me.

As the nearest of the two children passed by, I reached out. My fingers sailed through their arm and exited out their torso. The children kept moving until they faded from sight.

I rubbed my eyes. The hallucinations were starting to get the better of me. I reacted to those children as if they were real. Their screams had thrown me off focus.

I shook my head and hoofed it down the path the kids had taken. Hollow sounds thrummed through the wind. I felt like I was walking through a ghost town. Only, here, the ghosts still lingered—the ghosts of the asylum, the ghosts of

Babylon. There seemed to be no end to the remnants of the dead.

A thought crept into the back of my mind as I progressed down the road. My perception of time, among many things, was altered. The urge to check my forearm won over and I looked. For the first time in checking it, I was able to breathe a sigh of relief. My timeline remained the same.

Too bad the scenery hadn't.

A jarring flicker of color swept over me like a tsunami crashing over rocks. Someone left the faucet on near a megaphone. The magnified sound of water falling in steady drips echoed through my ears. Aged service lights cast an unreliable pale glow over wet stone, darkened to an iron gray. My head swam with the cavernous roaring.

Before I could exhale, the experience faded. I wasn't aware that I'd been moving during the mental onslaught. I couldn't have moved. Regardless, lengthy fingers of wheat surrounded me. I blinked and pinched the tip of the nearest stalk. It broke free with ease. I rolled it between my fingers before sending it tumbling through the air.

I craned my neck back to search for the city. An endless ocean of pale gold stretched out in every direction. Tufts of wheat waved. Something scraped against them and I braced.

Humming—melodic and feminine—graced my ears. She came into clarity. She was dressed like she had walked off the set of a Greco-Roman movie. Dark-featured and sun-weathered, unbound hair hanging past her shoulders. She ran her fingers over the tips of the golden stalks. The gentle hum increased.

Normally a person appearing out of thin air would get my heart thumpin' a bit. After the incident with the children, I didn't feel the need to invest any energy or time with this illusion.

I gave her a brusque nod. "Heya. You're gorgeous and all, and I know we're alone in a field and that's giving you ideas of a romantic nature. The thing is…" I cut off as she drew a sharp breath. Her head snapped up, eyes seeing me for the first time. Her pupils dilated. I snapped my fingers before her nose, causing her to recoil. "You…you can see me?"

Her eyes ballooned as she stood rooted to the spot.

"Hey," I breathed in a soft and reassuring voice. "It's okay." I extended an open hand. "I'm one of the good guys. I gank monsters." As I said it, another voice went through my head. *You're an idiot. You're talking to an illusion.* "Shut up." The woman took another step back. "Oh, sorry about that. Wasn't talking to you. That was directed to my cynicism angel. I've got one squatting inside my brainpan because he's too lazy to perch on my shoulder. Between you and me, he's an ass."

A hand flew to her chest, clutching it as if she were in pain. Her free hand shot up, fingers splayed. A clear message for me to back off.

"Okay." I held up my own hands in a gesture to calm her. "I get it. Graves no bueno here." I backed off a step.

Her mouth parted. The scream ricocheted through my eardrums and jarred my eyeballs. The girl had a set of pipes. She muttered something incomprehensible. It sounded like a prayer as she backpedaled.

The back of my neck tickled. The hairs located there shifted. Forget hearing the acute puffs of air behind me; I could feel them! I spat a curse and snapped around. My fist careened into the space behind me.

A rush of white mass hurtled at me, passing through my body without a problem—for the creature at least. Hands chipped out of ice gripped tight around the base of my throat and heart. I fell to a knee. The ground moved like it was set on a turntable. Still reeling, I fought to right myself and figure out what the hell happened.

A shriek helped clear the cobwebs. Her eyes were shut tight, as if that simple act could deny the reality of what was happening. The woman's hands thrashed, trying to bat the creature away. It didn't work. It was my first real look at the phage in action. That was the only thing holding me firmly in place.

I took it in as quick as I could. Some people tan; some people don't. This thing went overboard on the sunblock treatment. It had arms that belonged to a scarecrow. They were slender, twisted things that raked at the woman. Wine-colored tendrils flailed as it continued its assault.

Instinct took swings at reason within my skull. It told

me to charge the creature. Pinching the bridge of my nose, I inhaled and shut my eyes. *It's not real*, I reminded myself.

Another scream tore me from my reflection. "Damnit," I hissed. It didn't matter if it was real or not. If I see a monster or someone being mauled by one, I get involved. Too many cases. Too many monsters. It gets drilled into you. I rushed the creature and swept at the nearest of its tentacle-like appendages. My hand passed through it like I was grabbing fog.

Illusion or not, I had to try. I had to. You can't stand by watching something like that. Suffering is real. It doesn't matter if you're witnessing it from afar or right before you. It doesn't matter if it's suffering from the past or present. It all hurts.

The creature's tendrils stopped their flurried movement. They worked to restrain the woman.

I lashed out with a kick to the creature's sternum.

The woman released the sort of scream that tears the lining in your throat. It was peppered with sobs as her body shook. The phage's serpent-like appendages coursed over her body and toward her face. She ceased her frantic motions. Her lips trembled and tears streamed from her eyes. I could see her quit.

The phage wasn't content with silence—or sobbing for that matter. Tendrils slipped into every orifice of her face. Wet twigs cracked as the phage's limbs wormed their way up her nose. Cartilage and bone broke. Her lids parted and there was little white left in her eyes. The pupils were large and watery.

Her body convulsed like someone in the throes of an electric seizure. The phage's tendrils slithered into her ears next. The mouth followed. Dribbles of black grease formed in her tear ducts. They clung there, trembling, yet refusing to fall. Seeing someone of her complexion pale is enough to freeze your innards. It doesn't matter how many times you've seen monsters kill someone. It's never pretty. You never get used to it.

I could only hazard a guess as to what was going on inside of her. The phage's tendrils were high-powered jets, sending streams of pressurized toxins through her body. Her brain was engorged with tainted blood. Her sight flooded with the worst horrors she could imagine. Same with her touch, her sense of smell—all of it. She wasn't seeing nightmares; she was *living* them—dying in them.

Her eyes turned to me, registering my appearance. I met her gaze and couldn't tear myself away. The color in her eyes began to fade. She stopped moving.

The last bits of moisture in my throat fled in a shower of spittle. My tonsils felt sunburned. Something clawed at the lining of my esophagus, leaving it raw. Sand filled my lungs and dried them. I panted as my screams echoed over still fields of wheat.

Liquid wax, onyx in color, welled in her lids. It gushed forward to mask her face. Her ears leaked the same substance until tar-like bubbles frothed from her mouth. The phage withdrew its tendrils in a slow, almost pleasurable-looking fashion. Black mercury poured from her body and marred the gold of wheat surrounding her. A gust of wind rolled in. The small brush tops of grain bowed to it. It passed by and, with it, so did the dead woman and phage.

Sharp cracks sounded from within my knuckles. My fingernails dug into my palms. "Hey, douche canoe!" I roared. "When I find you, I'm going to shove my boot so far up your chalky white ass, you'll taste the Kiwi!"

Something scraped like dead leaves brushing over a sidewalk. Shifting my shoulders, I turned my head. Another phage loomed several paces away, hunched. For a thing without eyes, it looked at me like I was an Everlasting Gobstopper. Bodiless screams filled the air. I refused to look for their source.

"I get it," I snarled. "This is you showing me your greatest hits or something? The fall of Babylon?" My clap echoed around us. I paused before clapping again. "Congratulations for the epic effects. So, what, you wanted me to share in your nostalgia?"

The illusion didn't reply.

I exhaled through my nose and shook my head. I turned my back to the phage. My voice dropped to a whisper just loud enough for the phage to hear. "When I find you, I'm going to stake you, right through the chest. I'm going to tear your fucking heart out!" Each syllable dripped with venom. I took several steps before my back exploded in pain. The impact sent me stumbling. I regained my balance and sent my elbow crashing behind me without looking.

I connected.

Whirling about, I brought my hands up, fists clenched. I'd just smashed my elbow into the freak's face! A thin line made its way across its forehead, presumably from where I'd struck. A darkened jelly oozed from the cut. The phage made no sounds of anger. It didn't even seem to notice the cut. It blurred into motion that I couldn't register. All the air was driven from my lungs and my vision shifted.

Gray brick, waning lights, and the sound of dripping water replaced the fields of wheat. And faded just as quick. *The hell was that?* I shook off the phage's hit.

Breathing like I'd run a marathon with my mouth and nose duct taped, I glared at the phage as my body heaved. One second it was feet away; the next, its fingers dug into my arms. Each one felt like a blunt needle squeezing with hydraulic pressure. This thing was strong! But I was smarter and downright uppity.

Racking my throat, I worked up whatever mixture of saliva and bile I could. I spat. It struck the phage with a *thwook*, trailing over the thin skin where the phage's eyes should've been. My childish action hadn't elicited a reaction, so I used my head. My noggin snapped forward and crunched into the phage's skull. It reeled, its grip faltering.

Releasing a snarl, I covered the distance between us. I wrapped my arms around it. We tumbled to the ground. One of its tendrils brushed near my mouth. I got stupid. Opening my mouth, I clamped down, sinking my teeth into its flesh. The creature's body spasmed as I cut into the tendril.

It tasted like calamari...five years past its expiration date and filled with sewage.

I gagged and let the chunk fall from my mouth. Something with the consistency of cottage cheese flooded my pie hole. It squirmed within my mouth. The crap was alive! I strained the muscles in my throat, working to keep the monster gook from going down.

I retched. A torrent of colors shot out of me, courtesy of the Lucky Charms. A myriad of colors swam together and covered the phage. Bet it didn't expect me to upchuck all over it. My body heaved and something somersaulted in my gullet. The pit of my stomach felt hollow as I tried to keep myself from vomiting again. Something pushed against my ribcage and I tumbled off the phage. Another jolt arced through my body as I scrambled, trying to get to my feet. The phage bolted.

"That's right," I slurred, fighting a hiccup. "You better run!" Knuckling my eyes, I searched for the phage. There was no way it jumped me only to scamper when things got bad. Heck, it wasn't even a tough situation for it. I couldn't have killed the phage no matter how much I wanted to. All I managed to do was headbutt the sucker and puke my guts over it. My ribs shook as I laughed. I wondered if that's what caused the creature to panic. Between hurling on it and taking a literal chunk out of the thing, it probably viewed me in a more dangerous light.

Good. It better be as wary of me as I was of it. If it erred on the side of caution, I had a chance of surviving the hallucinations. If it decided to jump me again, things wouldn't go so well.

"Screw it," I panted and turned tail to wobble away. I had gotten as much as I could for the moment.

Remaining under the influence of the hallucinogen was becoming a hindrance rather than a boon. I had found the phage, it had kicked my ass, and I'd thrown up. Not the stunning victory I was looking for. At least I had come away with some knowledge. Seeing the phage let me know I was right about what we were dealing with. I sort of had an idea of where it was holed up. The deteriorating ruins at the heart of an ancient empire.

I'm sure there was a map that would lead me back there.

Endless kernels of wheat brushed against the back of my hands as I plowed on. With no bearings, it wasn't easy to navigate my way through the fields. Everything blurred into a smear of yellow-gold. Hollow dripping filled my head. My vision swam as I walked. The air felt like walking through low hanging fog. Dampness tickled my skin. The sun was overhead and I was walking through fields of grains. If anything, it should've felt warm and dry. Someone was playing competitive ping-pong within my skull. Sporadic bursts of impact jarred my head.

Cupping my hand over my eyes, I kept moving, trying to get clear of my surroundings. My vision snapped out of clarity like a nineties television with a bad antenna. I must've been burning through the phage's toxin, courtesy of my regenerative abilities. Whoever pulled my strings ensured my meat suits could take a pummeling. Guess they didn't want their toy broken so easily.

As my body worked the toxin out of my system, my muscles started feeling gummy. My legs turned to rubber and caused me to wobble. I peeked through the slit between my fingers. I shouldn't have. The world waned beneath me. Gold gave way to old concrete, not the marbled floors of the asylum I expected to see. Then it all snapped back into vibrancy. Stalks of wheat around me. The toxin wasn't letting go without a fight.

I pushed through it, eyes shut, willing my legs to carry me further. Nothing was going to stop me from making it back to Ortiz. *Nothing*, I resolved.

The pain intensified. Memories flooded my mind. Charles sat cross-legged on the floor of the rec room, hunched over paper and pad—coloring. He scribbled at a pace that would whittle the crayon to nothing. The image washed away like a stain splashed with bleach. Another filled its place. Charles huddled under his blanket, clutching at his head, twitching. His mouth was tight, the skin around his eyes wrinkled under the strain. Beads of sweat dotted his face. A leg kicked out in random intervals. He screamed in silence.

"Jesus," I breathed as I endured the broken slideshow of memories.

A plump nurse with the demeanor of a favored aunt smiled at Charles. His expression twisted as he spoke. It looked like he was struggling to remember how. Charles' mouth moved in odd shapes, sounding words out. The nurse patted her bun of hair, the color of a dulled penny. She gestured to her sides at nothing and Charles followed it, nodding at unoccupied space. That too rolled into another memory. Doctor Cartwright stood in Charles' room, hands digging into Charles' shoulders, fighting to restrain him. The doc's face slipped between a lined beaky looking one to paper white—devoid of most features. Tissue paper thin skin stretched over his eye sockets. It had a toothless mouth with thick bits of skin hanging between and connecting the lips.

I shook my head and wheezed from the onslaught of imagery and experiences. I stumbled. My hand lashed out to find balance on a textured surface that was like dried plaster. I removed the hand shielding my face. I blinked. Marbled floors. Drywall. A long corridor. I turned back to find that the hall ended in another split. There was no discernable way back to where I'd encountered the phage.

"Figures." Compulsion took over and I glanced down at my arm. Roaring, I sent my fist into the nearby wall. Another hour gone.

Twelve left.

Flecks of drywall fell as I pulled my fist from the cracked surface. Shoving my hands into my pockets, I moved at a brisk pace. It wasn't going to do me a whole lot of good to be found near a damaged wall and screaming. Straitjackets, anesthetic and restraints were not going to help this case. And I didn't need any more bondage experiences.

"Charles!"

"Ortiz?" I said, confused as to why she was running down the hall after me. "What's up?"

Her voice was neutral but her eyes shook. They were dilated. "It's Lizzie." She bit the corner of her lip, pausing. I could see she didn't want to go on.

"What?"

"She's been taken."

# Chapter Twenty-Three

"What?" I barked.

Ortiz flinched.

"Sorry. Sorry. I…" I trailed off, pressing my palm to my forehead.

"I don't know what happened. She was in bed. One second I was leaning against the wall in her room, and the next moment I felt like I hadn't eaten in days. I thought I was going blind at first. The room turned dark. It was like a cloud of ink…like before."

"Myrk." A guttural burble formed in my throat. "I don't get it." I pressed hard with my palm. "I just saw that freak not too long ago. Hell, I fought it."

"You what?" snapped Ortiz.

It was my turn to flinch. "When I was searching for where the phage could be hiding, I might've bumped into it…by accident."

Ortiz arched a single eyebrow. Her posture tightened and I noted subtle aggression in it. "Didn't you say something about not engaging the monster if you came across it?"

I let out a low mocking whistle. "Engaging, huh?"

Her eyes narrowed.

"Yeah, yeah." I tried to assuage her anger. "You wouldn't believe it all. Long story short, I tripped out, fell down some stairs, ended up in Babylon—"

"What?"

"Hallucination," I explained, spitting the word. "I saw Babylon. Bits and pieces of it anyways. It was broken down. I saw people. Memories of the phage, I think. Its greatest hits collection, reliving Babylon's collapse. I saw images of it attacking people." I stopped as I recalled the woman.

"Charles, what's wrong?"

I told her.

"I'm sorry, Charles. It must've been hard watching and not being able to do a thing."

"It was." My voice was raw. "Take me to Lizzie's room. Tell me everything that happened again, as it happened. Leave nothing out."

Ortiz nodded and took off. I followed, knuckling the sides of my head as I did. An imaginary congestion clouded all thought. I felt like a puppet being tugged along. I was going through motions. I kept walking best I could. The more I pushed, the more I felt like weak strings pulling on other bits of string. Despite all of it, there was a little girl out there in the hands of a monster.

Thoughts are powerful things. Never let anyone tell you different. That singular notion of Lizzie alone with the phage did more to wash away my weariness than anything else. My body tightened as I picked up my pace. It didn't take us more than a handful of minutes to get to Lizzie's room.

Ortiz went in first. I shadowed behind her. Upon entering, her body went rigid. Her hands balled tight by her sides. I could see the muscles in her neck and arms strain. The door crashed shut after I batted it with the base of my fist. I adopted a similar posture to Ortiz's when I saw who was sitting on Lizzie's bed.

She had swapped her pearl spun shift for simpler clothing, donning the outfit of an asylum nurse. And none of it did a thing to dull her unearthly beauty. Her hair hadn't changed. It was still done up with nine distinct tails of white which bobbed occasionally. She sat on the edge of the bed, leaning back with her legs crossed in comfort.

"You," I said without any particular fondness. We may have needed her, but she had damn well taken her time showing up. That wasn't winning her any points with me.

Lyshae's ears twitched. A lazy feline-like grin slid over her face. "Charles." She emphasized the name a bit more than I would've liked. She inclined her head in the slightest toward Ortiz. "Woman."

Ortiz's body and fists tightened further. "I have a name."

Lyshae's smile widened. "Oh, do tell?" Her eyes flashed with a hungry look.

"No!" My tone could have driven nails through a wall. Ortiz gave me a look. "Bad idea to trade names with someone like her." I made it clear how dangerous it was without having to elaborate further. Ortiz nodded.

Lyshae sniffed with an air of indignance.

"Why are you here?"

"To check on my investment of course."

Ortiz stiffened beside me.

"What's with the scrubs? Your cheap dress get dirty?" I said.

Lyshae's expression flickered before she addressed Ortiz. "Always so pleasant, isn't he?" Ortiz didn't reply. Lyshae turned back to me. "A choice. I felt it appropriate attire to wear as I sought to aid you in your case."

"Huh?" I replied with an abundance of Vincent Graves wit.

"Your case," she repeated in a voice reserved for someone rather dimwitted. "We struck an accord, did we not?"

I bristled under the reminder. Three favors. Three distinct, potentially dangerous favors that would be well out of my comfort zone. Lyshae would see to that.

"Yes."

She gestured to herself with a downward wave of her hands. "It was necessary. It would have been difficult to walk around the asylum and engage in conversation with people as my normal self."

"Normal self?" Ortiz piped up. "All she did was change her outfit. She doesn't look like anyone who works here."

Lyshae rolled her eyes. "Would you care to explain, or should I?"

"She's a master illusionist—"

"Thank you," she interjected.

I glared at her. "She can pass herself off as anyone she wants to—with a little magical help. To her, it's as natural as breathing."

"That's mildly unsettling," Ortiz murmured under her breath.

"Yeah, mildly." It definitely was.

Lyshae reached behind herself and pulled something into view. It would've been handy if we were hunting

Dracula. The stake was the length of my forearm and nearly as thick. The tip was charred black with—if Lyshae had done it right—olive oil. I don't make the rules on these things.

"Uh, do I want to know where you were hiding that? That seems like an awfully big piece of wood for you to have been hiding up your ass."

Lyshae ignored me. Good humor is wasted on the supernatural. "Take it." She reversed her grip on it and offered it to me. I accepted it with a slight bow of my head. Despite my occasional rudeness toward her, real respect is something that should be shown to many of the supernatural.

"Thank you."

Lyshae inclined her head as well. "As I made myself acquainted with the asylum and its many occupants, I came across several interesting things." She paused for a moment. "That was quite poetic, Charles—your writing on the wall. Accurate as well."

I blinked, trying to recall all Charles had scribbled down. Apart from the imagery, nothing of value came to me.

"I spoke with some of the staff here. They provided wonderful insight, and shared some rather touching photographs." Lyshae's eyes sparkled with something I couldn't quite pin down.

"Look," I cut in with a wave of my hand, "you have anything that's actually useful? You know, like a 'gank this person,' or 'the object you seek is here' sort of thing?"

She let out a rueful chuckle. "Now, when was that ever part of our bargain?"

"Get out."

Lyshae bowed her head once more. She passed by us with smooth, graceful steps. The Kitsune paused at the door and looked over her shoulder. "Remember." Lyshae rolled her hand with a bit of flair, displaying three fingers before tucking them away. "You owe me." She smiled. Each word felt like weighted shackles snapping onto me.

I let my anger slip by, resisting the urge to cave into it. Lyshae was a problem for another time. She had come through on her end, supplying us with the weapon to kill the phage. There was a young girl who needed my attention, all of it, focused and unclouded by frustration.

Lyshae opened the door, gliding through it with refined movements no mortal could match. A nurse with a pinched face walked by. She saw Lyshae and froze. Ortiz and I did as well. The nurse's eyes seemed unfocused as she regarded Lyshae.

Her head tilted to the side. "Have we…"

"I'm new here." Lyshae smiled, her voice sweet and bubbly. She went so far as to bob in place, oozing enthusiastic energy. The nurse shook her head, features still set in a mask of confusion.

"Oh, yeah, hi." She extended her hand to Lyshae. They shook, and the nurse moved on.

Lyshae shot us a pleased grin before moving out of view.

"Show off," I grumbled.

"Bitch," Ortiz mumbled and I snorted.

I moved to Lizzie's bed and fell onto it. My knuckles buried themselves into my eyes as I rested my head atop them. "So, tell me everything that happened." A yawn escaped my lungs and I forced myself up.

Ortiz positioned herself against the far wall, leaning against it. "I was here." She hooked a thumb to the wall she leaned against. "Lizzie—where you are now. She was resting, but still awake. It was like that for a while—quiet. No monsters. No trouble." There was a bitterness in the way she said *monsters*.

The pressure in my head increased. I roped Ortiz into this world not once, but twice. No matter what I did, I seemed to be dragging people into my hellish life of late. Ortiz, Lizzie, and God knew who'd be next.

"My head felt like I was wearing a ridiculously tight hat while the inside was being pumped full of air," she said. "That stuff—what'd you call it, Myrk?"

I nodded.

"It began filling up the room. I couldn't make out where it was coming from. It was like a gas grenade full of the crap had gone off. I pressed myself against the wall, trying to keep away from the stuff."

"Smart move," I said. "Then?"

"Part of the Myrk started acting out. Vines of it

whipped around the place like they were trying to grab something that wasn't there. One of them almost caught Lizzie across the face."

My body spasmed at the thought of Lizzie being struck by even a sliver of Myrk. It wouldn't have been pretty. I couldn't imagine the horrors she would've had to endure. A child exposed to this world, speaking with ghosts, seeing the things she had alongside me. The Myrk would have used all of those things against her. It could've subjected her to the sort of visions that leaves someone a dribbling mess. And, for someone her age, it could've shattered her mind completely.

"I would like to say that we were both calm as it happened, but I'd be lying." Ortiz went on. "I'm sure my heart was beating hard enough to be picked up by seismographs. Lizzie was frozen until that *thing* came in." Her mouth twisted in revulsion with the word *thing*. "That's when she screamed, Charles. Hearing someone scream like that, a kid no less…" Ortiz broke off as she shut her eyes, resting her forehead on her palm.

I crossed the distance in a few steps and put a hand on her shoulder. My fingers dug in with just enough force to make it a gentle squeeze. "I've heard kids scream like that before," I croaked.

It's never easy hearing it. It's not something you can forget no matter how much you want to. It's the sort of thing that digs in, roots itself in your mind, never letting go. The sort of thing that wakes you up at night, leaving you short of breath and your body drenched in cold sweat.

Ortiz's eyes widened. She stared at me in silence, mouth twitching on the verge of saying something.

"I'm sorry, Charles."

I gave her a weak smile.

"You've seen a lot of kids get wrapped up in stuff like this?"

"Enough." I frowned. "The list's long enough; too long for me." I cleared my throat to keep it from drying up completely.

"Lizzie's not being added to that list." Ortiz's voice changed from dry sorrow to steely resolution.

"No." I matched her tone. "She isn't."

Ortiz bobbed her head in agreement. "The one thing I don't get, though, is—"

"Why was she taken as opposed to"—I swallowed what little moisture was in my throat—"being killed here."

"We're missing something, Charles."

"Yeah." I nodded. "And it sucks." My fingers gripped tighter on the stake. "At least we have this." I raised the weapon. "It's something. When we find the phage, I'm going to jam it through its throat."

"Once we find it." Her tone wasn't accusing, but there was a hint of expectation in it. That maybe I should've found out more than I had. "Tell me about your acid trip again."

I repeated the details, going over them in my head as I did.

"So you think you were moving and seeing things in concert with the actual asylum?"

"I know I was. Remember, I had glimpses through it. I know what I saw."

"And the Babylon thing—where'd that come from?"

I shrugged.

"You said you remember climbing down stairs?" Her face slipped into a pensive mask.

I nodded.

Ortiz brushed the back of her hand against her mouth. "Doesn't fit. I've been here a while and I'm not aware of any stairs. You sure you're remembering it right?"

I glared.

She returned it. "You were hallucinating, remember?"

"I know."

"Okay," she relented. "You said something about old bricks, lights, and water? That mean anything?"

I shook my head. "No idea. I'll tell you this though: it felt real. It was like I was flashing to bits of the...." I blinked as I made sense of it all. I could feel my lips peeling back from teeth. The urge to scream was getting the better of me. The muscles in my forearm quivered, leaving me to clench my hand over and over until the shaking stopped. The far wall seemed the perfect place in which to bury my fist. So did the phage's face, repeatedly so, until I'd left it a bloody pulp.

"What's wrong, Charles?"

"How old is this place?" I said in a near whip crack like voice.

Ortiz reeled from the harshness of my outburst. She settled herself a second later. "Decades. I can't be sure exactly." She shrugged. "There was another building here before—a hospital. That's what I've heard."

"Of course there was," I growled. "The asylum was built atop the old building's foundations, wasn't it?"

She shrugged again. "Possibly. I'm not sure."

Ortiz didn't have to say anything. The fog that'd been mucking up my mind—cleared. It was easier to see what was really happening here. I pieced together one of Charles' cryptic clues. "Down below."

"So, theoretically, there's another level in this place." I lowered my eyes to regard the floor.

"Below us." Ortiz caught on and followed my gaze.

"Below us," I agreed. "Which explains my little descent earlier."

"The flashes of old stone and lighting," Ortiz added.

"Yeah," I said. "Seems like a place we should check out."

"Now that you're not tripping on monster booze," she interjected, grinning.

"Sobriety sucks."

She snorted.

I moved to the door and leapt out with a shout. "*Allons-y!*" I beckoned Ortiz with an exaggerated roll of my hand.

She rolled her eyes. "Do you even know what that means?"

"Course I do!" I said, my tone one of mock indignation. "It's like French for *ándale*, which is Spanish for something, or goading a bull." I rolled my shoulders in a mild shrug. "Either or."

She shook her head but I could see the edges of her mouth twisting into a smile. "You should think about trying electrotherapy when this is done. It might help."

"I once stuck a knife into a socket. That count?"

She laughed. "You're hopeless."

"Let's hope not," I said, moving the tone of the conversation to a darker one.

Ortiz followed in step as I led the way. I picked up my directional cues from the signs at the ends of the halls. Ortiz knew I had no idea how to find my way back to the sublevel, but she didn't comment on it. A desk came into view as we turned down another hall. I had seen it earlier.

I came to an abrupt halt, stowing the stake. I placed my palms over the wood and leaned against it. "Hey." My voice snapped the attendant out of her computer fixated reverie. It was the nurse with the pinched face.

"What?" she said in a waspish tone. Her eyes drifted back toward the screen.

"This place, the asylum," I said, "does it have a lower level?"

The nurse blinked several times. Her mouth moved with no sounds coming out. She was caught off guard and took a minute to collect herself. "Well, yes," she started. "The asylum was built on the foundations of the old one after the Second World War." Her voice lost the haughty tone as it shifted into one of enthusiasm. A self-satisfied grin slid over her face as she talked about the history of the location. I tuned it out.

The foundations housed the remnants of another asylum. That wasn't good news. This place was a bastion of illness. Especially ones of the mind. It's no wonder the phage was drawn to it. This place maintained a constant type of energy. Over the decades, an innumerable amount of patients had come in with various maladies and emotional instabilities. Every patient was sending out a message in their suffering. And all of them told the phage what it wanted to hear. Weakness, easy prey, and plentiful pickings. The perfect hunting ground.

Places can develop auras in tune with the dominant emotions within them. I'm not adept at picking up on that sort of thing. My talents lie elsewhere. But everyone's come close to feeling something like that. It's why you get that tingling down your spine when entering an abandoned place.

There's a good reason it's been abandoned. Some horror, tragedy or hardship was experienced there. That feeling lingers. It's also why when you visit your favorite aunt or grandmother, you get a sense of warm and comforting heaviness. The urge to fall asleep and doze. The familiar feeling of loved ones nearby. That smell homes of relatives always seem to have, no matter which relatives they are. You can't escape those. It's like being in the company of your best friend. You can just feel it.

The asylum—no, asylums—were breeding grounds of silent suffering. That kind of energy compounds and always ends up bringing some form of supernatural predator sniffing around. I permitted myself to shut my eyes, imagining how many people had lost their lives to the phage over the years. How many lived in mental agony and torment? How many died without closure? I didn't want to think about the numbers. They didn't seem bright, especially if the ghosts were any indication.

I sighed for the ghosts. I couldn't do much to help them. All I could do was tack on an extra ass-kicking for the phage atop the one I was going to give it for taking Lizzie.

My fingers dug into the desk, not going so far as to scratch the surface of the wood. "What's below this level?" I said, interrupting her history speech.

"The old foundations mostly. A bunch of stone, service lights, and plumbing."

Click—ding, and on went the frickin' light bulb. The minute muscles within my hands and fingers shook as my grip tightened. Charles' babble wasn't babble any longer. Every reference, every note was clear. Below the asylum, in the old foundations where the entire waterworks were. Where else would a Babylonian phage be more at home? Access to foul the water, dark, probably quiet, which would work to their auditory advantage. Not only that, but I wagered my ingestion of its toxin served to show me more than a hallucination of old Babylon.

The phage was a creature of the ancient empire, and it brought a piece along with itself. It had come over from its own pocket of the Neravene. The drug was a part of it as it was a part of Babylon. That's what I had seen. I peered into its part of the Neravene, hence Charles' reference to a world beside ours.

And now I knew how he had figured it all out. The same way I had. The more of the toxin he ingested, the more he saw. He didn't know what he was recording, or the value, but he knew enough of what he saw. Enough so Ortiz and I could act on it. And we were damn well going to.

"How do we get there?"

The nurse recoiled, sliding back in the chair. A slight pressure on my bicep prompted me to turn. Ortiz squeezed my arm, staring at me in concern. I flashed her a look. I didn't have time for niceties.

"How do we get there?" I lowered my voice, easing some of the harshness out of it.

"You can't go down there. Only maintenance is allowed."

I narrowed my eyes and leaned further in. "I'm going to ask you one last time, because a little girl is in danger. You know Lizzie? Yea high." I gestured her height. "Quiet, sometimes carries a toy."

"Elizabeth...Haylen?" she said.

I hadn't gotten Lizzie's last name in any of our prior exchanges. Making a mental note of it, I buried it for later. "Yes. She's down there." I wouldn't lose much in telling her the truth.

The nurse's eyes expanded in ballistic speed as her pupils followed suit. "What would she be doing there?"

"I heard her mention wanting to go down there." I grasped for any quick lie my brain could produce. "Tell me!"

She did. A wary look came over. "Charles, you're scaring me. I'm going to call Doctor Cartwright." The nurse reached for the nearby phone. I lunged, swinging my body onto the desk. My hand made it across, slapping it out of her hand and back into the set. She eyed me, staring like I was disturbed and needed the orderlies called on.

"Sorry." I threw up my hands. "Sorry." I went so far as to rub my arms. "New meds," I mumbled. "Take some getting used to."

She eyed me for several more moments before easing herself into the chair. Her gaze never left me however.

"We should go," suggested Ortiz, giving my arm another squeeze.

I nodded and started to move when I caught sight of something. A picture sat on the desk, the one I had seen earlier. It caused the joints in my hands to feel like they were near bursting. The skin around my knuckles felt too tight, like a plastic bag filled to the breaking point. My gums ached from the pressure of my grinding teeth.

"Lyshae," I whispered. "You clever, deceitful, wicked, wonderfully perceptive, twisted bitch!" She saw what should've been obvious to me this entire time and had been kind enough to point it out. I'd been too dense to pick up on it until seeing the photograph again.

I pushed myself away from the desk, legging it down the path the nurse had described. Ortiz caught up. Her hand fell on my shoulder as she walked beside me.

"What's wrong, Charles?"

"Nothing."

"Didn't I warn you about lying to me?" She accentuated her words by digging into the meat between my neck and shoulder with her fingers.

I winced and turned my neck to alleviate some of the pressure.

"I saw it on your face. Something's wrong."

"Ackh!" I sputtered. "Alright, alright, I give. Let go with the death touch, Lucy Lawless."

She let out a light war cry that was a shade from echoing down the halls.

I eyed her. "Anyone tell you how hot you are?"

Ortiz released a rather unladylike snort. "Yeah, being hit on by a guy in a mental institution is the stuff of dreams for women. Try again next time, crazy." She chuckled.

I arched an eyebrow. "Takes one to know one."

Her laughter stopped, she paused thoughtfully. "You know I can kick your ass, right?"

I smiled. "Save it for the monster, Ortiz." I picked up the pace when I noticed two vertical bars on my forearm.

Eleven hours left.

More than enough time to hunt down an ancient monster, find and save the young girl trapped in its clutches, and gank the aforementioned creature.

No sweat.

Ortiz and I rounded the corner. A pair of double doors stood at the hall's end. A fist-sized crack hung in the wall to my side. At least I knew I was heading down the right path. It wasn't likely that anyone else had made that indentation. As we drew closer to the double doors, I began to separate what I had seen from what was actually here. The dark pool of liquid that obstructed the path was likely my mind's warped version of the double doors ahead.

"Through there." I nodded to the doors at the end.

"Charles." A hint of wariness hung in her voice.

"Yeah?" I turned to face her.

Ortiz chewed on her lips again. She shot a furtive glance to the far doors but I caught it. Her fingers waggled before she clenched them into a fist.

"Lizzie's down there," she said. I could hear the myriad of emotions in her tone, all tangled about as one tried to voice itself above the rest.

"Yes, she is."

Ortiz folded the corner of her lip and bit down noticeably harder. "Lizzie's down there—alone—with a monster. A monster that, if we don't do something about, will make her see her worst nightmares—or worse. All the while, it'll be feeding on her, leaving a dead child behind."

"Yes." My voice sounded far away and removed. I didn't want to acknowledge the possibility of failing Lizzie. Of making our way down below only to find the body of a young girl. A kid who had become my friend. The whole of my body twinged like I had fallen into an ice bath. It wasn't an idea I was fond of thinking about. I found myself nursing the temptation to take Lizzie and run.

My job was to find Charles' killer—the phage—and destroy it. If it came down to a choice between getting Lizzie to safety or killing the creature, I knew which I'd choose. The phage could wait. Lizzie couldn't.

Ortiz's lips twitched. Her eyes shook and a something flashed through them. "Charles." She gave me a weak smile. "I'm… This is a lot of pressure."

"Yes. Yes, it is."

"You're going to think this is stupid," she said.

"No, I'm not. Trust me."

"I'm scared." Her words drove the strength out of my legs. My muscles turned to mush. Her gaze slipped away, turning to regard the floor.

Shame.

Camilla Ortiz was ashamed of the fact she was scared about what we were going to do. Iron bands wrapped tight around my lungs. It hurt and left my chest feeling heavy.

"So am I, Ortiz. So am I." The heaviness in my chest flooded my voice.

She looked up, staring me in the eyes. "Does it ever stop?"

"No. You never stop getting scared. Never. Not in this life. But you do get better at handling the fear. It does get easier to manage. It never goes away, not truly. The few moments of sleep I get to steal every now and again are always riddled with nightmares. You learn to bury them. I tell myself I see the horrible things I do so others don't have to. That I fight the nameless things out of stories so other people will never have to know they exist. That I'm burdened with the fear and knowledge that monsters exist so others can live in ignorance, enjoying the proverbial bliss that comes with it. When you think of it like that, it becomes a little easier to deal with, don't you think?" I flashed her a smile.

I realized as I was speaking to her, I was telling myself buried truths that I'd never really paid attention to. I spoke without thinking, a pure stream-of-consciousness. "And, like you said, if we don't do this," I broke off and inhaled. "A girl—Lizzie—our friend, will die. That doesn't leave us much choice, does it?"

The lost expression slid from her face, replaced by one I liked a whole lot more. A feral, wolfish grin I'd seen before. Aggressive, strong and one that completely rang of Camilla Ortiz. "No, it doesn't." She set her jaw. "So let's stop the chick flick, go kill a monster, and save our friend."

I returned her grin. "Damn right. And don't forget." I padded the massive bulge in my pants. "We have this." I gestured to the stake pinned in place by the elastic waistband.

Ortiz arched a singular brow, eyeing my pants askance. "Is that a charred stake for killing a phage in your pants, or are you just happy to see me?" She gave me a wry smile.

"Uh, both?"

She rolled her eyes and walked toward the doors.

"Hey!" I whipped out the stake. "A big piece of wood can be the answer to many of life's problems."

"Like inadequacy issues for which you're overcompensating?" Her voice was perfectly neutral, but her eyes danced.

I sniffed indignantly. I was not compensating.

"Whatever," I growled. "We've got a monster to shank and a kid to save. Let's get to it."

Ortiz's grin widened as we moved toward the end of the hall. We pushed our way through the doors, ignoring the "maintenance only" sign.

Time to dive into the dark below.

# Chapter Twenty-Four

The room wasn't what I was expecting. It certainly wasn't how I remembered it. Not that my memory of the trip could be trusted. The room was made of the same old stone I saw in my flashes. No attempt had been made to cover it up or modernize it. Copper piping, ranging in thickness from my pinky to my leg, filled the room. A lens the size of the bottom of a Coke bottle sat in front of a white circular plate. An arrow held steady between hash-like markings labeled with tiny numbers. It was attached to a barrel-like drum. All of it occupied the space of a small walk-in closet.

Something sharp glanced off my ribs. Nudging me again, Ortiz nodded to the corner of the room. "There."

The room didn't end there. It went off to some open space. Taking the lead, Ortiz crept over to the opening with measured caution. She beckoned me. Peering around the corner, we came across a corridor narrow enough that we couldn't walk side by side.

"Like the Sand People then," I murmured.

"What?"

"Sand People move in single file."

Ortiz shook her head but I saw her lips twitch, trying to break into a smile. She kept them in control.

"I'll go first." I brushed my way past her. "Watch my back?"

"You have to ask?" Her tone was without an edge. She slipped behind me, remaining a pace behind.

There was something comforting about her presence. It was like a familiar weight on my body. Almost like getting a tight hug from a close friend. It helped settle the steel cables tightening throughout my body. The lighting within the passageway stopped after the first few steps in, leaving the rest mired in darkness.

The front half of my foot lost contact with solid ground, hovering over empty space. The collar of my shirt stretched tight around my neck. My first thought was that my shirt was trying to strangle me.

It's not as stupid as it sounds. Not in my line of work.

Ortiz held me there, placing her other arm on my shoulder, pulling me back to stand.

"Found the stairs," I announced in a dry voice.

"Yeah, no kidding. Want to switch spots? We don't want you falling down the stairs…again." She worked to keep her voice neutral. She failed. I could hear the amusement in it.

I growled. "Yeah, right." Prodding with the tip of my foot, I found the next step and gauged its depth. After that, it wasn't difficult maneuvering my way down. I instructed Ortiz to keep a hand on my shoulder as we descended.

"I thought you said they were spiraled?"

"They were." Another thing I had gotten wrong because of the hallucinations. I prayed I wasn't making a mistake about anything else.

Flickering lights with the dull color of an aged porch lamp illuminated the place. Another step took me into the world of my delusion. We came into a hall of stone. It looked like a fantasy nerd's wet dream. All that was missing was the torches, booby traps, and monsters.

Well, if I was right about this, there would be at least one of those.

The hall was wide enough to park several cars side by side. The darkened stone did a great job at absorbing the poor lighting. We walked in silence. I managed to catch sight of something that caused the bones in my shoulders to slide a bit. In between the dismal flashes of amber light, I could see what looked like gnarled branches. I motioned Ortiz to follow as I stepped closer. I leaned forward, squinting to get a better look at the vine-like formations.

My shoulder crashed into Ortiz's chest as I leapt back. "Shit!"

"What is it?"

"Look!" I pointed at the wall.

Ortiz gave me a skeptical look and moved toward the wall, albeit with more caution than I had. Her head bobbed back a second later. "What the hell is that?"

I shrugged, peering closer. It registered seconds later. The lengthy, thin constructs had lost their prior purplish coloring. They resembled a set of once-gleaming teeth beneath layers of yellowish plaque. The flesh had lost its supple look, appearing like frayed rope. Others parts looked like cracked, dry branches. Where the tendrils had split open, a gelatinous sap oozed and congealed over the surface.

My sleeve slid across my skin as it was tugged. I turned to Ortiz, giving her a quizzical look.

She gestured with a single finger to the ceiling.

I followed it and looked up. I wished I hadn't. Plumbing crisscrossed above. Every pipe was festooned in more of the phage's elongated limbs. They had woven themselves around the metal tubing, growing like paranormal weeds. I could make out pebble-sized drops of moisture condensing over the pipes. With every snap of weak, bronzed light, I could make out more. The appendages looked like roots, fighting to take hold over and even in the pipes.

There were spots where bits of tendrils, thicker than my thumb, had wormed their way into the metal. A milky-white substance formed a ring where the tentacle met the piping. It formed some kind of anti-leak substance. The amount of water trickling out from the pipes was minimal. A few drops per minute at best.

"Whoa!" we exclaimed in unison, stepping back in synchrony.

"You see that, Charles?"

I nodded. The mass of intertwined tendrils pulsated like arteries pumping blood. Something coursed through them to make them bulge like that. The question was, what? I got my answer as soon as I asked.

Despite the dimness of the room, I noticed the glistening bead fall. Its black coloring was easy to spot amidst the lights. It landed and deformed into an inky smudge no larger than the tip of my pinky.

"So that explains a lot," Ortiz murmured.

"Yeah," I breathed. The phage was forcing its toxins into the water supply of the asylum via the piping. It should've been obvious, but, even so, seeing it was something else. As far as I could tell, the endless amount of tendrils snaking over everything weren't connected to the creature. They appeared to be separate entities. Though frail in appearance, they were clearly functioning.

"They aren't all, you know, still attached to the phage…are they?"

"No, Ortiz. No, they're not."

"Good," she said. "Because that would be pretty unsettling."

I raised an eyebrow and hooked a thumb to the tangle of thin limbs around us. "And this isn't?"

"Touché," she replied. "I didn't know it could do something like this."

"Neither did I." None of the lore mentioned it. Although, I should've suspected it. Nothing is ever simple with the paranormal. It's an unspoken law. And just because it isn't written anywhere for you to find, don't rule it out. In fact, it's better to assume it's possible—no matter how unlikely—than think it's impossible. Nowhere did it say that the phage *couldn't* pull a stunt like this. Hell, it was effective.

It's not a great idea to poison water supplies by scurrying around and dumping buckets of toxins in them. By leaving a growth of vines near water sources, they could taint things from a distance. Play it safe until it was chow time.

Chicken shits.

"So." Ortiz broke my silent train of thought. "This means that the phage really has polluted the asylum's water supply. All of it."

"Yes."

"That means everyone who's taken even a sip has some of this stuff in their body. Everyone has a little bit of the taint in them."

I didn't answer, knowing where Ortiz was going with this.

"There's some of it in me too, isn't there?" Her voice wavered.

I remained silent.

"In Lizzie?" she added.

My tongue found its way between the front row of my teeth and I bit down on it.

"Charles? The phage can reach out to us, can't it? Tamper with our minds? Make us see things?"

"Yes. Yes, it can."

Ortiz's shoulders shook for an instant. She pulled herself together after seconds in silence. "But you managed to deal with it."

"I had people counting on me. Didn't really have a choice." I smiled. It's always easier to bear difficult things when you're doing them for the people you care about.

She nodded. I could see her putting the disturbing line of thoughts in their place. "We'll deal with it if and when it happens, huh?"

I nodded. "Yeah. Let's keep moving. There's a kid needin' our help."

"So stop dicking around." She shook her head, going so as far as to roll her eyes.

I snorted and followed as she assumed the lead. We crept forward, hyperaware of our surroundings. The occasional twitch of tendrils caused us to mirror the sudden spasmodic movements. It's disconcerting to see tentacles on the walls move. It's the sort of thing to make you flinch.

Ortiz piped up after we had made it down half the length of the hall. "You said these things are blind, right?"

"As far as I can tell." I shrugged. "It had thin skin stretched over where its eyes should've been. My guess is the creatures are born blind. But like I said before, they don't need sight. They have ridiculous hearing and can hunt via pheromones. They can smell fear. Not to mention every single person in the asylum is harboring a conduit to the phage. That's what we get for drinking the Kool–Aid."

"So the phage could be stalking us right now."

I stopped. "Thanks for that," I muttered under my breath. "Way to destroy the calm."

"Man up," she retorted. "I just wanted to put the possibility out there. Better to be aware than caught with our pants down."

"It's happened before, literally," I grumbled. Ortiz showed no sign she had heard me.

I signaled in silence for us to switch places. She slipped behind me. I held the stake level, its point out like a rapier. It was important for us to keep changing positions. Keeping the same person in front leads to complacency. The best way to get the most out of our fear-driven awareness was to stay in motion and introduce changes. Falling into a routine would cause our senses to dull. All it would take is a second. That'd be enough to put the nails in our coffins.

The sound of tearing cloth emanated from around the hall. Our backs pressed against each other as we moved in a circular pattern, watching. Lights sputtered, revealing nothing more than tendrils moving over one another. Such an innocuous thing. Simple movements with such a disturbing sound. Ortiz's back heaved against mine.

"That freak you out as much as it did me?"

"Yeah," she breathed.

"Good. Didn't want to be the only one."

She snorted.

"If we keep getting worked up like this, the phage is going to know we're down here. Won't matter how quiet we are," I said.

"Technically, you wandered through here before. You just weren't aware of it. You came out fine."

"Ish," I replied. "I came out fine-ish." I moved again with one hand on the stake. I kept it out at arm's length. My other hand waved in the dark in an effort to gauge Ortiz's position. My fingers brushed against hers and both sets of digits locked. The tenseness in my muscles eased. My uncertainties faded.

It's one of the simple and wonderful things about life, about being human—the little things. Holding the hand of someone you trust—a friend. Getting the right sort of smile from the right kind of person. A hug. Simple gestures with an endless amount of strength in them. They can ease the heaviest of burdens and quell the darkest of fears...like walking into a nightmare's lair.

Holding her hand there, in the dark, gave me a sense of calm. It was an assurance that everything just might turn out okay in the end. That we would save Lizzie. We would gank the phage, and everything would be okay. It was the best reminder that I had Camilla Ortiz watching my back. Someone I could trust with my life. Someone I *had* trusted with it. She hadn't let me down yet and I didn't expect that to change.

I took another step and something prevented me from touching down on the concrete. My foot pressed down for a second before whatever it was gave out. There was a wet *squelch* like the sound of a water balloon bursting. I squinted and tried my best to make out what had just popped underfoot. Ortiz moved to my side. Her gaze followed mine to the floor. She swore and inched backward.

Hundreds of individual, worm-like limbs covered the floor. They knotted over one another to form some sort of grotesque mat. Unlike the tendrils over the walls that had an aged, dry look to them, these looked healthy. Still the color of a nasty bruise, they throbbed on occasion like each was nursing its own heartbeat. One squirmed and gave the illusion it was going to become a bit livelier. Worst of all, they were filled with the horrendous pus I'd come to despise and be wary of.

I grimaced and stepped back. Concrete friction fought my foot as I ground it over stone. I figured it best to get the phage's nightmare inducing gook off me as fast as I could. I counted six limbs moving of their own accord, slithering into new positions.

Ortiz eyed me. "You saw that, right?"

"Yeah."

"You think—"

"Dunno," I cut in. If the tendrils were moving on their own, unconnected and with no input from the phage, we were in deeper trouble. There was the chance that in navigating the snare formation before us, a rogue limb could grab us. Anything could happen after that. We could be dragged down, buried beneath the tangled mat and strangled. A walnut sized lump formed in my throat. I swallowed and shook my head clear. One thing burned my doubts away—Lizzie. We had come this far. She was still in danger. So we would go further. End.

"I hate to say this," Ortiz began.

"Then don't," I said.

"But I've got a bad feeling about this."

"Everything I do is inherently a bad idea. There's always going to be a bad feeling associated with it." I gave her a weak smile.

Ortiz stared at me for a second. Her body shook. The

next instant she broke into laughter that echoed down the hall. Realizing what she had done, she shut her mouth with a forceful *click* of teeth.

"Smooth," I whispered. The area just above my shoulder throbbed like I had taken a softball pitch to it. I rubbed it. "What happens if one of these days I punch back?" Ortiz gave me a look that made me reconsider the idea—permanently. "So, uh." I gave a flourish of my hands. "Shall we?" I gestured to the intricate weavings of tendrils. Stepping through was not going to be easy. One wrong step and game over, Graves.

Ortiz's chest rose as she inhaled several times, steeling herself. I mirrored her. Her fingers tightened around mine. I reciprocated and we took a step. We maneuvered ourselves so that each step put us in between the gaps of the net like pattern. My knuckles ground and my fingers rubbed against each other.

"Crap." Ortiz let out an irritated huff of breath, squeezing my hand as she did.

"What?"

"One of those things brushed up against my leg." She shivered.

I would've reacted the same way.

"So when we find her, what's the plan?"

I was tempted to tell her I hadn't gotten that far yet. My mind was solely occupied with Lizzie's safety. The phage, if we bumped into it, was a then and there sort of problem. "I'm going stab it." I punctuated my statement by jabbing the stake through the air.

"I was hoping for a little more than that."

"What do you want me to say?" I asked as we navigated the maze of limbs. "The truth is, Ortiz, you can't really plan for this stuff because, as soon as the shit hits the fan, all plans go south. We have a weapon. We know we can kill it. It's the best we can hope for. My priority, honestly, is to save Lizzie and, if possible, get out. We know the freak's nesting down here somewhere. We can always come back. I'm not risking a fight with a little girl down here." My voice took on a sharpened edge.

Ortiz's grip faltered for a second. "I'm not asking you to." Her voice was just above a whisper.

"Sorry."

She didn't reply but nodded.

"I don't know, Ortiz. I never know in this line of work. I just do the best I can and hope it's enough."

"Your best will be enough. We'll make sure of it." Her voice made steel seem soft.

*Let's hope so.* I didn't have the heart to tell Ortiz that my best hadn't always gotten the job done. "Thanks." I gave her the best grin I could manage. I was about to speak. I don't know what came first: the feeling that my wrist was connected by bits of breaking string or the scream. My entire arm wrenched and I was pulled to the side. The pressure built in my socket to the point where I was given a harsh reminder of how I had started this case—with the dislocation of my shoulder. I still refused to let go of her hand.

Ortiz tumbled into the bed of tendrils. They flared to life like writhing snakes. Slender rows of pain, like minute razor blades, pressed into my hand. Ortiz dug her fingernails into me. She fought to hold on as the limbs sought to bury her. They lashed themselves to her like bits of binding, restraining her by the waist, head and arms. Her legs kicked in desperation as she tried to fight her way out.

I took a death grip on the stake and plunged toward the tendrils. It severed one of the limbs with ease. I repeated the process, stabbing like a deranged killer absorbed in the act of burying the blade into whatever I could. For every one of the tendrils I cut, two more slid forward in its place. Ortiz's body was shrouded beneath the roiling mess. I did the only thing I could think of.

I let go.

A rubberband-like snap went off in my skull as it happened. I had let her fingers slip through mine. Willing the thought away, I went to work. I tugged my waistband and shoved the stake down my pants, taking care not to hit the important bits. Flexing my fingers, I formed stiff claws and raked at the tendrils. My goal wasn't to tear them apart. It was to pull them away. Hacking at them didn't seem to do any good. I burrowed through the tangled limbs until Ortiz's face was plainly visible. Satisfied I had loosened as many of the tendrils as I could, I grabbed hold of her legs and pulled.

"Get," she spat. "Me." She took another breath of air. "Out of this crap!"

It was tough, but she slid through most of it, swiping at whatever bits she could. I made the effort to stomp a few rogue tendrils that wormed their way toward me. Her body rose out of the mess. The tentacles stopped flailing as she was freed. Relinquishing my grip on her legs, I extended my hand and she took hold of it. I hauled her up and we watched as the tendril's undulating motions ceased. They receded toward the far end of the hall.

Ortiz and I were breathing heavily, but we managed to exchange a quick look of confusion. In truth, the phage's left-behinds were winning. I had no idea why they pulled away. It could have been that the net-like construction was exactly that—a snare trap. Good for one go. Once Ortiz and I had put up enough of a fight and the tendrils hadn't gotten what they wanted, they sank away. Not that I was complaining.

"Well," Ortiz panted, "that was unpleasant."

"Yeah. Phage—zip, dynamic duo—one."

"Good job, Robin," she quipped.

I glared. There is no reality, no train of thought, no plane of existence where I am not the goddamned Batman. I kept this to myself, of course. Batman doesn't tell others he's Batman. Everyone just knows it. And they should.

I sniffed and turned my head back to the clear hallway. Hooking a thumb inside my waistband, I tugged it away and removed the stake. Ortiz watched me, shaking her head in disappointment while nursing a small smile. She muttered something under her breath along the lines of, "Boys," and, "always playing with their wood."

I ignored it. "Keep an eye out. Likely that's not the only surprise lurking around."

Ortiz didn't reply. Her features tightened before slipping back into neutrality. The only thing that remained was a certain light in her eyes—widened, alert.

We moved on with our heads on a swivel. Every hint of motion from the tendrils on the walls caused my heart rate to spike. The appalling lighting didn't help in determining just how large the stone halls were. All I knew was that we'd been walking for longer than I wanted. In the next flicker of light, I turned over my forearm. My lips pressed tight.

Ten hours. It'd have to be enough.

"Charles?"

"What?"

She pointed off to the side. The wall was covered in tendrils like all the others. Through another burst of dismal lighting, I made out a thicker grouping of limbs. They were clustered together like webbing, much like the snare had done to Ortiz. An acidic coating lined my throat. It dried when I saw what Ortiz had.

Each bundle of tendrils held something within: men dressed in the overalls you'd see on mechanics or plumbers. At one point the man suspended on the right would have been dark-complected. His pal to the left was a pale associated with only one thing—death. A durable-looking canvas cinch bag lay at their feet. All manner of tools protruded from it. They must've been the resident maintenance. The asylum must've been having problems of late, and why wouldn't it?

"Damn." I spat. The word left a note of bitterness in my mouth.

"Poor guys," said Ortiz.

"Come on." My voice carried a hard edge. Ortiz didn't budge.

"Someone should cut them down."

"You're right," I said. "Later. Right now, Lizzie's the priority." I tried to keep my voice soft. I felt her pain.

I wasn't a fan of anyone dying, random civilians included. The hardened truth of the job is that it happens. It will happen. Always. There's no way around it. It wasn't that I was insensitive; there was a more pressing matter to attend to. Lizzie was still alive, and I hoped there was something we could do for her.

"Come on." I gestured with my hand.

Ortiz stayed rooted in place. She gave the two a final look before turning to me. With a slight nod, she gestured ahead.

I turned. Light shone with an almost paper white brightness in the dark. It came into the hall at a sharp angle, emanating from a room to the side.

Ortiz tilted her head to regard it. "If I were a spooky

monster hiding out in a sublevel—"

"That's where I'd be hiding." I grimaced.

I raced over and pressed my back against the wall near the doorframe. Ortiz moved to rush past the door and position herself on the other side. I shook my head to advise against it. She pulled up behind me, placing a hand on my shoulder. She'd follow me in as I turned the corner.

A lead balloon formed in my stomach as I rolled the stake in my palm. I looked back and gave Ortiz a steady look. I nodded and she returned it. My free hand gripped the doorframe like an anchor. I pulled off of it and swung around the corner. We charged into the room.

The lead balloon rose and settled into my throat.

A bare bulb hung from the ceiling, lighting the stone room. Opposite us was another throng of tendrils. A tawny young face protruded from them. A body was suspended a foot off the ground.

"Lizzie," Ortiz breathed.

I spat a string of curses.

Her face hadn't paled. It still retained its healthy coloration. Her mouth hung slack, the way you might expect when someone is deep in sleep. But her eyes were a different story. If Lizzie were a normal child, the look she wore would be like she'd seen a ghost. There was an alertness to them. I could see the whites shaking. She was looking straight at us. Or through us. I couldn't tell. Either she was seeing us or something else entirely. Given the phage's abilities, I was banking on the latter. Seeing her like that pushed me over the edge.

Acid seared my marrow. My heart beat with a diesel throb and the stake never felt more comfortable in my hands. Lizzie was still alive. The phage could wait.

"Ortiz." I reversed my grip on the stake. "Get her out of that crap!" Ortiz took the weapon without reply and inched her way to Lizzie. I stood back, watching in case the tendrils decided to flare into life and attack. Nothing of the sort happened as Ortiz seized the top corner of bundled limbs and hacked away.

"Stuff's tougher than I thought," she grumbled to herself. Ortiz cast a glance over her shoulder at me. Her eyes went wide. It set me in motion. I was turning before she shouted, "Charles!"

Tarnished silver flooded the corner of my view. It grew larger by the millisecond. Color warped from patinated metal to a rush of seventies disco assaulting my vision. The whatsit crashed home in a concerto of pain. It didn't glance off but deformed as it impacted my skull with a groan of objection. Thin, soft metal—a tray—I deduced as I stumbled sideways.

The flurry of disorienting dots cleared from my vision. Ortiz flew into motion, a near blur lashing out with a kick. It connected and drew a pained *oomph* from the woman as she tumbled into the wall. Caught up in the moment, Ortiz and I hadn't had the chance to register the stranger's identity. Plump, with a pear-shaped face and brown hair done up in a bun. She had a warm matronly look.

Ortiz's posture slipped from the tight, controlled fighting stance. Her arms wavered, and her head lowered a bit. "Katherine?"

"Yeah." I cleared my throat to get the words out.

"You knew?" she said, the whip crack question coming with a hint of accusation.

"I figured it out just before we came down here. I wasn't a hundred percent certain though."

A low groan of pain and exhaustion left Katherine's mouth.

"What should we do?" Ortiz's voice fluctuated. I could see her jaw tighten even as her eyes lost focus. She was having trouble believing Katherine was involved.

I wasn't. "I'm nursing the awful temptation to take the stake and—"

"I wouldn't do that if I were you," interrupted a soft, confident voice.

He was taller than anyone I'd seen in the asylum, with gentle cherubic features and cheeks made of pudgy flesh. The hefty guy blocked the door.

"Who's that?" Ortiz morphed back into an aggressive posture, stake held point out.

I buried my surprise that Ortiz could see him and turned my focus to Katherine lying slumped against the wall. "Gus," I said. "Gusbert Robinson." I kept my voice as flat as I could.

"Her son."

# Chapter Twenty-Five

Gus smiled. It was all teeth, disturbing to see on his face as his flabby features morphed. "When did you figure it out?"

"The photo," I said. "You have her eyes."

He arched an eyebrow. "That was enough for you?"

"Wait," Ortiz chimed in. "I thought her son was dead? One of the nurses said—"

"He is." I thrust my hand toward Gus' sternum. He never moved. My hand passed straight through.

His smile grew.

"Not going to lie. It took me a while to put it together. You only ever showed up after I drank water."

"Coincidence?" He gave a light shrug. Even he wasn't buying his own story.

"Yeah, I don't believe in those. Not with the life I lead."

"About that." Gus gave me an oblique stare. "How are you alive?"

Shit. Always the problem with my job: confronting the monster—or an extension of it—while inhabiting the body of someone it killed. I could almost hear the pneumatic drills Ortiz's eyes were using to glare at me.

I ignored his question. "Then I remembered our conversation with one of the orderlies. We were arguing. He looked at you, then back to me and called me a nut job. It didn't sink in until later. He couldn't see you, could he?"

Gus' smile stayed plastered on his face, but his eyes glimmered for a second.

"It wasn't until I took a nasty acid trip, courtesy of you, that I realized how powerful your illusions are. It's why I was able to touch you, feel you, and interact with you like you were real. I only thought you were. Now that's gone." I punctuated my statement with a swipe of my hand that sailed clear through his head.

"Charles, what are you talking about?" Ortiz asked.

"He's an illusion, Ortiz. Created by the phage...for her." I nodded to Katherine. "Gus was never real. He's a projection. Anyone who's drunk the water here has a chance of seeing him, so long as the phage wants them to. That's what Gus is—a tool, an extension of its powers." It dawned on me how obvious it should've been, all the clues. Lyshae's lectures on the power of illusions, everything the phage had thrown at me, and Katherine's treatment of Gus. "We took a trip into the Neravene, and we saw twisted versions of the asylum. We saw some people too."

Gus' expression remained the same, save for a slight tilt of the head.

"I saw Katherine. She looked broken. She was talking to someone, endearingly so. Someone we couldn't see. I saw her mouth a name—your name." I smiled.

He brought his hands together in a slow, heavy clap that echoed through the room. It wasn't real. It was just for show. Illusions exist through belief. So long as I thought Gus was real, I'd interact with him as such. The phage's toxin was powerful stuff. But the second I came to realize what he was, he couldn't touch me, couldn't hurt me. He was nothing. Gus was a cheap parlor trick at best.

"That's what you are, right? A crappy trick by a disgusting creature with a two-bit act!"

Gus' face contorted. Excess flesh bunched together as his skin flushed.

Guess I could make the apparition mad. Good. "Katherine was never 'cured,' was she?" I thought about what one of the nurses had told me earlier. Katherine Robinson was one of the asylum's greatest triumphs. "The phage—you—manipulated her. Gave her the illusion that her son lived on, even though, deep down, she knew he'd died. She was broken!" Spittle flew from my mouth. "You preyed on her, twisted her, pushed her. You kept her dangling on puppet strings!"

Gus' remained silent.

"She was your way in, your eyes in the asylum, using her to pick out targets!" I paused, realizing what else she'd done. "You used her to clean up your mess." I thought back to the smell of bleach, the removal of the markings in Charles' bedroom. "You took a mother's grief, her heartache, and used it to bend her to your will. You sick, twisted mother—" I stopped.

His body lost its appearance of solidity, looking all the more like a stage magician's conjuration. That's not what prompted me to stop though. As Gus' body became more like a fine mist, I could see past him. Behind him was a figure in need of a serious tan. Chalky white with tendrils protruding from its body.

"—fucker," I finished when I saw the phage. Its head fell to the side, much like Gus' had. It regarded me with eyeless sockets. Its mouth parted, opening halfway before it was stopped by the strands of skin connecting both lips. The phage released a dry breath that stirred the hanging strands of skin. Without turning my head, I shifted my gaze to Ortiz. "Ortiz, um, now might be a good time to go Xena on this thing's ass."

Gus clicked his tongue, waving his finger in warning as the phage stepped through him. "If you try…I can't guarantee young Elizabeth will be okay." A rustling forced Ortiz and me to look away from the phage to where Lizzie was held captive. The tendrils writhed, creeping over her face, and working toward her mouth and nose.

"Stop!" I barked. It did. The sinuous motions ceased. The tendrils stopped just below her bottom lip.

"Poor girl," Gus said, forcing a pitiful example of a sympathetic frown. "You have no idea what she's seeing right now."

"Bastard." I flexed my fingers as I controlled myself. Lengths of iron rods stiffened in my arm. I wanted to drive it right into his face. Not that it'd do any good. "If you hurt her…" My throat contorted. It felt like the muscles in my neck were cement that had begun setting. "There will be nothing stopping Ortiz from ganking your Pillsbury Doughboy ass!"

The phage bristled, taking a step forward. It stood face to face with me. "Nothing except me," called Gus from behind.

I leaned to the side and looked past the creature to Gus, then back to the phage. I blinked as it registered. "You're not just an illusion. You're its voice, aren't you?" Gus moved to the side, back in view and fixed me with a look that said I was a moron.

"Obviously," he answered.

Dick whistle.

"Pretty impressive. And here I thought you were a mindless shit for brains." I grinned. That wasn't wholly true. I was aware Babylonian phages were just as intelligent as humans. They just couldn't speak, or so I thought. That theory went down Hindenburg style thanks to Gus. "Why is she still alive?" I jerked a thumb over my shoulder to Lizzie.

Both the phage and Gus let their heads fall to the side in unison. One of its thin limbs slithered into motion, pointing toward the unconscious Katherine.

"Her?" I frowned in disbelief.

Gus intertwined his fingers, folding his hands. "Yes, she is my mother after all." He gave me a flabby smile. I was tempted to roll my eyes, but that would've meant taking my sight off the phage for a second. I reconsidered. "Katherine and I have formed a wonderful mother-son relationship over the decades. I looked out for her, gave her what she wanted—a relationship with her son. To watch him—me— grow up. To be happy, to be with her, to have some form of family. In turn, she did what any good mother does; she took care of her son. She kept me safe. Kept me fed." His smile grew wider.

Fake Gus continued to speak on the phage's behalf. I let it turn into white noise. I honed in on a single word: decades. The freakazoid had been skulking through the asylum for tens of years. The number of people it could've taken in that time made me wish the stake was back in my hands.

"Katherine dreamed of extending that family," the phage continued via its spectral puppet.

Ortiz glanced at Lizzie. "She wanted a daughter."

"Like any good son, I gave Ma what she wanted." He emphasized the *Ma* with an exaggerated southern drawl.

You could've bridged the gap between the phage and my nose with a penny. We were that close. I decided to get closer. I could almost feel the phage's skin against the tip of my nose. "She was broken!" I roared. "Do you understand that? Broken!" The lining of my throat went raw. "We saw her in the Neravene. She looked like glass that had been put back together too many times. Fishing line cracks—broken!" I shouted again. "And you kidnapped a little girl with the intention of giving her to a madwoman?" I jabbed a finger toward Katherine's limp form. "What's she going to do with Lizzie? She can't take care of herself. She's attached to a projection of her dead son. And she has to know—doesn't she—on some level deep down, that Gus is dead and not coming back?"

His grin grew, forcing the fat in his cheeks to press against his eyes until they became slits. "Of course, but you humans have always been adept at deluding yourselves. You'll tell any number of outrageous lies in order to believe what you want, what you can. You're adept at making the irrational—rational. Katherine Robinson wanted—needed— to believe that her son didn't die. I helped her do that. Now she pines for a daughter. I'm helping her get that."

"Yeah, you're a real flippin' saint, if you take away the fact you're a murdering monster."

"Monster?" Gus replied, a wry look on his face. "I'm giving a broken woman hope, keeping her together. What do you think her state would be without me? I'm giving her the family she wants—giving the girl the family she needs. I'm fully aware of Elizabeth Haylen's story."

Hearing that monster say Lizzie's full name made my spine feel like a phone had vibrated between the discs. "Yeah, what story is that?" I released a guttural snarl.

"I know what she sees, the loss of her family. She's as broken as Katherine, as broken as any other person in the asylum. As broken as you." The phage motioned to me with another tendril. A row of curved edges disfigured it. A mouthful-sized chunk was missing. "Oh," he trailed off, noticing my gaze. "This?" He raised the damaged tendril for Ortiz and me to see.

"Are those…teeth marks?" Ortiz shot a quick look from the tendril to me.

"School of McGruff," I quipped. "Take a bite outta crime!" I gave the phage a feral smile that was all teeth.

The phage's posture went rigid like a steel pipe had gone through its back. Guess I struck a nerve. It's been known to happen. "I planned on making you suffer for that.

To subject you to hours of your worst fears. Watch your mind and sanity crumble, your blood become engorged in endorphins—"

"Endorphins," I whistled. "Pretty big word for something that looks like Jack Skellington sans the pinstripe suit." *Come on, Graves, figure something out!* I told myself, trying to keep the phage talking until either Ortiz or I managed to find a way to free Lizzie. "I don't suppose if I check out your backside I'll find Tim Burton's hand up your ass?"

For the first time, it was the phage, not Gus that smiled. It was a strange thing to see on its face. Its feather-thin lips stretched, pulling the skin tight on its face. A dry succession of breaths came from its mouth like a dying man's coughs. Was it laughing?

"I was going to peel the layers of your psyche away, piece by piece, until nothing but a drooling shell was left. But, standing here, despite your flippant nature—"

Flippant. That's me.

"I'm going to let both of you go."

"Ah, what?"

"Provided you leave Elizabeth here, and you two leave the asylum, I will let you leave with your lives and minds intact."

Oh sure, it was one hell of an offer. Ortiz and I get to leave perfect and whole. No mind fuckery, no facial probe session. Nothing. All we had to do was leave a vulnerable young girl—one who'd lost her family—in the hands of a monster. Leave her with a madwoman who helped a walking nightmare kill people and feed on them. All I had to do was turn tail and walk out on a friend. Yeah, the phage was doing me a big fucking favor.

"You'll be doing her a great service. Her mind is a wreck. Now, go on," he ordered on behalf of the phage, clucking his tongue like urging a horse to trot off.

I don't know whose knuckles cracked louder—Ortiz's or mine.

"I'll do my best to put her back together. Do you have any idea the fears she harbors?" he asked, his voice rising in pitch. He sounded like a kid on the verge of spilling an exciting secret. "Do you? Do you want to know what buttons I can push to make her—"

He never finished the sentence. The phage couldn't move as fast in tight quarters, and I was grateful for it. I felt the impact from the wall shoot through phage's body and up my spine as I drove it into the concrete. Charles' body wasn't built like a linebacker, but I knew how to hit like one. One of my supernatural perks.

"Ortiz! Get Lizzie out of that crap." I held the phage pinned to the wall. Somehow—bad luck, I wager, the phage's head didn't cave in as I had hoped. It ricocheted off the wall, but the creature's skull remained whole. A fire built in my muscles as I held the phage's arms tight. I didn't need it swiping at my face with those elongated digits.

Tendrils moved with sinuous grace. Some lashed themselves around my arms. Python-like constriction made my limbs feel like twisted hoses about to burst. Another tendril slipped around my neck.

"Glurk!" I gasped as the noose tightened.

I registered Gusbert's ham-like fist arcing toward me and pushed it out of my mind. The heavy hand sailed through my temple with no effect. Even the phage looked stunned. For a monster with not much in the way of facial features, that was some feat.

I jumped and pulled my knees to my chest. My feet connected with the phage's chest and threw it back into the wall. It loosened its hold. I exhaled as the ground welcomed me with a chest bump.

I rolled over to face Ortiz. Lizzie's body hung lower on one side, protruding further from the nest of tendrils on the wall. Ortiz had hacked most of the material away. A little more time and Lizzie would be free. Just a little more time, a little longer of a tussle with tall, thin and scrappy.

Wonderful.

The phage lost no momentum after my drop-kick to the sternum. It was over me in a second. A fist hammered into my back as I tried to recover. The floor gave me another rough embrace. I was having my ass kicked more by the frickin' ground than anything else. Sounds like dried glue being peeled filled my ears as I lay on the floor. Ortiz was tearing Lizzie out of the phage's filth. Twisting, I snapped out with my legs, scissoring the monster. With a roll, I sent the creature falling to the ground alongside me.

Nothing should have been able to have its neck bent at an angle like that and survive. The phage's head was twisted forty-five degrees to the right and folded toward its shoulder. With an abrupt twist, it spun to its feet, making a show out of slipping its neck back into proper alignment.

*Great. I'm dealing with a Hot Topic and Gumby love child.*

"Got her!" Ortiz yelled and a fresh surge of adrenaline hit me. Lizzie was safe. Game on.

Roaring, I sprang to my feet a bit too fast and felt something twinge along my torso. I ignored it and pivoted with my hips. My fist sailed up toward the phage. Tissue strained as my blow failed to connect, leading my arm to hyperextend. My socket screamed. I whipped my head to the side. Ortiz laid Lizzie on the ground, a safe distance from the limb-infested wall. Since the phage hadn't carried through on its threat to Lizzie, she'd recover.

Capitalizing on my brief lapse in attention, the phage wrapped its fingers around my chin. If my mouth weren't open, my teeth would've ground to dust. I was flung to the side. Hot agony and static pulsing coursed through my shoulder. No screams left my mouth as the joint popped. All I managed to do was wheeze.

I don't possess the ability to sling fire, freeze things solid, or flatten someone with pure magical force. My only ability is to be a supernatural heavy bag. They hit. I take it. I heal and get back up for more. That's easier said than done. Two options were present. I could let my shoulder heal on its own. Or I was left with an immediate option. A painful one.

Ortiz leapt into the fray, stabbing with the stake. The phage, fixated on me, blurred into motion to avoid it. It failed. A sound like a crackling fire came from its shoulder. The tip of the stake glanced the creature, removing a golfball-sized lump of meat. A rush of air left its lungs, sounding like a dying hair dryer. The skin around the area morphed from white to charred black. Veins bulged under its tight skin, colored and pulsing like earthworms. The creature's body jerked like a marionette controlled by an amateur. It wasn't a killing blow, but I'd take it.

Seizing the moment, I repositioned myself to face the wall. I sucked in air through my teeth and braced. All it took was a sharp twist. My shoulder impacted the wall. I let out a dog-like whimper as my joint slammed back in place. Fingers waggling, I was satisfied that I'd done it right. I balled my fists and joined Ortiz.

She kept the phage on the defensive. The tip of the stake darted in and out like a fencer's sword. The monster was left with no option but to bob and backpedal.

"Nah-uh," I snapped as I blocked the exit. The last thing we needed was to give the freak room to maneuver. Not to mention the added darkness of the hall. Four of its slender limbs propelled toward my face. "Aiyah!" I yelped as I fell to a crouch, grabbing the creature by the waist. Feet scrabbling against the floor, I pushed, hoping to drive it back. And maybe, if I was lucky, into the stake Ortiz wielded.

The phage displayed the most impressive form of contortion yet. It split its legs at grotesque angles. The creature sunk out of my grip. Its torso twisted and its back pressed flat to the floor.

Those Cirque du Soleil acrobats had nothing on this monster.

It may have been too quick and nimble for me, but not for Ortiz. Flipping the stake in her hand, she dropped her weight, coming down fast. The phage twisted again, trying to slip past her strike. The stake didn't cut the phage. It slipped between the pencil-thin lengths of tissue connecting its mouth. A predatory smile spread over Ortiz's face. She wrenched the stake.

Forget nails on a chalkboard. The scream coming out of the phage's mouth was an entire nursery of kittens shrieking in unison over school desks being dragged across the floor. It doubled over and pawed at the area where the skin had been torn.

"Ehyuck." Ortiz's features twisted as she held the stake at a distance, shaking off the bits of tissue clinging to it.

The phage's frantic motions ceased. Its posture tightened as its freed lips peeled back. Gus' image flared in the far corner of the room, reminding me of a flickering screen. The creature's body quivered like a feral dog about to attack.

Guess it was pissed Ortiz did a number on its mouth.

"I am going to break your minds!" Gus seethed on behalf of the phage. "Tear away every layer of sanity you possess. Leave you broken—hollow things. Unable to function, to slip away from an eternity of horrors!" The phage matched his enraged motions.

That was a bit of an overreaction.

The phage blurred. Its claw-like hand reached for Ortiz. Contrary to belief, time does not slow in those moments. It hurtles past, leaving you burdened with trying to register what's happening. Two lightning-like steps were all it took for the monster to cross the distance between it and Ortiz. Pale fingers gripped her face, covering most of it. With an equally swift motion, it snapped its arm forward.

I dove, arms outstretched, hoping I'd acted in time.

Ortiz crashed into me. A rounded edge glanced off my ribs followed by pain. Lots of it. We hit the floor, tumbling. Every one of my joints felt like they were being rattled apart as we rolled. After the concrete floor had done its job pummeling us, we came to a stop a foot from Lizzie's prone form.

The corners of my eyes felt like they had been swabbed with rubbing alcohol. They burned and blurred near the edges. My field of vision narrowed and wobbled out of focus. Ortiz rocked within my grip.

"Hey." I shook her gently. "You good?"

"Wonderful," she groaned. "You?"

"Wonderful," I groaned back.

"You had your chance," Gus said, and I groaned a third time. Bad guys can't stop talking. It's like there's an official rulebook for them and incessant talking is a staple. Some people just won't shut up.

…Don't look at me like that.

"I allowed you to leave and you spurned my offer," he continued.

With a grunt, I worked my way up to my feet, steadying Ortiz as she rose alongside me. Her forearm tensed as she gripped the stake with renewed strength.

"Tell me," Gus went on. "Is it worth dying over? Was she worth it?" He gestured to Lizzie.

"Yes." Ortiz and I spoke in unison, our tones flat.

"Then die."

"Didn't you learn your lesson about flappin' your gums?" I quipped. It was short-lived.

Myrk, black as wet ink and formless as fog, seeped from its tendrils. Its mouth opened, parting wider without the strands of skin between its lips. A series of *pops* like bubble wrap emanated from its jaw. A plume of Myrk billowed out from it.

A roulette of obscenities spun through my mind. We couldn't slip past it. The freak was too agile and would catch one of us. Lizzie was out cold. We'd have to carry her, making it harder to get out.

There are moments where two people without any outward signs of communication, have the exact same notion.

This was one them.

Ortiz and I rushed into motion. She went high. I went low. Running toward the mass of black fog, I set my shoulders hoping to take the phage's legs out from under it. All I needed to do was keep it pinned while Ortiz drove the stake home. The first bits of Myrk hit us as we moved in for the kill. It was like hitting a brick wall at a hundred miles an hour in a frickin' shopping cart.

The muscles in my legs turned to putty and I rolled forward. A violent red snapped through my eyes and the side of my skull glanced off the floor. Blackness all around me. I was in the middle of the cloud of Myrk. I couldn't see Ortiz. I tried shouting for her. My mistake. Myrk sank into my mouth. It tasted like a mechanic's rag. Hot bile settled at the base of my throat.

Then it hit me. Cold grease slipped into my skull, prodding my brain. The phage was making good on its promise. Numbness overcame me. It wasn't the sort you feel when you're out with too little clothing in winter. It was bone deep. Like an arctic pipeline straight to your blood.

"You're going to die with this notion settled into your mind: that *you* are responsible for the death of young Elizabeth. That *your* arrogance is to blame for the deaths of all those occupying this building!"

Arrogance. Don't you hate the gloaters?

*Wait a tic. All those occupying this building?* I realized its intent and couldn't do a damn thing about it.

"I will reach out and touch every person's mind, enter them, shatter them. I will dance through their mangled minds and over their broken bodies!"

A bit overboard there, Darth Megalomaniac.

"I will feast!" Gus finished as the creature slathered. The sound of water draining was audible. I could see something flickering at the edge of the Myrk. Urging my non-responsive limbs to move, I clawed at the floor. My fingers felt so distant I thought they would sink through the stone as I pulled. I crept out from the Myrk. Softened wood brushed against my skin. I grabbed the stake and rolled out from the hallucinogenic trap. My head reeled from the toxin.

"Gluttony's suh sin," I slurred. The flickering intensified and I turned toward it. I sucked in a breath through my teeth. It was a Way into the Neravene. Nightmare Before Christmas was laying the psychic whammy on everyone in the asylum and was going to scuttle. The phage planned on returning after everyone in the building had been reduced to dribbling wrecks. After that, it was easy pickings.

Wobbling in place, I didn't pose much threat to the phage, even with the stake in my hand. Ignoring me, something I took great offense at, it jumped into the Way. I leapt after it, sending the weapon arcing after the creature. I felt the stake bite. It drove through the meat of the phage's calf. Hooked to the monster's leg, I was dragged along as it passed into the Way.

# Chapter Twenty-Six

The impact rocked my body, but I resolved to hold onto the stake. My eyes stayed shut. The muscles in my face contorted as the ligaments in my shoulder screamed. I twisted and wrenched the weapon from the phage's body. A death rattle came from its throat. It echoed around me.

Opening my eyes, I found myself in a place sapped of ordinary color. Well, that's not fair; it was ordinary for what it was. Ghostly blues and crumbling architecture surrounded me.

The place hadn't changed a bit since my last visit with Ortiz and Lizzie. Good. It was the break I needed.

The phage's pale form stood out like a candle in the night. I wasn't the only thing it had to worry about now. String-like trails of ichor streamed down one of its legs onto the deteriorating floor. The phage adopted the posture you'd expect—one of an injured, cornered animal. It was ready and willing to take any risks to survive.

Gulp.

The monster's head was on a swivel, like a small bird wary of an attack. A silhouette stood off a few feet behind the creature. Its eyes dilated, darting over our surroundings.

"What's the matter, Gus?" I panted. "Not where you were hoping to end up? Panicked and took a wrong turn?"

"Quiet, fool!" he hissed. "You'll attract them."

"Yeah." I smiled, giving the creature a light shrug. "It'd be a shame if someone went hollering after the residents. I could see how that'd be bothersome for you. I don't think the asylum ghosts will take too kindly to you trespassing in their domain."

Gus' eyes ballooned further. His lips trembled and he moved with jerky motions as he rubbernecked to look behind. The phage mirrored his every move.

I cupped a hand to the side of my mouth.

"Yodelayheehoo—mph!" My triumphant exclamation was cut short as the air left my lungs. A dull fire ebbed in my gut as the phage grew further away. I was vaguely aware of the stake falling from my hands and the fact that my feet were no longer touching the floor. My hip took the brunt of the landing as I rolled over broken ground.

And then the ground was gone.

The ceiling pulled away as I sank. I reached out. Fingernails struck the jagged drop-off, and slipped. In situations like this, the last thing you're supposed to do is look down.

I looked down.

Crap.

Blackness, the sort that's so deep you get the idea that it doesn't have an end, filled the area below me. Clawing at the edges of the destroyed floor, I fought for whatever grip I could. The insides of my palms felt like I'd been holding barbed wire as I climbed back up. My elbows creaked from the exertion.

*I'm too old for this shit.*

The phage stood still. Its body was tight and hunched, waiting for any surprises. As long as it was preoccupied with being on the lookout for ghosts, I could take advantage of the situation. My chest ached for a reprieve I couldn't give it. One deep breath wasn't enough to soothe the stretched feeling in my lungs, but it'd have to do. My legs wobbled the first few steps as I broke into a run. All I had to do was grab the stake, overpower the phage, stab it and win.

Easy…

A thin line of tissue within my calf chose that moment to feel like a fraying cable. I willed it out of mind and sprinted toward the phage. The stake was only a dozen feet away and the phage's attention was elsewhere.

The fraying cable snapped.

My calf shuddered and seized. Every step caused the area to pulse with an acid burn.

The apparition of Gus spun about. His lips peeled away as he snarled. Following its illusion, the phage moved to face me. Its arms splayed out like it was waiting to hug an old friend. Never mind the horrible array of hallucinogenic carrying tendrils whipping about its body. It rushed to meet me, passing the stake as it did.

I set my teeth as my speed increased. We were about six feet apart and closing fast when I left the ground. My shoulder burrowed into the creature's gut. A rubbery impact followed as it doubled over. I drove it to the ground. Spittle left my mouth. A satisfying ache filled the small bones in my left fist as the phage's head snapped to the side. The ache and pleasure jumped hands as I knocked its skull to the other side.

"Whaa!" I swatted at the slender appendages as they tried roping themselves around me. The phage seized the opportunity and bucked. The right side of my body hit the ground a foot behind the creature. Before it could get to its feet, I scrambled, clawing at the ground on all fours.

"There's nowhere you can run from me in this place!" Gus called. The phage's rasping followed the declaration.

A series of steps echoed behind mine as I continued my frantic scuttle. Casting a nervous glance back, I could see the phage closing in on me. I took a literal leap of faith and dove. My arm shot out and I hoped for success.

It felt like someone had broken a two by four across my chest as I thudded to the floor. A five-fingered shackle locked itself around my ankle. The creature gripped with enough force to crumble stone. And my fingers scraped across wood.

I offered no resistance as my leg was yanked. The limb was nearly pulled from the socket. The small of my back twinged as I squirmed. I swung as hard as I could. My ankle was relieved of the hydraulic-like pressure and I hit the floor, again.

Gus screamed out with the sort of rage that leaves your tonsils feeling swollen. The monster clutched its wrist in its good hand, breathing like it was having an asthma attack.

Suck it, Vader!

Ragged breaths left its lungs as its hands quivered. Dark fluid dripped from its palm. The only thing stemming the torrent was the object lodged in it. In a single motion, the creature grasped the stake, wrenched it free, and flung it toward me. Splintering wood filled my ears as the stake hit the ground where I had stood a second earlier. I stopped rolling and leapt to my feet. A razor-lined hammer struck the side of my head. The world spun. Maybe I was spinning. It was probably both. Remembering how to stand was an issue as I rubbed a hand across my cheek. Salty moisture from my fingers found its way into the talon-like marks on my face.

The lower half of my jaw clicked as the muscles in my neck fought to keep my head attached from the following backhand. My back came to rest against the wall and the phage seemed to rise. Slumped against the hall, I regarded the only advantage I had. The point of the stake had shattered, as well as a good fourth of the upper portions of the weapon. A much cruder thing was left behind. The tip now resembled a jagged crown of wood. Not ideal for impaling a monster.

Gus followed my gaze to the ruined stake. His lips spread wide into a smile that was all teeth. "It's over."

He was wrong. It wasn't over. I had lost the only object capable of killing the creature is all. *It's not over.*

Holding up its punctured hand for me to see, Gus spoke on behalf of his creator. "To do unto you as you have done unto me." The hole in the phage's hand leaked streams of plum colored ichor. Each of its fingers jerked like the severed tail of a lizard.

I groaned and pushed against the wall in an effort to get to my feet. No dice. It wasn't over. A chilling band formed around my neck. The tip of the phage's tendril settled near my temple.

Stroking my skull in a major display of creepitude, Gus continued speaking. "Relax," he urged. "It's *over.*" He spoke as if he could read my thoughts. "Young Elizabeth will die. Your friend Ortiz will die. Every single person in the asylum will die. Maybe I'll end Katherine as well, start anew somewhere else."

The grip around my neck wasn't tight. I had no gas left in the tank and the bastard knew it. I struggled nonetheless.

"You let them down," Gus went on. A growl formed in my throat as I fought harder. The noose tightened, cutting off the snarling protest. As I sputtered, the phage's slit of a mouth twisted into a skeletal smile. "But it's not the first time is it?"

The muscles in my throat rippled as I summoned what

moisture I could. A globule of foamy spit struck the phage's abdomen.

The phage made good on its threat. The edges of my vision dimmed. It was like ink clouding through water. Everything went black. My head felt like it was in a clamp. Hot wax replaced my blood, too thick and scalding to be pumped properly. I felt heavy. My insides burned and I saw all the wrong things.

A pale greenish-blue blanket was kicked to the floor. My gaze was drawn to what was happening on the bed. The pastel purple nightgown rippled as a woman thrashed against an unseen assailant.

"Marsha!" I breathed.

Her hands clasped her throat. The woman's heart shaped face lost color, and her eyes bulged.

My heart skipped as I clambered atop the bed, shouting, "Ortiz!" Marsha's eyes bulged. Adrenaline fueled her frantic motions as I struggled to pin her down. Recognition flooded Marsha's face. She understood what was going to happen. Her features slipped into a silent plea for help, one I knew I couldn't answer.

"My God!" came a voice behind me.

"Help me!" I begged Ortiz, my voice strained. "Help!" I shouted as best I could.

Ortiz was there in an instant. She held Marsha down while I tried to figure out what was choking her. Finding nothing, I switched to administering abdominal thrusts. Marsha's gasping slowed. My tempo quickened in response. The gasping stopped prompting me to breathe a sigh relief until I heard something else. Marsha's motions ceased and a sound like gurgling water came from her throat.

"No, no, no, no, no!" I dribbled.

Reality snapped back into jarring clarity. My lungs felt leaden as I breathed against the wall. The phage's limb was still wrapped around my throat. Gus looked like he'd just enjoyed a five course meal. The disconcerting smile only grew. "Painful memory?"

"Fuck you," I gurgled in an ever-so-witty riposte.

"Marsha Morressy died six months ago—because of you."

I wanted to tell him that he should've been more

concerned about himself. After all, I was going to kill him, too. I just needed to be free of his grasp, his mind fuck abilities, and get my hands on the stake.

Details...

"Get. Out. Of. My. Head," I said in a tone that could've scoured steel.

Gus chuckled. "Oh no. It's such an interesting place to be. Remember, I'm in everyone's head here. But yours—yours is a particularly desirable place to be. The guilt! Oh, the guilt. All the others you've let down. The ones you've failed..." He trailed off as he touched on something else. "The ones you've lied to." His smile transcended a human look altogether. The phage wore the same expression. Imagine the smile painted onto a scarecrow, thin and stretched too far across. "All the suffering." He released a pleasurable moan.

"You need a new fetish," I muttered.

"I like my vices the way they are. They're so fulfilling, and you seem to be forgetting something."

"Oh yeah?" I spat.

"Before departing the asylum"—he stopped and cast a look around the halls—"the real asylum, I reached out and touched the minds of everyone within its walls."

I swallowed, knowing where this was going.

"How long do you think it's been for them?" Gus and his scarecrow-esque puppeteer smiled. "An hour—*hours?*" he stressed the plural. "Days? Time has a way of slipping by rather fast in this place. Do you think there's anything left of a single person back there? Do you want to go back and find out?"

Bristling, I balled my fists as my weight shifted from bracing against the wall.

The phage breathed and dark vapor came over me once again. Everything warped.

Something acrid clung to the inside of my nose. Anyone who's burnt their finger knows the particular smell of burning flesh. Multiply it a hundredfold. Particulate matter sticks to your nostrils, refusing to let go. It's a cocktail of iron-rich blood and bodily gasses. The body, if you could call it that, looked like something from Pompeii, minus the coating of volcanic ash. The figure was positioned much the way a toddler would sleep when having a bad dream. Curled tight and pulling away from something.

Rick. He was a security guard at the museum during my last case in New York. He was a complete tool. A porcine-faced dude with a bad attitude. But he didn't deserve to die the way he did. Another tally on the list of casualties over my cases. Every death of an innocent was like an iron weight pulling me down. And I was already drowning.

The images were pulled as fast as I had seen them. The phage's tendril shivered in excitement against my throat. "They're palpable, you know?" Gus said. "Fear. Anguish. Suffering. Even to your kind. You just have to open up to it." Gus ran a tongue over his lips as the phage leaned in closer. It lowered itself so its head was on the side of mine. It opened its mouth and inhaled. Both of them shivered in pleasure as the phage breathed in.

"I'm flattered. Creeped out a little, too, but I don't swing that way."

"Don't worry," Gus assured. "You're not to enjoy this anyway. This is more for me than you."

*Selfish prick.*

"How about another?" he asked.

"How about you take your tendrils and—" I never finished my sentence.

*No!*

Ortiz stood a dozen paces away from the Ifrit. She was strong, confident and without a weapon. I tuned out the exchange of words. Shutting my eyes did nothing to stop the images. Ortiz's face twisted into a mask of revulsion and pity as she regarded the creature. A figure lay on the floor, pointing a revolver at someone past the Ifrit. I watched myself smile, holding the gun in a quivering grip. The Ifrit's black lips peeled into a smile. A horrible pulsing white light hovered above its palm. The Ifrit's smile widened and the throbbing light fled from its place atop the creature's hand.

And struck the area above Ortiz's left breast.

I waited for the scene to pull away like the others but the phage had no intention of letting that happen.

Ortiz's eyes lost their focus. They widened in search of an answer to a question she couldn't understand. Then...Camilla Ortiz fell.

The distant me on the floor exhaled. "Oh, God."

Black swirls of ink overtook my sight and I tensed, waiting for it to return to normal. Every ounce of my body contorted. I prepared to charge the phage and bash its brains out.

Ortiz stood about a dozen paces away from the Ifrit, chin thrust up, iron tones in her voice. There was an exchange of words and glances. The vision of me on the floor wore a wolfish grin. A hideous orb of white light hissed past and buried itself in Ortiz's chest. She fell in slow motion. A snowflake melting before the Ifrit's fire.

It looped again.

The muscles in my eyes ached. My throat felt stripped of lining. I couldn't find my voice to scream.

Phages are assholes. Nothing made it more evident than when the memory looped for the fifth time.

Gus' voice slithered into my ear like cold oil, slimy and prompting my body to jerk. "You'll endure it. You'll endure *all* your failures until there's nothing left of you."

I wanted to spit back a reply, but it felt like I had stepped into an industrial freezer. The tips of my fingers tingled, and a winter morning's air stung the insides of my throat. It was irrefutably spring in New York, yet a December chill filled my body, dulling my senses. The cold helped ease me out of the phage's mind trip.

It faded and I was back in the warped asylum. I looked past the phage, taking note of the walls. Crystalline structures formed over them. It was beginning to look like glass screens in the frozen food aisle. My breath came out in a plume of fog. I couldn't help it. A few coughs left my lungs before clearing into laughter.

Gus and the phage took a step back in unison, eyeing me like I was insane. I laughed harder. The icy coating on the walls grew, layering until the inevitable happened. The sound of glass cracking filled the halls in perfect synchrony. The laughter was possessive now. It took hold of me and ran away. My laughter rang over the shattering ice to the point they became giggles.

"Stop laughing," Gus bellowed.

My head rocked to the side as the phage's fist drove me to the ground. Copper filled one of my cheeks. Spitting, I let out a weak chuckle. "Oh, man," I groaned. "You're not seeing it, are you?"

Gus remained motionless, but the phage titled its head, turning slowly to look around.

"This isn't your domain." I dropped my voice to a dangerous whisper. "And you're trespassing."

It happened without transition. Gus, the phage, and I weren't the only things in the hall anymore. By my count, at least a dozen beings stood twenty paces off from us. All of them were dressed in simple garments resembling asylum attire. All of them stood eerily motionless. All of them exuded a haunting beauty. All of them were pissed.

The cold ring around my neck disappeared as the phage pulled its tendril away. It turned to face the crowd of newcomers.

"You…" I coughed. "You're a popular fella, it seems." Gus glared cold murder at me. The ghosts inched forward with hungry looks in their eyes. "Think about it. I'm pretty sure you're responsible for a fair few of these folks and their ghostly predicament. So I imagine they ain't too happy to see you here unannounced and all." I grinned.

Gus' appearance waned. Out of all the things occupying the hall, he became the most ghost-like. Hunched, arms out wide, the phage looked like it was ready for one hell of a fight. One it was, by the look of things, definitely going to get.

Coughs shook my body as I rose to my feet with support from the wall. Cold needles pricked at my fingers. I yanked my hand away from the frost-caked hall. I shook my freezing hand. "This is the part where you might want to turn tail and run."

The phage whipped its head to look at me. A low hiss passed its lips before it turned back to the ghosts. Every one of them moved toward the phage.

"Think about it, man," I said. "They're stuck like this, in here, because of you. They're broken, *angry*, because of you! And now you're in their domain. Powerful creature or not, you're not playing with the home field advantage."

The creature turned to sneer at me, which takes skill when you have no eyes and a paper-cut-thin mouth.

"Best get a-bouncin', man," I advised. "Open a Way

and get out of here. You might not want to ever come back."

Gus flashed back into clarity. His neck tensed and teeth bared. "You'd like that wouldn't you? Have a chance to escape, maybe get back with your friends. If I perish, you'll follow!"

"Uh, pretty sure I won't, pal. See, I made good with the ghosts here on account of my good friend, Lizzie."

Both the phage and Gus flinched.

"Yeah." My voice took an edge. "You remember her, don't you? Innocent young girl you tied up below the asylum. Were planning on doing God-knows-what to. A little girl who'd just been through hell to get her sister back!"

Gus lost the clarity he had just regained. The phage took a step back from the approaching cluster of ghosts. "If anything happens to me, there'll be nothing left of her. Of your friend—of anyone back there." His lips peeled back as he snarled.

"Something's going to happen to you. I just can't guarantee what exactly. I've never seen ghosts pick a phage apart before. Should be…informative. Plus, what can you do to stop them?" I stopped as a thought occurred to me. "You can't, can you?"

Gus' eyes grew wider than before. He looked like he was hunting for a bomb shelter.

"They're not living any longer. You can't feed off ghosts, meaning…you can't affect them. You *can't* hurt them—at all!"

The phage took another step back and something clattered against its heel.

Burying the numbness, and the pain, I rushed forward, crashing with the phage into the wall. "Get 'em!" I roared, hoping it wasn't presumptuous of me to order around the gaggle of ghosts. Pain raced through my collarbones as the phage's forearm smashed into the top of my chest. Stumbling backward, I let myself fall to get clear of the oncoming horde. It's never a good idea to stand in front of a group of pissed off paranormal entities.

Heels kicking against the floor, I pushed myself away from the phage as the first of the ghosts made contact. What I saw next made it feel like I was breathing compressed oxygen. Chilling air nipped my insides as the spectral being swiped at the phage. Four lines appeared across the phage's chest, deep, oozing more of its blood before slowing. The fluids crystallized into icy streams over its body.

Ortiz and I had gone through one helluva time trying to hurt the sucker as much as we did. Heck, just one of the ghosts managed to put a hurting on it. And that was all it took.

A scene from a wildlife documentary unfolded around me. Tendrils shot out trying to grab the ghost, passing through without effect. More ghosts crowded around, like hyenas surrounding a wounded animal. Every visible inch of Gus' body quivered. The phage's body mimicked him. It was about time the bastard got a taste of fear.

The phage made no attempt to move. It was motionless inside a group of hostile spirits. I rose to my feet and walked over to retrieve the broken stake. It may not have been perfect, but I was banking on the notion that it still held the potential to gank the phage.

A flash of light pulled my attention away from the weapon. Space tore; a Way hung past the group of ghosts. The phage made its move, blurring into motion.

Big mistake.

Fast movements are not the best course of action when surrounded by multiple predators. Especially when you're on their turf.

With a unison that had to be telepathic, the asylum's ghosts converged on the phage. Frickin' shark-week happened before me. My eyes struggled to keep up with the amount of action. Ghosts rushed the phage, clawing, snarling. Hell, some were biting. Tooth-and-nail fighting. A cloud of Myrk puffed into existence causing me to lose sight of the phage.

As the ghosts reeled away from the toxic gas, I bolted toward the doorway suspended in the air. Tall, thin and ugly burst out from the dark mass of smog. It hoofed it toward the opening. My lungs squeezed tight in effort. My legs and joints howled in protest from the temperature. I ignored them all, focusing solely on catching the phage before it crossed through the Way.

Being trapped in the twisted asylum did not seem like a

good idea.

I gained on the phage, its movements slowed by the Sixth Sense beat-down it had received. The creature's left arm looked like a twig someone had stepped on, multiple breaks in the bone. It hung in a grotesque fashion. Lengthy gashes marred its back, looking like it'd been mauled by a big cat.

I smiled and pumped my legs harder as my hand tightened on the stake. *Just a bit closer.* One swift plunge and the stake would be buried in the back of the phage's skull. The phage turned its head, never breaking its stride as its appendages flared into motion. Myrk rushed to fill the space between the monster and me. It seeped into my nostrils and mouth, burying itself in my lungs.

I fell.

A flurry of nightmares sprang to greet me. It was a cocktail of everything Charles and I feared. Dim halls with shadows darting through them. The skin at the base of my neck pricked. The lights waned further. Darkness consumed me. All of it transpired within a second.

"No," I breathed.

I pulled myself back, leaping out of the fumes. The phage stopped a little more than a dozen paces away. Its slender lips stretched. It leapt—

—the magical passageway flared like a crack of lightning in the dark.

The Way had shut.

Concrete solidified in my gut. The phage was wounded and needed to heal. To feed. And there was an entire asylum full of people waiting on the other side.

Ortiz.

Lizzie.

I'd failed.

# Chapter Twenty-Seven

Freon pumped through my arteries. My insides went cold. An army of woodpeckers assaulted my skull. A staccato beat of knocking was all I could hear. I stood motionless, staring at the empty space where the Way had been seconds before.

"No," I breathed, harder this time, as if my denial would force the pathway open again. My knuckles ached from how tight my fists were balled. A pressure cooker nestled in my heart. "No!" My fist bounced off the nearest wall. The roar tore through the halls, followed shortly by its echo. With military snap precision, I turned to face the remaining ghosts.

They were immobile, blending into the eerie surrounding like fixtures. Spooky, spectral, dangerous fixtures.

"What?" I barked.

Every ghost bristled in unison.

It's never a smart idea to yell at a bunch of ghosts, especially when you're standing in their living room.

Cold vapors emanated from their bodies and crept along the hall. Another layer of ice formed over the already frozen walls.

*Holy shit!*

I didn't budge, at least visibly. "Do something." The ghosts had no obligation to me. I may have helped with the Shadowvore problem but that was more Lizzie's doing. And I wasn't Lizzie. She was trapped with a hungry supernatural horror. "Do something!" My throat ached, my body quivered and I could feel my heart quicken. The muscles in my jaw went rigid for a few seconds. I didn't have Lizzie's gift of communicating with ghosts, all I had was my anger. I used it.

"What? You bastards can only do something if the

phage is prancing around in your stinkin' corner of the Neravene?"

Their faces flashed, eyes narrowing as they stepped closer.

I swallowed. "Lizzie fought to save your intangible asses. I fought to save your asses! If you don't want to leave and face the phage outside your plane, fine! I get it; I really do. I'm not asking you to fight. I'm asking you to just do something!" My voice cracked. "Please."

The ghosts continued their silent march toward me.

I wasn't going to fail another person. Not again. My feet shifted of their own accord, bringing me closer to them. "That thing is responsible for so many deaths. For making some of you like this. There are innocent people back there. People I'm supposed..." I trailed off.

Moving became more difficult. My skin grew paler and frost lined my lashes. My teeth chattered. "If...if you let this thing get away..." I broke off as I fought to breathe. The temperature plummeted further. "You'll be just as responsible for any future deaths. You'll be no different," I said, letting as much heat as I could fill my voice. "And I'll come after you next!"

It wasn't as intimidating as it could've been, what with me being a Gravescube. My clothes stiffened. A coating of soft ice formed over them. We moved another step closer to each other. "That child," I began, my voice hardening as I spoke. "That little girl is braver than all of you put together. You have power. Real fucking power! And you can't use it to help a child? You're not people! You're hollow shells. Empty, cowardly, self—"

The air in my lungs felt solid, freezing and cutting off my voice. One of the ghosts appeared beside me. I hadn't registered its movement. Fingers brushed across my throat, causing my neck to harden.

*Let's rumba, spooky.* I shifted my weight to strike. Looking into the ghost's eyes, I stopped. They were downcast. The former man's head was bowed. Pale eyes looked away as his mouth twisted into a grimace. Looking past him, I saw that every other ghost wore a similar expression—pain, sadness, regret...shame.

The ghost before me pointed to a spot behind my head.

He gestured with a slow wave as I turned around. Stark white light cleaved through the air with the sound of tearing fabric. Invisible talons raked the space behind me. An opening was gouged into existence.

A Way.

For once, I had a good idea of where this particular one would lead me. I turned a fraction, looking over my shoulder. "Thank you." I inclined my head. The ghosts returned the gesture, some of their lips even spread into smiles.

Turning back to the Way, I set my jaw and the muscles in my hand contracted. I threw myself into the opening with a snarl, hoping the phage would hear me before I emerged.

\* \* \*

It was like a train leaving the station and entering the darkness of a tunnel. The brightness of the Way was replaced by the dimness of the Asylum under-works. My vision adjusted and part of me wished it hadn't. An itch drew my gaze to my forearm. A whole hour had passed in about fifteen minutes of dealing with the phage in the Neravene.

Nine hours was still plenty of time. I hoped.

Katherine Robinson was curled on the floor like a sleeping infant. I would've thought it peaceful if it weren't for the slender white being crouched over her. The phage's remaining tendrils wormed their way into Katherine's nostrils, ears and mouth. One of the limbs found a way to burrow into the soft tissue of her trachea.

"Just in time for the finale," said a smug voice from behind me.

Impulse took hold and I spun around, swinging with a haymaker. I might as well have tried to punch smoke.

"Lizzie!" Her body slumped against the wall. At first glance she would've appeared to be at rest. First glances are often wrong in my business. Her body jerked at random intervals, beads of sweat fell down her face. I turned to the far side of the room where another figure sat. Her arms were hugging her knees tight to her chest; worse, unlike

Lizzie, her eyes were open.

"Ortiz!" My scream failed to register with her.

Her eyes were unfocused like she was under the influence of some drug. She muttered something that only she could hear. Ortiz looked like a child in the midst of a silent nightmare, rocking slightly as she endured the mental terror.

"Stop it, now!" My voice dropped to a low, threatening growl.

Gus broke into laughter. "Or what?"

I waved the stake. "Or I'm going to redefine what it means to have a woody. I'm going to jam this through your windpipe!" A soft sigh, much like relief, pulled me away from threatening Gus.

An ink-like discharge pooled from Katherine's ears as the first two tendrils slipped out of her skull. The ichor leaked from her tear ducts, mouth and the hole in her throat. Her body lost what remaining strength it had and collapsed entirely. The phage took her by the shoulders, easing her fall to the ground with more care than I would've expected from a monster.

Another person dead on the job. Katherine may have been responsible for other deaths, but she wasn't exactly in her right mind. She was driven to do those things by the phage's manipulations. The muscles in my throat knotted, choking out most of what I wanted to say. "Bastard!"

"Me? Why?" Gus thrust his chin in defiance. "I didn't kill her. You did."

"Yeah? How do you figure that one?

Gus' image blurred out of sight. A flicker over my shoulder told me where I'd find it. I moved in a cautious turn, working not to prompt the phage into any sudden action. The creature took its time rising to full height to face me. With an exaggerated wave, it turned its wounded hand over for me to see. Viscous fluid no longer wept from the puncture. The edges of were stitching closed by some unseen force. The rest of the phage remained the grisly battered sight it had been upon leaving the Neravene.

"You'll never have any idea how hard it was feeding on her, putting her through that." Gus dropped his gaze to the ground.

"Whose fault was that?"

"Yours," he countered in a matter-of-fact voice. The monster looked poised to jump me any second now. My palm itched from the stake. Its weight was reassuring. "Think about it. I took on the appearance and personality of her son."

"Her son died!" I snarled. "You're a bastardization. You toyed with her head, made her think she was okay! You preyed on the love she had for her son and the pain his loss caused her. You gave her a glimmer of hope and strung her along with it!"

"I saved her from becoming a nonfunctional mess," he argued. "I gave her happiness and she, in return, did what any mother would. She took care of me, fed me. Looked out for me, cleaned up after me. In the end, she was ready to die for me. She *wanted* to give her life for me. She was protecting her son, giving her life—"

Charging forward, I drove the stake toward its heart. My rage echoed through the room. The phage bobbed to the side but wasn't quick enough to avoid the splintered edges of the weapon. Reeling back, it cupped the area around its brow where the wooden implement had glanced it. A serpentine hiss came from the surrounding flesh. The skin crackled and looked like necrosis would begin any moment now. "You're a monster!" I declared.

A battering ram impacted my gut. Hell, my feet left the floor. Electric jolts sparked throughout the vertebrae in my neck as an explosion went off beneath my chin. I didn't remember the flight but I sure as hell remembered the landing. Someone was playing the xylophone on my flippin' ribcage. I couldn't make out the damage to the supporting bones. Ow seemed like as good a prognosis as any.

"Monster?" Gus spat back. A cold, damp rag fell atop my brain. Everything went numb. Thinking became cloudy and my body convulsed. "You pushed me to this. If you had left well enough alone, my *mother* would still be alive!" he screamed. I managed to groan between the fit of coughs jarring my ribs as I lay on the ground. "The only deaths I've caused are to feed and to sustain myself. What about the ones you've caused?"

I sputtered a trio of coughs. They translated to: "Shut

the fuck up." So I was a cough off. I didn't have it in me.

The feeling inside my skull grew. A nauseating oily presence snaked around my thoughts. "You want to know what a monster is—a real monster?" he asked.

Planting the butt of the stake against the stone tiling, I pushed down, using it to help me rise. But the phage had other ideas. The small bones in my wrists ground as it clamped down on them. With another ribcage-shaking *thud*, the phage pinned me to the floor again. Its pale, puppet-like face was inches from mine.

"Ugh." I coughed and turned from its breath. "The hell did you eat for breakfast—garbage?"

Ignoring my insult, Gus continued talking me to death. "A monster is something that gives false hope to someone. Let's them believe in something better, and pulls a wool of lies over their eyes. A monster hides them from the terrible truth. It lets them think they will come out okay."

The pressure inside my head increased. The worms roiled my brain.

"Look at them." Gus pointed to Ortiz and Lizzie.

I spat on the creepy Muppet's face.

"Look!" he ordered. My neck felt like a rusted motor as it was forced to turn by the phage. Ortiz sat there, eyes looking right at me—through me—still shaking. "A monster brings people like that into danger with no way out. It's been an hour since we departed to the Neravene and back. What do you think is left of her, of young Elizabeth? Anything at all? Who involved them in this?"

*You, you twisted freak.*

"I probed every recess of their thoughts. You don't think I know who's responsible for their predicament? It's certainly not me. I am doing what I've always done—surviving. If you hadn't come along—who knows—I might not have harmed these two at all. There's no end to the people I could have chosen. It's possible these two would've left the asylum before I had a chance. And if I did feed on them, it would've been quick."

"Liar. You get off on making people suffer. It gets your pasty rocks off!" I shot back.

"True. Fine, not so quick. But look at them now. Suffering because of you. You don't honestly believe they are here on their own whim, do you?"

"They made a choice! They *wanted* to help. They're good people." I thrashed in the creature's grip.

"Really? You believe that? At any time you could have removed them from your search. Did they force themselves into it...or did you allow them to? I read their minds, remember? They urged, they argued, but you could have easily withheld information. You could have left them in the dark and proceeded without them. You didn't. You involved them, turned to them for help, guidance, asked favors of them. Subtly so. It was craftier manipulation than anything I have ever done."

He was lying. That's what phages do. Lie. They twist your mind and the facts.

"Answer me. Could you have spared them this?"

Icicles pierced my skull and forced me to answer. "Yes!"

Oh, hell. Oh, hell. The phage was right. I could've pushed Ortiz away. I tried to at first, but part of me wanted her help. It was just like with the Ifrit. Only now, if she died, there wasn't any way to bring her back. Lizzie. She was just a kid. How in the name of heaven and hell did I think it was okay to get a kid involved in this?

"*You* murdered them." I could hear the heat in the phage's voice. The damp feeling in my brain grew colder and wetter.

Everything became heavy. The air felt like a lead blanket falling to snuff me out. I've dealt with death a lot. It's not a new experience for me, and, now, it was rather comforting. Too many people had died on my watch. This was easier. All I had to do was lay there. It would be over soon. The serpents moving through my skull flared in activity, pulsating.

*Oh crap*, I realized. *I've been whammied!* "Rawgh!" I flailed, trying to free my hand. The bellow was replaced by a high pitched scream as the bones in my wrist failed. Heat, the uncomfortable, painful sort, filled the joint as the stake was yanked from it. My hand dislocated at the wrist from the violence in which the phage pulled the weapon away. Gus' lips peeled into a sneer as the phage tossed the wood aside, letting it clatter near Ortiz's feet.

"Figured it out, hmm?" Gus asked.

"Get out of my head!"

"Why would I do that? We're back where I have the power and your ghost friends cannot intervene. They're too terrified of facing me here. This is my domain. A house of fear. Even they can feel it here. Would you like a taste?"

"How about I give you a taste of my foot up—" The phage cut me off. Myrk spilled from its mouth and tendrils. The toxin invaded me.

I shook my head as the foul stuff entered my body. The weight came off my arms and the creature stood above me. I may have been free, but moving was out of the question. The Myrk began its work a bit too quickly for my tastes. Images swirled, distorting reality and imagination. I was able to make out the phage as it stepped past me. Rolling onto my stomach, I watched as he approached Lizzie.

The monster gave Lizzie a sharp tug. She shrieked as the creature hauled her by her hair. It shoved her toward me with a callous thrust of its hand.

I gurgled an incoherent stream of obscenities. The only clear bit was, "Leave her alone."

I was ignored. Go figure.

Myrk obscured my thoughts and my grasp of what was real. I felt myself slipping into a dreamlike state. Lizzie was only an arm's length away but seemed to be pulling away from me somehow. Her eyes opened, pupils dilating, whites trembling in terror. The phage went to work. Its strand-like limbs wrapped themselves around her face. Lizzie's body jerked as the appendages made contact.

"You're going to watch as I make her suffer through the worst her mind has to offer. Then when she's all but spent...I'll finish her."

Something expanded in my stomach. A primordial wave of anger filled me up. When it was too much to keep contained, I let it out. The scream must've been heard through the entire building. "Let her go!" I bellowed, trying to inch forward. My senses left me, switched out for what the phage wanted me to see.

Lizzie lay broken and twisted on the ground. The extra padding of fat in her cheeks was now gone. Emaciated, gaunt, like a wet cloth wrung dry. Her eyes lost the childlike brightness they'd had earlier. They were a hollow gray, the sort that comes with bleak weather. Her skin was devoid of that unique complexion of hers. A wine-colored syrup bled out from her eyes, mouth and ears, congealing on the floor.

You might as well have ripped my heart out. It would've hurt a helluva lot less.

"Ortiz?" I screamed through the vision. The phage was not going to have the satisfaction of turning Vincent Graves into a crying pansy. "Ortiz?" I called again. "Please!"

"She can't hear you," Gus answered through my imaginings.

"Can it! Ortiz!" I shifted my neck so I could see her. Ortiz's chest was rising faster. Her breathing quickened. Maybe I was getting through. "Ortiz, come on. Fight it. I don't know what this thing is doing to you, but fight it. You can beat this mind game crap. You're too hotheaded, too stubborn for this shit. Come on!"

The Myrk tried to cloud my head with more images. I fought back. A pinpoint piercing pain erupted in my tongue. I tasted copper. I winced as I bit harder. "Ortiz." I tried to speak clearly with my impaired tongue. "Ortiz, listen to me!" I snapped. Her head jolted for a fraction of a second, but I saw it. That was enough.

"Charles?" Her words slurred like she'd had a heavy night of drinking.

"That's right. Me. Annoying, smart ass, insufferable and ever-so-awesome me!"

She groaned.

I tried not to take it personally.

"Listen to me. You've been whammied by the phage." Her eyes fluttered and she looked like she was about to nod back off. "Listen!" I screamed. "You wanted to know why I do this, how I do this. About always feeling outmatched and outclassed. Well, I am. We are. In this life you always are, but so what? Against the supernatural, you're always fighting out of your weight class. What matters is that you fight, because what else is there to do? We don't curl up into balls and bitch; we fight! Ortiz!"

"She. Can't. Hear. You," Gus repeated. "But little Elizabeth can. She can hear you trying and failing. Would you like to hear her?" The phage gripped her head tighter. She screamed. God, was it awful. Hearing a child make a noise like that—someone pretty much took a power drill to my ears.

"Ortiz, we fight to keep freaks like this at bay, ganking them whenever we can. Yes, this world is scary. You think knowing about it helps. Well, it does, but it also makes things worse. I know tons and, hell, I'm terrified by what I know—about what's out there. But so what? It's not about being afraid for ourselves. It's about being afraid for others, and fighting for them. It's about keeping monsters from hurting people—hurting children! Ortiz, it's about putting your fear in a place where it works for you, not against you!" I continued, helping myself as much as I aimed to help her with my words. I don't know where they came from. All I knew was that they were true.

And that if I didn't do something, Lizzie, Ortiz and I were going to die.

"Silence!" The phage gave Lizzie another shake. She yelped once again.

"If I don't kill you, Ortiz will!"

The threat passed idly by the phage's ears. It remained keen on tormenting Lizzie. I was watching the live-action version of the image the phage had forced me to see before. Lizzie's complexion was losing its youthful glow. A shade of yellow associated with illness began to seep in. Her cheeks lost their mass. It didn't look so much like Lizzie was dying so much as she was aging.

There's a kind of anger that comes from somewhere bone-deep inside you. It's the kind people are afraid to let out. It's the sort that threatens to tear you apart at the seams. Your body becomes the housing for a crematorium-level fire. Kept inside, it's the type of thing that'll consume you. So there's only one thing to do.

Let it out.

So I did.

"Ortiz!" I barked, my voice harsh enough to strip paint from metal. "Snap out of it, right now! You want to play in my world, get involved and be the hero? Well toughen up, sister, because this life is hard. People count on you. They depend on you all the damn time and you *can't* let them down. It's not an option. You think because you're having a rough time inside your head right now that you're—what—

excused? Fuck that! You're not. You wanna act tough in front of me, then fine; show me! Show me!" I screamed.

"Cute," Gus chimed in.

"Shut it, Skeletor. You think you're this terrifying boogey monster that should be feared. You're not. Your kind may have survived the collapse of Babylon—"

"We caused it!" Gus seethed. Even the phage paused from its torment of Lizzie.

I sneered. "Of course you did. Insects always cause the infestation. Congrats; you weren't exterminated. Know what that makes you? A cockroach. A pest. A dirty little bug scuttling around for whatever scraps of food it can find! You're filth; you're—"

The side of my skull exploded in pain. Something went *crack*, either the ground or me. Smart money was on both. I could see the phage towering above me, one hand cocked for another blow, the other wrapped in Lizzie's hair.

My body shook as I tried laughing through the coughs. "Touched a nerve, pasty?" I arched as a shockwave went through the broad of my back. The phage could seriously throw a punch.

"Shut up!" Gus ordered. Each word was punctuated with another strike to my body.

Violence is never the key to good communication.

The bits of my body that weren't broken or dislocated ached like I had gone bungee jumping without the harness. Getting up was out of the question, and fighting the phage was laughable at best.

"Damnit, Camilla Ortiz, get up! If you don't put on your big girl pants right now, a little girl is going to die! And you know what? It's not going to be on the phage. It's not going to be on me. It's going to be on you!" My insides stung spouting the lie, but I didn't know what else to say. Fingers dug into my throat, cutting off any further reply. I tried anyways. "Blurkh!" My feet were still anchored to the ground as the phage lifted me to waist height solely by my neck. Three of the phage's tendrils remained free. Guess what it decided to do with them? I gurgled and beat my feet as the first limb wound its way over my face. Coldness spread through that half of my face. A slow paralysis worked to lull me back into the phage's nightmares.

Fear is many things. A killer of the mind and function according to some. A necessity to others. Fear is the grindstone that turns a dull edge into one of diamond hardness. Fear is the poison that erodes resolve. And fear is not without a killer of its own.

Hope.

It's that little root protruding from the rocks on the cliff face you're dangling from. Not much of a thing, but it's all you have to reach for, and you grab it. It's that tiny piece of vegetation that keeps you from falling.

I looked out of the corner of my eyes to the spot where Camilla Ortiz had been. I smiled and clung to hope.

My smile was torn from me as the phage's fingers tightened across my voice box. Pounding my fists against the creature's arm was no good. It was like beating on steel railings with a stick. Struggling was too difficult. I let my arms fall to my sides and forced out a weak laugh.

"What's so funny?" Gus sneered.

Another laugh left my lungs. Well, it was more like a death wheeze trying to be a laugh. It's the intent that counts.

"Nothin'," I managed to rasp. "I was just wondering...what happened to Ortiz?"

Gus never had the chance to answer. It sounded like someone drove over a rotting melon. There was a wet *squelch* of a noise as the phage's body jerked. Its fingers loosened their grip around my throat. Catching myself as I fell, I looked up to see a jagged crown of wood burst through the phage's chest.

"Boo," whispered Ortiz. In one swift motion, she pulled the stake from the monster's chest and sent it plunging into the side of its throat. The phage lost all composure, like a rag doll with no one holding it. The monster crumpled to the ground. Another body followed the monster's fall and I rushed to catch her.

"Lizzie!" I shouted through a couple of coughs. My joints and muscles screamed as I cradled her in my arms.

It didn't matter. I would heal. I always heal. I pushed every bit of pain as far down as I could, blinking through the few tears.

I shook Lizzie as I looked at Ortiz. I placed an ear to her mouth and sucked in a breath through my teeth. "She's not breathing!"

Ortiz fell into a crouch by my side. The stake left her grip and her hands eased their way under mine to support Lizzie. I lowered Lizzie to the ground. We slipped our hands out from beneath her and went to work.

I pinched her nose shut and inhaled, hoping this was all I needed to do. I exhaled, forcing the proper amount of breath into her. An image of a young woman in a pastel gown swam before me.

*Not again!* I inhaled a second time. *Please let this work.* I breathed into Lizzie. First the Ifrit and Marsha. Now the phage and Lizzie. I wasn't going to let a monster take another person. Not like this.

"Her heart's still beating," said Ortiz.

"Damnit!" I snapped. "The hell's going on here?" There was no reason for Lizzie's lack of breathing. The phage certainly hadn't finished its job on her. She was still alive...for now. Hands fell on my shoulders and squeezed tight for a moment.

"Charles, move over," Ortiz urged in a voice too soft for the situation before us.

Huffing out a breath, I pushed myself to my feet and crossed the short distance to the phage's body. Its pale skin looked like ash. It had dried to the point where it had cracked. Bits of tissue looked like they were being eroded away by invisible waves. I took hold of the phage's mangled throat and shook the creature. "What did you do to her?" I knew I'd get no answer. I squeezed harder. My fingers were wound tight into a fist with dust slipping between them. The phage's neck crumbled like centuries' old paper. The rest of its body followed.

I sighed. "Of course."

Sharp, dry coughing prompted me to turn. Lizzie's body shook. She shook! "Lizzie!" I scrambled over to her. "Ortiz, what'd you do?"

"I just kept breathing?" She shrugged.

I bowed my head. "Thank you."

Lizzie made the sort of sound you'd expect a child to make when forcing them to eat their vegetables. "Yeeackh!" she retched. The bile was water-like in consistency, tinged with strings of black-syrupy gunk. She wiped her mouth with the back of her wrist. "Why does my mouth taste like grape cold medicine?"

I couldn't help it. I lost it. I fell back to the floor. A pang went through my ribs as I burst into laughter. Ortiz joined me. It's moments like that, after a terrible ordeal, where laughter truly helps. It's one of the purest things in the world. Laughter heals a lot, even the troubles of the paranormal world at times.

Moments later, the cool tingling like that of an alcohol swab washed over a small area on my forearm. I glanced at the spot to see my tattoo lose its clarity until nothing was left. With a sigh of relief, I hobbled over to Lizzie. I pressed one of my hands to my aching ribs. "Come on." I smiled and extended a hand. It felt good when I took her hand in mine, hauling Lizzie to her feet. Even with my ribs and wrist lighting up in pain, I didn't bat an eye. I held my smile through it all.

I could feel the warmth of Ortiz's breath on my ear when she whispered. "Is she going to be fine?"

My voice was louder and harsher than it should've been. "Yes." I could feel Ortiz's eyes widening as she took a step back. Looking at Lizzie, I told her, "You're going to be fine." I flashed her the largest and goofiest grin I could manage. Lizzie's smile wasn't quite as wide or full as it had been before, but I took it. "Ortiz," I said, "what about you? You good?"

She bit her lip but didn't answer.

I kept my voice neutral when I said, "You were out for an hour. Both of you were, you know that?"

"That long?" There was a hint of disbelief in her voice.

"After we started walloping the phage, it bounced to the Neravene." I paused for a moment when Ortiz shuddered. "You two, and maybe the entire asylum, were under the phage's influence while we were there."

"What about now?"

I shrugged. "I don't know. Not really, at any rate. But Ortiz, an hour...an hour under that monster's influence can dredge up your worst fears and memories. What did you see?"

"What I needed to." The tone in which she said it sent the message. I didn't pry any further.

"Well, I'm glad you came out of it."

"Thanks." She flashed a quick smile. "And thanks for what you said. For all of it."

"Heard that, huh? Hey!" I rubbed my arm where her elbow had struck. "The heck was that for?"

"I heard *all* of it." A challenging light gleamed in her eyes. "Put on your big girl pants?" She arched an eyebrow.

"Glad you did." I smirked before my arm throbbed again. Ortiz grinned. "Come on. Let's get out of the creepy basement of doom."

"Charles." Ortiz nodded in the direction of a slumped form. "What about Katherine?"

"I don't know—" I started, my hands clenching on their own. People and monsters aren't as different as some would like to make out. I've met my fair share of monstrous people. I've also met a handful of supernatural beings that showed a great deal more humanity than many people.

Katherine Robinson was manipulated by a real monster, but that didn't excuse what she did. On some level, no matter how far down, Katherine knew she was involved in the deaths of innocent people. Maybe she thought she was doing it for her long-lost, twisted son. Whatever. Wrong is wrong.

At least, I'd like to think it is. Nothing is ever so cut and dry with the paranormal, and certainly not with people.

"She's dead." I moved to leave the room.

Lizzie settled the matter for us. "We should carry her out," she said as if it were obviously the right—and only—thing to do.

A lopsided smile spread over my face. Elizabeth Haylen kept me from stepping over the line into becoming a monster. She reminded me that no matter Katherine's actions, warped or not, I didn't have to be the same. Kneeling by her body, I beckoned to Ortiz. "Help me get her onto my shoulders."

Getting Katherine onto my shoulders wasn't the easiest of things. My knees bent further as her weight caused a few of my aching joints to grind. It felt like someone had tapped my ribs with a mallet.

"Let's get out of here."

# Chapter Twenty-Eight

"Ay yai yai yeow!"

"God," Ortiz exhaled after my exclamation.

"Wow," followed Lizzie.

The asylum halls looked like a hurricane had blown through with the windows left open. Clothing, plastic cutlery, broken glass, and food was everywhere. Every now and again we came across a person slumped against a wall or on the floor. Some were out cold, others babbled to themselves. They all sported cuts and bruises. It was like the aftermath of a prison brawl scene from a movie. An occasional flare of red and blue lights shone through the windows onto the asylum walls.

I released an inner sigh.

A woman staggered around the corner, hands pressed to her skull as if trying to keep it from splitting. The tops of her forearms bore lengthy shallow cuts. The tips of her nails were encrusted in the blood that also matted bits of her wheat hair. I let out a sharp whistle to draw the nurse's attention. Her body jerked in reaction to the piercing sound. The nurse pulled her hands away from her face. It was tear-stained. Grime marred her cheeks and forehead, as well as bits of her own blood.

"Hey." I lowered my voice to a more soothing tone. "You okay?" I eyed her arms.

"This?" She blinked several times as if trying to remember how to speak. She cleared her throat. "I think so. Now, at least. I don't know what happened. It's like the whole place went nuts at once. I started seeing things. People were fighting. I saw things—monsters...and things on my arms."

"Things?"

She nodded. "Don't ask me what they were. I just... I had to get them off." The nurse held up her bloodied nails.

"We're sorry," Ortiz whispered.

If the nurse heard Ortiz's apology, she didn't show it. Her gaze was fixated above my shoulder. "Oh, my God." She threw her hands up to her mouth.

Totally unsanitary when they're covered in blood.

"Is that Katherine?"

I grimaced. "It is."

"What's wrong with her?"

I didn't want to tell her. Death is never easy to deal with, especially after what had transpired in the asylum. Fortunately, I didn't have to. Lizzie stepped forward. She wrapped her arms around the nurse's waist.

The nurse got the message. Her lips quivered and her eyes fluttered. She took shallow breaths before shutting her eyes tight. The nurse shook her head as if the act of doing so could change the fact.

Denial is one of the most complicated tools the mind has to offer. A man can deny his perceived fate and whatever others believe, be they human or monster. He can fight against the odds, no matter how grim, and win. All by denying the horrendous odds stacked against him. And then there are the moments where denial can do nothing. It can't bury the pain of losing a friend or colleague. You can't push those things aside.

Ortiz placed a hand on the nurse's shoulder and helped guide her into a nearby room. I followed behind and waited till the nurse had taken a seat before I lowered Katherine Robinson to the bed. The young nurse cradled her head in her hands again. Her body shook and we could hear the sobs. Ortiz gave me a silent tilt of the head. We left the room, heading toward the exit of the asylum.

* * *

If the insides of the asylum were one helluva mess, then the front grounds were a veritable fustercluck. Everyone imaginable was there. Patients, staff, and medical first responders were helping out. A flash of blue lights peppered the overwhelming red emitted by the ambulances.

"Wonderful," I grumbled.

Officers sifted through people, helping sort things out. Some gathered statements. Cutting through the mass of people with a bit more purpose were men and women dressed in cheap suits of the same color.

"And there's the Feds," I sighed.

Ortiz rubbernecked and let out a hiss. The sort you'd get from a pissed off cat.

"Something wrong?"

She gave me a look.

"Oh, right, you're here on the down low." I grinned. "Nobody knows. So I suppose if I hollered real loud and pointed to you—"

"You'd be a dead man." She glared. It was a look that could've stripped paint and primer off cars.

"Hehe." I took a step back, raising my hands in surrender. "Wouldn't dream of it." She kept staring however.

Ortiz turned her head back to the crowd. "We should go." Her tone and stare told me it wasn't a good idea to argue with her. So we moved aside.

I led as we pushed our way through tight-knit groups within the already massive gathering. Ortiz stepped up to my side and spoke over the raucous noise around us.

"About Lizzie. Honestly, do you think she'll be fine?"

I cleared my throat. It was a hard question. Harder still because I didn't know the truth. God, I wish I did. "I don't know." My voice was weak. "I don't know and I hate it. When that thing was in her mind... I mean, for Christ's sake, she's a kid. She didn't deserve that. And that's the sort of stuff that sticks with you, especially children. They're more impressionable."

Ortiz nodded in silence.

"But I hope so. I really do." I threw a look back to Lizzie, who was trailing a few feet behind us. The kid was content in whatever was going on in her head. "There's something else, Ortiz, and it's not good. I told you how the phage taints things—corrupts them."

Ortiz nodded again.

"It got inside the mind of a child, Ortiz. A child who's already been through a lot. Losing her family, her beloved sister—twice technically. Getting locked up for what she can do, cut off from the outside world...”

“You're saying it could have done something to her. Something...permanent?”

“I don't know. That’s what scares me.”

Ortiz chewed her lip, mulling for a moment in silence. Her nose and lips twitched. “So...what about the phage? What happens now? I mean, look what it did, Charles. People are going to come asking questions, and I’m not sure they’re going to like the answers...or find them. That thing’s body crumbled to dust. What do...”

“You know the funny thing I’ve learned doing this?”

Ortiz arched an eyebrow, waiting for my answer.

“People are obsessed with causality. Everything has to have a reason. Cause and effect. One thing leads to another. And, in all of that, people want the answers they want to hear, want to believe, *need* to believe. The answers have to fit their paradigms. And here’s the scary thing: if things don’t add up, humans are great at making up their own explanation, one that everyone’s okay with. So long as everyone comes out happy and things are somewhat believable, no matter the holes, people don’t push it.”

“You’re right. That *is* scary.”

“Ignorance normally is, Ortiz, especially when people choose to be.”

“Lizzie!” someone called, drowning out every other voice nearby. Lizzie snapped out of her reverie and turned to the source of the voice with an alertness I hadn't seen before. Her mouth quirked into a smile and she tore past us, pushing people away by the waist. Ortiz and I exchanged a look before we chased after her. The voice called out again.

A squat woman with the complexion of rich clay bulldozed her way through a small group of people. Her skin was old leather, tanned, wrinkled and hardened. She had the same eyes as Lizzie. Quick and warm. Thinning hair and a powerful look.

She barely came up to my chest in height.

“Move!” she barked, shoving an officer out of the way. The cop turned with a snarl, looking the elderly woman in the face. The pint-sized woman shot him a look that could've turned granite to dust. The cop paused before deciding it was better for his health to turn around and forget what happened.

Lizzie screamed in delight and threw herself against the diminutive woman's chest. "Grandma!" she squealed. Her grandmother returned the pleased look and beamed. She squeezed the kid back. The embrace lasted for ten seconds or so before Lizzie pulled away. "Grandma, these are my friends." She gestured to us with a sweep of her arm.

Her grandmother eased out of Lizzie's hug, moving towards us with a penguin-like gait. I stiffened in response, equal parts respect—any woman who stares down a cop like that deserves mountains of respect—and fear. She stopped a finger's length away from Ortiz, hands on hip, chin upthrust as she turned her head to regard us.

I could feel the weight of the appraisal...and the judgment. Oh, the weighty judgment of family members.

Ortiz didn't smile. She dipped her head in a polite nod of respect. "Ma'am." Lizzie's grandmother continued to stare up at Ortiz, thinking in silence for a minute that felt like an hour.

The old woman's mouth quirked at the edges, making the lines in her face more visible. "I like you. Polite, honest"—she paused for a moment before adding—"strong."

Ortiz's lips twitched, not quite spreading into a pleased grin, but a hint of it was there. Her eyes gleamed at the compliment.

Lizzie's grandmother rounded on me and I swallowed the lump forming in my throat. Her hands balled into fists that rested on her hip. She marched over to me. I dwarfed the elderly woman by a couple of feet, yet I got the feeling she was the one looking down at me.

I followed Ortiz's earlier lead. I lowered my head in respect, working hard to keep my expression neutral. "Ma'am," I said, echoing Ortiz's tone.

She said nothing. Just an exhale of breath through the nose. This was going well.

I cleared my throat awkwardly. "You have an amazing granddaughter, ma'am. She's smart, kind, tough and brave, even where others wouldn't be."

Her grandmother blinked. A smiled cracked that hardened face. "Yes, she is."

I breathed a sigh of relief.

"And you," her tone turned accusatory, "are trouble!"

Am not.

"But," she continued. "You are strong. Brave, like my little Lizzie. A good man with a good heart." She jabbed a finger at the left side of my chest to make her point.

"Ow." I rubbed the spot.

"And a crybaby," she added. All three women broke out into varying degrees of laughter.

I sniffed indignantly. "Am not."

The laughter subsided and Lizzie crept up beside her grandmother, putting an arm around her. It was a nice thing to see, especially after what we all went through. It killed me to ruin it. "Ma'am, there's something I need to tell you about your granddaughter." Lizzie watched me without a fleck of concern on her face. "She's special, and she doesn't belong in a place like this, no matter what—"

Her grandmother made a slashing movement with her hand and cut me off. "I know."

Ortiz and I responded at the same time. "You do?"

Lizzie bobbed her head. "Yup. I told her a long time ago. She believes me." Her grandmother nodded in affirmation.

"So why..." I was unable to finish the question.

"Was she in this place?"

I nodded.

Her grandmother's body sank with a sigh. "The state. Too many hoops to jump through. But I have her back now. Thank you." She gave us a smile that touched her eyes.

"Hey, Camilla. Hey!" A voice shouted over the crowds. "That you?"

Ortiz swore. She threw her hands up to cover her mouth. "Sorry," she said to both Lizzie and her grandmother before rubbernecking toward the direction of the voice.

"What's up?" I asked.

"Harrison," she spat. "Guy I worked with at the Bureau. Good guy, but Christ, is he a loudmouth. If he catches me here, it'll spread through the Bureau. My job will be at risk." She gave me a dagger and nails look. "Wait here. I'm going to duck this clown, but you and I have things to discuss."

Ortiz's voice was ice.

"Camilla!" he called again. Ortiz shook her head and slipped through the crowd, heading in the opposite direction.

A silent thanks went through my head as she disappeared. It was the bout of good luck I needed. My pants stretched as something tugged at them. Lizzie was staring at me. "What's up, Short Round?"

"I have something to tell you," she said. I arched an eyebrow. "Well, not me really." She looked over her shoulder at someone.

The woman's appearance remained the same as when I saw her last. A mature version of Lizzie. Long-haired, large eyes, and beautiful. A member of the nursing staff passed through the spot Lizzie's sister occupied. The man reacted as if someone had dumped ice water on him. He stood there for a moment, eyeing the space. He frowned, shaking his head before moving on. "People can't see her," Lizzie explained.

"Uh, yeah. I, uh, got that." I blinked. "Hi." I waved. Her sister smiled and returned my wave.

Lizzie's sister's face scrunched up in effort as her lips moved. "Sorry."

She said—she spoke—and I heard it! Her voice wasn't the waning, garbled echoes people expect ghosts to speak in. It was strained but clear. "Sorry?" I asked.

"She's trying to talk. It's hard for her to do it this way, but she wants you to hear her," said Lizzie.

"She doesn't need to. Look, I get it. You don't need to push it." I raised a calming hand to her sister. Her lips quirked into a lopsided smile and she inclined her head. That was more than enough for me.

"She says thank you...not Charles." Lizzie gave me the same lopsided grin as her sister.

"I know, Lizzie, and thank you. Believe it or not, you helped me a lot on this case too. More than you know and..." I stopped as I became aware of another person standing to Lizzie's side. He was dressed exactly like me, a bit more disheveled though. His face bore the same hawkish features as the one I was borrowing.

"She's not the only one who wants to say thanks."

Lizzie gave me a smile wide enough to bring out her dimples.

I blinked. My mouth moved, trying to sputter a single word.

He flashed me a grin, winking as he turned to Lizzie.

"He says 'thank you', too, for figuring out what he left behind. For stopping the pain."

I nodded like an idiot as he waved. His appearance dimmed from sight until it was gone. Lizzie leapt, throwing her arms around me in a tight hug which I was too out of sorts to return. I stood there gawking as she took her grandmother's hand and left. The entire scene had unfolded before dozens of people, and not a single one saw what I had.

"Sunuvabitch." I laughed. *That was a first.*

# Chapter Twenty-Nine

Everyone knows that feeling when you're being watched. It's that itch in the back of your skull prompting you to turn. I'd worked my way to the edge of the asylum grounds. I stuck close to the woods as I moved back toward the building. The sensation became too much. It felt like there was a hook tugging on the back of my head. I turned.

"Lyshae." I frowned. "What now?"

"You're welcome, Vincent Graves." She sounded like she expected a thank you.

"For what?"

Her voice changed, and I shivered as she called, "Hey, Camilla. Hey!"

"That was you?"

She nodded.

"How did you—"

"Know?" She gave me a self-satisfied smile. "I learned a great deal about your female friend. Her name, occupation, people in her life. While you were busy with the phage, I was rather busy myself."

*Bitch.* Saying it aloud wouldn't have served any purpose besides self-satisfaction. "Bitch." I felt better.

I'm petulant. Sue me.

"Why though, Lyshae?"

"Your ability to perform whatever tasks I have in mind needs no further complications. A particular woman discovering the truth of who and what you are, for example."

"Uh, thanks?"

She bowed her head. "I also witnessed your exchange with Elizabeth Haylen."

Oh, bitch squared!

"Leave her alone, Lyshae." I kept my voice level but she knew it was a threat despite the tone.

"I will, for now. But if it ever serves my purpose...I won't." She gave me a foxlike smile.

I bristled. "The hell you will, I'll—"

"Stop me?" She laughed, throwing up a hand to cover her mouth. "You're in my service now. Your case is done, remember that. I could compel you to fetch her right now if I wished."

An animalistic sound formed in my throat. "Is that why you came here, to dangle this over my head?"

"To let you know that when I come asking, you will do as I say, regardless of the case at hand. You know the price of breaking a pact." It wasn't a question. "I also came to share something with you. A token. Something to let you know that I'm not all you make me out to be."

"Oh?"

"Yes, Vincent. A bit about your old life."

My thoughts turned into the static of a dead radio station.

"The Watcher of the Ways has all your answers." She smiled before shifting. A fox of pure white with nine golden tails sat before me. Lyshae bounded into the woods an instant later.

"Triple bitch." I scowled and headed back toward the asylum. It was time to wrap things up.

I pushed through the chapel doors and released a pleasurable groan of relief. Church wasn't in sight.

The chapel was empty. It's never completely empty.

"Church? Tall, blonde and nerdy—you here? Goldilocks?" I made my way toward the middle of the pews.

"I told you not to call me that," came a soft voice.

"Gyah! Church, I... And you stop doing that!" My chest heaved.

"Sorry, Vincent," he apologized.

I grunted in acceptance. I couldn't be all polite and understanding with Church. It would set a dangerous precedent for him.

Church snorted as if I'd said that aloud. He crossed his legs as he sat and clasped his hands. "Will you sit with me, Vincent?"

That didn't sound odd at all. "Well, when you put it that way, how can I say no?" Placing a hand on the back of the pew for support, I eased myself into a comfortable position on the wooden bench. I had to shift a bit before my butt stopped complaining. You'd think they'd find softer seating for a place offering comfort to troubled people.

"So, Vincent?" Church let the question hang in the air.

"So, Church?"

"You usually have questions after an assignment. Has that changed?"

*Oh, God, do I ever, Blondie. Where do I start?*

"With whatever is first on your mind, Vincent."

"You know, I'd appreciate you not reading my mind."

"I'm not. It's complicated, an explanation best saved for another time. For now, let us stick with what you have to ask about this case. Are you fine with that?" he asked in his always-soft tone of voice.

I unleashed my inner caveman, grunting once again. There's no dignified way to answer when he's speaking to you like you're a child. "Okay." I exhaled. "Ah, hell, I don't know. Lizzie! She's been through a lot—"

"Yes, she has," he interjected. I glared at him for doing so until I noticed the intensity of his reaction. His head looked heavy. He was drilling a hole through the floor boards. "Harder things than anyone her age should have to endure, and harder things to come."

"What?" I snapped. "No. She's out now. This was her crucible. That little girl is going home to a life full of boring school, thinking boys are idiots, and, one day, an awkward prom."

"If the world worked that way, then, yes, she would. She deserves as much, Vincent. As you know, this life isn't easy to leave. Many people have their roles to play."

I buried my face in my hands. I didn't need to hear this crap, not about Lizzie. I blew a breath through my fingers. "Lizzie, will she—"

"She will be fine, Vincent. Her grandmother is a strong and caring woman. She will take care of Elizabeth."

"Oh, okay, Church, another thing. I don't know if you *can* do this, if it's allowed in whatever rules you play by, but—"

"I will spare what time I can to keep an eye on her, Vincent, for you. You've earned that much." His tone made it clear he would do exactly that. Church was honest as far as I could tell.

"Thank you."

He didn't respond.

I pulled my hands away. "Speaking of roles, Church... What role does Ortiz have to play in this? This is the second time she's popped up in one of my cases and I'm starting think it's more than coincidence."

"Her role"—he mulled—"is whatever she decides it should be."

"Cryptic..."

"She's free to choose her own path, but we both know the sort of woman she is, don't we, Vincent?"

"She's tenacious," I said as Church nodded. "She won't stay out of this world. She said it herself. She can't, not really." Church gave me a knowing look. "You didn't answer my question though, not all of it at least. Why was she here?"

"Because of what happened with the Ifrit. It took quite the toll on her. She was here to recover."

I snorted. "Yeah, some recovery. Damned phage mucked that up."

"Did it?"

I blinked. "Uh, well...yeah, I think? She went through hell again on this one. She didn't need that, Church."

"Different people need different things. You think of her as a woman of steel, don't you?"

"Yeah, so?"

"Fire tempers steel. She needed this, to be thrown back into this world. Yes, it was hard on her, Vincent, but she had friends to help her through it."

"Oh, yeah, I did a great fucking job. She nearly died...again! She nearly lost it, Church. If I had screwed up, Ortiz, Lizzie, and God knows how many more people, would've wound up brain dead. Worse, they could've been stuck in a coma reliving their worst fears!" I stood over him, seething.

Church was calm as ever. "But you didn't screw up. You helped her through it, helped both of them through what they needed, Vincent..." His voice sounded strained near the end. "Your job isn't simply killing monsters. It is not about just saving people. It's helping them, helping yourself, helping people on a level beyond the physical."

"Eh?" was my brilliant response.

"Vincent, tell me what you think you accomplished here today."

"I, well, kicked the phage's ass..." I trailed off as Church eyed me, arching a singular pale eyebrow. I cleared my throat. "Ahem, sort of. Ortiz, you know, did the important part," I mumbled. "I wore it down. She killed it. But I helped save Lizzie, her sister too. I saved a couple people."

"You saved every living person in the asylum. You helped Camilla Ortiz work through her most paralyzing fears. You reunited a girl with her departed sister. You worked through many of your own fears as well."

"You mean when I thought my borrowed body was falling apart?"

"Yes, Vincent. Part of this case was to help you learn to face and deal with your fears."

"Church, I'm afraid all the time, damn it. That's nothing new!"

"But setting your fears aside for the sake of others is." His words dropped like a hammer.

"Oh." I blinked. I hadn't realized it at first, but he was right. I was terrified throughout this case. I didn't tough it out because of my own fortitude. I did it because I was more afraid of what would happen to Lizzie and Ortiz if I didn't. I did it for them.

"Exactly," Church commented and I glared at him. This mind reading shit was getting old fast. "That's something you needed to go through—feeling fear, having it paralyze you, and pushing it aside for the sake of others. There's something else you're overlooking as well, Vincent."

I remained silent.

"The asylum's ghosts. You gave them closure. The creature that caused so many of their deaths, so many of them pain, is gone. You saved them from the shadowed—"

"Shadowvores!" I said.

Church stared at me like I had said something incredibly stupid. "Vincent," he sighed. Church removed his glasses to polish them with his shirt. "There is a good reason why some creatures do not receive a definitive name throughout the ages."

"Lack of creative inspiration?"

"Because, sometimes, when people try, they come up with terribly stupid names." He eyed me like I had done exactly that.

"Whatever." I waved a dismissive hand. "I fought 'em. I kicked their shady butts. I get to name them."

"That...was a horrendous pun, Vincent."

I smiled. Suffer as I do, Church. Suffer!

"As I was saying, you saved them from those creatures. They may not be what they once were, but that doesn't make them any less than what they were. Do you understand?"

I frowned. "I think so?" The corners of Church's mouth quirked into a slight smile. "Church, why aren't I a ghost?"

His thin smile vanished.

"I died too, once. I know that. I still don't know what did it. I never got my closure. So why aren't I one? Shouldn't I be?"

"A ghost can't be formed if there's still something whole to cling to."

The air in my lungs froze.

"My body," I whispered. "It's still out there."

"Yes." Church looked away.

"Where?" My voice hardened.

"Safe."

"That's not an answer, Church! Damn it, that's not the one I deserve."

"It's the one you are going to get, Vincent, for now." Church's tone hadn't changed from whisper soft, but it was clear that he wasn't going to discuss it any further. "You need to trust me."

"No. No, Church, I don't. I bleed for you. You know that. And you're not doing a good job earning my trust right now."

"But you're doing a great job earning mine." He sounded like he meant it.

"This is about that whole shadows in the dark, menacing forces crap." I waggled my fingers in an ominous gesture. "Isn't it?"

"Yes."

"And you still can't tell me what it is?"

"No, Vincent."

"Why not?"

"Because, I don't know myself. Not all of it." His voice wavered when he said it. Church was scared!

Holy shit. This was serious.

"For now, Vincent, keep doing what you are doing. Save people. Keep being yourself. I know it's hard not knowing what happened to you, where your body is, but believe me, one day you will."

"But it is not this day, huh?"

"No, Vincent." He was oblivious to the reference.

"If you keep stringing me along like this, Ortiz is going to figure it out before I do. It'll be quite the blow to my investigator ego."

"I'm sure you'll survive."

"She deserves to know, Church. Ortiz risked her neck for me. Twice now. I want to tell her, but I don't know if she'll trust me after that."

"And her trust means that much to you?"

"Yes."

"Vincent, in the few moments you have to spare in your cases, when you are given a slight reprieve from things, have you ever stopped to just think? Have you ever asked yourself if some things will work themselves out? That maybe it is a good thing that you are torn over telling Camilla Ortiz your secret. You value her trust. Have you considered that maybe you are not supposed to tell her?"

"What? Keep her in the dark? You're kidding, right? I seriously thought about staying put and not coming to visit you until Lyshae pulled that stunt." I broke off to look at the floor for a moment. "I don't have enough real, honest, *human* friends that I can afford to lose them."

"You're not listening, Vincent. Have you ever wondered if Camilla Ortiz is meant to figure it out in her own time? That she needs to get to the bottom of the mystery that is you—by herself?"

"I...uh...erhm...no?" I mean what the hell do you say to that?

"If she intends to be part of this world, Vincent, she will have to begin learning on her own. You cannot expect to explain everything to her, prepare her for everything. Life doesn't work that way."

"I know," I whispered. "Ughf." I exhaled as I plopped back onto the pew, rolling my neck and kicking out my legs.

Church's hand rested on my collar. He gave me a bro squeeze. "She's a smart and resourceful woman."

I chuckled. "I know. That's half the reason I'm afraid of her."

"Give her the time and space she needs, Vincent. She still needs to wrap her mind around a great many things. Camilla Ortiz will make the best decision for herself in time."

"Yeah," I said. My heart wasn't completely in it though.

"Is there anything else on your mind, Vincent?"

"Thanks, I guess. Pretty generous timeline you gave me. Last time it was thirteen hours. Not cool by the way."

"The Neravene can be a troublesome place to navigate. And I seem to remember extending your timeline during your last case in New York." Church's face remained neutral save for a glint in the eyes.

"Of course. You *knew* I'd wind up in the Neravene." I sighed. "Church, promise me one of these days you'll be straight with me, seriously."

"One of these days, Vincent. In the meantime, might I suggest keeping a closer eye on these?" He brandished a pair of leather bound journals. "Found by the wrong beings, these could lead to a lot of trouble."

I nodded in dumbfounded silence. I had no idea how he knew where I'd hidden them.

"And a final piece of something to think on. New York. The place has many more surprises in store for you."

Fatigue took hold and I breathed out through my nose, closing my eyes as a yawn escaped me. "Yeah, Church, I'll keep that in mind," I said through another yawn. I opened my eyes and looked to where Church was sitting. I blinked.

Alone again. I shook my head and let out a rueful chuckle. I thought about the past six months as I waited to leave Charles' body. First the Ifrit, now a phage. My life was certainly becoming more interesting.

And Church said there were more surprises on the way.

"Ah." I sighed. "New York. It's a helluva place."

## ABOUT THE AUTHOR

**R.R Virdi** is the author of *The Grave Report* series and many short stories. He has worked as a mechanic, in retail, and now spends his weekends helping others build gaming PCs, all while continuing to write. An avid mythology buff, he keeps a journal following the fictional accounts of his character, Vincent Graves, and all the horrible monsters he comes across. He lives in Falls Church, Virginia, tinkering with cars, gaming computers, and chasing after his dog.

Thank you for taking the time to read this novel.
If you would like to know more about the author,
please visit:

**http://www.rrvirdi.com/**

Follow me on Twitter: **https://twitter.com/rrvirdi**

Follow me on Facebook:
**https://www.facebook.com/rrvirdi**

If you enjoyed this book, please consider leaving a
review!